PENGUIN BOOKS

The Castle

Franz Kafka was born of Jewish parents in Prague in 1883. The family spoke both Czech and German; Franz was sent to German-language schools and to the German University, from which he received his doctorate in law in 1906. He then worked for most of his life as a respected official of a state insurance company (first under the Austro-Hungarian Empire, then under the new Republic of Czechoslovakia). Literature, of which he said that he 'consisted', had to be pursued on the side. His emotional life was dominated by his relationships with his father, a man of overbearing character, and with a series of women: Felice Bauer from Berlin, to whom he was twice engaged; his Czech translator, Milena Jesenská-Pollak, to whom he became attached in 1920; and Dora Diamant, a young Jewish woman from Poland in whom he found a devoted companion during the last year of his life. Meanwhile, his writing had taken a new turn in 1917 with the outbreak of the tubercular illness from which he was to die in 1924. Only a small number of Kafka's stories were published during his lifetime and these are published in Penguin as *Metamorphosis and Other Stories*. He asked his friend, Max Brod, to see that all the writings he left should be destroyed. Brod felt unable to comply and undertook their publication instead, beginning with the three unfinished novels, *The Trial* (1925), *The Castle* (1926) and *Amerika* (1927). Other shorter works appeared posthumously in a more sporadic fashion, and a representative selection of them is collected in *The Great Wall of China and Other Short Works*, also published in Penguin.

J. A. Underwood, who was born in London in 1940, has worked as a freelance translator (from French as well as German) since 1969, translating texts by a wide variety of modern authors, including Elias Canetti, Jean-Paul Sartre, Julien Green, Alain Robbe-Grillet and Kafka. *The Castle* was joint winner of the 1998 Schlegel-Tieck Prize for translation from the German.

Idris Parry was born in 1916 and educated in Wales and at the universities of Bonn and Göttingen. After war service he became a university teacher at Bangor, moving in 1963 to Manchester, where he was Professor of

Modern German Literature, until he retired in 1977. His essays have been collected in *Animals of Silence* (1972), *Stream and Rock* (1973), *Hand to Mouth* (1981) and *Speak Silence* (1988). He has also translated Kafka's *The Trial* for Penguin.

FRANZ KAFKA

THE CASTLE

A new translation by
J. A. UNDERWOOD
with an introduction by
IDRIS PARRY

PENGUIN BOOKS

PENGUIN BOOKS

Published by the Penguin Group
Penguin Books Ltd, 80 Strand, London WC2R 0RL, England
Penguin Putnam Inc., 375 Hudson Street, New York, New York 10014, USA
Penguin Books Australia Ltd, 250 Camberwell Road, Camberwell, Victoria 3124, Australia
Penguin Books Canada Ltd, 10 Alcorn Avenue, Toronto, Ontario, Canada M4V 3B2
Penguin Books India (P) Ltd, 11 Community Centre, Panchsheel Park, New Delhi – 110 017, India
Penguin Books (NZ) Ltd, Cnr Rosedale and Airborne Roads, Albany, Auckland, New Zealand
Penguin Books (South Africa) (Pty) Ltd, 24 Sturdee Avenue, Rosebank 2196, South Africa

Penguin Books Ltd, Registered Offices: 80 Strand, London WC2R 0RL, England

www.penguin.com

Published in Penguin Books 1997
Reprinted in Penguin Classics 2000

004

Translation copyright © J. A. Underwood, 1997
Introduction copyright © Idris Parry, 1997
All rights reserved

The moral right of the translator and editor has been asserted

Set in 10/12.5pt Monotype Janson
Typeset by Rowland Phototypesetting Ltd, Bury St Edmunds, Suffolk
Printed in England by Clays Ltd, St Ives plc

ISBN-13: 978–0–14–119755–5

www.greenpenguin.co.uk

CONTENTS

Translator's Note   vii
Introduction by Idris Parry   ix

1 Arrival   3
2 Barnabas   18
3 Frieda   33
4 First Conversation with the Landlady   41
5 At the Mayor's   52
6 Second Conversation with the Landlady   68
7 The Schoolmaster   80
8 Waiting for Klamm   89
9 Resisting Interrogation   97
10 In the Street   106
11 At the School   111
12 The Assistants   121
13 Hans   127
14 Frieda's Reproach   136
15 At Amalia's   146
16   154
17 Amalia's Secret   168
18 Amalia's Punishment   181
19 Approaches   190
20 Olga's Plans   197
21   211
22   219
23   228
24   242
25   256

TRANSLATOR'S NOTE

Kafka never finished this book. In fact, it breaks off in the middle of a sentence. He did not finish any of his three novels; they and many of his stories remained unpublished during his lifetime. Dying of tuberculosis in 1924, he asked his writer friend Max Brod to burn his papers. Brod did not do so (nor, surely, can Kafka seriously have expected him to) but instead edited much of Kafka's work after his death and published it bit by bit.

In this, Max Brod's contribution was immense; without Brod, Franz Kafka might be a minor name, known only to a few specialists. In other respects, however, scholars wishing to uncover Kafka's original intentions have had to undo a lot of what Brod did, patiently stripping away the textual adjustments and layers of interpretation that, with the best of intentions, he and those who followed him had imposed on the dead man's prose (and that, for example, inevitably affected the way in which Kafka's first English translators, Willa and Edwin Muir, approached their task).

A good marker for the turning-point is perhaps Erich Heller's provocative comment (in *The Disinherited Mind*, 1952): 'Kafka is the least problematic of our modern writers.' In a sense, there is no 'problem' of 'what Kafka meant': he meant what he wrote. The original on which this translation is based is, as nearly as we can tell, *The Castle* as Kafka left it; I hope the translation will give English readers a glimpse of the original's freshness.

J.A.U.

INTRODUCTION

Has there ever been so convoluted a mind revealed in utterance? Kafka believed his situation was unique. Nobody else could be so tormented by fear, the 'secret raven' he talks about in his diaries. Does he exaggerate? 'I am given to exaggeration,' he writes to Milena Jesenská, 'but all the same I can be trusted.'

During the months from January to September 1922 when he is writing *The Castle* the most important person in his life is Milena Jesenská. Over this period he writes to her constantly and without reserve. She is necessary to him. 'To you,' he says, 'I can tell the truth, for your sake as well as mine, as to nobody else. Yes, it's possible to find one's own truth directly from you.' In October 1921 he gave her all his diaries and never asked for them back – an almost unbelievable act of trust for such a private person. But this action was a logical consequence: in the diaries he reveals his introspective self; in the letters to Milena he exposes his fears (and therefore himself) as to no other correspondent. Nothing was to be hidden from her. His intention seemed so interlocked with her understanding that there was nothing to conceal, everything to discover. 'I can't listen simultaneously to the frightful voices from within and to you,' he tells her, 'but I can listen to those and impart them to you ... to you as to nobody else in the world.' These letters to Milena tell us about the state of mind he projects into prose as this novel. The frightful voices from within could after all be imparted to others.

This intense relationship seems to have been an attraction of opposites. Milena was further from Kafka in external circumstances than any other woman in his life. She was twelve years younger; that would hardly matter to us, but he, at thirty-eight, thought she belonged to a different generation. She was already married, but unhappily, and the marriage was breaking up. He was Jewish, she was Christian and seems to have been an extrovert. She lived in Vienna, inaccessible to the man from Prague except through complicated and baffling arrangements. There were no simple arrangements in Kafka's life. 'Today I saw a map of Vienna. For a moment I couldn't understand why they built such a great city when after all you need only one room.'

His letters are charged with painful analysis of the obstacles between them. For Kafka any surface, even the surface of love, can generate its black swarm of disturbing possibilities. This is how life seems to him. Obstacles start from the ground wherever he looks – his Jewishness, passport difficulties, trains, lack of sleep, her husband, his own office obligations, his state of health, his sister's wedding. Disaster or distraction (and for him there is little difference between the two) surround him like a design for living. This is the design found in his fiction, which reflects a view of life as a proliferation of obstacles splitting off into more obstacles, bewildering the brain by their multiplicity and movement. His fears become almost laughable when he tells Milena he is afraid of lifting a tumbler of milk to his mouth 'because it could easily explode in my face, not by chance but by design, and throw the splinters into my face'.

His letters (hers have been lost) show their relationship growing into passionate and, for him, tormented love. Who else but Kafka could find hostility in happiness? It could burst in his face and really consist of the fragments into which he analyses it. He reviles himself for his inadequacy, for his fears, for the corrupting influence he brings to a life as natural and open as hers. This happiness is too terrifying. 'Love is to me that you are the knife which I turn within myself.'

In his diary when he is writing *The Castle* he describes his life as a hesitation before birth. 'Not yet born and already compelled to walk the streets and talk to people.' As usual, he exaggerates. All art has been called opportune exaggeration, and Kafka carries this to extremes. It is his method. In the novels and letters as well as his diaries, feeling is given extraordinary form. Talking about hesitation before birth is his way of saying life appears to be a succession of loose ends, always provisional, a hesitant progression, seemingly without connection or conclusion. Is this chance or design? He must believe in design behind the apparently accidental, or he would not assume birth beyond hesitation. He is not yet complete, not yet born. His correspondent is perhaps one who can complete him. He can address her as 'Mother Milena'. He speaks of her 'life-giving power'. She becomes for him a kind of earth-mother who can smooth into oblivion the hesitations of consciousness. He tells her he wants only 'to lay my face in your lap, feel your hand on my head and stay like that through all eternity'.

Kafka and Milena met in Vienna for four days, the longest time they spent together. Later Milena told a friend that Kafka forgot his fears. 'There was no need for the slightest effort,' she said, 'everything was simple and straightforward . . .' His nervousness disappeared. But fear is not so easily lost, especially fear bred in the bone. 'I am always trying to convey something that can't be conveyed,' he writes to her, 'to explain something which is inexplicable, to tell about something I have in my bones, something which can be experienced only in these bones.'

After Vienna, alone in his room with the paper on which he writes, he abandons himself again to fear. He confesses that the possibility of living with Milena does not exist. Those happy days become in retrospect merely a time when 'I looked over my fence . . . I held myself up by my hands, then I fell back again . . .' To Kafka the torment of love was that, like practically everything else, it created an indefinite fear which threatened the bounds of his strength. It is as if relationships, to objects and events as well as people, are visible to him only in the hieroglyphs of fear.

Kafka's writing is an effort to find meaning in the central fact of his existence, and this central fact is inexplicable fear. In a strange way, this fear justifies his existence too, and we have the seeming paradox of the man who claimed he had spent his life resisting the temptation to end it also claiming that without fear he could not live. 'My life consists of this subterranean threat. If it stops, I'll stop too. It's my way of taking part in life. If it stops, I'll give up living as easily and naturally as a dying man closes his eyes.'

When life comes to him only as emanations of fear, it is important that this fear should be accurately observed: it is the material for his work and hope. He either gives up or goes on. Kafka goes on. His fear, he tells Milena, is 'fear extended to everything, fear of the greatest as well as the smallest, fear, convulsive fear of pronouncing a word'. If there is hope, it is here, in its apparent opposite. One must give praise in spite of everything, says Rilke; and by praise the poet means unqualified acceptance of the material of life, however frightful or inexplicable. Truth cannot be found through omission or editing. In spite of everything, Kafka remains the curious observer: 'You forget, Milena, that we are standing side by side, watching this creature on the ground which is me.'

The importance of these letters, apart from their evocative brilliance as human documents, is that here Kafka reveals exactly what he is transposing into the fictional skin called *The Castle*. In his fiction he is always talking about himself. He told Felice Bauer, to whom he was twice engaged before he met Milena, that she had no cause to be jealous of the novel he was then writing (the book later called *Amerika*). 'The novel is me,' he said. 'I am my stories.'

Several entries in Kafka's diaries and notebooks show what a fascination the ancient myths had for him. Kafka's fictional writings often seem like modern legends or folk-tales about fear. This is no accident. The myth is a legend whose survival tells us it has enduring implications for the human mind. Here events may seem impossible, but they linger in the deepest recesses of consciousness, pure fabrications – that is, fabrications recognizably pure. We are attracted outside reason to these clear statements which are simple with a simplicity beyond our formulation of truth and therefore inexplicable. These gods, messengers, impossible animals, impossible transformations (Daphne into laurel tree, Arethusa into fountain of fresh water) are fantasy made precise, but fantasy related to a conviction of truth. It is organic fantasy. If these are attempts to probe the mystery which is the relationship of the individual to his world, the images must seem to the rational mind remote and unreal. But they are not attempts to 'probe' the mystery, they are attempts to present it, to give us a picture, to organize instinct into form, to explain by not explaining – which is the essence of poetry and the justification for art.

In the same way, Kafka's stories are not explanations but pictures. His heroes submit and endure. He writes and rewrites his versions of ancient legends, clearly looking for some meaning to connect them with his own experience. He has no difficulty in seeing himself, this creature writhing on the ground, as a modern Prometheus tormented by eagles tearing at his vitals which never cease to grow. The legend of Prometheus is one Kafka rewrote for his own satisfaction – still writing about himself. The conclusion of his version is that 'the legend tries to explain the inexplicable.' As he has said to Milena, he himself is always trying to explain something which is inexplicable. But he never explains in the intellectual sense. 'True reality is always unrealistic,' a friend records him as saying. 'Look at the clarity, purity and truth of a Chinese coloured woodcut. To talk like that – that would be something.' Kafka makes pictures.

Can there be hope if truth ends as it begins, in the inexplicable? Or do we misunderstand the nature of hope? Writing is a positive and optimistic act, and Kafka must write or die. He is on record as saying the pen is not an instrument but an organ of the writer's. In the month in which he starts to write *The Castle* he speaks in his diary of 'the strange, mysterious, perhaps dangerous, perhaps saving comfort there is in writing'. And in that letter to Milena where he talks of listening to 'the frightful voices from within', he also speaks of his conviction that the fears themselves form a path to truth. Either that, or he has no access to truth: he has no other material.

'It is true,' the letter continues, 'that this fear is perhaps not only fear but also a longing for something which is more than all the things which produce fear.' His life is fear, but is it possible that fear is simply a false interpretation of events? In *The Castle* we find a double-aspect surface which reflects duality in the writer. In one aspect the surface as experienced seems fragmentary, disconnected, and therefore inexplicable, a source of anxiety. In the other there is dream-like acceptance which implies belief in harmony beyond intellectual perception. The book is charged with essential fear, but also with essential hope, both together as they exist in the man.

It is easy to classify Kafka's novels as catalogues of woe and handbooks of frustration. But he is presenting the evidence, the only evidence we have, and the writer starts from here. This evidence has to be absorbed. 'Accept your symptoms,' says Kafka in his diary. 'Don't complain about symptoms, immerse yourself in your suffering.' This faith that revelation must and can come only from immediate suffering, the assault of experience, underlies many diary entries which seem puzzling if the images are not accepted as form given to innate belief, pictures of thought. 'Mount your attacker's horse and ride it yourself. Only possibility. But what strength and skill that demands! And how late it is already!' And perhaps most pathetic and inspiring: 'Somewhere help is waiting and the beaters are driving me there.' The beaters are his experience of life, there to be endured in every trifling detail, for no detail is trifling.

The Castle is nonsensical by rational standards. This is Kafka's way of saying reason is not enough. He has told us through Milena that he is always trying to explain the inexplicable. But he never explains. In *The Castle* he makes no attempt to persuade the reader that events should follow like this. We are given a picture and told in effect: 'This is how it is.' The absurd is presented with such assurance, fantasy made so precise, that we are moved to follow as if by a law of induction.

Perhaps art is simply induction. The picture in prose or paint or stone touches vibrations in us we did not know existed. We respond and understand, beyond explanation. The secret understanding induced by art changes the structure before us from the absurd to the magical, and we know there is a common relationship between parts even if it can't be understood, a unity or coalescence like the one suggested when K. tries to telephone the castle and hears only a buzzing sound quite unlike anything he has ever heard before when using the phone, and it seems to him, the attentive listener, as if from this strange sound there emerges 'in a quite impossible fashion a single high-pitched yet powerful voice that struck the ear as if demanding to penetrate deeper than into mere hearing'. In a unified world nothing can be separate, not even the senses. Vibrations are common, and commonly observed; and it is primarily through sound that vibrations are perceptible, can even be seen to shake affected objects. Who can tell if the violin is silent when untouched by the bow?

In *The Castle* K. lives in a space where magical connection is taken for granted. The strong erotic charge in the novel, which is a transposition of Kafka's passion for Milena, finds its climax when K. and Frieda make love amid the rubbish and puddles of beer on the floor of the bar at the Count's Arms, and K. 'constantly had the feeling that he had lost his way or wandered farther into a strange land than anyone before him, a strange land where even the air held no trace of the air at home, where a man must suffocate from the strangeness yet into whose foolish enticements he could do nothing but plunge on, getting even more lost.' Apart from being a reasonably accurate description of the physical form of the novel as a strange land, this can also be taken as yet another commentary on the central theme of familiar and strange, reason and fantasy, caution and ambition, doubt and certainty.

To understand beyond understanding we too must be in a mood of acceptance. Our reason is bounded by perceptions which cover part of reality, not the whole. Kafka as an individual is not protected by the skin of habit and selective awareness. Each sentence in his works uncovers him, and one phrase in particular in his letters to Milena, given in parenthesis, seemingly an afterthought, suddenly illuminates his writing: 'Sometimes I think I understand the Fall of Man better than anybody else.'

What he means is that he is abnormally sensitive to the damage caused by consciousness of self. We are told in Genesis how Adam and Eve eat of the fruit of the Tree of Knowledge and are suddenly aware of themselves in their surroundings. This awareness is the real expulsion from Paradise. Unconscious harmony is traded for conscious intellect, and mankind finds itself opposite and always opposite. From the darkness of harmony we move to the faint light of knowledge and the fractures of definable experience. This is the Fall Kafka understands so well.

For Kafka's heroes, as it happens, especially in *The Trial* and *The Castle*, the shades of night are always falling fast, no matter what time of day it is. They grope through the dark as if in search of a truth reluctant to appear in the illuminated segment we call intellect. It's as if they are always searching for the state of unconscious harmony before 'their eyes were opened and they knew that they were naked'. *The Castle* in particular often seems a study in shadows, as if the hero is aware of dark harmony at the end of his quest, beyond the frustrating complications of the present. K. is always making for the remote castle on the hill, always on the point of achieving something, never quite getting there. As he looks at the castle, 'the longer K. looked, the less he could make out, and the deeper everything sank into semi-darkness'. The effort itself is an obstacle because, as a conscious expression of individual and separate entity, it remains a denial of harmony.

In this novel even the physical movements of the hero seem to be affected by the peculiar regulations of dreams. Everybody else can skim over the surface of snow, it is only K. who flounders. 'There is a goal but no way,' says Kafka in one of his notes: 'What we call a way is hesitation.' K. drags his feet as he hesitates before choice. He does not know if any one way is better than another. His perplexity is transposed (as everything in this book is a transposition of mood) into the suffering character who sinks at every step into the deep snow which is a firm crust for everyone else. In every moment of life the material is the same, only judgement differs.

Standing in the snow, K. sees the twins Arthur and Jeremiah glide past him at speed. He has not seen them before, he now learns their names, he knows they are from the castle. When he hears they have business at the inn he shouts that he has business there too. They do not stop. What happens next reveals the attitude of total acceptance which, because it is normally excluded by man contemplating his disturbed surroundings, is presented here as an incident which must seem rationally incomprehensible.

K. reaches the inn. Arthur and Jeremiah are waiting for him. 'Who are you?' says K. They tell him they are his assistants. K., nominally a land surveyor, is expecting the arrival of his old assistants, but these two are strangers. They come from the castle. K. knows this, and we know that he knows it. In a rational human context we should expect him to laugh at their impudence or ignore them or kick them out as impostors. He does none of these things. 'What?' he asks, 'you're my old assistants whom I had follow me, whom I've been expecting?' They reply that they are. 'That's good,' K. says after a pause, 'it's good that you've come.'

Is he mad or blind? The pause is put there by Kafka. It seems to betray his awareness of human imperfection. In the realm of total acceptance there are no accidents. He once told a friend accidents do not exist in the world but only in our heads. There is no world without causation, and the idea of accident reflects the limits of human perception, our inability to know all connections and so pursue total causality. No contradictions can exist where connection is complete. The same friend took Kafka to an exhibition of Picasso paintings and expressed his opinion that this artist is guilty of wilful distortion. Kafka said he did not think so: 'He merely notes the abnormalities which have not yet penetrated our consciousness. Art is a mirror which "runs fast" like a clock – sometimes.'

Kafka's images are of a world not yet discovered. Here the understanding is stretched beyond rational comprehension, beyond the limits of perceptible experience. Nobody has been here before. We are in the realms where imagination is waiting for life to catch up. It is a world where things just happen and are not committed in advance to the limits of human understanding. This makes the difficulty. How do we comprehend what is deliberately beyond our comprehension? The reader too needs a sense of wonder, belief that there is truth in the inexplicable rock to which this modern Prometheus is chained.

In the incident about the assistants who are at the same time both known and unknown Kafka the novelist brings together in one image the seeming contradiction of uncertainty and confident trust which exists in him and drives him on. It has to be one image because these are two faces of the same situation. But what sense are we to make of confident uncertainty? And how else can we describe hope, the faith which transcends all immediate disheartening evidence?

The story of Eden appeals to Kafka because it contains the duality he is always presenting: on the one hand unconscious harmony, on the other the concept of disintegration. He understands the Fall as a present situation, our condition of self-awareness, not as an event which took place on a particular day in the remote past when man's nature suddenly switched from insight to introspection, and integration fell to pieces. 'Only our concept of time,' he says in one of his notes, 'leads us to call the Last Judgement by that name. In fact, it's a court in standing session.' In other words, it's taking place now, all the time. Kafka might also have said (but did not) that it is only our concept of time which makes us think of the expulsion from Paradise as a kind of 'first judgement'. It is another court in standing session, which his central character faces every day, waking into the strange country of dream, at the same time both familiar and foreign. The Fall as seen by Kafka is a legendary image of a perpetual human condition now experienced by an individual in Prague and projected as literature.

Man knows about disintegration (it is his world) and he inexplicably senses concealed harmony. In *The Castle* these ideas are presented in tandem because they exist together in our perception (where else can they be?). The idea of harmony can only be a projection from what we know, so the duality of divine and devilish or Apollo and Dionysus is a duality only in the mind. These are two aspects of the same world, the god with two faces. Apollo is Dionysus organized. Goethe knew at eighteen that hell and heaven are not separate places but a divided perception of the same world, and Kafka writes to Milena: 'Nobody sings as purely as those in deepest hell. What we take for the song of angels is their song.'

Kafka makes several references to the Fall, and consequently to his ideas on the nature of sin, in *Reflections*, a series of his aphorisms collected by himself from scattered sources and so (one may believe) considered by him to be of special importance. Here he ascribes the Fall of Man and the catastrophe of consciousness to impatience, classified as the main human sin. 'It was because of impatience they were expelled from Paradise, it is because of impatience they do not return there.' What he means by impatience is seen from another entry: 'All human errors are impatience, a premature breaking-off of the methodical, an apparent fencing-in of the apparent issue'. The 'methodical' must be the continuous process of life, running constantly from one organic manifestation to another. (It is impossible to speak of unity except through the language of division, our only semantic tool.) Method is the pattern of causation broken by man through classification by thought. Experience is reduced to the limits of human perception, phenomena are segments fenced-in from the flow.

These segments are however our only experience and our only approach. The truth is already there. Nobody makes it. It is waiting to be found along the lines of causation, beyond the accidental limits of individual perception.

'One must write into the dark,' says Kafka, 'as if into a tunnel.' And in another place: 'My stories are a kind of closing one's eyes.' He is yearning for the state before the Fall, the satisfaction of the dark unconscious. And in his diaries he uses words which must come as a surprise to those who think of him as a drab pessimist: 'It is entirely conceivable that life's splendour forever lies in wait about each one of us in all its fullness, but veiled from view, deep down, invisible, far off. It is there though, not hostile, not reluctant, not deaf. If you summon it by the right word, by the right name, it will come. This is the essence of magic, which does not create but summons.'

The writer as magician. Kafka's works are a continuous effort to find the right word, the right name. To a friend he spoke of the act of writing as a conjuration of spirits, and in his notebooks he describes it as a form of prayer. In Kafka's novels there is no complexity of prose surface to puzzle us; we are puzzled by its simplicity. Here feeling is form, and form is feeling, indistinguishable. And the simplicity of this prose reflects the fundamental attitude of acceptance.

This acceptance, or patience, follows from the conviction that life is greater and better than the intellect allows. But impatience is the normal human characteristic – or the story of the Fall would not exist. Kafka's fiction represents life by showing impatience and patience as a running pair, to reflect the dual aspect of life as he finds it. When he describes his writing as 'an assault on the frontier' he is talking about the frontier of rational perception. His conjuration of spirits is an effort to follow causation across that frontier into the dark.

In *The Castle* we encounter a proliferation of obstacles, endless conversations, perpetual possibilities which hook on to each other as if intent to go on until the end of time. And with it all, and because of it all, quiet acceptance. The seeming contradiction in K. of questioning and acquiescence has its origin in the man who believes he is uniquely battered by the puzzles, perplexities, horrors and injustices of life but can also speak of glory and claim that 'he who does not seek will be found'. The truth that emerges from his letters to Milena is universal. He finds it difficult to utter, but his life depends on this utterance. 'There is only one truth,' he tells her, 'but it is alive and therefore has a vividly changing face.'

IDRIS PARRY

Milena Jesenská died in the Nazi concentration camp at Ravensbrück on 17 May 1944.

THE CASTLE

I

ARRIVAL

It was late evening when K. arrived. The village lay deep in snow. Nothing could be seen of Castle Hill, it was wrapped in mist and darkness, not a glimmer of light hinted at the presence of the great castle. K. stood for a long while on the wooden bridge that led from the main road to the village, gazing up into the seeming emptiness.

Then he went to look for somewhere to spend the night; they were still awake at the inn, the landlord did not have a room to rent but was willing, the late guest having very much surprised and confused him, to let K. sleep on a palliasse in the lounge, K. accepted. A few peasants still sat over their beer but he did not feel like talking to people, he fetched the palliasse from the attic himself and lay down near the stove. It was warm, the peasants were quiet, he scanned them for a while with tired eyes, then he fell asleep.

Shortly afterwards, however, he was woken up. A young man in town clothes with a face like an actor, eyes narrow, eyebrows powerful, stood beside him, accompanied by the landlord. The peasants were still there too, some had turned their chairs round in order to see and hear better. The young man apologized most courteously for having woken K., introduced himself as the son of the castle governor, and went on: 'This village belongs to the castle, anyone living or spending the night here is in a sense living or spending the night in the castle. No one may do that without a permit from the count. You, however, possess no such permit or at least have not produced it.'

K. had risen to a seated position and smoothed his hair tidy, he looked up at the people and said: 'What village have I strayed into? You mean there's a castle here?'

'There certainly is,' the young man said slowly, while here and there heads were shaken over K., 'Count Westwest's castle.'

'And you need a permit to spend the night here?' K. asked as if seeking to convince himself that he had not perhaps dreamed the earlier statements.

'You need a permit,' came the answer, and there was a certain rude mockery in the way the young man held out one arm and asked the landlord and the guests: 'Or is a permit perhaps not required?'

'Then I shall have to get a permit,' K. said with a yawn, pushing back the blanket as if to rise.

'And who will you get a permit from?' the young man asked.

'From the count,' said K., 'there's nothing else for it.'

'Now, at midnight, get a permit from the count?' the young man cried, stepping back a pace.

'Is that not possible?' K. asked composedly. 'Why did you wake me, then?'

But here the young man lost his temper. 'You've the manners of a tramp!' he shouted, 'I demand respect for the count's office! I woke you to say you must leave the count's territory immediately.'

'Enough of this farce,' K. said with remarkable gentleness, lying down again and pulling the blanket over him. 'You're going a little too far, young man, and I shall have more to say about your conduct in the morning. The landlord and the gentlemen here are my witnesses, in so far as I need witnesses at all. For the rest, I would have you know that I am the land surveyor the count sent for. My assistants will be following in the carriage tomorrow with the instruments. I was keen not to miss the walk through the snow, but unfortunately I wandered off the road a few times, which is why I was so late getting here. I knew for myself it was too late then to report to the castle, even before your lecture. That is also the reason why I was content to spend the night here, the night you have had the – to put it mildly – discourtesy to disturb. That is all I have to say. Good night, gentlemen.' And K. rolled over to face the stove.

'Land surveyor?' he heard someone ask hesitantly behind him, then all was quiet. However, the young man soon pulled himself together and, in tones that were sufficiently muted to pass as consideration for K.'s sleep and loud enough to be audible to him, said to the landlord: 'I'll telephone and inquire.' What, there was even a telephone in this village inn? They were very well equipped here. Specifically, this surprised K., in a general way he had expected it, of course. The telephone turned out to be almost above his head, in his drowsiness he had failed to notice it. If the young man now had to telephone, he could not with the best will in the world have avoided waking K. up, the only question was whether K. should let him telephone, he decided to allow it. That meant, of course, there was also no point in pretending to be asleep, so he rolled over on to his back again. He watched the peasants move cautiously together and confer, the arrival of a land surveyor was no small thing. The door to the kitchen had opened, the mighty figure of the landlady stood filling the frame, the landlord tiptoed over to tell her what was happening. And at this point the telephone conversation began. The steward was asleep, but an under-steward, one of the under-stewards, a man called Fritz, was there. The young man, who gave his name as Schwarzer, told how he had found K., a man in his thirties, quite ragged-looking, lying peacefully asleep on a palliasse, with a tiny rucksack for a pillow, a heavy walking-stick within reach. Well, he had looked suspicious, naturally, and since the landlord had clearly neglected his duty it had been his, Schwarzer's, duty to get to the bottom of the matter. K., he said, had taken the rousing from sleep, the interrogation, and the obligatory threat of expulsion from the county with a very bad grace, though as things turned out perhaps justifiably, since he claimed to be a land surveyor appointed by the count. It was of course at least technically necessary for this claim to be checked, and Schwarzer was therefore requesting Mr Fritz to make inquiries in the main office as to whether a land surveyor of this kind really was expected and to telephone the answer through immediately.

Then there was silence, Fritz was making inquiries at the other end and here an answer was awaited, K. stayed as he was, not even turning round, seemingly quite incurious, just looking. Schwarzer's account, a blend of malice and circumspection, gave him some idea of the almost diplomatic training, as it were, that even people as unimportant as Schwarzer could easily possess in the castle. Nor was there any lack of diligence there, the main office had a night shift. And evidently replied very promptly, because Fritz was already ringing back. This report seemed to be a very brief one, though, since Schwarzer immediately slammed the receiver down in a fury. 'Didn't I say so?' he cried, 'land surveyor? – nothing of the sort, a common, lying vagrant, probably worse.' For a moment K. was sure all of them, Schwarzer, peasants, landlord, and landlady, were about to fall on him, and to escape at least the initial onslaught he was crawling right under the blanket when – as he slowly poked his head out again – the bell rang a second time, particularly shrilly, K. thought. Although this was unlikely to concern K. again, everyone fell silent and Schwarzer returned to the telephone. There he listened to a lengthy explanation, then said quietly: 'A mistake, you say? This puts me in a most embarrassing position. The office manager phoned in person? Odd, very odd. Yes, but how am I going to explain that to the land surveyor?'

K. began to take notice. So the castle had appointed him land surveyor. On the one hand that was to his disadvantage, since it showed they knew all they needed to know about him at the castle, had weighed up the balance of forces, and were entering the fray with a smile. But on the other hand it was also to his advantage, because it showed, he felt, that they underestimated him and that he was going to have more freedom than he might have hoped for at the outset. And if they thought that with this intellectually no doubt superior recognition of his land-surveyorship they could keep him in a permanent state of fright, then they were wrong, it sent a little shiver down his spine, that was all.

As Schwarzer tentatively approached, K. waved him away; he declined to move into the landlord's room, as he was urged to do, he simply accepted a nightcap from the landlord and a washbasin with soap and towel from the landlady and had no need even to ask for the lounge to be vacated because they were all pushing through the door with faces averted, possibly to avoid being recognized by him in the morning, the lamp was extinguished and he was finally left in peace. He slept well, only fleetingly disturbed by the occasional rat scurrying past, until morning.

After breakfast, which like all K.'s board was (said the landlord) to be paid for by the castle, he wanted to go straight into the village. However, since the landlord, with whom in the light of his behaviour the previous day K. had so far exchanged only the most essential remarks, persisted in hovering about him, mutely pleading, he took pity on the man and made him sit down beside him for a moment.

'I've not met the count before,' said K. 'He's said to pay well for good work, is that right? When you travel as far from wife and child as I've done, you want to have something to bring home.'

'Sir need have no worries on that score, you hear no complaints about poor pay.'

'Well,' said K., 'I'm not a shy man and can speak my mind even to a count, but it's far better, of course, to deal with the gentlemen in peace.'

The landlord sat on the edge of the windowseat facing K., not daring to make himself more comfortable, and he spent the whole time looking at K. with large brown, fearful eyes. Initially he had thrust himself on K., and now it seemed he wanted nothing so much as to run away. Was he afraid of being questioned about the count? Did he fear the untrustworthiness of the 'gentleman' he took K. to be? K. needed to distract him. He glanced at the clock and said, 'My assistants will be arriving soon, will you be able to put them up here?'

'Certainly, sir,' he said, 'but won't they be staying with you in the castle?'

Was he so ready and willing to turn away guests and particularly to turn away K., whom he was urgently referring to the castle?

'That's not certain yet,' said K., 'I first have to find out what sort of job they have for me. If I'm to be working down here, for instance, it will make more sense to live down here, too. I'm also afraid that life up in the castle would not agree with me. I'm keen to stay free.'

'You don't know the castle,' the landlord said quietly.

'Granted,' said K., 'one shouldn't jump to conclusions. I mean, all I know about the castle at the moment is that they know how to choose the right land surveyor. The place may have other merits.' And he stood up to give the landlord, who was chewing his lips uneasily, his release. It was not going to be easy, gaining this man's trust.

As K. walked away, his attention was drawn to a picture on the wall, a dark portrait in a dark frame. He had noticed it before, from his bed, but at that distance, unable to make out details, he had thought the actual painting had been removed from the frame, leaving only a black backing-sheet visible. However, it was in fact a painting, as now emerged, a half-length portrait of a man of perhaps fifty. The head was sunk so low on the breast that very little could be seen of the man's eyes, the apparent cause of the sinking being the high, heavy

7

forehead and the large hooked nose. The beard, forced in at the chin by the way the head was held, stood out farther down. The left hand lay splayed in the thick hair but was no longer capable of lifting the head. 'Who is that?' K. asked, 'the count?' Planted in front of the picture, K. did not even look round at the landlord. 'No,' said the landlord, 'the governor.' 'They've a handsome governor up at the castle, that's a fact,' said K., 'pity his son turned out so badly.' 'No,' said the landlord, pulling K. down to him slightly and whispering in his ear: 'Schwarzer was exaggerating yesterday, his father is only an under-governor, and one of the lowest at that.' Just then, for a moment, the landlord looked to K. like a child. 'The rascal!' K. said with a laugh, but the landlord did not join in the laughter, saying only: 'Even *his* father is powerful.' 'Go on!' said K., 'you think everyone's powerful. Me too, I suppose?' 'You,' he said shyly but in earnest, 'I do not consider powerful.' 'In that case you're a very observant man,' said K., 'because powerful, between you and me, is something I really am not. And I probably, as a result, have no less respect for the powerful than you do, only I'm not as honest as you and won't always admit it.' And to console the landlord and make him more kindly disposed towards him, K. patted him on the cheek. At this, he did give a little smile. He was very much a youth with his soft almost beardless face. How had he come by his fat elderly wife, now visible through a hatch in the next room, elbows held wide, bustling about in the kitchen. But K. decided not to press him any further just now, not dispel the smile he had at last elicited, so he simply signalled to him to open the door for him and stepped out into the fine winter's morning.

Now he could see the castle up above, sharply outlined in the clear air and made even sharper by the thin layer of snow that covered everything, duplicating every shape. There seemed in fact to be far less snow up on the hill than here in the village, where K. found progress no less laborious than out on the main road the day before. Here the snow came up to the windows of the cottages and then immediately lay heavy again on their low roofs, but up on the hill everything rose freely and airily skyward, at least so it appeared from below.

On the whole, seen from this distance, the castle matched K.'s expectations. It was neither an old-style knight's stronghold, nor a modern palace, but an extended complex consisting of a few two-storeyed but a great many lower buildings set close together; had you not known it was a castle, you might have taken it for a small town. K. saw only one tower, there was no telling whether it belonged to a residential building or to a church. Flocks of crows wheeled around it.

His eyes fixed on the castle, K. walked on, nothing else concerned him. As he came closer, however, the castle disappointed him, it really was just a wretched-looking small town, a collection of rustic hovels, its only distinction being that, possibly, everything was built of stone, though the paint had peeled off long since and the stone looked as if it was crumbling away. K. had a fleeting memory of his own home town, it was scarcely inferior to this so-called castle, if K. had been interested only in sightseeing it would have been a waste of all the travelling, he would have done better to revisit his old home, where he had not been for so long. And he drew a mental comparison between the church tower of his home town and the tower above him. The tower at home, neatly, unhesitatingly tapering straight upward, ending below in a red-tiled expanse of roof, an earthly building – what other kind can we build? – yet with a loftier goal than the squat jumble of houses and making a clearer statement than the drab working day. The tower up above – it was the only one visible – the tower of a dwelling, as could now be seen, possibly the main body of the castle, was a uniform, circular structure, part cloaked in ivy, with small windows that gleamed in the sun – there was a crazy quality about this – and a balcony-like rim with battlements that jutted uncertainly, unevenly, brittlely, as if drawn by the timid or slapdash hand of a child, up into the blue sky. It was as if some gloomy inmate, who by rights should have remained locked away in the farthest room in the house, had burst through the roof and raised himself high in order to be seen by the world.

Once again K. stood still, as if standing still sharpened his judgement. But he was interrupted. Round the back of the village church, beside which he had come to a halt – it was only a chapel, actually, enlarged like a barn to accommodate the congregation – was the school. A long low building, oddly blending characteristics of the temporary and of the very old, it lay beyond a fenced garden that was now an expanse of snow. The children were just emerging with the schoolmaster. They surrounded the schoolmaster in a dense mass, all eyes fixed on him, chattering incessantly from all sides, K. understood nothing of their rapid speech. The schoolmaster, a young, short, narrow-shouldered man who, without appearing ridiculous, nevertheless held himself very straight, had already spotted K. from a distance, true, apart from his own group, K. was the only person about. K., as the stranger, gave his greeting first, particularly to so commanding a little man. 'Good morning, sir,' he said. At a stroke the children stopped their chatter, the abrupt silence was no doubt pleasing to the schoolmaster as a prelude to his words. 'You're here to view the castle?' he asked, more gently than K. had expected yet in a tone that suggested disapproval of what K. was doing. 'Yes,' said K., 'I'm a stranger here, I only arrived last night.' 'You don't like the castle?' the schoolmaster asked quickly. 'What's that?' K. asked back, somewhat startled, and he echoed the question in a milder form: 'Do I like the castle? Why should you assume I don't?' 'Visitors never like it,' said the schoolmaster. To avoid saying anything unwelcome at this point, K. changed the subject and asked: 'You know the count, presumably?' 'No,' the schoolmaster said and was about to turn away, but K. did not give up and asked again: 'What? You don't know the count?' 'How should I know him?' the schoolmaster said under his breath, adding aloud, in French: 'Remember there are innocent children present.' K. used this as an excuse to ask the schoolmaster: 'Could I come and see you some time, sir? I'm here for a while and am already feeling a bit lonely, I'm not one of the peasants and hardly belong in the castle either.' 'There's no difference,' the schoolmaster said, 'between peasants and castle.' 'Maybe,' said K., 'that doesn't alter my situation. Might I come and see you some time?' 'I live in Swan Lane, at the butcher's.' This was more a statement than an invitation, but K. still said: 'Fine, I'll be there.' The schoolmaster nodded and moved on with the mass of children, who immediately resumed their shouting. They soon disappeared down a lane that dropped away sharply.

But K. was distracted, the exchange had irritated him. For the first time since his arrival he felt real weariness. The long journey to this place seemed to have left him quite unaffected at first – how he had tramped through the days, stride by smooth stride! – now, however, the effects of that huge effort were making themselves felt, it was a bad time for it, of course. He was irresistibly drawn towards seeking out fresh acquaintanceships, yet each fresh acquaintanceship increased his weariness. In his present state, if he pushed himself to extend his walk as far as the castle entrance at least, that would be more than enough.

On he went, then, but it was a long way. This road, the village high street, did not in fact lead to Castle Hill, it only went close to it but then curved away, as if on purpose, and although it took one no farther from the castle, nor did it come any nearer. K. constantly expected the road to turn in the direction of the castle at last, surely it would, and it was only because he expected it that he kept going; obviously, given his weariness, he was reluctant to leave the road, he was also surprised at how long the village was, it went on and on, nothing but tiny houses and iced-up windowpanes and snow and nobody around – finally he tore himself loose from the grip of the high street, a narrow lane swallowed him up, even deeper snow, his feet sank in, it was hard work extracting them, he began to perspire, abruptly he came to a halt and could go no farther.

He was not alone, though, humble cottages stood on either side, he made a snowball and hurled it at a window. The door opened immediately – the first to have done so the whole way through the village – and there, wearing a brown fur jacket, his head cocked on one side, friendly and frail, stood an aged peasant. 'May I come in for a minute?' said K. 'I'm very tired.' Not even hearing what the old man said, he gratefully accepted a board being pushed towards him, this promptly retrieved him from the snow and with a couple of steps he was inside.

A large room, dimly lit. Coming in from the lane, one saw nothing at first. K. stumbled against a washing-trough, a woman's hand restrained him. Much shouting of children came from one corner. From another corner steam billowed, turning the half-light into darkness, K. was standing in clouds, as it were. 'He's drunk,' someone said. 'Who are you?' a peremptory voice called, presumably then turning to the old man: 'Why did you let him in? Are we to let in everyone prowling the streets?' 'I am the count's land surveyor,' said K., seeking to justify himself to the still invisible questioner. 'Oh, it's the land surveyor,' said a female voice, then there was complete silence. 'Do you know me?' K. asked. 'Of course,' the same voice said briefly. The fact that K. was known seemed not to recommend him.

Eventually the steam dispersed somewhat and K. was gradually able to get his bearings. It appeared to be a communal washday. By the door, laundry was being washed. However, the steam had been coming from the left-hand corner, where in the largest wooden tub K. had ever seen, it was about the size of two beds, two men sat in steaming water, taking a bath. But even more surprising, without one quite knowing what was surprising about it, was the right-hand corner. There a large opening, the only one in the rear wall of the room, let in, presumably from the yard, pale snow-reflected light that, falling on the dress of a woman so weary she was almost lying in a tall easy-chair right in the corner, gave it a sheen like silk. The woman held a baby to her breast. Around her, several children were playing, peasant children evidently, yet she seemed not to belong to them, though of course disease and fatigue make even peasants look delicate.

'Sit down,' ordered one of the bathers, a man with a full beard and a moustache as well, below which his panting mouth was held permanently open, and he pointed, it was a comical sight, over the edge of the tub towards a chest, spraying K. full in the face with warm water as he did so. On the chest, already dozing, sat the old man who had let K. in. K. was grateful to be allowed to sit down at last. Now no one took any further notice of him. The woman at the washing-trough, fair-haired, plumply youthful, sang softly as she worked, the men in the bath stamped and turned about, the children tried to approach but were repeatedly driven back by great splashes of water that hit K. too, the woman in the easy-chair lay as if life had left her, not even looking down at the child at her breast but vaguely up in the air.

K. had spent some time, possibly, contemplating this unvarying, lovely, melancholy spectacle but must then have fallen asleep, because when he started up, having been summoned by a loud voice, his head was resting on the shoulder of the old man beside him. The men had finished their bath, the children were now romping around in it under the eye of the fair-haired woman, and they were standing in front of K., fully dressed. The noisy one with the beard proved to be the slighter of the two. The other, who was no taller than the full-bearded one and had far less facial hair, was in fact a silent, slow-thinking man, broad in the body, broad-faced too, with lowered head. 'Sir,' he said, 'you can't stay here, Mr Land Surveyor. Pardon the discourtesy.' 'I didn't mean to stay,' said K., 'only to rest a little. That I've done, and now I'm off.' 'You're no doubt surprised at the lack of hospitality,' said the man, 'but hospitality is not one of our customs, we don't need visitors.' Somewhat refreshed by his sleep, his hearing rather keener than before, K. was delighted by these frank words. He moved about more freely, planting his stick here and there, approaching the woman in the easy-chair, he was also the biggest person in the room, physically.

'Of course,' said K., 'why should you need visitors. Now and again, though, you do need one, me for instance, the land surveyor.' 'I don't know,' the man said slowly, 'if you've been summoned you probably are needed, that may well be an exception, but we lesser folk, we stick to the rules, you can't blame us for that.' 'No, no,' said K., 'I'm only grateful to you, you and everyone here.' And K. surprised them all by positively leaping round to face the woman. She looked at K. out of tired blue eyes, a transparent silk headscarf came down to the middle of her forehead, the baby slept at her breast. 'Who are you?' asked K. Disdainfully, it was not clear whether the scorn was aimed at K. or at her own response, she said: 'A girl from the castle.'

All this had taken no more than a moment, already K. had one of the men on either side of him and, as if there had been no other means of communication, was silently but with full force being dragged to the door. Something about this delighted the old man and he clapped his hands. The woman doing the washing laughed too as the children suddenly began shouting like mad.

K., however, was soon standing in the lane, the men eyeing him from the doorway, snow was falling again although it did seem a little brighter. The one with the beard called out impatiently: 'Where do you want to go? This way leads to the castle, that way to the village.' Him K. did not answer, but to the other, whom for all his superior air he took to be the more obliging of the two, he said, 'Who are you? Who should I thank for having me?' 'My name is Lasemann, I'm the tanner,' came the reply, 'but you don't need to thank anyone.' 'Fine,' said K., 'perhaps we'll meet again.' 'I don't think so,' said the man. Just then the bearded fellow raised a hand in the air and called out: 'Morning Arthur, morning Jeremiah!' K. turned, so people did actually show themselves on the street in this village! Coming from the direction of the castle were two young men of medium height, both extremely slim, dressed in tight-fitting clothes, facially very similar too, with dark-brown complexions against which goatee beards nevertheless stood out with especial blackness. They were moving astonishingly fast, given the road conditions, swinging their slim legs rhythmically. 'What's up?' the bearded man shouted. Shouting was the only way to communicate with them, they were walking so fast and did not stop. 'Business,' they called back with a laugh. 'Where?' 'At the inn.' 'That's where I'm going too,' K. suddenly shouted out louder than everyone else, he was aware of a deep yearning to be taken along by the two men; as acquaintances, they did not seem to him to have much to offer, but they were clearly fine enlivening escorts. However, they heard what K. said but merely nodded and were gone.

K., still standing in the snow, had little desire to heave one foot out of the snow in order to plunge it back in a bit farther on; the tanner and his companion, happy to have got rid of K. for good, slowly pushed their way, keeping their eyes on K., through the only slightly open door into the house, and K. was alone with the snow enveloping him. 'Occasion for a moment's despair,' he thought, 'if I'd been standing here purely by chance, not from choice.'

Then a tiny window opened in the cottage on his left, while closed it had looked dark-blue, possibly in the light reflected off the snow, and was so tiny that, now that it was open, rather than the whole face of the person looking out only the eyes, elderly brown eyes, could be seen. 'There he is,' K. heard a shaky female voice say. 'It's the land surveyor,' said a man's voice. Then the man came to the window and asked in a not unfriendly way, but still as if he was keen that everything should be in order in the street outside his house: 'Who are you waiting for?' 'For a sledge to pick me up,' said K. 'No sledges come along here,' said the man, 'there's no traffic here.' 'But this is the street leading to the castle,' K. objected. 'Even so,' the man said with a certain relentlessness, 'even so, there's no traffic here.' They both fell silent. But the man was evidently thinking something over because the window, from which smoke was pouring, stayed open, with him holding it. 'Difficult going,' K. said to prompt him. But all he said was: 'Certainly is.' After a while, though, he came out with: 'If you like, I'll drive you in my sledge.' 'Please do,' K. said delightedly, 'what will it cost me?' 'Nothing,' said the man. K. was amazed. 'You're the land surveyor,' the man said in explanation, 'and belong to the castle. Where do you want to go, then?' 'To the castle,' K. said quickly. 'In that case I'm not going,' the man said promptly. 'But I belong to the castle,' said K., echoing the man's own words. 'Maybe,' the man said coldly. 'Then take me to the inn,' said K. 'All right,' said the man, 'I'll bring the sledge round.' The whole episode gave an impression not of any particular friendliness, rather of a sort of wholly self-centred, fastidious, almost pedantic concern to get K. away from the area in front of the house.

The yard gate opened and a small goods sledge came out, quite flat without any sort of seat, drawn by a frail pony, and behind it the man, not old but frail, bent, lame, with a thin red peevish face made to look particularly small by a woollen scarf wound tightly around the neck. The man was clearly ill and had come out purely to be able to get K. away from there. K. mentioned something to that effect, but the man waved it aside. All K. learned was that the man was Gerstäcker the carter and that he had taken that uncomfortable sledge because it had been standing ready and because getting another one out would have taken too long. 'Have a seat,' he said, using the whip to point to the sledge behind him. 'I'll sit beside you,' said K. 'I'm walking,' said Gerstäcker. 'But why?' asked K. 'I'm walking,' Gerstäcker repeated, promptly suffering a coughing fit that shook him so badly he had to thrust his legs into the snow to brace himself and hang on to the side of the sledge with both hands. K. said nothing more, sat on the sledge behind him, the coughing gradually subsided, and off they drove.

The castle above, already strangely dark, which K. had been hoping to reach that day, receded again. But as if he was meant to be given a signal at this provisional leave-taking, the sound of a bell rang out there, gaily vibrant, a bell that for a moment at least sent a tremor through the heart, as if it was threatened – for the sound was also painful – with the fulfilment of what it vaguely yearned for. Before long, however, this big bell fell silent and a feeble monotonous tinkling took its place, possibly also up above but possibly down in the village. This smaller bell was more in keeping, of course, with the slow drive and the wretched yet relentless driver.

'I say,' K. cried suddenly – they were near the church already, it was not much farther to the inn, K. could afford to take a risk – 'I'm most surprised you should dare to drive me about on your own responsibility. Is that allowed?' Gerstäcker took no notice and walked calmly on beside the pony. 'Hey,' K. called, and he made a snowball from some of the snow on the sledge and hit Gerstäcker right on the ear with it. At this he did in fact halt and turn around; but when K. now saw him so close to – the sledge had glided on a little way – that bent, as it were abused figure, the red tired narrow face with the two cheeks somehow not matching, one flat, the other sunken, the open attentive mouth with only a few isolated teeth in it, he had to repeat what he had earlier said with malice, this time with compassion, asking whether Gerstäcker might not be punished for carrying K. 'What do you expect?' Gerstäcker asked blankly, but without waiting for any further explanation he called to the pony and they drove on.

When they – K. realized this at a bend in the road – were almost at the inn, to his amazement it was already completely dark. Had he been gone so long? Surely only one, say two hours, by his reckoning. And it had been morning when he left. Nor had he felt any need to eat. And until recently it had been constant daylight, the darkness falling only now. 'Short days, short days,' he said to himself as he slid off the sledge and walked towards the inn.

At the top of the modest front steps of the building stood the very welcome figure of the landlord, lighting his way with upraised lantern. Briefly recalling the carter, K. halted, heard coughing somewhere in the darkness, that was him. Well, he would be seeing him again soon. Only when he had climbed the steps and joined the landlord, who murmured a humble greeting, did he notice two men, standing one on each side of the door. Taking the lantern from the landlord's hand, he shone its light on them; they were the men he had come across before, when they had been hailed as Arthur and Jeremiah. They now saluted. Remembering his army days, those happy times, he gave a laugh. 'Who are you?' he asked, looking from one to the other. 'Your assistants,' they replied. 'These are the assistants,' the landlord quietly confirmed. 'What?' K. asked, 'you're my old assistants whom I had follow me, whom I've been expecting?' They said they were. 'That's good,' K. said after a pause, 'it's good that you've come.' 'Actually,' K. said after a further pause, 'you're very late, you've been extremely negligent.'

'It was a long way,' one of them said. 'A long way,' K. echoed, 'but I met you coming from the castle.' 'Yes,' they said, without further explanation. 'Where have you got the equipment?' asked K. 'We have none,' they said. 'The equipment I entrusted you with?' said K. 'We have none,' they repeated. 'Well, you're fine fellows!' said K. 'Do you know anything about land surveying?' 'No,' they said. 'But if you're my old assistants, you must know something about it,' said K. They were silent. 'Come on, then,' K. said, pushing them ahead of him into the building.

2

BARNABAS

They were sitting in the lounge of the inn over their beer, saying little, the three of them at a small table, K. in the middle, the assistants on either side. Otherwise only one table was occupied by peasants, as on the previous evening. 'It's difficult with you,' K. said, comparing their faces as he had already done many times, 'how am I to tell you apart? The only difference between you is in your names, otherwise you're as alike as' – he hesitated, then continued involuntarily – 'otherwise you're as alike as two snakes.' They smiled. 'Other people can tell us apart,' they said to justify themselves. 'I believe you,' said K., 'I witnessed that myself, remember, but I see only with my eyes and with them I can't tell you apart. So I shall treat you as one man and call you both Arthur, that's what one of you is named – you, am I right?' K. asked one of them. 'No,' the man said, 'I'm Jeremiah.' 'All right, never mind,' said K., 'I shall call you both Arthur. If I send Arthur off somewhere, you both go, if I give Arthur a job, you both do it, for me that has the big disadvantage, of course, that I can't use you for separate jobs, on the other hand it has the advantage that, for every task I set you, you both share undivided responsibility. I don't care how you split the work between you, only you mustn't ever use each other as an excuse, to me you're one man.' They thought about this and said: 'We wouldn't like that at all.' 'Of course you wouldn't,' said K., 'how could you help not liking it, but that's the way it's going to be.' For some time now, K. had been aware of one of the peasants prowling round the table, eventually the man made up his mind, went up to one assistant, and was about to whisper something to him. 'Excuse me,' K. said, striking the table with his hand and standing up, 'these are my assistants and we are just having a discussion. No one has any right to interrupt us.' 'Sorry, sorry,' the peasant said anxiously, backing away towards his table companions. 'One thing you must look out for above all,' K. went

18

on, resuming his seat, 'you may not speak to anyone without my permission. I'm a stranger here, and if you are my old assistants, then you're strangers, too. So we three strangers must stick together, I want you to shake on that.' Rather too readily they offered K. their hands. 'Put your paws down,' he said, 'but what I say goes. Now I'm off to bed and I advise you to follow my example. We've missed one working day today, tomorrow work has to start very early. You must get hold of a sledge to drive to the castle and be ready with it outside here at six o'clock.' 'Right,' said one. The other, however, broke in: 'You say "Right", but you know it can't be done.' 'Calm down,' said K., 'I suppose you're just trying to show that you're different.' But now the first one also said: 'He's right, it can't be done, strangers aren't allowed into the castle without permission.' 'Where does one apply for permission?' 'I don't know, to the governor, possibly.' 'Then we'll telephone and apply, go and ring the governor immediately, both of you.' They ran to the telephone, requested the connection – how they pushed and shoved, on the face of it they were absurdly biddable – and asked whether K. might come up to the castle with them tomorrow. K. heard the answering 'no' from where he was sitting, but the reply went into greater detail, adding: 'neither tomorrow nor any other time.' 'I'll telephone myself,' K. said and stood up. Whereas previously, the incident of the one peasant aside, K. and his assistants had attracted little notice, his last remark aroused general attention. They all rose to their feet with K. and, despite the landlord's attempts to restrain them, gathered in a group near the telephone, forming a tight semicircle around him. The prevailing view among them was that K. would not even get a reply. K. had to ask them to be quiet, he had no wish to hear their views.

The earpiece emitted a buzzing sound unlike anything K. had heard before when using the telephone. It was as if out of the buzzing of countless children's voices – but again, this was no buzzing, this was the song of distant, utterly distant voices – as if out of this buzzing there emerged in a quite impossible fashion a single high-pitched yet powerful voice that struck the ear as if demanding to penetrate deeper than into mere hearing. K. listened without telephoning, he had rested his left arm on the telephone console, and he listened like that.

He was not aware for how long, he was still listening when the landlord tugged at his jacket to say a messenger had arrived for him.

'Go away,' K. shouted, beside himself, possibly into the telephone because at that point someone did come on the line. The following conversation ensued: 'Oswald here, who's that?' a voice shouted, a harsh, arrogant voice carrying, as it seemed to K., a minor speech defect for which it tried involuntarily to compensate with added harshness. K. hesitated to give his name, he was defenceless so far as the telephone was concerned, his interlocutor might shout him down, lay the earpiece aside, and K. would have blocked what was perhaps quite an important channel for him. K.'s hesitation made the man impatient. 'Who's that?' he repeated, adding: 'I'd be very glad if a little less telephoning was done from that end, there was a call only a moment ago.' K. ignored this remark and announced with sudden decision: 'This is the land surveyor's assistant.' 'What assistant? What land surveyor?' K. recalled the previous day's telephone conversation: 'Ask Fritz,' he said briefly. This worked, to his own amazement. But what amazed him even more than that was the coherence of the operation up there. The answer came back: 'I know. The land surveyor again. Don't tell me. Go on. Which assistant?' 'Joseph,' said K. He was slightly disturbed by the muttering of the peasants behind him, clearly they disagreed with his not announcing himself correctly. However, K. had no time to worry about them, he was too involved in the conversation. 'Joseph?' the voice asked back. 'The assistants' names are' – a short pause, he was obviously asking someone else for the names – 'Arthur and Jeremiah.' 'Those are the new assistants,' said K. 'No, those are the old ones.' 'They're the new ones, I'm the old one, I rejoined the land surveyor today.' 'No,' the voice now shouted. 'Who am I then?' K. asked, still as calmly. And after a pause the same voice with the same speech defect, except that it was like another, deeper voice, one commanding greater respect, said: 'You're the old assistant.'

K., concentrating on the tone of voice, almost missed the question: 'What do you want?' What he really wanted was to lay the receiver aside right then. He expected nothing further from this conversation. Under some strain, he asked quickly: 'When can my boss come to the castle?' 'Never,' was the reply. 'Right,' said K., and hung up.

Behind him the peasants had already pressed right up close. The assistants, with frequent sideways glances at him, were busy keeping the peasants away from him. It looked like pure pretence, however, and in any case the peasants, satisfied with the outcome of the conversation, were slowly giving ground. At this point their group was parted from behind with swift strides by a man who came up to K., bowed, and handed him a letter. K. kept the letter in his hand and looked at the man, who for the moment seemed to him more important. There was a great similarity between him and the assistants, he was as slim as they were, his clothes fitted as tightly, he was also as nimble and quick as they were, yet he was quite different. How K. would have preferred him as an assistant! He reminded him slightly of the woman with the baby whom he had seen at the tanner's house. He was dressed almost in white, the suit was not silk, presumably, it was a winter suit like all the others, but it had the delicate, festive quality of a silk suit. His face was bright and open, with huge eyes. His smile was extraordinarily encouraging; he passed a hand over his face as if wishing to banish the smile, but this he failed to do. 'Who are you?' K. asked. 'My name is Barnabas,' he said, 'I'm a messenger.' It was manly yet gentle, the way his lips opened and closed as he spoke. 'Do you like it here?' K. asked, indicating the peasants, in whose eyes he had lost none of his fascination and who with their positively tortured faces – the skulls looking as if they had been smashed flat on top and the features had taken shape in the agony of being struck – their thick lips, and their open mouths continued to watch but then again were not watching because their gaze sometimes went wandering off and dwelled, before returning, on some trivial object, and K. then also indicated the assistants, who were clasped in an embrace, leaning together cheek to cheek and smiling, whether humbly or derisively there was no telling, he indicated them all as if introducing an entourage that had been forced on him by particular circumstances and expecting Barnabas – there was a familiarity in this, which was what mattered to K. – to draw a sensible distinction between himself and them. But Barnabas – in all innocence, of course, that much was clear – did not even take up the question but let it pass over him, as a well-trained servant does with a word from his master that was only seemingly meant for him, and merely looked around in the spirit of the question, waving to acquaintances among the peasants and exchanging a few words with the assistants, all this freely and independently without mingling with them. K. returned – dismissed but unabashed – to the letter in his hand

and opened it. It read: 'Dear Sir, as you know, you have been admitted to the count's service. Your immediate superior is the mayor of the village, who will also give you all the details of your job and the terms of payment and to whom you will also be accountable. Nevertheless, I shall also be keeping an eye on you myself. Barnabas, the bearer of this letter, will make inquiries of you from time to time in order to discover your wishes and communicate them to me. You will find me ever ready to oblige you so far as possible. I like to have contented workers.' The signature was illegible but printed beneath it was: Chief Clerk, X. Office. 'Wait,' K. told Barnabas as the man bowed, then he summoned the landlord to show him to his room, he wished to be alone with the letter for a while. At the same time he remembered that Barnabas, for all the fondness he felt for him, was in fact no more than a messenger, and he had a beer brought for him. He watched to see how he would receive it, clearly he did so with great pleasure and drank some immediately. K. then went with the landlord. All they had been able to make available to K. in that tiny house was a little attic room, and even that had caused problems, because two maids who had been sleeping there up to now had needed to be accommodated elsewhere. Actually, nothing had been done beyond getting rid of the maids, the room was otherwise unchanged, presumably, no linen on the one bed, only a couple of pillows and a horse blanket in the state they had all been left in after the previous night, a few holy pictures and photographs of soldiers on the walls, the room had not even been aired, clearly it was hoped that the new guest would not be staying long and nothing was being done to keep him there. K., however, was quite happy with everything, wrapped himself in the blanket, sat down at the table, and began by the light of a candle to reread the letter.

It was not consistent all the way through, there were places where he was addressed as a freeman might be addressed whose own will was acknowledged and accepted, the 'Dear Sir' was like that, as was the bit about his wishes. But there were other places where he was frankly or by implication treated as a minor employee, barely noticeable from where this chief clerk sat, the chief clerk had to make an effort to 'keep an eye on' him, his superior was simply the mayor, to whom he was even accountable, possibly his only colleague was the village policeman. These were undoubted contradictions, so obvious they must have been intentional. The idea, crazy in relation to such an authority, that indecision may have played a part here scarcely occurred to K. Instead he saw it as a choice freely offered him, it was up to him what he wished to make of the arrangements contained in the letter, whether he wished to be a village workman with a certainly distinctive yet purely ostensible connection with the castle or an ostensible village workman who in reality allowed the news brought by Barnabas to govern his entire employment. K. did not hesitate over his choice, he would not have hesitated even without his experience hitherto. Only as a village workman, as far removed as possible from the gentlemen of the castle, was he in a position to achieve something in the castle, these folk in the village, so mistrustful of him as yet, would start to talk once he had become, if not their friend, at least a fellow-citizen, and was indistinguishable from, say, Gerstäcker or Lasemann – and that must happen very soon, everything hung on that – then all avenues would doubtless open to him at a stroke that, had it depended solely on the gentlemen up there and their favour, would have remained not only permanently closed but permanently invisible to him. There was a risk, of course, and it was well emphasized in the letter, it was even set out with a certain relish as if it was inescapable. This was the fact of being a worker. Service, superior, job, terms of payment, accountable, workmen, the letter teemed with such expressions and even if other, more personal things were said they were said from that standpoint. If K. wished to become a worker he could do so, but it must be in all appalling earnest, with no other prospect whatever. K. knew the threat was not one of real coercion, he was not afraid of that, here least of all, but the power of the depressing surroundings, the growing inured to disappointment, the power of the imperceptible effects of each moment, those he was afraid of, but it was a risk he must boldly combat. Nor, after all, did the letter hide the fact that, should it come to a fight, K. had had the temerity to start it, this was said subtly and only an uneasy conscience – uneasy, not guilty – could have noticed, it lay in the three words 'as you know', with reference to his acceptance for work. K. had announced his presence and since then had been aware, as the letter put it, that he had been accepted.

K. took a picture down from the wall and hung the letter on the nail, this was the room he would be living in, this was where the letter should hang.

Then he went down to the lounge, Barnabas was sitting at a little table with the assistants. 'Ah, there you are,' K. said for no reason, simply because he was glad to see Barnabas. He leaped to his feet immediately. As soon as K. entered the room, the peasants stood up to approach him, they were already in the habit of running after him the whole time. 'What is it you constantly want from me?' K. shouted. They took no offence at this, slowly turning back to their places. One said as he went, casually, by way of explanation, with an inscrutable smile that was taken up by several others: 'One's always hearing something new,' and he licked his lips as if news were something to eat. K. said nothing placatory, it was fine if they were starting to have a bit of respect for him, but hardly had he taken a seat beside Barnabas when he felt one of the peasants breathing down his neck, he said he had come over to fetch the salt cellar, but K. stamped his foot in irritation and the man ran off without actually taking the salt cellar with him. K. was really easy to get at, all that was needed, for example, was to stir up the peasants against him, their obstinate interest seemed to him more malevolent than the others' reserve, and in any case it was itself reserve because had K. sat down at their table they would certainly not have stayed sitting there. Only the presence of Barnabas stopped him making a fuss. He did turn threateningly towards them, they were now facing him too. But seeing them sitting there, each in his place, not consulting amongst themselves, with no visible link between them, the only thing linking them the fact that they were all staring at him, it struck him that it was not malevolence that made them pursue him, maybe they really did want something from him only could not say so, and if it was not that, it might be mere childishness; a childishness that seemed to be at home in this place; was not the landlord being childish too, holding in both hands a glass of beer that he was supposed to be bringing to some customer, coming to a halt, looking in K.'s direction, and ignoring a shout from the landlady, who was leaning out of the kitchen hatch.

Calmer, K. turned to Barnabas, he would gladly have got rid of the assistants but could think of no excuse, anyway they were staring silently into their beer. 'I've read the letter,' K. began. 'Do you know what's in it?' 'No,' said Barnabas. His look seemed to express more than his words. K. may have been mistaken here about good as he had in the peasants' case about evil, but the agreeableness of his presence remained. 'The letter mentions you too, it says you're to pass information between me and the chief clerk from time to time, that's why I thought you knew what was in it.' 'My instructions,' said Barnabas, 'were simply to hand you the letter, wait until it had been read, and, if you felt it necessary, bring back a verbal or written reply.' 'Fine,' said K. 'Writing's not necessary, just give the chief clerk – what's his name, in fact? I couldn't read the signature.' 'Klamm,' said Barnabas. 'Right, thank Mr Klamm for my acceptance as well as for his especial kindness, which as someone who has yet to prove himself here I greatly appreciate. I shall conduct myself entirely in accordance with his intentions. For the moment, I have no special wishes.' Barnabas, who had been paying close attention, asked to be allowed to repeat the message for K.'s benefit, K. gave permission, and Barnabas repeated everything word for word. Then he stood up to take his leave.

K. had been studying his face throughout, now he did so one last time. Barnabas was about the same height as K. yet appeared to look down on K., it happened almost humbly, though, there was no chance of this man ever embarrassing anyone. He was only a messenger, of course, not knowing what was in the letter he had been given to deliver, yet his look, his smile, his whole bearing seemed themselves to constitute a message, even if he knew nothing of that one, either. And K. offered him his hand, which clearly surprised him, because he had only meant to bow.

As soon as he had gone – before opening the door he had leant his shoulder against it for an instant and, with a look that was no longer aimed at anyone in particular, taken in the room – K. said to the assistants: 'I'll fetch my drawings from my room and we'll discuss the next job.' They made as if to go with him. 'You stay here,' K. ordered. Still they made as if to go with him. K. had to repeat the command even more sternly. Barnabas was no longer in the hallway. Yet he had only just that minute left. Even outside – fresh snow was falling – K. could not see him. He called out: 'Barnabas!' No reply. Was he still inside the building? It seemed the only possibility. Even so, K. shouted the name again with all his strength, sending it booming into the night.

And this time, out of the distance, there did come a feeble reply, that was how far off Barnabas was already. K. called him back and at the same time set out to meet him; where they met, they were no longer visible from the inn.

'Barnabas,' said K., unable to suppress a tremor in his voice, 'there's something else I wanted to say to you. This makes me realize what a very poor arrangement it is that I should be wholly dependent on your chancing to turn up when I need something from the castle. If I hadn't chanced to catch up with you just now – how you fly, I thought you were still inside the building – who knows how long I'd have had to wait for your next appearance?' 'Well,' said Barnabas, 'you can ask the chief clerk for me always to come at specific times laid down by yourself.' 'That wouldn't do either,' said K. 'I might go for a year without wanting anything said, then have something really urgent a quarter of an hour after you've gone.' 'In that case,' Barnabas inquired, 'shall I inform the chief clerk that a different contact should be established between him and you than through me?' 'No, no,' said K, 'certainly not, I only mention the matter in passing, this time I luckily managed to reach you.' 'Shall we,' asked Barnabas, 'return to the inn so that you can give me my new instructions there?' He had already taken a step in that direction. 'Barnabas,' said K., 'there's no need, I'll walk a little way with you.' 'Why don't you want to go to the inn?' Barnabas asked. 'The people there bother me,' said K. 'You saw for yourself how pushy the peasants are.' 'We can go to your room,' said Barnabas. 'It's the maids' room,' said K., 'dirty and dreary; it was to get out of staying there that I wanted to walk along with you for a bit, but you must just,' K. went on in a final bid to overcome his hesitation, 'let me slip my arm through yours, you're steadier on your feet.' And K. took his arm. It was quite dark, K. could not see his face at all and his figure only vaguely, the arm he had already tried to feel for earlier.

Barnabas gave in to him, they left the inn behind them. K. felt, of course, that despite his best efforts he could never keep up with Barnabas, that he hindered his freedom of movement, and that under normal circumstances everything must surely founder on this trifle alone, particularly in those side-streets like the one where K. had sunk into the snow that morning and from which he would escape only if Barnabas carried him. However, he kept such worries at bay for the

26

present, he was also comforted by the fact that Barnabas said nothing; if they walked in silence, then possibly for Barnabas, too, simply walking on was in itself the purpose of their being together.

On they walked, but K. did not know where they were going, he recognized nothing, he was not even aware whether they had passed the church yet. The effort that the mere act of walking cost him made him incapable of controlling his thoughts. Instead of staying trained on the object, they became confused. His home kept cropping up, and memories of it filled his mind. There too a church stood in the main square, partially surrounded by an old cemetery and the cemetery by a high wall. Only very few boys had climbed that wall, K. himself had never yet managed to do so. It was not curiosity that drove them to it, the cemetery held no secrets for them any more, they had often got in through its small iron gate, all they wanted was to conquer the smooth high wall. One morning – the silent, empty square was flooded with light, when had K. ever seen it like that, before or since? – he managed it with surprising ease; at a spot where he had often been turned back before, carrying a little flag between his teeth, he scaled the wall first go. Rubble was still clattering down beneath him when suddenly he was on top. He stuck the flag in, the wind pulled the material taut, he looked down and all around, even back over his shoulder at the crosses sinking into the earth, no one, just then, in that place, was taller than him. The schoolmaster happened along at that point, forced K. down with an angry look, K. hurt his knee landing, it was an effort getting home, but he had been up on the wall, the feeling of that triumph seemed to him then to offer support for a long life, which had not been entirely silly because now, many years on, there in the snowy night on Barnabas's arm, it came to his aid.

He held on tighter, Barnabas was almost dragging him along, the silence was uninterrupted; of their route, all K. knew was that, judging from the state of the road, they had not so far turned up any side-streets. He swore to let no difficulty in the journey or indeed concern about the return journey deter him from pressing on; no doubt his strength would suffice to enable him, ultimately, to be dragged on. And the journey could not be endless, surely? In daylight the castle had lain before him like an easy target, and the messenger was bound to know the shortest route.

Abruptly, Barnabas halted. Where were they? Was this the end of the road? Would Barnabas be taking leave of K.? He would never succeed. K. clung to Barnabas's arm, almost hurting himself. Or had the impossible happened and they were already in the castle or at its gates? Yet so far as K. was aware, they had done no climbing. Or had Barnabas brought him by a route that climbed so imperceptibly? 'Where are we?' K. asked quietly, more to himself than to him. 'Home,' Barnabas said as quietly. 'Home?' 'But mind you don't slip now, sir. It's downhill here.' Downhill? 'Just a couple of steps,' he added, then he was knocking at a door.

A girl opened it, they were standing on the threshold of a large room in near-darkness, with only a tiny oil lamp hung above a table in the background to the left. 'Who's this with you, Barnabas?' asked the girl. 'The land surveyor,' he said. 'The land surveyor,' the girl repeated more loudly in the direction of the table. At this, two old people rose to their feet there, a man and a woman, as did another girl. They greeted K. Barnabas introduced him to everyone, the people were his parents and his sisters Olga and Amalia. K. hardly glanced at them, his wet coat was taken from him to be dried by the fire, K. did not resist.

They were not both at home, then, only Barnabas was at home. But why were they here? K. took Barnabas aside and said, 'Why have you come home? Or do you actually live in the castle precincts?' 'In the castle precincts?' Barnabas repeated as if not understanding K. 'Barnabas,' said K., 'you meant, surely, to go from the inn to the castle.' 'No, sir,' said Barnabas, 'I meant to go home, I only go to the castle first thing, I never sleep there.' 'I see,' said K., 'you weren't intending to go to the castle, only here' – his smile seemed fainter, he himself less prepossessing – 'why didn't you tell me?' 'You didn't ask me, sir,' said Barnabas, 'you simply wanted to give me further instructions, but neither in the lounge nor in your room, so I thought you could give me the instructions here at my parents' house, undisturbed – they'll all leave at once if you order them to – you could even, if you prefer it here, spend the night with us. Did I do something wrong?' K. was unable to reply. So it had been a misunderstanding, an ordinary, petty misunderstanding, and K. had surrendered to it utterly. Had let himself be charmed by Barnabas's tight-fitting shiny silk jacket, which the latter now unbuttoned to reveal a coarse, dirty-grey, heavily mended shirt, covering the powerful square chest of a farmhand. And everything around not only matched but actually surpassed this, the old gouty father making progress more with the aid of his groping hands than with the slow shuffle of stiff legs, the mother with her hands folded over her bosom, so stout she could take only the tiniest steps, they had both, father and mother, been advancing on K. from their corner since his entry into the room and had not nearly reached him yet. The sisters, both blonde, resembling each other and Barnabas, but with harder features than Barnabas, big strong wenches, stood around the new arrival, expecting some sort of greeting from K., but there was nothing he could say, he had thought everyone here in the village mattered to him, and so they did, presumably, it was just that these people were of no concern to him whatsoever. Had he been in a fit state to make the journey to the inn on his own, he would have left immediately. The chance of going to the castle with Barnabas first thing did not tempt him at all. It was now, at night, unobserved, that he had wanted to penetrate the castle, guided by Barnabas, but by Barnabas as he had appeared to him previously, a man to whom he felt closer than to anyone he had met here up to now, and of whom he had at the same time believed that he had intimate links with the castle, far beyond his apparent rank. However, with the son of this family, to which he belonged utterly and with which he was already sitting at table, with a man who, significantly, was not even allowed to sleep in the castle, marching into the castle in broad daylight on the arm of such a man was out of the question, was a ludicrously hopeless undertaking.

K. sat down on a window seat, determined to spend the night there, too, and not take advantage of any other service offered by the family. The villagers who sent him away or were afraid of him seemed to him less dangerous, because basically they were only throwing him back on himself, helping him to keep his strength together, but such ostensible helpers, who led him not to the castle but with something of a masquerade to their family home, they were a distraction, whether intentionally or otherwise, they were working to ruin his strength. A shouted invitation from the family table he ignored completely; head lowered, he stayed where he was.

Then Olga, the gentler of the sisters, she even showed a trace of girlish embarrassment, stood up, came over to K., and asked him to sit at table, bread and ham were already set out, she said, and she was just off to fetch beer. 'Where from?' K. asked. 'From the inn,' she said. Delighted to hear this, K. asked her not to fetch beer but to accompany him to the inn, he had some important jobs still to do there. However, it turned out she was not going that far, not to his inn but to another, much nearer one, the Count's Arms. K. still asked if he could accompany her, thinking there might be a chance of a bed there; whatever it was like, he would have preferred it to the best bed in that house. Olga did not answer immediately, she turned and looked towards the table. There her brother, already on his feet, nodded readily and said: 'If it's what the gentleman wants – .' This agreement might almost have persuaded K. to withdraw his request, nothing of value could be agreed to by Barnabas. However, when the question was discussed as to whether K. would be allowed into the inn and they all expressed doubts, he did most urgently insist on going along, though without bothering to invent an intelligible reason for his request; the family must accept him as he was, he felt no shame in their presence, so to speak. The only one who confused him slightly in this respect was Amalia with her serious, level, imperturbable, possibly also rather stolid gaze.

On the short journey to the inn – K. had taken Olga's arm and was drawn along by her, he could not help it, almost as he had been earlier by her brother – he learned that this inn was actually reserved for gentlemen from the castle, who when they had things to do in the village ate there and sometimes even spent the night there. Olga spoke quietly, almost intimately to K., it was pleasant, walking with her, much as it had been with her brother, K. fought the feeling of well-being, but it persisted.

The inn was very similar in appearance to the inn where K. was staying, probably there were no very great external differences in the village, but small differences were noticeable immediately, the front steps had a banister, a splendid lantern was fixed above the door, as they entered a piece of fabric flapped above their heads, it was a flag in the count's colours. In the hallway they were met immediately by the landlord, he was clearly on a tour of inspection; his small eyes searchingly or sleepily took in K. as he passed, and he said: 'The land surveyor's allowed as far as the bar only.' 'Of course,' said Olga, sticking up for K. immediately, 'he's with me, that's all.' K., however, ungratefully removed his arm from Olga's and took the landlord aside, meanwhile Olga waited patiently at the end of the hallway. 'I should like to spend the night here,' said K. 'That's not possible, I'm afraid,' said the landlord, 'you seem to be unaware that this place is for the exclusive use of gentlemen from the castle.' 'That may be what the rules say,' K. countered, 'but surely it must be possible for you to let me sleep in a corner somewhere.' 'I should be delighted to oblige you,' said the landlord, 'but even apart from the stringency of the rules, which you speak of as a stranger would, it is also not feasible because the gentlemen are extremely sensitive, I'm convinced they could never, at least not without warning, stand the sight of a stranger; so if I did let you spend the night here and by some accident – and accidents are always in the gentlemen's favour – you were discovered, not only should I be lost but so would you. It sounds absurd, but it's true.' This tall, tightly buttoned-up fellow who stood with one hand braced against the wall, the other on his hip, legs crossed, stooping slightly towards K., addressing him confidentially, seemed almost not to belong to the village any more, even if his dark suit did simply look like a peasant's Sunday best. 'I quite believe you,' said K., 'and I certainly don't underrate the importance of the rules, either, even if I did express myself carelessly. There's just one thing I'd like to draw to your attention, I have valuable contacts in the castle and shall have even more valuable ones, they will guard you against any danger that might arise out of my spending the night here and be your guarantee of my ability to give adequate thanks for a small favour.' 'Yes, I know,' said the landlord, repeating: 'I do know that.' K. could of course have put his request more forcefully, but this reply from the landlord distracted him, so he simply inquired: 'Do many gentlemen from the castle spend the night here?' 'In that respect today's a good day,' the landlord said almost enticingly, 'only one gentleman has stayed.' K. was still incapable of insisting, also he now had hopes of having almost been accepted, and he merely asked the gentleman's name. 'Klamm,' the landlord let fall as he turned to his wife, who came rustling up in curiously worn and old-fashioned – they were full of ruches and pleats – but still fine-looking town clothes.

She asked the landlord to come, the chief clerk wanted something. Before he went, however, the landlord turned to K. again as if the decision about staying the night was no longer for him but for K. to make. But K. was beyond speech; the fact that his own superior was here perplexed him; without knowing quite why, he did not feel as free where Klamm was concerned as he did with regard to the rest of the castle, to have Klamm catch him here would not, for K., have meant the kind of alarm the landlord had been talking about, but it would certainly have been an embarrassing inconvenience, rather as if he had thoughtlessly pained someone to whom he owed a debt of gratitude, though it depressed him very much to find that the dreaded consequences of subordinancy, of being a worker, clearly showed in such misgivings and that not even here, where they were so much in evidence, was he able to overcome them. So he just stood, biting his lips and saying nothing. One more time, before he vanished through a door, the landlord looked back at K., K. watched him go, not stirring until Olga came and pulled him away. 'What did you want from the landlord?' Olga asked. 'I wanted to stay the night here,' said K. 'But you're staying the night with us,' said Olga, astonished. 'Yes, of course,' said K. and let her make of his words what she would.

3

FRIEDA

In the bar, a large room quite empty in the centre, several peasants sat around the walls, at and on barrels, but they looked different from the people at K.'s inn. These were more neatly and uniformly dressed in coarse cloth of a greyish yellow, the jackets full, the trousers tight-fitting. They were small men, very like one another at first glance, with flat, bony, but still round-cheeked faces. All were quiet and moved little, only their eyes tracking the people who had just come in, though slowly and without interest. Nevertheless, because there were so many of them and because they were so quiet, they had a certain effect on K. He took Olga's arm again as a way of explaining to them why he was there. Over in one corner a man stood up, someone who knew Olga, and made as if to approach her, but with his arm in hers K. steered her in a different direction, no one else could have been aware of it, she acquiesced with a smiling sideways glance.

The beer was dispensed by a girl named Frieda. An insignificant little fair-haired girl with mournful features and pinched cheeks but with a striking look in her eye, a look of unusual superiority. When that look fell on K., he had the feeling it had already dealt with matters concerning him, matters of whose existence he himself knew nothing as yet, but of whose existence the look convinced him. K. continued to gaze at Frieda from the side, even after she had started talking to Olga. Friends they clearly were not, Olga and Frieda, exchanging only a few cool words. K. wished to help, so asked abruptly: 'Do you know Mr Klamm?' Olga laughed out loud. 'Why do you laugh?' K. asked crossly. 'I'm not laughing,' she said, but went on doing so. 'Olga is still a very childish little girl,' K. said, leaning right over the counter in order to draw Frieda's look firmly back to himself. She, though, kept her eyes lowered, saying softly: 'Do you want to see Mr Klamm?' K. asked if he might. She pointed at a door immediately to her left.

'There's a little spyhole here you can look through.' 'And the people here?' asked K. Pursing her underlip, she drew K. towards the door with a hand that felt unusually soft. The little hole, which had clearly been drilled for observation purposes, gave him a view of almost the whole of the next room. At a desk in the centre of the room, seated in a comfortable round-backed easy chair, starkly lit by an electric light bulb dangling in front of him, was Mr Klamm. A fat, big-bodied man of medium height. The face was still smooth but the cheeks already sagged slightly with the weight of age. The dark moustache was drawn out wide. A pince-nez, worn askew, reflected the light and so hid the eyes. Had Mr Klamm been sitting up at the desk, K. would have seen only his profile, but since Klamm was turned well towards him he was seeing the man full-face. Klamm had his left elbow on the desk, his right hand, holding a cigar, rested on one knee. On the desk stood a beer glass; the desk had a high rim, so K. could not quite make out whether there were any papers lying there, but he had the impression it was empty. To make sure, he asked Frieda to look through the hole and tell him what she saw. She had been in the room only recently, however, and could confirm at once that no papers lay there. K. asked Frieda if he should move away now, but she said he could go on looking for as long as he liked. K. was alone with Frieda now because Olga, as he swiftly ascertained, had got together with her friend after all and was sitting up on a barrel, kicking her legs. 'Frieda,' K. said in a whisper, 'do you know Mr Klamm very well?' 'Oh yes,' she said, 'very well.' She leaned towards K. and playfully rearranged what K. now noticed, for the first time, was a lightweight, low-cut, cream-coloured blouse, which lay against her poor body as if it did not belong there. Then she said: 'Don't you remember Olga laughing?' 'I know, the naughty girl,' said K. 'Well,' she said in a placatory tone, 'she had reason to laugh, you'd asked if I knew Klamm and in fact I'm' – here she involuntarily straightened up a little and again her triumphant look, quite unconnected with what she was talking about, passed over K. – 'in fact I'm his mistress.' 'Klamm's mistress,' said K. She nodded. 'In that case,' said K. with a smile, to prevent things from becoming too serious between them, 'in my eyes you're a most estimable person.' 'Not just in your eyes,' said Frieda in a friendly enough way, though without responding to his smile. K. had a remedy against her arrogance and he used it, asking: 'Have you ever been in the castle?' It did not work, though, because she answered: 'No, but isn't it enough that I'm here in the bar?' Her ambition was clearly crazed, and she seemed to have decided to use K. to feed it. 'Certainly,' said K., 'I mean, here in the bar you're doing the landlord's job.' 'That's right,' she said, 'and I started as a milkmaid at the Bridge Inn.' 'With those delicate hands?' K. half asked, himself unaware whether this was mere flattery or whether he really had been captivated by the girl. Her hands were in fact small and delicate, though they might equally have been described as weak and uninteresting. 'No one noticed them at the time,' she said, 'and even now –' K. looked at her inquiringly, she shook her head and would not go on. 'Of course,' said K., 'you have your secrets and are not going to discuss them with someone you've known for half an hour and who has not yet had a chance to tell you how things really stand with him.' As it turned out, this was an inappropriate remark, it was as if he had woken Frieda from a drowse that had been to his advantage, she took a piece of wood from the leather bag that hung from her belt, used it to plug the peephole, and said to K., visibly making an effort to conceal her change of mood: 'As far as you're concerned I know all there is to know, you're the land surveyor,' adding: 'now I must get on,' and she moved to her place behind the counter as several people rose to have her refill their empty glasses. Wanting another chance to speak to her unobtrusively, K. took an empty glass from a rack and went up to her: 'Just one more thing, Miss Frieda,' he said, 'it's most unusual and requires exceptional strength to work one's way up from milkmaid to barmaid, but has such a person then reached the ultimate goal? The question is absurd. Your eyes, don't mock me, Miss Frieda, say less about the past struggle, more about the one to come. But the resistance put up by the world is great, it grows greater, the greater the goals, and there is nothing shameful about securing the assistance even of a small, ineffective, but correspondingly combative man. Perhaps we could talk in peace some time without so many eyes staring at us.' 'I don't know what you're after,' she said, and this time her tone seemed to convey, against her will, not the victories in her life but the endless disappointments, 'are you trying to take me away from Klamm, by any chance? Oh good heavens!' and she clapped her hands. 'You've guessed it,' said K. as if weary of so much mistrust, 'that was precisely my most secret intention. You were to leave Klamm and become my mistress. Now I can go. Olga!' K. shouted, 'we're going home.' Obediently, Olga slipped down from the barrel, though she did not immediately escape from the friends surrounding her. Just then Frieda said quietly, with a threatening look at K.: 'When can I talk to you?' 'Can I spend the night here?' K. asked. 'Yes,' said Frieda. 'Can I stay now?' 'You leave with Olga, let me get rid of the people here. Then in a little while you can come.' 'Fine,' said K. and waited impatiently for Olga. But the peasants were not letting her go, they had contrived a dance of which Olga was the centre of attention, they danced in a circle and whenever they all shouted one stepped up to Olga, grasped her firmly about the hips with one hand, and whirled her around several times, the circle moved faster and faster, the shouts, like groans of hunger, gradually merged almost into a single cry, Olga, who earlier had tried smilingly to break out of the circle, now simply went staggering from one to the next with her hair all undone. 'That's the kind of people they send me,' said Frieda, biting her thin lips in anger. 'Who are they?' asked K. 'Klamm's staff,' said Frieda, 'he always brings this rabble with him, their presence destroys me. Sir, I hardly know what I've been saying to you today, if it was anything bad do please forgive me, the presence of these people is to blame, they're the most contempt-ible, most disgusting thing I know, and I have to fill their beer glasses. The times I've begged Klamm to leave them at home, if I have to put up with other gentlemen's staffs, he at least could show me some consideration, but all my begging is wasted, an hour before he arrives they come storming in like cattle into a barn. Well, now they really can go in the barn, where they belong. If you were not here, I'd pull this door open and Klamm would have to drive them out himself.' 'Can't he hear them, then?' asked K. 'No,' said Frieda, 'he's asleep.' 'What!' exclaimed K., 'he's asleep? When I looked into the room he was still awake, he was sitting at his desk.' 'He always sits like that,' said Frieda, 'even when you saw him he was asleep – would I have let you look in otherwise? – that was his sleeping position, the gentlemen sleep a great deal, it's hard to know why. Come to think of it, if he didn't sleep so much, how could he stand these people. But that means I'll have to drive them out myself.' She took a whip from the corner, and with a single, soaring, slightly unsteady leap, rather like the way a lamb leaps, she leapt towards the dancers. At first they turned to face her as if a fresh dancer had arrived, and for a moment it looked as if Frieda meant to drop the whip, but then she raised it again, 'In the name of Klamm,' she shouted, 'into the barn, all of you into the barn,' now they could see it was serious, showing a fear K. found incomprehensible they began to push towards the back of the room, under the impact of the first of them a door there opened, night air swirled in, they all vanished with Frieda, who was clearly driving them across the yard into the barn. In the sudden hush that followed, K. heard footsteps from the hallway. To give himself some protection, he leapt behind the counter, beneath which was the only possible hiding-place, he was not banned from the bar but since he wished to spend the night here he must avoid being seen at this stage. He therefore slid, when the door was actually opened, under the table. Being found there was also a risk, of course, though in that case a not implausible excuse would be that he had been hiding from the rampaging peasants. It was the landlord, 'Frieda!' he called and paced up and down the room a few times, fortunately Frieda soon arrived and made no mention of K., she only complained about the peasants and in an attempt to find K. went round behind the counter, there K. was able to touch her foot, and from then on he felt safe. Since Frieda did not mention K., the landlord eventually had to do so himself. 'And where is the land surveyor?' he asked. He was altogether a polite and, from his constant and relatively free dealings with vastly superior beings, very well-trained man, but with Frieda he spoke in a particularly respectful manner, this was chiefly apparent in the way in which, while talking, he nevertheless remained an employer in conversation with an employee, and a very cheeky employee at that. 'I'd forgotten all about the land surveyor,' Frieda said, placing her tiny foot on K.'s chest. 'He'll have left ages ago.' 'I didn't see him, though,' said the landlord, 'and I was in the hallway nearly all the time.' 'Well, he's not here,' Frieda said coolly. 'Perhaps he's hiding,' said the landlord, 'the impression I had of him is that he's capable of many things.' 'He wouldn't be as bold as that, surely,' said Frieda, pressing her foot harder down on K. There was a cheery independence about her that K. had never noticed before, it broke through in a most unlikely fashion when suddenly, with a laugh and the words: 'Maybe he's hiding under here,' she ducked down towards K., gave him a quick kiss, and bounced back up to say sadly: 'No, he's not here.' But the landlord, too, gave cause for amazement when he said at this point: 'It's very awkward for me, not knowing for certain whether he's gone. It's not just a question of Mr Klamm, it's a question of the rules. However, the rules apply to you, Miss Frieda, as they do to me. The bar is your responsibility, I shall search the rest of the building. Good night! Sleep well!' He could not have been out of the room before Frieda had switched off the light and joined K. under the counter, 'Darling, oh my darling,' she whispered, but without touching K. she lay on her back as if swooning with love and threw her arms wide, doubtless time stretched eternal before her blissful love, she sighed more than sang some little ditty. Then she started up, K. having remained lost in thought, and began to tug at him like a child: 'Come, it's suffocating under here,' they embraced, the little body burning in K.'s hands, in a state of oblivion from which K. tried repeatedly yet vainly to extricate himself they rolled several steps, thudding into Klamm's door, then lay in the little puddles of beer and the rest of the rubbish covering the floor. There hours passed, hours of breathing as one, hearts beating as one, hours in which K. constantly had the feeling that he had lost his way or wandered farther into a strange land than anyone before him, a strange land where even the air held no trace of the air at home, where a man must suffocate from the strangeness yet into whose foolish enticements he could do nothing but plunge on, getting even more lost. So initially, at least, it caused him no alarm but was like a reassuring dawn when from Klamm's room a deep, commandingly indifferent voice summoned Frieda. 'Frieda,' K. said in Frieda's ear, passing on the summons. Showing a truly innate submissiveness, Frieda was about to leap to her feet but then remembered where she was, stretched, chuckled softly, and said: 'Don't think I'm going, I'll never go to him.' K. wanted to counter this, wanted to urge her to go to Klamm, began collecting together the remnants of her blouse, but he could not speak, he was too happy to be holding Frieda, and too anxious as well, for it seemed to him that if Frieda left him, everything he had would be leaving him. And as if Frieda had drawn strength from K.'s assent she clenched her fist, pounded on the door, and called out: 'I'm with the land surveyor! I'm with the land surveyor!' At this Klamm fell silent. K., though, rose to a kneeling position beside Frieda and looked around in the dim, pre-dawn light. What had happened? Where were his hopes? What could he expect of Frieda now, with everything given away? Instead of advancing with the greatest care, in keeping with the magnitude of the enemy and the objective, he had spent the night romping in pools of beer, the smell of which was now overpowering. 'What have you done?' he said aloud. 'Now we're both lost.' 'No,' said Frieda, 'I'm the only one who's lost, but I have won you. Hush, be quiet. Look at those two laughing, though.' 'Who?' asked K., and he turned round. Sitting on the counter were his two assistants, somewhat bleary-eyed but cheerful, with the kind of cheerfulness that comes from loyally doing one's duty. 'What are you doing here?' K. exclaimed as if they were to blame for everything, he searched about him for the whip Frieda had had the previous evening. 'We had to come looking for you,' said the assistants, 'you didn't come down to us in the lounge so we looked for you at Barnabas's place and finally found you here, we've been sitting here all night. It's not an easy job, this.' 'I need you during the day, not at night,' said K., 'be off with you!' 'It's day now,' they said, not moving. And so it was, the doors to the yard were thrown open, the peasants and Olga, whom K. had quite forgotten, came streaming in, Olga was as lively as she had been the night before, however untidy her clothes and hair, right from the door her eyes searched for K. 'Why did you not come home with me?' she said, almost in tears. 'Because of that slut!' she said then, repeating it several times. Frieda, who had disappeared for a moment, came back with a small bundle of clothes, Olga stepped glumly aside. 'We can go now,' said Frieda, she meant of course to the Bridge Inn. K. with Frieda, behind them the assistants, such was the procession, the peasants showing great contempt for Frieda, understandably since she had kept them under strict control until then, one even took a stick and made as if to refuse to let her go until she had jumped over it, but a glance from her was sufficient to repulse him. Out in the snow, K. breathed a sigh of relief, the joy of being outside was so great that it made the difficulty of the journey bearable this time, if K. had been alone it would have been even easier. At the inn, he went straight to his room and lay down on the bed, Frieda made a bed for herself on the floor beside him, the assistants had pushed their way in too, were driven out, but came back in through the window. K. was too weary to drive them out again. The landlady came up especially to welcome Frieda, Frieda called her mummy, there was an incomprehensibly cordial welcome with kisses and prolonged hugging. There was not much quiet in the little room generally, every now and then the maids too came crashing in wearing their men's boots to bring something or take something away. If they needed something from the bed, which was stuffed full of various items, they pulled it from beneath K. regardless. Frieda greeted them as her own kind. Despite the upheaval, K. stayed in bed all day and all night, with Frieda providing small services for him. When at last he got up next morning, much refreshed, it was already the fourth day of his stay in the village.

4

FIRST CONVERSATION WITH
THE LANDLADY

He would have liked to speak to Frieda in private but the assistants, with whom in fact Frieda even joked and laughed from time to time, prevented him from doing so simply by their obtrusive presence. Not that they were at all demanding, they had installed themselves on the floor in a corner, using two old dresses, it was their ambition, as they discussed with Frieda from time to time, not to get in the land surveyor's way and to take up as little room as possible, to this end they tried various methods, always of course with much whispering and giggling, they crossed their arms and legs, they crouched down together, the two of them, at dawn and dusk all that could be seen in their corner was one big huddle. Nevertheless, daytime experiences had unfortunately shown that they were most attentive observers, always staring across at K., even if in what looked like childish play they used their hands as a telescope, say, and did other such silly things, or if they merely darted a glance across, appearing chiefly concerned with grooming their moustaches, which were very important to them and which they compared with each other countless times in terms of length and thickness and had Frieda judge. K. often, from his bed, watched the antics of the three of them with complete indifference.

Now that he felt strong enough to get out of bed, they all rushed over to serve him. Not yet quite strong enough to be able to defend himself against their services, he could see that this made him dependent on them in some way, which might have dire consequences, but he had to let it happen. Nor was it at all unpleasant to sit at table drinking the good coffee that Frieda had brought, warm himself at the stove that Frieda had lit, have the assistants in their clumsy eagerness run downstairs and up again ten or a dozen times to fetch water for him to wash in, soap, comb, and mirror and eventually, K. having voiced a quiet wish capable of being interpreted to that effect, a little glass of rum.

In the middle of all this giving of orders and receiving of services K. said, more from contentment than with any expectation of success: 'Off you go now, you two, there's nothing I need for the moment and I'd like to talk to Miss Frieda alone,' and when he saw no actual resistance in their expressions he went on, by way of offering a reward: 'The three of us will then go and see the mayor, wait for me down in the lounge.' Remarkably, they obeyed, merely putting in before they left: 'We could have waited here,' and K. replied: 'I know, but I don't want you to.'

However, K. found it irritating if in a way also welcome when Frieda, who as soon as the assistants had gone sat in his lap, said: 'Darling, what have you got against the assistants? We need have no secrets from them. They're loyal.' 'Huh, loyal,' K. said, 'they're forever lying in wait for me, it's pointless, but it's awful.' 'I think I know what you mean,' she said, throwing her arms around his neck, she was about to say more but could not go on, and since the chair was right beside the bed they rolled over and fell on it. There they lay, though not as abandoned as they had been that night. She was in search of something and he was in search of something, enraged, pulling faces, burrowing into each other's breasts they searched, and their hugging and their heaving bodies brought them no oblivion but reminded them of their duty to search, the way dogs scratch desperately in the earth they scratched at each other and in helpless disappointment, still pursuing final bliss, now and again swept their tongues over each other's faces. Only weariness quietened them and made them grateful to each other. The maids came up then, too, 'look at them lying there,' one said and compassionately threw a shawl over them.

When, later, K. freed himself from the shawl and looked around, there – it came as no surprise to him – were the assistants back in their corner, each exhorting the other, pointing at K., to be serious now, both of them giving salutes – but also the landlady, sitting beside the bed and knitting a sock, a tiny task that hardly suited her huge, almost room-darkening bulk. 'I've been waiting for ages,' she said, lifting her broad, much age-lined, but by and large still smooth, possibly once beautiful face. The words sounded like a reproach, one that was out of place since, after all, K. had not asked her to come. So he merely acknowledged her words with a nod and sat up, Frieda got up too but left K. and went and leaned against the landlady's chair. 'Is there any chance, ma'am,' K. said distractedly, 'of what you have to say to me being put off till I come back from the mayor's? I have an important appointment there.' 'This is more important, sir, believe me,' said the landlady, 'what's at issue there is probably just a job, but here it's a person, Frieda, my very dear maid.' 'I see,' said K., 'all right, then, only I don't know why the matter is not left to the two of us.' 'For reasons of love, reasons of concern,' said the landlady, drawing Frieda's head, which reached only to the seated landlady's shoulder, towards her. 'Since Frieda trusts you so much,' said K., 'I must too. And since Frieda only recently referred to my assistants as loyal, well, we're all friends together. In which case, ma'am, I can tell you that I should think it best if Frieda and I got married, and married soon. Sadly, very sadly, I shall not be able to make up to Frieda what she has lost through me, namely her job at the Count's Arms and the friendship of Klamm.' Frieda looked up, her eyes were full of tears, there was no trace of triumph in them. 'Why me? Why am I chosen in particular?' 'What?' asked K. and the landlady simultaneously. 'She's confused, poor child,' the landlady said, 'confused by too much happiness and unhappiness coming together.' Here, as if confirming these words, Frieda fell on K., kissing him furiously as though no one else had been in the room, then sank weeping, still with her arms around him, down on her knees before him. As he stroked Frieda's hair with both hands, K. asked the landlady: 'You seem to agree with me?' 'You are a man of honour,' said the landlady, she too had tears in her voice, looked a little crumpled, and was breathing heavily, yet she still found the strength to say: 'Now we need only consider certain assurances you must give Frieda, because however much I respect you, you're still a stranger, you have no references, your domestic circumstances are unknown here, so assurances are in order, you do see that, sir, don't you, after all, you stressed yourself how much Frieda is losing through her association with you.' 'Right, assurances, of course,' said K., 'they'd best be given in the presence of the notary, presumably, though other agencies of the count's may of course become involved. Incidentally, before the wedding there's something I simply have to do. I must speak to Klamm.'

43

'That's impossible,' said Frieda, rising slightly and pressing herself against K., 'what an idea!' 'It's essential,' said K., 'if I'm unable to arrange it, you'll have to.' 'I can't, K., I can't,' said Frieda, 'Klamm will never talk to you. How can you even think Klamm is going to talk to you!' 'And to you he would talk?' K. asked. 'No,' said Frieda, 'not to you, not to me, they're both sheer impossibilities.' She turned to the landlady with outstretched arms: 'Oh ma'am, you see what he's asking?' 'You're extraordinary, sir,' said the landlady, and there was something alarming about the way she now sat more erect, legs apart, powerful knees thrust forward through the thin dress, 'you're asking for the impossible.' 'Why is it impossible?' asked K. 'I'll explain,' said the landlady in a tone of voice that suggested the explanation was not one last favour, as it were, but in fact the first punishment that she was handing out, 'I'll gladly explain that to you. All right, I don't belong to the castle and I'm only a woman and only a landlady here in an inn of the lowest class – it's not the lowest class but not far off it – so you may not attach much importance to my explanation, but I've kept my eyes open through life and come across a lot of people and borne the whole burden of the inn by myself, because my husband may be a good fellow but he's no innkeeper and responsibility is something he will never understand. For instance, you have only his negligence to thank – I was so tired that evening I could have collapsed – for the fact that you're here in the village, that you're sitting on this bed here in peace and comfort.' 'What's that you say?' asked K., roused from a certain absent-mindedness more by curiosity than by annoyance. 'It's his negligence you have to thank, that's all,' the landlady repeated in a loud voice, and she pointed a forefinger at K. Frieda tried to calm her. 'What's the matter with you?' the landlady said, swiftly pivoting her whole body, 'the land surveyor asked me and I have to give him an answer. How else is he going to understand what to us is obvious, that Mr Klamm will never speak to him, what do I mean "will", can never speak to him. Listen to me, sir. Mr Klamm is a gentleman from the castle, that in itself, quite apart from his position otherwise, signifies very high rank. But what are you, whose marriage permit we're so humbly applying for here. You're not from the castle, you're not from the village, you're nothing. Unfortunately there's one thing you are, though, namely a stranger, an outsider, someone who's superfluous to require-

44

ments and in everybody's way, someone who's a constant source of trouble, on whose account the maids have to be moved out, someone whose intentions are unknown, someone who has seduced our dear little Frieda and to whom she must unfortunately be given in marriage. Not that I'm basically reproaching you for any of this; you are what you are; I've seen too many things in my life not to be able to bear this sight as well. But imagine for a moment what you're asking, in fact. A man like Klamm is supposed to speak to you. It pained me to hear that Frieda had let you look through the peephole, she'd already, when she did that, been seduced by you. But tell me, how could you bear the sight of Klamm? You needn't answer, I know, you bore it very easily. The fact is, you're quite incapable of seeing Klamm properly, that's not arrogance on my part because neither am I capable of it myself. You want Klamm to speak to you, but he doesn't even speak to people from the village, never has done, not even to someone from the village. It was Frieda's greatest honour, one I shall be proud of till my dying day, that he used at least to call Frieda's name and that she could speak to him as much as she wanted and was given the freedom of the peephole, but he never spoke to her, either. And the fact that he did occasionally call Frieda need not in fact mean what one would like it to mean, he simply called the name Frieda – who knows what he had in mind? – the fact that Frieda naturally came running was her affair, and her being allowed without protest to go in to him was due to Klamm's kindness, but we cannot claim that he was calling her, not as such. Of course, even what used to be has now gone for ever. Klamm may go on calling the name Frieda, it's possible, but she certainly won't be allowed to go in to him any more, not a girl who has associated with you. And there's just one thing, just one, that my poor brain can't understand, that a girl who was said to be Klamm's mistress – I regard that, by the way, as a very exaggerated description – should let you even touch her.'

'It certainly is strange,' said K. and drew Frieda, who promptly complied, if with head bowed, on to his lap, 'but it shows, I believe, that in other respects too, things aren't all quite as you think. For instance, you're certainly right when you say that compared with Klamm I'm a nobody, and despite the fact that I'm now asking to speak to Klamm and am not even dissuaded by your explanations, that's not to say that I am capable of bearing so much as the sight of Klamm without a door between us, nor whether I shan't run from the room the moment he appears. However, such a fear, even if justified, is not in my view a reason for not risking the thing anyway. But if I do manage to stand up to him, there won't be any need for him to speak to me, I shall be satisfied with seeing the impression my words make on him, and if they make none or if he doesn't even hear them, I shall still have the benefit of having spoken freely in the presence of someone powerful. But surely you, ma'am, with your great knowledge of life and of people, and Frieda, who only yesterday was Klamm's lover – I see no reason for dropping the word – can easily create an opportunity for me to speak to Klamm, if it's the only way possible then at the Count's Arms, maybe he's still there today.'

'It's not possible,' said the landlady, 'and I can see that you lack the ability to understand that. But tell me, what do you want to speak to Klamm about?'

'About Frieda, of course,' said K.

'About Frieda?' asked the landlady blankly, and she turned to Frieda. 'Do you hear, Frieda, it's about you that he, he, wants to speak to Klamm, to Klamm.'

'Ah ma'am,' said K., 'you're such a shrewd woman, you inspire such respect, yet every trifle alarms you. Look, I want to speak to him about Frieda, that's not so very dreadful, in fact it stands to reason. Because I'm sure you're wrong, too, if you think that from the instant I appeared Frieda lost all importance for Klamm. You underestimate him, if that's what you think. I quite realize it's presumptuous of me to try to put you right on this point, but I have to do it. I cannot have made any difference to Klamm's relationship with Frieda. Either no relationship to speak of existed – which is in fact what they're saying, the people who strip Frieda of the title of mistress – in which case none exists today, or it did exist, in which case how could I, a nobody in Klamm's eyes, as you rightly said, how could I have disrupted it? Those are the things one thinks in the first moment of alarm, but the slightest reflection will correct them. Anyway, let's ask Frieda what she thinks.'

With a wandering, faraway look in her eyes, her cheek on K.'s chest, Frieda said: 'It's as mother says, I'm sure: Klamm wants nothing more to do with me. But not because you came along, darling, of course not, nothing like that could have upset him. No, I believe it is his doing that we found ourselves together under the counter there, oh blest, not cursed, be that hour.'

'If that is the case,' K. said slowly, for Frieda's words were sweet, he closed his eyes for a second or two to allow them to sink in, 'if that is the case, there's even less reason to be afraid of a discussion with Klamm.'

'Quite honestly,' said the landlady, looking down her nose at K., 'you remind me of my husband at times, you're as awkward and childish as he is. You've been here a couple of days and already you think you know it all better than folk who were born here, better than an old woman like me, better than Frieda, who's seen and heard so much up at the Count's Arms. I'm not denying it's possible, sometimes, to achieve something even completely contrary to regulations and in defiance of tradition, I've not experienced anything of the kind myself, though there are said to be instances of it happening, that's as may be, but it certainly doesn't happen the way you're going about it, by constantly saying No, no, and not taking anyone's word for anything, ignoring even the best-intentioned advice. Do you think it's you I'm worried about? Did I take any notice of you, as long as you were alone? Despite the fact that it would have been a good thing if I had, and certain things might have been avoided? The only thing I said to my husband about you at the time was: "Keep away from him." I'd have been the same way today, had Frieda not been drawn into your life as she has. It's her you have to thank – whether you like it or not – for my attention, even my consideration. And you can't simply brush me aside, because you have a heavy responsibility towards me as the only one who watches over little Frieda with a mother's concern. It may be that Frieda is right, and everything that's happened is the will of Klamm, but Klamm I know nothing about, now, I shall never speak to him, he's utterly beyond my reach, whereas you, you're sitting here, claiming my Frieda and – why should I hide the fact? – being kept by me. Yes, kept by me, because just you try, young man, if I turn you out of the house, to find a place to stay anywhere in the village, even in a dog kennel.'

'Thank you,' said K., 'those are frank words and I quite believe you. My position is that insecure, then, and with it Frieda's too.'

'No,' the landlady interrupted angrily, 'Frieda's position has nothing to do with yours in this respect. Frieda is part of my household, and no one has the right to call her position here insecure.'

'Fine, fine,' said K., 'I'll grant that too, particularly since for reasons unknown to me Frieda seems too frightened of you to intervene. All right, let's stay with me for the time being. My position is highly insecure, you don't deny that, in fact you're making every effort to prove it. As with everything you say, this again is only very largely true, not completely. For instance, I know of a very good billet I can go to.'

'Where? Where?' cried Frieda and the landlady as near-simultaneously and as eagerly as if their motives for asking had been the same.

'With Barnabas,' said K.

'The rogues!' cried the landlady, 'the cunning rogues! With Barnabas! Do you hear –' and she turned towards the assistants' corner, but they had long since emerged from it and were standing arm in arm behind the landlady, who now, as if needing support, seized the hand of one of them – 'do you hear where the gentleman has been hanging around, with Barnabas's family! Of course he'll find a billet there, if only he'd stayed there instead of at the Count's Arms. Where were you two, though?'

'Madam,' K. told the landlady before the assistants replied, 'they're my assistants, yet you treat them as if they were your assistants but my keepers. In everything else, I'm prepared at least to discuss your opinions in a civil manner, not as regards my assistants, though, because in this area things are really too clear-cut. So I would ask you not to talk to my assistants, please, and if asking is not enough, then I forbid my assistants to answer you.'

'So I mayn't talk to you,' said the landlady to the assistants, and the three of them laughed, the landlady mockingly but much more gently than K. had expected, the assistants in their usual suggestive and at the same time meaningless way, refusing all responsibility.

'Don't be cross,' Frieda said to K., 'you have to understand what it is that's upset us. If you like, it's all Barnabas's doing that we now belong to each other. When I saw you in the bar for the first time – you were coming in with your arm through Olga's – I knew something

48

of you already, I admit, but by and large you didn't matter to me at all. Well, it wasn't just you that didn't matter to me, hardly anything did, hardly anything mattered. There was also a lot I was unhappy about at the time and much that used to irritate me, but what sort of unhappiness was it, what sort of irritation. For instance, a customer in the bar would insult me – they were always on at me, you saw the fellows there, but much worse ones than that used to come, Klamm's staff were not the worst – so one of them insulted me, what was that to me? It felt as if it had happened years back or as if it hadn't happened to me at all or as if I'd only heard about it or as if I personally had forgotten it already. I can't describe it, though, I can't even picture it to myself any more, that's how much everything's changed since Klamm left me –'

And Frieda broke off her account, bowing her head in sorrow and holding her hands folded in her lap.

'There you are,' cried the landlady, acting as if she was not speaking herself but simply lending Frieda her voice, she also moved up till she was sitting right beside Frieda, 'look at the consequences of what you've done, sir, and let your assistants, whom I mayn't talk to, of course, let them look too, they'll learn something. You snatched Frieda away from the most blissful circumstances she had ever known, and what enabled you to do so was mainly that Frieda, in her childishly exaggerated compassion, couldn't stand seeing you on Olga's arm, looking as if you were at the mercy of Barnabas's family. She came to your rescue, sacrificing herself in the process. And now that it's happened and Frieda has exchanged everything she had for the happiness of sitting on your knee, now you come along and play as your trump card the fact that you once had the opportunity to spend the night at Barnabas's place. I assume you're trying to show you're not dependent on me. Well, yes, if you really had spent the night at Barnabas's place, you'd be so independent of me that you'd have had to leave my house immediately, and I mean at the double.'

'I don't know what Barnabas's family has done wrong,' said K. as he carefully lifted an apparently lifeless Frieda, slowly laid her on the bed, then stood up, 'you may be right there, but I was most certainly right when I asked you to leave our affairs, Frieda's and mine, to us alone. You mentioned something about love and care at the time, but

I've not noticed much of either since, it's been more hatred and contempt and banishment from the house. If what you were trying to do was to make Frieda change her mind about me or me about Frieda, it was cleverly enough done but you will not, I think, succeed, and if you should succeed you will come – if you'll allow me a dark threat of my own – to regret it bitterly. As for the accommodation you're providing for me – you can only be referring to this loathsome hole – it is by no means certain that you're doing it of your own volition, it looks to me more like a ruling from the count's office. I shall now inform the office that I have been given notice here, and if I am then assigned alternative accommodation you'll no doubt breathe a sigh of relief, but I shall breathe an even deeper one. And now I'm going to see the mayor about this and other matters, please at least look after Frieda, whom you've been treating pretty roughly with what you call your motherly words.'

He turned to the assistants. 'Come,' he said, took Klamm's letter down from the hook, and moved to go. The landlady had been watching him in silence, his hand was already on the doorhandle when she said: 'Sir, I've one more thing to say to you before you go, because however you may talk and whatever insults you may wish to hurl at an old woman like me, you're still Frieda's husband-to-be. The only reason I tell you this is that your ignorance regarding the way things are here is appalling, it makes one's head spin to listen to you and then mentally compare what you say and think with the actual situation. Such ignorance is not going to be remedied at a stroke, and maybe not at all, but much can be improved if you'll only believe me a little and bear your ignorance constantly in mind. You'll then immediately become fairer to me, for instance, and begin to form some idea of the shock I received – and the after-effects of that shock are still with me – when I realized that my darling little girl had, so to speak, left the eagle to form an attachment with the slow-worm, yet the actual relationship is worse than that, far worse, and I must constantly try to put it out of my mind, otherwise I couldn't speak a calm word to you. Oh, now you're cross again. No, don't go yet, hear this one plea: Wherever you fetch up, always remember that you're the most ignorant person in the place and be careful; here with us, where Frieda's presence shields you from harm, by all means talk away to your heart's content, here, for instance, you can show us how you mean to speak to Klamm, but in reality, in reality, please, please don't do it.'

She stood up, a little unsteady in her agitation, went over to K., took his hand, and gave him a pleading look. 'Madam,' said K., 'I fail to understand why for something like this you lower yourself to pleading with me. If, as you say, it's impossible for me to speak to Klamm, then I shall not manage to do so whether I'm pleaded with or not. But if it is in fact possible, why shouldn't I, particularly since, with your main objection ceasing to apply, your other fears also become highly dubious. Of course I'm ignorant, that remains true at all events and is extremely distressing for me, but it does have the advantage that the ignorant man dares more, so I shall gladly put up with ignorance and its undoubtedly dire consequences for a while, as long as my strength lasts. In essence, though, those consequences affect only me, which is mainly why I fail to understand your request. For Frieda, you'll of course go on caring for ever and if I disappear completely from Frieda's sight that can only, in your terms, be a stroke of luck. So what are you afraid of? You're surely not afraid – to the ignorant, anything seems possible' – K. was already opening the door – 'you're surely not afraid for Klamm?' The landlady stared after him in silence as he ran down the stairs, the assistants behind him.

5

AT THE MAYOR'S

The interview with the mayor, almost to K.'s own amazement, hardly worried him at all. He tried to explain this to himself by the fact that his previous experiences had shown official dealings with the count's authorities to be, for him, very simple. This was on the one hand because, with regard to the handling of his affairs, clearly a firm and, on the face of it, so far as he was concerned, very favourable ground rule had been laid down once and for all, on the other because of the admirable uniformity of the organization, which particularly where it was not in evidence one suspected of being particularly complete. K. came close, thinking at times about these things only, to finding his situation satisfactory, although he was always, following such bursts of contentment, quick to tell himself that that was just where the danger lay. Direct dealings with authorities were never too difficult because, however well organized those authorities were, they only ever had to defend remote, invisible matters on behalf of remote, invisible masters, whereas K. was fighting for something of the most lively proximity, namely himself, and what is more, at least right at the beginning, doing so of his own volition since he was the aggressor, nor was he the only one fighting on his behalf, apparently other forces were too, forces unknown to him but in which the authorities' actions had made it possible for him to believe. However, by being so accommodating to K. from the outset over less important matters – all that had been at issue up to now – the authorities were depriving him of the opportunity for small, easy victories and with such opportunity also the attendant satisfaction and, arising out of it, well-founded confidence for further, greater struggles. The fact was, they were letting K., if only within the confines of the village, slip through wherever he wished, spoiling and undermining him in consequence, eliminating any kind of struggle here completely and shifting him instead into the non-official, wholly unclear, clouded, alien life-sphere. In this way it might well, if he was not constantly on the alert, happen that one day, despite all the authorities' kindness and despite full discharge of all these exaggeratedly easy official obligations, deceived by the apparent goodwill being shown him, he conducted his other life so incautiously that he broke down in this place, and official authority, still gentle, still friendly, was compelled, almost against its will but in the name of some public ordinance he knew nothing about, to come and clear him out of the way. And in fact what was it here, that other life? Nowhere before had K. seen officialdom and life as interwoven as they were here, so interwoven that it sometimes even looked as if officialdom and life had changed places. What was the meaning, for example, of the hitherto purely formal power that Klamm wielded over K.'s work, compared to the very real power Klamm possessed in K.'s bedroom? It followed that it was only in direct dealings with the authorities that a slightly less cautious approach, a degree of relaxation were in order here, whereas otherwise great care was called for at all times, a quick glance about one prior to each step.

Initially, K. found his view of the authorities in this place very much confirmed at the mayor's. The mayor, a fat friendly cleanshaven man, was sick, he had a bad attack of gout, and he received K. in bed. 'So this is our land surveyor,' he said as he tried to rise in welcome, failed to manage it, and with an apologetic gesture towards his legs threw himself back against the pillows. A silent woman, almost a shadow in the dimness of the small-windowed room, which curtains darkened even further, brought K. a chair and set it beside the bed, 'Sit down, sir, sit down,' the mayor said, 'and tell me what it is you want.' K. read out Klamm's letter and added one or two remarks. Once again he had that sense of how extraordinarily easy it was, dealing with the authorities. They literally bore every burden, you could place everything on their shoulders, leaving yourself unaffected and free. As if the mayor felt this as well in his way, he turned awkwardly in bed. Eventually, he said: 'As you've realized, sir, I was aware of the whole thing. The reason why I've done nothing myself as yet is first my illness and second the fact that you've been so long in coming, I assumed you had dropped the matter. However, now that you've been good enough to call on me yourself, I must of course tell you the whole unpleasant truth. You've been taken on as a land surveyor, you say, but unfortunately we don't need a land surveyor. There'd be nothing for him to do here at all. The boundaries of our small farms are marked out, everything is properly registered, changes of title rarely occur, and we resolve minor boundary disputes ourselves. So what would we want with a land surveyor?' K. was convinced, deep down, though without its having occurred to him before, that he had been expecting some such news. That explains why he was able to say immediately: 'I'm very surprised to hear it. This upsets all my calculations. I can only hope there has been some misunderstanding.' 'Unfortunately not,' said the mayor, 'it's as I say.' 'But how can it be,' K. exclaimed, 'I've not made this endless journey to be sent back again now.' 'That's another matter,' said the mayor, 'and not for me to decide, but what I can tell you is how the misunderstanding was possible. In an authority as large as the count's, it can sometimes happen that one department arranges this, another that, neither is aware of the other, and although overall control is most precise, by its very nature it comes too late, so that a degree of confusion may arise none the less. It is only ever in the tiniest minutiae, of course, your case for example, I've never heard of a mistake being made in major matters, but the minutiae are often awkward enough. As regards your own case, I should like without making any official secrets – I'm not civil servant enough for that, I'm a farmer and always will be – to tell you quite frankly what happened. A long time ago, I'd only been mayor for a few months then, an order arrived, I forget from which department, saying in the categorical fashion peculiar to the gentlemen there that a land surveyor was to be appointed and the municipality was instructed to have in readiness all the plans and drawings required for the jobs he was to do. That order cannot have concerned you, of course, because this was many years ago and I shouldn't have recalled it were I not now indisposed and had time enough in bed to think about the silliest things. Mizzi,' he said, suddenly breaking off his account to address the woman, who was still flitting about the room in incomprehensible activity, 'look in that cupboard, would you, maybe you'll find the order. It's from my early days, you see,' he explained to K., 'I still kept everything then.' The woman promptly opened the cupboard, with K. and the mayor watching. The cupboard was completely stuffed with documents, two large bundles of files rolled out as it was opened, they were bound up in cylinders the way kindling-wood is often tied; the woman sprang to one side in alarm. 'At the bottom, it's probably down the bottom,' said the mayor, directing the operation from the bed. Obediently, grasping armfuls of files, the women threw everything out of the cupboard to get at the documents underneath. Documents covered half the floor already. 'A lot of work was done,' said the mayor, nodding, 'and that's just a small part. I kept the bulk of it in the barn, and the greater part has of course been lost. One can't hang on to everything! There's still a great deal in the barn, though.' He turned back to his wife: 'Shall you be able to find the order? You must look for a file with the words "Land Surveyor" underlined in blue.' 'It's too dark here,' said the woman, 'I'll fetch a candle,' and stepping over the documents she left the room. 'My wife is a great help to me,' said the mayor, 'in this onerous official work that is in fact all supposed to be done on a part-time basis, though for the written work I do have an aide, the schoolmaster, but it's still impossible to get everything done, there's always a lot left unattended to, I accumulate that in there,' and he indicated another cupboard. 'And now that I'm ill, it's getting really out of hand,' he said, lying back wearily but also with some pride. 'Could I not,' K. asked when the woman, having returned with the candle, was kneeling in front of the cupboard, looking for the order, 'help your wife in her search?' The mayor shook his head with a smile: 'As I said, I have no official secrets from you, but letting you search the files yourself is really a bit further than I can go.' It became quiet in the room now, the rustle of papers the only sound, the mayor may even have dozed a little. A faint knocking at the door made K. turn. It was the assistants, of course. Still, they did have some manners, not barging straight into the room but first whispering through the slightly opened door: 'It's too cold for us out here.' 'Who's that?' the mayor asked, starting up. 'It's only my assistants,' said K., 'I don't know where to have them wait for me, it's too cold outside and in here they're a nuisance.' 'They don't bother me,' said the mayor pleasantly, 'let them come in. Anyway, I know them. Old friends.' 'To me they're a nuisance, though,' K. said frankly, glancing from the assistants to the mayor and back to the assistants and finding all three smiles indistinguishably similar. 'But now that you're here,' he went on tentatively, 'stay and help the mayor's wife there look for a file with the words "Land Surveyor" underlined in blue.' The mayor made no objection; what K. was not allowed to do, the assistants were, and they threw themselves on the documents immediately, but they rummaged in the piles more than searched, and when one was spelling out a text the other always snatched it from his hand. The woman, however, kneeling before the empty cupboard, appeared to have quite given up the search, at any rate the candle stood a long way from her.

'So the assistants,' said the mayor with a self-satisfied smile, as if everything went back to his instructions but no one was capable of even suspecting as much, 'are a nuisance to you. But they are your own assistants.' 'No,' said K. coldly, 'they only attached themselves to me here.' 'How attached themselves?' he said, 'were assigned, you presumably mean.' 'All right, were assigned to me,' said K., 'but they might as well have fallen with the snow, it was done that thoughtlessly.' 'Nothing here happens without thought,' said the mayor, he even forgot the pain in his foot and sat up straight. 'Nothing,' said K., 'and what about my appointment?' 'Your appointment too was thoroughly considered,' said the mayor, 'it's just that minor details intervened confusingly, I shall prove it to you with the aid of the files.' 'But the files won't be found,' said K. 'Not be found?' exclaimed the mayor, 'Mizzi, look a bit faster, please! For now, though, I can tell you the story even without the files. We replied to the order I mentioned by saying thank-you but we did not need a land surveyor. However, our reply appears not to have found its way back to the original department, I'll call it A, but to another department B by mistake. So department A got no reply, but unfortunately nor did B receive our full reply; whether the contents of the file never left here or whether they got lost on the way – certainly not in the department itself, I'll vouch for that – anyway, all that arrived at department B was a folder on which was marked simply that the accompanying but in reality unfortunately missing file concerned the appointment of a land surveyor. Meanwhile department A was awaiting our reply, they did have some notes on the matter but, as happens with understandable frequency and quite admissibly, given the precision with which everything is dealt with, the head of department relied on our replying and his then either appointing the land surveyor or, if necessary, corresponding with us further on the subject. Consequently, he ignored the notes and the whole thing was forgotten so far as he was concerned. In department B, however, the folder reached an official who is renowned for his conscientiousness, Sordini by name, an Italian, even to an initiate like myself it is incomprehensible why a man of his abilities is left in almost the most subordinate position of all. Sordini, of course, sent the empty folder back to us for completion. However, many months if not years had passed by now since that initial letter from department A, understandably so, because when, as usually happens, a file follows the correct channel it reaches its department in a day at most and is dealt with that same day, but if it happens to go the wrong way, and such is the excellence of the organization, it has literally to seek out the wrong way with some zeal, otherwise it will not find it, then in that case, admittedly, it does take a very long time. So when we received Sordini's memorandum, we could only very vaguely recall the affair, there were only two of us doing the work then, Mizzi and myself, the schoolmaster had yet to be assigned to me, we kept copies only in the most important matters – in short, we were able to reply only very vaguely that we knew nothing about such an appointment and that there was no call for a land surveyor here.'

'But,' the mayor interrupted himself at this point, as if in the heat of narration he had gone too far, or as if it was at least possible he might have gone too far, 'is the story not boring you?'

'No,' said K., 'I find it entertaining.'

At which the mayor: 'I'm not telling it for your entertainment.'

'I'm entertained by it only in the sense,' said K., 'that it gives me an insight into the ludicrous confusion that may possibly determine the existence of a human being.'

'You've been given no insight as yet,' the mayor said seriously, 'and there's more I can tell you. Our reply did not satisfy a man like Sordini, of course. I admire the man, even though he's a torment to me. He distrusts everyone, you see, even if, for example, he's met a person on countless occasions and come to know him as the most trustworthy of men, on the next occasion he'll distrust him as if he didn't know him at all, or rather as if he did know him for a scoundrel. I think that's right, an official has to act like that, unfortunately my nature is such that I'm not able to follow that principle. I mean, you see how I treat you, a stranger, setting everything out frankly, I just can't help it. Sordini, though, immediately distrusted our reply. A substantial correspondence ensued. Sordini inquired why it had suddenly occurred to me that no land surveyor should be appointed, I replied with the help of Mizzi's exceptional memory that the initial suggestion had come from the authority itself (the fact that a different department had been involved was something we'd of course long since forgotten), Sordini countered: why did I mention this official letter only now, I wrote back: because I had only now remembered it, Sordini: that was most remarkable, I: it was not at all remarkable in so long-drawn-out an affair, Sordini: yes it *was* remarkable, because the letter I had remembered did not exist, I: of course it did not exist, the whole file had been lost, Sordini: but there ought to be a note about that first letter and there was none. At that point I wavered, not daring either to assert or to believe that a mistake had occurred in Sordini's department. You, sir, are perhaps mentally reproaching Sordini, you feel that regard for my assertion should at least have prompted him to make appropriate inquiries with other departments. But that is just what he'd have been wrong to do, I want no stigma to attach to this man, even if only in your thoughts. It is an operating principle of the authority that no allowance is made for possibilities of error. The principle is justified by the excellent organization all round, and it is necessary if extreme swiftness of execution is to be achieved. Sordini could therefore not make any inquiries with other departments, in any case those departments would have given him no answer because they would have spotted immediately that what was being investigated was a possibility of error.'

'Mr Mayor, if I may interrupt you with a question,' said K., 'did you not earlier mention a control authority? I mean, the organization as you describe it is such that one feels sick at the thought that there might be no overall supervision.'

'You're very severe,' said the mayor, 'yet multiply your severity a thousandfold and it will still be nothing compared to the severity that the authority applies to itself. Only a complete outsider could ask your question. Are there control authorities? There are nothing but control authorities. Of course, their purpose is not to uncover errors in the ordinary meaning of the word, since errors do not occur and even when an error does in fact occur, as in your case, who can say conclusively that it is an error?'

'That would be something entirely new,' exclaimed K.

'To me it is something very old,' said the mayor. 'Not so very differently from yourself, I am convinced that an error occurred and Sordini became extremely ill as a result of his despair at that fact and the first control bureaux, which we have to thank for discovering the source of the error, also acknowledge the error here. But who is to say that the second control bureaux will form the same judgement and then the third and subsequently the others?'

'That's as may be,' said K., 'I'd really rather not get involved in such considerations just yet, also this is the first I've heard of these control bureaux and naturally I don't understand them as yet. It's just that I think two things need to be distinguished here, first what goes on inside the offices and is then capable of this or that official interpretation, and second my actual person, I who stand outside the offices and am threatened by the offices with an interference so nonsensical that I am still unable to believe in the seriousness of the danger. With regard to the first, what you tell me, sir, with such amazing and extraordinary expertise, is doubtless true, only I should like subsequently to hear something about myself as well.'

'I'm coming to that,' said the mayor, 'but you'd not be able to understand it if I did not say certain other things first. Even my mentioning the control bureaux at this point was premature. So I'll go back to the differences of opinion with Sordini. As I was saying, my opposition gradually decreased. But once Sordini has got hold of the slightest advantage against somebody, victory is already his, because now his attention, energy, presence of mind are enhanced and for the person under attack he is a dreadful sight, for the enemies of the person under attack a splendid sight. It is only from having had this latter experience too in other cases that I am able to talk about him the way I do. Incidentally, I have never yet managed to set eyes on him, he isn't able to come down here, he's too overwhelmed with work, his room has been described to me as having all its walls covered with columns consisting of great bundles of files stacked one on top of another, those are just the files Sordini's currently working on, and since files are forever being pulled out of bundles and pushed back in, and it is all done in a tremendous hurry, the columns are forever collapsing, in fact this continual crashing sound, repeated at rapid intervals, has come to characterize Sordini's office. You see, Sordini is a worker and devotes to the smallest case the same care as he does to the biggest.'

'Sir,' said K., 'you constantly refer to my case as one of the smallest, yet it has meant a great deal of work for a large number of officials, and while at first it may have been very small, the zeal of officials of Mr Sordini's stamp has in fact made it a major case. Unfortunately so, and very much against my will; because my ambition is not to give rise to and bring crashing down great stacks of files concerning me but to work away quietly at a small drawing-board as a humble land surveyor.'

'No,' said the mayor, 'it is not a major case, you have no grounds for complaint in that respect, it is one of the smallest of small cases. The amount of work does not determine the standing of the case, you're still a long way from understanding the authority if that's what you believe. But even if it were a question of the amount of work, your case would be one of the least, the ordinary cases, meaning the ones without so-called errors, give much more work and of course also work of a far more productive kind. Anyway, you still have no idea of the actual work your case has caused, that's what I want to tell you about now. At first, then, Sordini left me out of it, but his officials came, every day there were minuted hearings involving respected councillors at the Count's Arms. Most of them stood by me, only a few became suspicious, the question of land surveying is one that concerns a peasant farmer, they scented secret agreements and injustices of some kind, what is more they found a leader and Sordini was inevitably persuaded by their statements that, if I had brought the matter up in council, not everyone would have been against appointing a land surveyor. In this way a self-evident truth – namely that no land surveyor is required – was rendered doubtful to say the least. Someone who stood out particularly in all this was a man called Brunswick, you probably don't know him, he's not necessarily a bad man but stupid and over-imaginative, he's a brother-in-law of Lasemann.'

'The tanner?' asked K., and he described the bearded man he had seen at Lasemann's house.

'Yes, that's him,' said the mayor.

'I know his wife, too,' said K., slightly at random.

'That's possible,' said the mayor and fell silent.

'She's lovely,' said K., 'but a bit pale and not in good health. She's from the castle, presumably?', this was said half as a question.

The mayor looked at the clock, poured some medicine into a spoon, and gulped it down.

'I suppose all you know in the castle are the offices?' K. asked abruptly.

'Yes,' said the mayor with an ironic but none the less grateful smile, 'they are also the most important part. And so far as Brunswick is concerned: if we could ban him from the council, nearly all of us would be happy, not least Lasemann. But Brunswick gained a certain influence at the time, not that he's a speaker, more of a heckler, but even that's enough for some. That's how it came about that I was forced to bring the matter before the council, which incidentally was Brunswick's only success at first, because of course the vast majority of the council did not want to have anything to do with a land surveyor. Even that is years ago now, but the whole time the matter has not been allowed to rest, partly through the conscientiousness of Sordini, who tried by means of the most painstaking inquiries to probe the motives both of the majority and of the opposition, partly through the stupidity and ambition of Brunswick, who has various personal contacts with the authorities, which he activated with ever fresh figments of his imagination. Sordini, though, refused to let Brunswick deceive him – how could Brunswick deceive Sordini? – however, precisely in order to avoid such deception fresh inquiries were necessary, and before these were complete Brunswick had already dreamed up something new, he's very nimble-minded, you see, it's part of his stupidity. And at this point I must mention a peculiar feature of our official machinery. In keeping with its precision, it is also extremely sensitive. When a matter has been under consideration for a very long time, it can happen, even without the considerations having been completed, that suddenly, with the speed of lightning, at an unforeseeable and subsequently also untraceable point a settlement emerges that concludes the affair usually quite properly, I grant you, but none the less arbitrarily for that. It's as if the official machinery, no longer tolerating the tension, the years of irritation resulting from the same perhaps in itself insignificant affair, had taken the decision spontaneously without the aid of the officials. No miracle has occurred, of course, and certainly some official or other will have put the settlement in writing or taken an unwritten decision, but anyhow it's not possible, at least from our end, from here, indeed even from the top, to find out which official decided in this case and on what grounds. Only the control bureaux find that out, much later, but we no longer hear about it, anyway it's unlikely to interest anyone by then. As I was saying, these decisions in particular are for the most part excellent, the only disturbing thing about them is that, the way things usually work out, people hear about them too late, so that in the meantime an affair that has long since been decided still forms the subject of heated discussion. I don't know whether such a decision has been made in your case – a number of things suggest it has, a number suggest not – but if it had, the summons would have been sent to you and you would have made the long journey to come here, much time would have passed in the process, and meanwhile here Sordini would still have worked to the point of exhaustion and Brunswick have intrigued over the same matter, and I should have been pestered by both. This possibility I merely hint at, but what I do know for certain is this: in the meantime a control bureau discovered that department A had sent the municipality a formal request concerning a land surveyor many years ago without a reply having yet been received. An inquiry was recently sent to me, and of course the whole matter was then cleared up, department A was satisfied with my answer that no land surveyor was needed and Sordini was compelled to admit that he had not had competence in this case and, quite blamelessly of course, had done so much unnecessary and soul-destroying work. Had not fresh work, as ever, come crowding in from all sides and had your case not, as it happens, been only a very small one – almost, it might be said, the smallest of the small – we should no doubt all have breathed a sigh of relief, even Sordini himself, I should think, only Brunswick grumbled, but that was simply absurd. So imagine my disappointment, sir, when now, after a happy end to the whole affair – and again much time has passed, even since then – you suddenly appear and it looks very much as if the business is about to start all over again. You will surely understand that, so far as it's up to me, I'm quite determined not to let that happen?'

'Of course,' said K., 'but I understand even more clearly that an appalling abuse is being perpetrated here against myself, possibly even against the laws. I shall know, as regards myself, how to combat this.'

'How?' asked the mayor.

'That I can't give away,' said K.

'I don't wish to impose,' said the mayor, 'I'll just give you one thing to think about, that in me you have – I won't say a friend, since we're total strangers – but a business associate, so to speak. I'll not let you be taken on as a land surveyor, I won't allow that, but otherwise you can always turn to me with confidence, within the limits of my power, of course, which is not enormous.'

'You speak repeatedly,' said K., 'of my needing to be taken on as a land surveyor, but I have already been taken on, here is Klamm's letter.'

'Klamm's letter,' said the mayor, 'is valuable and commands respect because of Klamm's signature, which appears to be genuine, but otherwise – no, I don't dare express myself on the subject on my own. Mizzi!' he called and then: 'Whatever are you all doing?'

The assistants and Mizzi, unobserved for so long, had clearly not found the file they were looking for, they had then tried to shut everything back in the cupboard, but because of the untidy profusion of files had been unable to do so. It was probably this that had given the assistants the idea they were now putting into execution. They had laid the cupboard on the floor, stuffed all the files inside, had then sat themselves, with Mizzi, on the cupboard doors, and were now trying gradually to press them down.

'So the file has not been found,' said the mayor, 'pity, but you already know the story, we don't really need the file any more, anyway, I'm sure it won't be found, it's probably with the schoolmaster, a great many files are still with him. But bring the candle over here now, Mizzi, and read this letter with me.'

Mizzi came, looking even greyer and less prepossessing than before as she sat on the edge of the bed and pressed up against this powerful man, so brimming with life, who had placed an arm round her. Only her small face now stood out in the candlelight, its clear, severe lines softened only by the effects of age. No sooner had she glanced at the letter than she lightly clasped her hands together, 'from Klamm,' she said. They then both read the letter, whispered together for a moment, and eventually, as the assistants shouted hurrah, having pushed the cupboard doors to at last, and Mizzi looked across at them in silent gratitude, the mayor said:

'Mizzi shares my view entirely, and I suppose I now dare voice it. This letter is not an official missive at all but a private letter. That much is clear simply from the form of address, "Dear sir". Nor is there a single word in it to say that you have been taken on as a land surveyor, instead it merely talks in general terms about his lordship's service and even that is not stated definitely, you are simply admitted "as you know", in other words the burden of proof that you have been taken on is upon you. Finally, you are being referred, for official purposes, exclusively to me, the mayor, as your immediate superior, who is to give you all the details, which to a great extent has already occurred. For someone who knows how to read official missives and by extension reads non-official letters even better, the whole thing is all too obvious; that as an outsider you fail to see that, does not surprise me. Altogether, the letter means simply that Klamm intends to take a personal interest in you in the event of your being admitted to his lordship's service.'

'Sir,' said K., 'you interpret the letter so thoroughly that in the end nothing is left of it but the signature on a blank sheet of paper. Don't you see how your doing so disparages Klamm's name, which you claim to respect?'

'That is a misunderstanding,' said the mayor, 'I don't underestimate the significance of the letter, I'm not belittling it with my interpretation, on the contrary. A private letter from Klamm clearly has a lot more significance than an official missive, it's just that it does not have the significance *you* attach to it.'

'Do you know Schwarzer?' asked K.

'No,' said the mayor, 'how about you, Mizzi? Likewise. No, we don't know him.'

'That's odd,' said K., 'he's the son of an under-governor.'

'My dear man,' said the mayor, 'how am I supposed to know all the sons of all the under-governors?'

'Right,' said K., 'then you must take my word for it that he is. I and this Schwarzer had an unpleasant scene the day I arrived. He then telephoned an under-governor by the name of Fritz to inquire, and he was told I'd been taken on as land surveyor. How do you explain that, Mr Mayor?'

'Very easily,' said the mayor, 'you have never yet come properly into contact with our authorities. All these contacts are merely apparent, but you with your ignorance of the circumstances regard them as real. As for the telephone, look: here, and I certainly do have dealings with the authorities, there is no telephone. In bars and the like it may provide a useful service, much as a music box does, no more than that. Tell me, have you ever telephoned here? Then you'll perhaps understand what I'm saying. In the castle, the telephone clearly works very well indeed; I'm told that people are constantly telephoning there, which of course greatly speeds up the work. We hear this constant telephoning on our telephones here as hissing and singing, you'll have heard it yourself, I'm sure. But, you see, that hissing and that singing are the only real and reliable things that the telephones here tell us, everything else is illusory. There is no specific telephone connection with the castle, no exchange that puts our calls through; when you call someone in the castle from here, it rings on all the telephones in the lowest departments there, or rather it would ring on all of them were it not for the fact, which I know for certain, that on nearly all of them the bell is switched off. Every so often, though, an overtired official feels the need for a little distraction – particularly in the evening or at night – and switches the bell on, then we get an answer, except it's just a joke. And that's very understandable, after all. Who has any right to ring in about his private little troubles in the middle of the most important jobs, which are invariably being done in a tearing hurry. Nor do I understand how even an outsider can think that, when he calls Sordini, for instance, it really is Sordini that answers. It's much more likely to be a minor clerk in quite another department. On the other hand, it may happen in a lucky moment that, when you call the minor clerk, Sordini himself replies. Of course, it's better then to run away from the telephone before you hear the first ring.'

'That's not the way I saw it, though,' said K., 'I had no means of knowing these details, but I did not have a lot of confidence in those telephone conversations and was aware all the time that real significance attaches only to what one learns or achieves actually in the castle.'

'No,' said the mayor, seizing on the words, 'real significance attaches to these telephone replies, certainly, how could it not? How should a piece of information provided by an official from the castle be without significance? It's as I was saying in connection with Klamm's letter. All these statements have no official significance; if you attribute official significance to them, you are making a mistake, on the other hand their private significance in terms of friendliness or hostility is very great, usually greater than any official significance could ever be.'

'All right,' said K., 'assuming that is how things are, I have many good friends in the castle; strictly speaking, the idea of that department many years ago that a land surveyor might one day be sent for was already an act of friendship towards me, and after that, one followed another, except that I was then lured here to a bad end and am now under threat of being thrown out.'

'There's an element of truth in your view,' said the mayor, 'you are right in thinking that castle statements cannot be taken entirely literally. However, caution is necessary everywhere, not just here, and the more so, the more important the statement concerned. But what you go on to say about being lured here makes no sense to me at all. Had you been following my explanations more closely, you'd surely be aware that the question of your being summoned here is much too difficult for us to be able to answer here in the course of one short conversation.'

'So the end result,' said K., 'is that everything is very unclear and insoluble, right down to my being thrown out.'

'Who do you suppose would dare to throw you out, sir,' said the mayor, 'the very unclarity of the previous questions guarantees you the most courteous treatment, only you seem to be oversensitive. No one is keeping you here, but that doesn't mean you're being thrown out.'

'But Mr Mayor,' said K., 'now it's you again, seeing some things all too clearly. I shall tell you something of what is keeping me here: the sacrifice I made to get away from home, the long hard journey, the legitimate hopes I had as a result of being taken on here, my total lack of assets, the impossibility of my now finding another suitable job back home, and last but not least my intended, who is a local girl.'

'Ah, Frieda!' said the mayor without any surprise, 'I know. But

Frieda would follow you everywhere. As to the rest, of course, certain considerations are in fact necessary here and I shall be reporting to the castle on the subject. If a decision should arrive or if it should become necessary to interrogate you again first, I shall send for you. Is that all right with you?'

'No, not at all,' said K., 'I want no favours from the castle, I want my rights.'

'Mizzi,' said the mayor to his wife, who still sat pressed against him and was playing dreamily with Klamm's letter, which she had fashioned into a little boat, K. now took this from her in alarm, 'Mizzi, my leg is starting to hurt very badly again, we must renew the poultice.'

K. rose, 'in that case, I'll take my leave,' he said. 'Yes,' said Mizzi, who was already preparing an ointment, 'there's also an awful draught.' K. turned, the assistants, with their invariably inopportune zeal, had already, the moment K. spoke, opened both leaves of the door. K. was unable, if he wished to preserve the sickroom from the cold that was driving in, to give the mayor more than a cursory bow. He then ran, pulling the assistants with him, out of the room and quickly shut the door.

6

SECOND CONVERSATION WITH
THE LANDLADY

The landlord was waiting for him outside the inn. Unasked, he would not have dared to speak, so K. asked him what he wanted. 'Have you found somewhere else to live yet?' the landlord asked, looking at the ground. 'You're asking because your wife told you to,' said K., 'you're very dependent on her, aren't you?' 'No,' said the landlord, 'I'm not asking because she told me to. But she's very nervous and unhappy because of you, can't work, lies in bed sighing and complaining the whole time.' 'Shall I go to her?' asked K. 'Please do,' said the landlord, 'I meant to fetch you from the mayor's, listened at the door there but you were talking, I didn't want to butt in, also I was concerned about my wife, came running back here, she wouldn't let me in, though, so I'd no alternative but to wait for you.' 'Come on, then,' said K., 'I'll soon calm her down.' 'Let's hope you can,' said the landlord.

They passed through the bright kitchen, where three or four maids, a long way apart, literally stiffened in what they happened to be doing at sight of K. Even in the kitchen, the landlady could be heard sighing. She lay in a windowless area partitioned off from the kitchen by a thin wooden wall. There was room in it only for a large double bed and a wardrobe. The bed was positioned in such a way that from it the whole kitchen could be seen and the work supervised. From the kitchen, however, very little could be seen in the partitioned area, it was very dark in there, only the red and white bedclothes made a faint gleam. It was not until you were inside and your eyes had accommodated that you could distinguish details.

'You've come at last,' said the landlady feebly. She lay prostrate, breathing was clearly a problem for her, she had thrown the quilt back. She looked much younger in bed than in her clothes, but a delicate little lace nightcap that she wore, despite the fact that it was too small and sat unsteadily on her coiffure, made the sunkenness of her face pitiful. 'How was I supposed to come?' said K. gently, 'you didn't send for me.' 'You shouldn't have made me wait so long,' said the landlady with the obstinacy of the sick. 'Sit down,' she said, indicating the edge of the bed, 'you others go away, though.' In addition to the assistants, the maids had meanwhile come crowding in as well. 'Shall I leave too, Gardena?' said the landlord, this was the first time K. had heard the woman's name. 'Of course,' she said slowly, and as if preoccupied with other thoughts she added absent-mindedly: 'Why should you stay, of all people?' But once they had all retreated into the kitchen, this time even the assistants promptly did as they were told, granted they were after one of the maids, Gardena was in fact alert enough to realize that every word spoken in here could be heard from the kitchen, the partition having no door, so she ordered them all to leave the kitchen too. This they did immediately.

'Sir, please,' Gardena said then, 'there's a shawl hanging in the front of the wardrobe, pass it to me, I want to put it over myself, I can't stand the quilt, I have such difficulty breathing.' And when K. had brought her the shawl, she said: 'Look, isn't this a lovely shawl?' To K. it seemed an ordinary woollen shawl, he felt it once again, purely to oblige, but said nothing. 'Yes, it's a lovely shawl,' Gardena said, and wrapped herself up. She lay there peacefully now, all suffering apparently taken from her, indeed she even thought about her hair, ruffled from her lying in bed, she sat up for a moment and made some small improvements to her coiffure around the lace cap. She had luxuriant hair.

K., growing impatient, said: 'You wanted to know, ma'am, whether I had somewhere else to live yet.' 'I wanted to know?' said the landlady, 'no, that's not right.' 'Your husband has just asked me.' 'I quite believe it,' said the landlady, 'we've had a row. When I didn't want you here, he kept you here, now that I'm glad you live here, he's driving you away. He's always doing that sort of thing.' 'Does that,' said K., 'mean you've changed your mind about me so much? In an hour or two?' 'I've not changed my mind,' said the landlady, her voice weaker again. 'Give me your hand. There. And now promise me to be completely honest, I want to be completely honest with you, too.' 'Fine,' said K., 'but who's going to start?' 'I am,' said the landlady, giving the impression not that she was seeking to meet K. halfway but that she was eager to speak first.

She pulled a photograph out from beneath the pillow and handed it to K. 'Look at this picture,' she pleaded. To see it better, K. stepped into the kitchen, but even there it was not easy to make out anything in the picture, because it was faded with age, badly cracked, creased, and blotchy. 'It's not in very good condition,' said K. 'Sadly not, sadly not,' said the landlady, 'when one carries a thing around constantly for years, that's what happens. But if you look at it closely, sir, you'll make everything out, I'm quite sure. I can help you, anyway, tell me what you see, I adore hearing about the picture. What do you see?' 'A young man,' said K. 'Right,' said the landlady, 'and what is he doing?' 'He's lying on a board, I think, stretching his limbs and yawning.' The landlady laughed. 'That's quite wrong,' she said. 'But here's the board and here he is, lying,' K. insisted. 'Look more closely,' said the landlady, annoyed, 'is he really lying?' 'No,' K. now said, 'he's not lying, he's in the air and I can see now, it's not a board, it's probably a rope and the young man is doing the high jump.' 'There you are,' said the landlady, pleased, 'he's jumping, that's how the official messengers practise, I knew you'd see it. Can you make his face out, too?' 'I can see very little of the face,' said K., 'he's clearly making a great effort, his mouth is open, his eyes screwed up, and his hair streaming.' 'Very good,' the landlady said appreciatively, 'that's all someone who's not seen him in person could make out. But he was a handsome young man, I only glimpsed him once, and I'll never forget him.' 'So who was he?' asked K. 'He,' said the landlady, 'was the messenger Klamm had summon me to him the first time.'

K. was prevented from listening closely by a distracting rattle of glass. He located the cause of the disturbance immediately. The assistants were standing outside in the courtyard, hopping from one foot to the other in the snow. They acted as if they were pleased to see K. again, delightedly pointing him out to each other and tapping constantly on the kitchen window as they did so. At a threatening gesture from K. they stopped at once, attempted to push each other back, but one promptly eluded the other and in no time they were both back at the window. K. hurried behind the partition, where the assistants could not see him from outside and he need not see them. But the faint, almost pleading rattle of the windowpane continued to haunt him for a long time even there.

'The assistants again,' he told the landlady by way of excusing himself and pointed outside. She, however, took no notice of him, she had taken the picture from him, looked at it, smoothed it out, and pushed it back under the pillow. Her movements had become slower, not from weariness but under the weight of memory. She had wanted to tell K. a story, and in the telling had forgotten about him. She played with the fringe of her shawl. A moment passed before she looked up, drew a hand over her eyes, and said: 'This shawl is from Klamm, too. And the cap. The picture, the shawl, and the cap, they're the three mementoes I have of him. I'm not young like Frieda, I'm not as ambitious as she is, nor as sensitive, she's very sensitive, what I mean is, I'm able to resign myself to life, but one thing I must say: without these three things I shouldn't have lasted so long here, in fact I probably shouldn't have lasted a day here. These three mementoes may not seem much to you, but Frieda, you see, who was going with Klamm for so long, has no mementoes at all, I've asked her, she's too infatuated as well as too demanding, whereas I, who was with Klamm only three times – after that he stopped sending for me, I don't know why – brought away these mementoes as if sensing how short my time would be. You have to attend to it yourself, of course, Klamm will volunteer nothing, but if you see something suitable lying around there you can ask for it.'

K. felt uncomfortable, hearing these stories, however much they concerned him too. 'How long ago was all this?' he asked with a sigh.

'Over twenty years,' said the landlady, 'well over twenty years.'

'So that's how long women stay faithful to Klamm,' said K. 'But are you also aware, ma'am, that with confessions like this you give me serious cause for concern when I think of my own forthcoming marriage?'

The landlady felt it was improper for K. to seek to butt in here with his own affairs, and she gave him a furious sideways glance.

'Don't be angry, ma'am,' said K., 'I'm not saying a word against Klamm, but through force of circumstances I've entered into a certain relationship with Klamm; not even Klamm's greatest admirer could deny that. So. It follows that at every mention of Klamm I must also think of myself, there's no altering that. And anyway, ma'am' – here K. grasped her hesitant hand – 'think how badly our last conversation turned out and how this time we want to part in peace.'

'You're right,' said the landlady, bending her head, 'but don't be hard on me. I'm not more sensitive than other people, quite the contrary, everyone has sensitive spots, I have just this one.'

'Unfortunately, at the same time it is also mine,' said K., 'though I shall certainly control myself; but will you now explain to me, ma'am, how I am to bear, in marriage, this appalling faithfulness toward Klamm, always assuming Frieda resembles you in this.'

'Appalling faithfulness,' the landlady echoed angrily. 'Do you call that faithfulness? I'm faithful to my husband, but Klamm? Klamm once made me his mistress, can I ever lose that rank? And how are you to bear it with Frieda, you say? Sir, who are you to dare ask such a thing?'

'Madam!' said K. in warning.

'I know,' said the landlady meekly, 'but my husband never asked such questions. I don't know whom to call more unhappy, me then or Frieda now. Frieda, who deliberately left Klamm, or myself, whom he stopped sending for. Possibly Frieda, in fact, even if she seems not altogether to realize it as yet. But my thoughts were more exclusively dominated by my unhappiness at the time, because I had constantly to ask myself and basically have never stopped asking myself, even now: why did it happen? Three times Klamm sent for you and a fourth time not, never again, there was no fourth time! What was more on my mind back then? What else was I to talk about with my husband, whom I married soon afterwards? During the day we had no time, we had taken over this inn in a pitiful state and had to try to bring it up to scratch, but at night? For years, our nightly talks centred only on Klamm and the reasons for his change of heart. And if my husband fell asleep during these conversations, I woke him and we went on talking.'

'I shall now,' said K., 'if I may, ask a very rude question.'

The landlady was silent.

'I mayn't ask, then,' said K., 'that'll do me too.'

'Of course it will,' said the landlady, 'that especially. You misinterpret everything, even silence. You can't help it, you see. Yes, you may ask your question.'

'If I misinterpret everything,' said K., 'maybe I'm also misinterpreting my question, maybe it isn't so rude. I merely wanted to know how you met your husband and how this inn came into your possession.'

The landlady frowned but said composedly: 'It's a very simple story. My father was a blacksmith and Hans, now my husband, who was groom to a big farmer, came to my father from time to time. This was after the last meeting with Klamm, I was very unhappy and shouldn't really have been so, since everything had been done quite properly and my no longer being permitted to go to Klamm was Klamm's own decision, in other words quite proper, only the reasons were obscure, those it was all right for me to probe but I shouldn't have been unhappy, I was, though, and couldn't do any work and used to sit in our front garden all day. Hans saw me there, came and sat beside me sometimes, I didn't complain to him, but he knew what was up, and being a generous young man he wept with me occasionally. And when the then innkeeper, whose wife had died and who therefore had to give up the business, he was also an old man by that time, when he passed our garden one day and saw us sitting there, he stopped and offered us a lease on the inn there and then, he said he trusted us so wanted no money in advance and charged very little for the lease. I didn't wish to become a burden on my father, I didn't care about anything else, and so, thinking of the inn and the chance that a new job might bring some oblivion, I gave Hans my hand. That's the story.'

There was silence for a moment, then K. said: 'The innkeeper's behaviour was handsome but rash, or did he have particular grounds for his confidence in you both?'

'He knew Hans well,' said the landlady, 'he was Hans's uncle.'

'Then presumably,' said K., 'Hans's family set great store by the connection with you?'

'Possibly,' said the landlady, 'I don't know, I never bothered about that.'

'But they must have done,' said K., 'if the family was prepared to make such sacrifices and simply hand the inn over to you with no security.'

'It wasn't rash, as things transpired,' said the landlady. 'I threw myself into the work, I was a strong girl, the blacksmith's daughter, I needed neither maid nor manservant, I was everywhere, in the bar, in the kitchen, in the stables, in the yard, I cooked so well I even took custom away from the Count's Arms, you've not been in the lounge at lunchtime yet, you don't know our lunchtime customers, there used to be even more of them, a lot have trickled away since then. And as a result, not only did we manage to keep up the lease, after a few years we were able to buy outright and today the inn is virtually free of debt. Also as a result, of course, I ruined my health in the process, began to have heart trouble, and am now an old woman. You think, perhaps, that I'm much older than Hans, but in fact he's only two or three years younger, and anyway he'll never grow old, because doing the job he does – smoking a pipe, listening to the customers, then knocking out the pipe and occasionally fetching a beer – doing that job, you don't grow old.'

'What you've achieved is admirable,' said K., 'no doubt about it, but we were talking about the days before your marriage, and at that time it would have been remarkable, would it not, if at some financial cost to themselves, or at least while assuming so big a risk as handing over the inn, Hans's family had urged marriage with no other hope than your capacity for work, of which nothing was known as yet, and Hans's capacity for work, which they must surely have known then was non-existent.'

'All right,' said the landlady wearily, 'but you see, I know what you're getting at and how wide you are of the mark. Klamm had nothing whatever to do with any of this. Why should he have provided for me or rather: how could he have provided for me? He knew nothing else about me. His no longer sending for me was a sign that he'd forgotten me. A person he stops sending for, he forgets all about. I didn't want to mention that in front of Frieda. But it's not just forgetting, it's more than that. A person you've forgotten, you can always get to know again. With Klamm, that's not possible. A person he stops sending for, he has utterly forgotten not only so far as the past is concerned but literally for all future time as well. If I make a big effort, I can in fact think myself into your thoughts, thoughts that make no sense here but may have their validity in the foreign parts you come from. Possibly, your presumption extends to the mad belief that Klamm had given me a man like Hans for a husband precisely in order that I should have little to hinder my coming to him if he did ever summon me in future. That really is as far as even madness can go. Where's the

74

husband who could stop me running to Klamm, if Klamm gives me a sign? Nonsense, utter nonsense, it's asking for confusion, toying with such nonsense.'

'No,' said K., 'we don't want to confuse ourselves, I'd got nothing like so far in my thinking as you suppose, though to tell the truth I was on the way there. For the present, though, I was merely surprised that the relatives had such high hopes of the marriage and that those hopes were in fact fulfilled, if at the cost of your heart, your health. The idea of a connection between these circumstances and Klamm did in fact occur to me in the process, but not or not quite with the coarseness you use to describe it, clearly for the sole purpose of being able to have another go at me, because it's something you enjoy doing. Well, good luck to you! However, what I was thinking was this: firstly, Klamm is clearly the reason for the marriage. But for Klamm you'd not have been unhappy, not have sat idle in your front garden, but for Klamm Hans would not have seen you there, but for your sadness the shy Hans would never have dared to talk to you, but for Klamm you would never have been found in tears with Hans, but for Klamm the kindly old uncle-innkeeper would never have seen Hans and you sitting there peacefully together, but for Klamm you would not have been indifferent to life so would not have married Hans. I should have thought there was plenty of Klamm, just in all that. But that's not the whole story. Had you not been trying to forget, you would surely not have worked with such disregard of self and improved the inn so much. In other words, Klamm again. But quite apart from that, Klamm is also the cause of your illness, because even before your marriage your heart had been worn out by unrequited passion. That leaves only the question of what so tempted Hans's relatives about the marriage. You once mentioned yourself that being Klamm's mistress means an irrevocable increase in status, so maybe that was what tempted them. But also, I think, the hope that the lucky star that had led you to Klamm – assuming it was a lucky star, but you insist it was – belonged to you and would therefore be bound to stay with you and not, say, abandon you as swiftly and suddenly as Klamm had.'

'Are you serious about all this?' asked the landlady.

'I'm serious,' K. said quickly, 'only I think that Hans's relatives were neither entirely right nor entirely wrong in their hopes, and I also

75

think I see the mistake they were making. Outwardly it all seems a success, Hans is well looked after, has a splendid wife, commands respect, the inn is out of debt. In reality, though, it is not a complete success, with a simple girl whose first great love he'd been he would certainly have known far greater happiness; if, as you reproach him for, he sometimes stands in the bar looking lost, it's because he actually feels lost – without being unhappy about it, certainly, I do know him that well – but what is equally certain is that this handsome, intelligent young man would have grown happier, by which I mean at the same time more independent, more industrious, more manly, with another woman. Nor, surely, are you happy yourself, as you were saying, but for the three mementoes you had no wish to go on living, plus you have a heart condition. So were the relatives wrong in their hopes? I think not. You'd been blessed all right, they just didn't know how to take advantage of the fact.'

'So what did they not do?' asked the landlady. She was now lying flat on her back, staring up at the ceiling.

'Inquire of Klamm,' said K.

'Which brings us back to you,' said the landlady.

'Or to you,' said K., 'our affairs overlap.'

'So what is it you want with Klamm?' said the landlady. She had sat up, plumped up the pillows to enable her to lean against them in a sitting position, and was looking K. full in the eye. 'I've told you frankly about my case, from which you might have learned a thing or two. Now you tell me as frankly what it is you want to ask Klamm. I had trouble persuading Frieda to go up to her room and stay there, I was afraid you wouldn't speak frankly enough in her presence.'

'I have nothing to hide,' said K. 'First, though, there's something I want to draw your attention to. Klamm forgets immediately, you said. For one thing that seems to me highly unlikely, but for another it can't be proved, it's clearly no more than a story, thought up by the girlish minds of those who happened to be in favour with Klamm at the time. I'm surprised you believe so trite a fancy.'

'It's no story,' said the landlady, 'it's drawn from common experience.'

'So can be refuted by fresh experience,' said K. 'But there's another difference, too, between your case and Frieda's. It didn't, so to speak, ever happen that Klamm stopped summoning Frieda, he summoned her all right, but she didn't go. He may even still be waiting for her.'

The landlady was silent, merely looking K. up and down attentively. Then she said: 'I shall listen calmly to everything you have to say. Speak frankly rather than spare my feelings. Just one request. Don't use Klamm's name. Refer to him as "him" or whatever, but not by name.'

'Fine,' said K., 'but what I want from him is hard to say. To begin with, I want to see him close to, then I want to hear his voice, then I want to know from him how he feels about our marriage; what I may then ask of him will depend on the course the discussion takes. Lots of things may come up, but the most important thing from my standpoint is that I shall be in his presence. You see, I haven't yet spoken directly to a single genuine official. It seems to be harder to achieve than I thought. However, it's my duty to speak to him as a private individual, and as I see it that is far easier to accomplish; as an official, I can talk to him only in his quite possibly inaccessible office, in the castle or, questionably, in the Count's Arms, but as a private individual, anywhere in the building, on the street, wherever I succeed in bumping into him. That I shall then, incidentally, have the officer before me too, is something I shall be glad to accept, but it's not my main goal.'

'All right,' said the landlady, pressing her face into the pillows as if she was saying something indecent, 'if through my contacts I manage to get your request for a discussion passed up to Klamm, promise me that until the reply comes back down you'll do nothing on your own initiative.'

'I can't promise that,' said K., 'much as I'd like to meet your request or gratify your whim. The matter's urgent, you see, particularly after the unfavourable outcome of my meeting with the mayor.'

'That objection doesn't apply,' said the landlady, 'the mayor is someone entirely without consequence. Didn't you realize? He couldn't keep his job for a day if it weren't for his wife, who runs every-thing.'

'Mizzi?' K. asked. The landlady nodded. 'She was there,' said K.

'Did she say anything?' asked the landlady.

'No,' said K., 'but nor did I have the impression she could have done.'

'I see,' said the landlady, 'well, that's how wrongly you view every-thing here. Anyway: whatever action the mayor has taken concerning you is unimportant, and I'll be talking to the wife some time. And if I also promise you that Klamm's response will be here in a week at most, you presumably have no further reason not to let me have my way.'

'None of that makes any difference,' said K., 'my decision stands and I should seek to implement it even if a negative response came back. But if that's my intention from the outset, I can't put in a request for a discussion first. What without the request is perhaps a bold experiment, though one made in good faith, would after a negative response be open insubordination. That would be far worse, of course.'

'Worse?' said the landlady. 'It's insubordination either way. Just do as you wish. Pass me my dress.'

Disregarding K., she pulled the dress on and hurried into the kitchen. For some time now, noise had been audible from the lounge. Someone had knocked at the little window. The assistants had pushed it open once and called through that they were hungry. Other faces too had appeared there subsequently. Singing could even be heard, quiet but involving a number of voices.

K.'s conversation with the landlady had of course seriously delayed the cooking of lunch; it was not yet ready but the customers were assembled, though none had ventured to enter the kitchen against the landlady's orders. However, now that the watchers at the little window reported that the landlady was coming, the maids ran into the kitchen immediately, and as K. entered the lounge the surprisingly large crowd, more than twenty persons, men and women, provincial in their dress, certainly, but not rustic, not like peasants, were flocking from the little window, where they had been gathered, over to the tables in order to secure themselves places. Only one little table in a corner had a couple already sitting at it with several children, the man, a cheerful-looking, blue-eyed gentleman with dishevelled grey hair and a beard, was on his feet, bending over the children and beating time with a knife to their singing, which he kept trying to mute. Possibly he was using the song to try to make them forget their hunger. The landlady apologized to the company with a few carelessly uttered words, no one reproached her. She looked around for the landlord, but he had presumably long since fled from the difficulty of the situation. She then moved slowly into the kitchen; K., who was hurrying to his room to see Frieda, she ignored completely.

7

THE SCHOOLMASTER

Upstairs K. met the schoolmaster. Fortunately, the room was scarcely recognizable, so busy had Frieda been. It was well aired, the stove generously stoked, the floor washed, the bed tidied, the maids' things, odious trash, their pictures included, had gone, the table, which had previously, no matter which way you turned, literally stared after you with its filth-encrusted surface, was covered with a white crocheted cloth. They could now receive visitors, K.'s small store of underwear, which Frieda had clearly washed that morning and hung by the stove to dry, was hardly in the way. The schoolmaster and Frieda were sitting at table, they stood up as K. came in, Frieda greeted K. with a kiss, the schoolmaster gave a small bow. K., his mind elsewhere and still restless from the conversation with the landlady, started to apologize for not having managed to call on the schoolmaster as yet, it was as if he assumed that the schoolmaster, impatient at K.'s non-appearance, had decided to make the call himself. However, the schoolmaster in his measured way seemed only now slowly to recall that some sort of visit had once been agreed between himself and K. 'Indeed, Mr Land Surveyor,' he said slowly, 'you're the stranger I spoke to in Church Square a couple of days ago.' 'Yes,' K. said curtly; what in his desolate state he had tolerated at the time, he did not have to put up with here in his room. He turned to Frieda and conferred with her regarding an important call he had to make immediately and for which he must look as smart as possible. Frieda immediately, without quizzing K. further, called to the assistants, who were busy examining the new tablecloth, and told them to give K.'s clothes and boots, which he began removing at once, a good clean down in the yard. She herself took a shirt from the line and ran downstairs to the kitchen to iron it.

K. was now alone with the schoolmaster, who again sat in silence at the table, he left him waiting a while longer, took off his shirt, and began to wash in the washbasin. Only now, with his back to the schoolmaster, did he ask him why he had come. 'I bring a message from the mayor,' he said. K. was prepared to listen to the message. However, since K.'s words were hard to make out through the splashing, the schoolmaster had to come closer and leant against the wall beside K. K. apologized for his washing and his agitation on the ground of the urgency of the call he planned to make. The schoolmaster disregarded this, saying: 'You were rude to the mayor, who is an elderly, experienced, deserving, and venerable man.' 'I wasn't aware of having been rude,' K. said as he dried himself, 'but it's true I had other things to think about than good behaviour, because what was at stake was my livelihood, under threat from a humiliating official system, the details of which I need not set out for you since you are an active arm of that authority yourself. Did the mayor complain about me?' 'Whom should he have complained to?' said the schoolmaster, 'and even if he did have someone, would he ever complain? I merely drafted a small minute about your discussion from his dictation and learned sufficient from that about the mayor's kindness and the style of your replies.' As K. searched for his comb, which Frieda must have tidied away somewhere, he said: 'What did you say? A minute? Drafted in my absence, after the event, by someone who was not even at the discussion. That's not bad. And why a minute, anyway? Was it official business?' 'No,' said the schoolmaster, 'semi-official, the minute too is only semi-official, it was made only because with us there has to be strict order in everything. Anyway, there it is and it does you no honour.' K., who had finally found the comb, it had slipped into the bed, said more calmly: 'All right, there it is. Is that what you came to tell me?' 'No,' said the schoolmaster, 'but I'm not an automaton and I had to tell you what I thought. The message I bring is, on the contrary, yet further proof of the mayor's kindness; I stress, such kindness is incomprehensible to me, and I execute this commission only under the constraint of my office and out of admiration for the mayor.' K., washed and combed, was now sitting at the table waiting for his shirt and suit, he felt little curiosity regarding what the schoolmaster had brought him, he was also under the influence of the landlady's low opinion of the mayor. 'It's gone noon, presumably?' he asked, his mind on the journey in prospect, then he corrected himself and said: 'You had a message for me from the mayor.' 'Well, yes,' said the schoolmaster with a shrug, as if shaking off any responsibility of his own. 'The mayor is afraid that, if the decision regarding your case is too long in coming, you will do something rash on your own initiative. I don't myself know why he's afraid of that, in my view your best course would be to do what you want. We're not your guardian angels and have no obligation to go running after you down every avenue you take. Still. The mayor thinks otherwise. The decision itself, which is a matter for the count's authorities, he's of course not in a position to expedite. However, within his sphere of influence he does want to make what is a truly generous interim decision, it's purely up to you whether you accept it, he's offering you a temporary position as school caretaker.' What he was being offered made little immediate impression on K., but the fact that he was being offered something seemed to him not without significance. It suggested that in the mayor's view he was capable, in his own defence, of doing things of a kind that, so far as the municipality was concerned, safeguarding itself against them even justified a certain amount of expense. Also, how seriously the matter was being taken. The schoolmaster, who had already been waiting here for a while and before that had drafted the minute, must have been sent round here by the mayor very urgently.

When the schoolmaster saw he had succeeded in making K. think, he went on: 'I made my objections. I pointed out that no school caretaker had been needed hitherto, the sexton's wife tidies up from time to time and Miss Gisa, the schoolmistress, supervises, I have enough trouble with the children, I don't want to be getting cross with a caretaker too. The mayor replied that it was in fact very dirty in the school. I responded truthfully that it was not too bad. And, I added, will things be any better if we do make the man caretaker? They most certainly will not. Apart from the fact that he knows nothing about such work, all the school has are two large classrooms, with no side rooms, consequently the caretaker and his family will have to use one of the classrooms to live in, sleep in, possibly even cook in, which will of course hardly enhance cleanliness. However, the mayor pointed out that this job was a lifeline in distress for you and you would therefore make every effort to do it well, the mayor also thought that with you we also gain the energies of your wife and your assistants, so that not only the school but also the school grounds can in future be kept in exemplary shape. I rebutted all that with ease. Eventually the mayor, unable to say anything more in your favour, laughed and said simply that as a land surveyor you'd be able to draw the beds in the school garden especially nice and straight. Well, there's no answer to jesting so I left to bring you the message.' 'You needn't worry, sir,' said K., 'I've no intention of taking the job.' 'Excellent,' said the schoolmaster, 'excellent, you unreservedly turn it down' and he took his hat, bowed, and left.

Immediately afterwards Frieda came upstairs, her face haggard, the shirt unironed in her hand, she refused to answer questions; to distract her, K. told her about the schoolmaster and the offer, the instant she heard it she threw the shirt on the bed and ran out again. She soon returned, but with the schoolmaster, who looked annoyed and did not even offer a greeting. Frieda asked him to be patient for a moment – she had clearly done this several times already on the way here – then pulled K. through a side door he had not even known existed into the adjacent roof space and there at last, flustered and breathless, told him what had happened to her. The landlady, furious at having lowered herself in K.'s presence to confessions and, even more irritatingly, to compliance with regard to a discussion between Klamm and K. and at having achieved nothing thereby but, as she said, cold and furthermore insincere rejection, was evidently determined no longer to tolerate K. in her house; if he had contacts with the castle, let him make use of them and let him be quick about it, because this very day, this very hour he must quit the house, and only at the direct command of the authorities and under duress would she have him back, but she hoped it would not come to that, because she too had contacts with the castle and would know how to bring them to bear. In any case, he had only got into the inn as a result of the landlord's carelessness, nor was he in any distress because only this morning he had been boasting about other accommodation for the night being available to him. Frieda should stay, of course, were Frieda to move out with K. she, the landlady, would be deeply unhappy, she had just then, down in the kitchen, collapsed in tears by the cooking-stove at the mere thought, the poor woman with her heart condition, but how could she do otherwise now that, to her mind at least, it was almost a question of

83

the honour of Klamm's memory. That, then, according to Frieda, was where the landlady stood. She, Frieda, would of course follow K. wherever he wished, through snow and ice, there was no more to be said on that score, of course not, but anyway, the situation was very grim for them both, which was why she had welcomed the mayor's offer so gladly, she said, and although the position was perhaps an unsuitable one for K. it was, after all, this was stressed specifically, only provisional, they would gain some time and would easily find other possibilities, even if the final decision should turn out unfavourably. 'If we have to,' Frieda ended up crying into K.'s neck, 'we'll emigrate, what's to keep us in the village here? In the meantime, though, all right sweetheart, we accept the offer, I've brought the schoolmaster back, you tell him "done", that's all, and we move into the school.'

'That's awful,' said K., not entirely seriously since he did not much care where they lived, he also felt very chilly in his underwear out here in the roof space, which with no wall and window on two sides had a fiercely cold through draught, 'you've got the room arranged so nicely and now we're to move out. I'm reluctant to take the job, I really am, my present humiliation in front of this little schoolmaster is embarrassing enough for me, and now he's to be my boss. If we could stay here just a little longer, my situation may change this very afternoon. If at least you stay here, we might hang on and just give the schoolmaster a vague answer. I'll always find a bed for myself, if I really have to with Bar –' Frieda put a hand over his mouth. 'Not that,' she said fearfully, 'please don't say it again. That apart, I'll do everything you tell me to. If you want, I'll stay here alone, however sad that would be for me. If you want, we'll turn the request down, however wrong that would be, to my mind. Because look, if you do find another possibility, even this afternoon, well, it goes without saying that we'll give up the school position immediately, no one's going to stop us doing that. And as for humiliation in front of the schoolmaster, let me see to it that there isn't any, I'll speak to him myself, you'll simply be standing there, saying nothing, and afterwards too it'll be no different, you'll never have to speak to him yourself if you don't want to, only I shall be his subordinate, really, and not even I shall be, since I know his weaknesses. So nothing is lost if we accept the job, but a lot will be if we refuse it, above all you truly would not, even just for yourself, unless you get somewhere with the castle today, find a place to sleep anywhere in the village, not anywhere, I mean a place to sleep that I as your wife-to-be needn't feel ashamed of. And if you find nowhere to sleep, will you then really expect me to sleep in the warm room here, knowing that you are wandering about outside in the cold and dark?' K., who the whole time had had his arms crossed over his chest and had been slapping his back with his hands to warm himself a bit, said: 'Then there's nothing for it but to accept, come on!'

In the room he hurried straight over to the stove, taking no notice of the schoolmaster; the schoolmaster was seated at the table, took out his watch, and said: 'It's getting late.' 'Yes, but we're now in complete agreement, sir,' Frieda told the schoolmaster, 'we accept the job.' 'Fine,' said the schoolmaster, 'but the job was offered to the land surveyor, he must say himself.' Frieda came to K.'s aid, 'of course,' she said, 'he accepts the job, don't you K.?' In this way, K. was able to limit his statement to a simple yes, which was not even directed at the schoolmaster but at Frieda. 'In that case,' said the schoolmaster, 'it remains only for me to inform you of your duties, I want us to agree on this point once and for all: you are required, Mr Land Surveyor, to clean and heat both schoolrooms every day, carry out minor repairs to the building as well as to teaching and gymnastic equipment yourself, keep the garden path clear of snow, run errands for myself and the schoolmistress, and in the warmer season see to all the gardening. In return, you have the right to live in one of the schoolrooms at your discretion; however, when both rooms are not being taught in simultaneously and you happen to be living in the room we are teaching in, you will of course be required to move into the other room. You're not allowed to cook in the school, instead you and your dependants will be fed here in the inn at the council's expense. That you must behave in a manner befitting the dignity of the school and that in particular the children must never, and most certainly not during lessons, be permitted to witness unpleasant scenes in your domestic life, say, are points I shall mention only in passing, because as an educated man you will surely be aware of them. In this connection, I further point out that we must insist you regularize your relations with Miss Frieda as soon as possible. Regarding all these matters and one or two details besides, a contract of employment will be drawn up that you must sign as soon as you move into the schoolhouse.' To K. this all seemed unimportant, as if it did not concern him or at least was not binding on him, but the schoolmaster's bragging irked him and he said lightly: 'Well yes, those are the usual duties.' To try to cover up this remark, Frieda asked about salary. 'Whether a salary will be paid,' said the schoolmaster, 'will be considered only after a month-long probationary period.' 'That's rather hard on us,' Frieda said, 'we're to marry with almost no money, set up house on nothing. Could we not, sir, perhaps petition the council for a small immediate salary? Would you advise us to do that?' 'No,' said the schoolmaster, who was still directing his words at K., 'such a petition would be complied with only if I recommended it, and I should not do so. Indeed, the grant of this position is merely a favour to you, and favours, if a person remains aware of his public responsibility, mustn't be pushed too far.' Here K. did butt in, almost in spite of himself. 'As to favours, sir,' he said, 'I believe you're making a mistake. The favour in this case is possibly more on my side.' 'No,' said the schoolmaster with a smile, he had got K. talking after all, 'my information is precise on that point. We need the school caretaker about as urgently as the land surveyor. School caretaker and land surveyor alike are a burden around our necks. It will take a lot of thinking about, how I'm to justify the expenditure to the council, the best and most truthful course would be simply to throw the request on the table without any grounds at all.' 'That's what I mean,' said K., 'it's against your will that you have to take me on, it causes you serious misgivings but you have to take me on. Well, if someone is forced to take another person on and that other person allows himself to be taken on, then he's the one doing the favour.' 'Curious,' the schoolmaster said, 'what should compel us to take you on, it's the mayor's kind, over-kind heart that is compelling us. You, sir, I can see, will need to part with a good many fancies before you're any use as a school caretaker. And as regards the allocation of a possible salary, remarks like that naturally generate little enthusiasm. I'm also sorry to note that your behaviour is going to give me a great deal of trouble, you've conducted this whole conversation with me, I have the sight constantly before me and can scarcely believe my eyes, in your vest and underpants.' 'Right,' said K., laughing and clapping his hands together, 'those terrible assistants, what's keeping them?' Frieda ran to the door, the schoolmaster, realizing that, so far as he was concerned, there was no more talking to K. just now, asked Frieda when they would be moving into the school, 'today,' said Frieda, 'then I'll be round tomorrow to check things over,' said the schoolmaster, waved a hand in farewell, tried to go out through the door, which Frieda had opened for herself, but bumped into the maids, who were already arriving with their belongings to reoccupy the room, and was obliged, since they would never have stepped aside for anyone, to slip between them, Frieda following in his wake. 'You're in a hurry,' said K., this time very content with them, 'we're still here and you have to move in already?' They did not answer, merely spun their bundles in embarrassment, K. spotted the familiar filthy rags hanging out of them. 'I don't suppose you've ever washed your things,' said K., not maliciously but with a certain affection. Sensing this, they simultaneously opened their hard mouths to show beautiful, powerful, animal teeth, and laughed soundlessly. 'Come on, then,' said K., 'make yourselves at home, it's your room.' But when they still hesitated – presumably their room struck them as rather too much changed – K. took one by the arm to lead her farther. He promptly let go of her, however, so startled was the look that, after a swift mutual consultation, both girls now fixed on K. and kept there. 'Right, you've looked at me long enough,' K. said, fighting off a vaguely unpleasant feeling, then took the clothes and boots that Frieda, followed shyly by the assistants, had just brought, and got dressed. Once again, as always, he found Frieda's patience with the assistants incredible. After a protracted search she had located them, at a time when they were supposed to have been cleaning the clothes in the yard, sitting happily downstairs over lunch, the still dirty clothes crumpled up in their laps, she had then had to clean everything herself, and yet she refrained, well knowing how to control common folk, from the least reproach, talked, even in their presence, of their gross negligence as a minor laughing matter, and went so far as to pat one of them lightly, almost caressingly on the cheek. K. intended to chide her about this very soon. Now, though, it was high time he went. 'The assistants will stay here to help you with the move,' K. said. They took exception to this, replete and happy as they were, they would have liked a bit of exercise. It was only when Frieda said: 'Of course, you stay here,' that they obeyed. 'Do you know where I'm going?'

asked K. 'Yes,' said Frieda. 'You mean, you'll no longer stop me?' asked K. 'You will meet so many obstacles,' she said, 'what difference would anything I said make!' She kissed K. goodbye, handed him, since he had eaten no lunch, a small package containing bread and sausage that she had brought for him from downstairs, reminded him that he should no longer return there but go straight to the school, and accompanied him, one hand on his shoulder, out of the building.

8

WAITING FOR KLAMM

At first, K. was glad to be out of the crush of the maids and assistants in the warm room. It was also freezing slightly, the snow was firmer, the going easier. But of course it was beginning to get dark already, and he quickened his pace.

The castle, its outlines already beginning to dissolve, lay still as ever, K. had yet to see the least sign of life there, maybe it was impossible to make out anything at all from this distance, but the eyes kept wanting to, they refused to accept the stillness. Looking at the castle, K. felt at times as if he was watching a person who was sitting there quietly, staring straight ahead, not so much lost in thought and hence cut off from everything as free and unconcerned; as if the person had been alone, with no one watching him; he must be aware that he was being watched, but it did not affect his calm in the least and in fact – there was no telling whether this was cause or effect – the watcher's gaze found no purchase and kept sliding away. This impression was reinforced today by the early dusk, the longer K. looked, the less he could make out, the deeper everything sank into semi-darkness.

Just as K. arrived at the Count's Arms, where there were no lights on yet, a first-floor window opened and a young man, fat, cleanshaven, and wearing a fur coat, leaned out and then remained in the window opening, K.'s hello seemed not to elicit from him even the faintest answering nod. Neither in the hallway nor in the bar did K. encounter anyone, the smell of stale beer in the bar was worse than before, no doubt that sort of thing never happened at the Bridge Inn. K. went straight to the door through which he had observed Klamm last time, carefully pressed the latch down, but the door was locked; he then felt for the place where the peephole was, but probably the shutter fitted so well he was unable to find the place like this, so he struck a match. He was startled by a cry. In the corner between the door and the sideboard, crouching by the stove, a girl was staring at him in the flare of the match with eyes she held open with difficulty, they were dazed with sleep. This was Frieda's successor, obviously. She soon pulled herself together, switched on the light, the look on her face was not angry because she recognized K. 'Ah, the land surveyor,' she said with a smile, holding out a hand to him and introducing herself, 'hello sir, I'm Pepi.' She was short, ruddy, healthy-looking, her thick reddish-blond hair was woven into a heavy plait as well as curling round her face, she wore an extremely ill-fitting dress of shiny grey material that fell straight, it was gathered at the hem with childish clumsiness by means of a silk ribbon ending in a bow, the effect was to hamper her. She asked after Frieda and whether she would not be coming back soon. It was a question that verged on the malicious. 'I was summoned here in a hurry,' she said then, 'immediately after Frieda left, because they can't use just anyone here, I was a chambermaid before but it's not a good swap I've made. You work lots of evenings and nights here, it's very tiring, I'll probably find I can't take it, I'm not surprised Frieda quit.' 'Frieda was very happy here,' said K. in order finally to draw Pepi's attention to the difference between her and Frieda, which she was overlooking. 'Don't you believe her,' said Pepi, 'Frieda has great self-control, more than most. She'll not admit what she doesn't want to, and you won't even realize she has anything to admit. Look, I've worked with her here for several years now, we've always slept in the same bed, but we're not close, she's bound to have forgotten all about me already. Possibly her only friend is the old landlady from the Bridge Inn, and that says a lot in itself.' 'Frieda and I are engaged,' said K., still looking for the place in the door where the peephole was. 'I know,' said Pepi, 'that's why I'm telling you this. Otherwise it wouldn't matter to you, would it?' 'I see,' said K., 'you're telling me I can be proud of having won myself so reserved a girl.' 'Yes,' she said, and smiled happily, as if she had won K. round to a secret understanding about Frieda.

However, it was not really her words that preoccupied K. and distracted him slightly from his search, it was more her appearance and her presence in this place. She was much younger than Frieda, of course, almost a child still, and her dress was ludicrous, clearly she had dressed in accordance with the exaggerated notions she held of the importance of a barmaid. And she was even, in her way, quite right to hold such notions, since the appointment, for which she was quite unsuited as yet, had doubtless been unexpected and unmerited and the job was hers only provisionally, she had not even been given the leather pouch Frieda had always worn at her waist. And her alleged dissatisfaction with the job was pure presumption. Nevertheless, for all her childish lack of judgement, even she probably had contacts with the castle, after all, if she was telling the truth, she had once been a chambermaid, unaware of what she possessed, she was sleeping away her life in this place, but to gather that dumpy, slightly stooping body in one's arms, while it could not wrest from her the thing she possessed, might just touch that thing, supplying courage for the difficult journey. In which case, was this perhaps no different than with Frieda? Oh yes, it was different. The mere thought of Frieda's eyes made that clear. K. would never have touched Pepi. Just now, though, he had to cover his eyes for a moment, so lustfully was he eyeing her.

'There's no need for the light to be on,' said Pepi, turning it off again, 'I only switched it on because you gave me such a fright. What are you doing here, anyway? Did Frieda leave something behind?' 'Yes,' said K. and indicated the door, 'in the next room there, a tablecloth, a white crocheted tablecloth.' 'Right, her tablecloth,' said Pepi, 'I remember, a lovely piece of work, I even helped her with it, but it's hardly likely to be in there.' 'Frieda thinks it is. Whose room is that, then?' K. asked. 'No one's,' said Pepi, 'it's the smoking room, it's where the gentlemen drink and eat, or rather, it's supposed to be, but most of the gentlemen stay up in their rooms.' 'If I knew,' said K., 'that there was no one in there at the moment, I'd very much like to go in and look for the tablecloth. But one can't be sure, for instance Klamm often likes to sit in there.' 'Klamm's certainly not in there now,' said Pepi, 'he's just leaving, the sledge is already waiting in the yard.'

Promptly, without a word of explanation, K. went out of the bar, turned in the hallway not towards the entrance but towards the interior of the building, and in a few steps had reached the courtyard. How calm and beautiful it was out here! A rectangular courtyard, bounded on three sides by the building and towards the street – a side-street K. did not know – by a high white wall with a tall heavy gate, which now stood open. Here at the back, the building seemed taller than at the front, at least the first floor was built right out and looked bigger, being surrounded by a wooden gallery that was totally enclosed but for a tiny gap at eye level. Obliquely across from K., still in the central wing but right in the corner where the lateral wing opposite joined it, there was an entrance to the building, open, with no door. Outside it stood a dark, enclosed sledge with two horses harnessed up. Apart from the driver, whom at that distance, given the twilight, K. imagined more than made out, there was no one to be seen.

Hands in pockets, looking carefully about him and keeping close to the wall, K. walked round two sides of the courtyard until he reached the sledge. The driver, one of the peasants who had recently been in the bar, sat slumped in his furs, apathetically watching K.'s approach like someone following the progress of a cat. Even when K. was standing beside him, saying hello, even with the horses showing signs of restiveness because of this man looming up out of the darkness, he remained wholly unconcerned. K. was very glad of this. Leaning against the wall, he took out his food, thought gratefully of Frieda, who had provided for him so well, and peered into the interior. A staircase led down, turning at right angles, at the bottom meeting a low but evidently deep passageway, everything was neat, whitewashed, sharply and precisely defined.

The wait was longer than K. had expected. He had long since finished eating, it was bitterly cold, dusk had given way to total darkness, and still Klamm did not come. 'Could be a long while yet,' a rough voice said suddenly, so close that K. jumped. It was the driver, who was stretching and yawning noisily, as if he had just woken up. 'What could be a long while yet?' asked K., not ungrateful for the interruption, because the continual silence and suspense had been tedious. 'Before you go away,' said the driver. K. did not understand him but asked no further questions, thinking this would be the best way to make the arrogant fellow talk. A failure to answer here in the darkness was almost a provocation. And indeed, the driver did after a moment ask: 'Like some brandy?' 'Yes,' said K. without thinking, the offer was too tempting, he was frozen. 'Open the sledge, then,' said the driver, 'there are some bottles in the side pocket, take one, have a drink, and then pass it to me. The fur makes it too much bother for me to climb down.' It irked K. to lend a hand in this way, but having already let himself get involved with the driver he did as he was asked, even at the risk of Klamm possibly catching him at the sledge. He opened the wide door and could have pulled the bottle straight out of the pocket on its inner face, but with the door now open he felt so strong a pull from the interior of the sledge that resistance was beyond him, he wanted to sit in it, just for a moment. He darted inside. The warmth in the sledge was extraordinary and remained so despite the fact that the door, which K. dared not close, hung wide open. There was no telling whether you were sitting on a seat, you were so deep in blankets, cushions, and furs; you could turn and stretch whichever way you wished, you always sank in soft and warm. His arms outspread, his head propped on cushions that were always there, ready, K. glanced out of the sledge into the dark building. Why was Klamm taking so long to come down? As if stupefied by the warmth after standing in the snow for so long, K. wished Klamm would finally arrive. The thought that it would be preferable if Klamm did not see him in his present situation came to him only vaguely, as a faint ruffling of awareness. Support for this state of oblivion came from the behaviour of the driver, who must have known he was in the sledge but let him stay there, not even asking for the brandy. This was considerate, but K. in fact wished to be of service to him; awkwardly, without altering his position, he reached for the side pocket, not in the open door, which was too far away, but behind him in the closed one, it did not matter, there were bottles in this pocket too. He pulled one out, unscrewed the cap, and took a sniff, he had to smile, it smelled so sweet, so caressing, as when you hear praise and fine words from someone of whom you are very fond and you are not at all sure what it is about and do not wish to know and are simply happy in the knowledge that it is the loved one speaking. 'That's brandy?' K. wondered in some doubt, and tasted it out of curiosity. Yes, it was brandy, astonishingly, it burned and it warmed. The way it changed as you drank it, from something that was little more than a source of fragrance into a drink fit for a sledge-driver. 'Can this be?' K. asked himself, almost in self-reproach, taking another drink.

Suddenly – K. was just taking a good swig – everything went bright, the lamps had been lit on the stairs, in the passage, in the hallway, outside above the entrance. Footsteps could be heard descending, the bottle slipped from K.'s grasp, the brandy went pouring over a fur, K.

leapt out of the sledge, he had just managed to slam the door, which made a booming noise, when shortly afterwards a gentleman slowly emerged from the building. The only apparent consolation was that it was not Klamm, or was that a matter for regret? It was the gentleman K. had seen before at the first-floor window. A young man, extremely good-looking, white and red, but very earnest. K. gave him a bleak look of his own, though the look was intended for himself. He should have sent his assistants instead, they could have conducted themselves as well as he had done. The gentleman still stood before him in silence, as if he did not have the breath in his enormously broad chest for what needed to be said. 'This is just awful,' he said, pushing his hat a little way back off his forehead. What? Knowing nothing, as seemed likely, of the time K. had spent in the sledge, the gentleman still found something awful? The fact that K. had penetrated as far as the courtyard, perhaps? 'How did you get here?' the man asked then, already more softly, already breathing out, resigning himself to the inevitable. What questions! What answers! Should K. himself expressly confirm to the gentleman that his journey, begun with such hopes, had been in vain? Instead of answering, K. turned to the sledge, opened it, and retrieved the hat he had left inside. He noticed, uneasily, how the brandy was dripping on to the running-board.

Then he turned back to the gentleman; showing the man that he had been in the sledge caused him no misgivings now, nor was it the worst thing; if he was asked, though only then, he would not conceal the fact that the driver himself was responsible, at least for his opening the sledge. But what was really bad was that the gentleman had taken him by surprise, that there had been no time to hide from him and go on waiting for Klamm undisturbed, or that he had not had the presence of mind to stay inside the sledge, shut the door, and wait for Klamm there, on the furs, or at least stay there as long as this gentleman was around. True, he could not have known whether Klamm himself was not perhaps already on his way, in which case it would have been far better, of course, to receive him outside the sledge. There had indeed been a number of things to think about here, but now there was nothing more, it was all over.

'Come with me,' said the gentleman, not actually ordering K., but the order lay not so much in the words as in a cursory, deliberately indifferent accompanying wave of the hand. 'I'm here waiting for someone,' said K., no longer in hope of any success, purely on principle. 'Come,' the gentleman said again, quite unflustered, as if wishing to show he had never doubted that K. was waiting for someone. 'But I'll miss the man I'm waiting for,' said K. with a movement of his whole body. Despite everything that had happened, he felt that what he had achieved so far was a kind of possession that, though his hold on it was only apparent as yet, he ought not to surrender at just any command. 'You'll miss him in any case, whether you wait or leave,' said the gentleman, brusque in voicing his opinion but remarkably indulgent with regard to K.'s train of thought. 'Then I'd rather miss him waiting,' K. said defiantly, he was certainly not going to let any mere words from this young man drive him away. At this, the gentleman tilted his face back with a superior expression, closed his eyes for a moment as if wishing to quit K.'s foolishness and return to his own good sense, ran the tip of his tongue round slightly parted lips, and told the driver: 'Unhitch the horses.'

The driver, submissive towards his master but with a nasty sideways glance at K., did now have to climb down in his fur and began very hesitantly, as if expecting not a countermand from the gentleman but a change of mind on K.'s part, to lead the horses backwards with the sledge towards the lateral wing of the building, where a tall door evidently led to the stable and coach-house. K. saw himself being left behind alone, with the sledge moving away on one side and the young gentleman, using the route K. had come by, on the other, both of them going very slowly, though, as if wishing to show K. that it was still in his power to fetch them back.

Maybe he had that power, but it could have done him no good; fetching the sledge back meant banishing himself. So he stayed where he was, the only one standing his ground, but it was a victory that brought no joy. He looked by turns after the gentleman and after the driver. The gentleman had already reached the door through which K. had first entered the courtyard, he glanced back once more, K. thought he saw him shake his head over such stubbornness, then he turned with a quick, firm, conclusive movement and stepped into the hallway, where he promptly disappeared. The driver stayed in the courtyard longer, he had a lot of work with the sledge, he needed to open the heavy stable door, reverse the sledge into its place, unhitch the horses, lead them to their stalls, he did it all with great seriousness, utterly self-absorbed, all hope of a speedy departure now abandoned; this silent busying of himself without a single sideways glance at K. struck the latter as a far harsher reproach than the way the gentleman had behaved. And as the driver, his work in the stable completed, now crossed the courtyard with his slow, rocking walk, closed the tall gate, then came back, doing everything slowly and really only contemplating his own tracks in the snow, then shut himself in the stable, and as all the lights went out as well – for whom should they have gone on shining? – and only the gap up in the wooden gallery remained bright, just catching the wandering eye, it seemed to K. then as if all contact with him had been severed and he was now freer than ever before, no question about it, and might wait in this otherwise forbidden place for as long as he liked and had fought for and won this freedom as few others could have done and none might touch or banish him, barely even address him, but – this conviction was at least equally strong – as if at the same time there was nothing more futile, nothing more desperate than this freedom, this waiting, this invulnerability.

9

RESISTING INTERROGATION

And he tore himself away and went back into the building, not along the wall this time but straight through the snow, in the hallway he met the landlord, who greeted him wordlessly, pointing to the door of the bar, he took the hint, because he was cold and because he wanted company, but was very disappointed to see there, sitting at a little table that had no doubt been placed there specially, since otherwise people made do with barrels here, the young gentleman and, standing in front of him – a depressing sight for K. – the landlady from the Bridge Inn. Pepi, proudly, head flung back, forever smiling the same smile, unchallengeably conscious of her dignity, her pigtail swinging with each change of direction, darted to and fro, fetching beer and then pen and ink, because the gentleman had spread papers out in front of him, was comparing information that he found first on one sheet and then again on a sheet at the other end of the table, and now wished to write. The landlady, tall and silent, lips slightly pursed as if in repose, looked down at the gentleman and the papers as if she had already said everything that needed saying and it had been duly noted. 'Ah, Mr Land Surveyor, at last,' said the gentleman as K. entered, glancing up briefly before sinking back into his study of the papers. The landlady, too, gave K. only a casual glance, showing no surprise. As for Pepi, she seemed quite unaware of K.'s presence until he stepped up to the bar and ordered a brandy.

K. leaned on the bar, pressed a hand to his eyes, and ignored them all. Then he took a sip of the brandy and pushed it back, saying it was undrinkable. 'All the gentlemen drink it,' Pepi said briskly, and she poured the rest away, rinsed the glass, and stood it on the shelf. 'The gentlemen have better stuff, too,' said K. 'Possibly,' said Pepi, 'but I don't,' with that she had dealt with K. and was once again at the gentleman's service, but he needed nothing so she simply paced back and forth in an arc behind him, trying in a respectful way to see over his shoulders and catch a glimpse of the papers; but it was only empty inquisitiveness and swagger, of which the landlady in fact expressed frowning disapproval.

Suddenly, however, something caught the landlady's attention, and she began to stare into space, listening intently. K. turned around, he could hear nothing in particular, the others apparently heard nothing either, but the landlady ran on tiptoe, taking great strides, to the door in the background, which led out to the courtyard, she peered through the keyhole, then looked back at the others with eyes wide, face flushed, beckoned them over with a finger, and now they took turns peering, the liveliest interest remained the landlady's but Pepi too became thoughtful each time, of the three of them the gentleman was the least involved. Pepi and the gentleman also came back before long, only the landlady still strained to look through, bent double, on her knees, almost, it was almost as if all she was doing now was begging the keyhole to let her through, because presumably there had been nothing more to see for some time. When she did at last get up, run her hands over her face, tidy her hair, and take a deep breath, having first, apparently, to let her eyes readjust to the room and the people here, which they were reluctant to do, K. said, not in order to have something he already knew confirmed but to forestall an attack he almost feared, so vulnerable was he at this point: 'Has Klamm gone, then?' The landlady walked past him without a word, but the gentleman said from his table: 'He certainly has. You having quit your sentry post, Klamm was able to drive off. But the amazing thing is how sensitive the man is. Did you notice, ma'am,' he asked the landlady, 'how nervously Klamm looked about him?' The landlady had not noticed this, apparently, but the gentleman went on: 'Well, fortunately there was nothing more to be seen, the driver had even smoothed away the footprints in the snow.' 'The landlady noticed nothing,' said K., though not with any kind of hope, purely out of irritation at the gentleman's assertion, intended to sound so final and beyond appeal. 'Maybe I wasn't at the keyhole just then,' the landlady said at first, taking the gentleman's part, but then, anxious to give Klamm his due too, she added: 'Mind you, I don't believe in this great sensitivity of Klamm's. We worry about him, of course, and do our best to protect him, so we assume enormous sensitivity on Klamm's part. That's fine, and it is certainly what Klamm wants. But what the real situation is, we don't know. Granted, Klamm will never talk to someone he doesn't want to talk to, however hard that someone tries and however unbearably he thrusts himself forward, but that fact alone, that Klamm will never speak to him, never allow him into his presence, is surely enough, why should he really not be able to bear the sight of a person. At least it can't be proved, since it will never be put to the test.' The gentleman nodded eagerly. 'That's of course basically my view, too,' he said, 'if I expressed it in slightly different terms, it was in order to be understood by the land surveyor here. The truth is, though, that as Klamm stepped into the open he several times looked around him in a half-circle.' 'Maybe he was looking for me,' said K. 'It's possible,' the gentleman said, 'I didn't think of that.' They all laughed, Pepi, who understood very little of this, loudest of any of them.

'Now that we're so happily gathered here,' the gentleman said then, turning to K., 'I should be most grateful, sir, if you'd give me one or two details to complete my files.' 'There's a great deal of writing done here,' K. said, glancing over at the files. 'I agree, a bad habit,' said the gentleman and gave another laugh, 'but perhaps you don't even know yet who I am. I'm Momus, Klamm's village secretary.' At these words, a seriousness fell on the room; the landlady and Pepi knew the man well, of course, but were still deeply affected by the mention of the name and title. And even the gentleman himself, as if he had said too much for his own ability to take things in, and as if at least seeking refuge from any additional solemnity inherent in his own words, became engrossed in the files and began to write, so that only his pen was heard in the room. 'What's that, then: village secretary,' K. asked after a moment. Speaking for Momus, who now that he had introduced himself no longer felt it fitting to offer such explanations himself, the landlady said: 'Mr Momus is Klamm's secretary like any of Klamm's secretaries, but his office and if I am not mistaken also his official duties' – Momus, still writing, shook his head vigorously and the landlady corrected herself – 'only his office, then, not his official duties are confined to the village. Mr Momus takes care of such written work of Klamm's as becomes necessary in the village and receives all requests to Klamm from the village as first instance.' When K., little affected by any of this as yet, gave the landlady a blank look, she added in some embarrassment: 'That's how it's organized, every gentleman from the castle has his village secretary.' Momus, who had been listening a lot more attentively than K., told the landlady further: 'Most village secretaries work for only one master, but I work for two, for Klamm and for Vallabene.' 'Yes,' said the landlady, remembering this herself now and turning to K., 'Mr Momus works for two masters, for Klamm and for Vallabene, so is a village secretary twice over.' 'Twice over, eh,' said K., giving Momus, who was now almost bent double, looking right up at him, a nod of the kind one gives a child whom one has just heard praised. If there was a certain contempt in it, this either passed unnoticed or was positively asked for. None other than K., who was not even worthy to have Klamm catch so much as a chance glimpse of him, had been treated to a full description of the services of a man from Klamm's immediate circle with the undisguised intention of inviting K.'s appreciation and praise. K., however, simply lacked the proper feeling for it; here he was, trying his hardest to get a look at Klamm, yet he did not rate the position of a man like Momus, say, who was allowed to live in Klamm's sight, at all highly, he was far from feeling admiration, let alone envy, because it was not mere nearness to Klamm he thought worth striving for but rather that he, K., he alone and no one else, should with his and no one else's desires get close to Klamm, and get close to him not in order to come to rest in his presence but in order to go on, past him, into the castle.

And he looked at his watch and said: 'I have to go home now, though.' Instantly, the relationship shifted in Momus's favour. 'Of course you do,' said the latter, 'a school caretaker's duties call. But you must give me a moment more. Just a couple of quick questions.' 'I don't feel like it,' said K., starting towards the door. Momus slammed a file down on the table and stood up: 'In Klamm's name I demand that you answer my questions.' 'In Klamm's name?' K. echoed, 'you mean my affairs concern him?' 'As to that,' said Momus, 'I am no judge and you, presumably, even less so; so I think we can safely leave it to him. I do, however, call on you in the position bestowed upon me by Klamm to stay and answer.' 'Sir,' the landlady butted in, addressing K., 'you can be sure I'll give you no more advice, for my suggestions up to now, which could not have been better meant, I've been quite outrageously rejected by you, and I have now come to see the secretary here – I've nothing to hide – purely to give the office due notification of your conduct and intentions and to protect myself for the rest of my days against your ever being billeted on me again, that's how we stand, you and I, probably that's the way things will stay, so if I now speak my mind it is not for your benefit but in order to make a difficult job, namely dealing with someone like yourself, a little easier for the secretary here. There is a possibility, though, just because of my complete candour – I can't help being candid with you, and even so it occurs against my will – of you turning my words to advantage for yourself as well, you only have to want to. If you do, let me point out that the only way to Klamm, so far as you are concerned, is through the reports of the secretary here. But I don't wish to exaggerate, maybe the way doesn't lead to Klamm, maybe it stops long before him, that's for the secretary in his wisdom to decide. But at any rate it's the only way that, for you, leads at least in the direction of Klamm. And you mean to dispense with that only way, for no other reason than contrariness?' 'Oh ma'am,' K. told the landlady, 'it's neither the only way to Klamm, nor is it worth any more than the others. And you, sir' – turning to the secretary – 'decide whether what I may say here is allowed to reach Klamm or not.' 'That's right,' said Momus, glancing with proudly lowered gaze to right and left, where there was nothing to be seen, 'why else should I be secretary?' 'You see,' said K. to the landlady again, 'it's not Klamm I need a way to, I first need a way to the secretary.' 'I wanted to open that way for you,' said the landlady, 'didn't I offer this morning to pass your request on to Klamm? That would have happened through the secretary here. You, though, rejected the offer, yet now you'll have no alternative but this one, single way. After your performance today, of course, that attempt to waylay Klamm, with even less prospect of success. However, this last, least, dwindling, strictly speaking non-existent hope is all you have.' 'Why is it, ma'am,' said K., 'that at first you tried so hard to stop me getting through to Klamm, yet now you take my request so very seriously and should my plans fail seem to see me as somehow lost? When at one time I could be sincerely advised against trying to reach Klamm at all, why am I now, as regards the way to Klamm, which you admit may not even lead that far, being with apparently equal sincerity almost propelled forward?' 'I'm doing that?' said the landlady, 'is it propelling you forward to tell you your efforts are futile? That really would be the ultimate audacity, if you tried to shift the responsibility for yourself on to me like that. Is it perhaps the presence of the secretary here that gives you that urge? No, Mr Land Surveyor, I'm not forcing you into anything. I've only one confession to make, and it is that I may, the first time I saw you, have overrated you somewhat. Your swift conquest of Frieda startled me, I didn't know what else you might be capable of, I was keen to avoid further damage and thought the only way I could achieve that was by trying to unsettle you with pleas and threats. I've since learned to think more calmly about the whole thing. You can do what you like. Your actions may leave deep footprints in the snow out in the yard, but that's all.' 'The contradiction is not quite cleared up, it seems to me,' said K., 'but I'll be satisfied with having drawn attention to it. However, would you please now tell me, Mr Secretary, whether madam is right in thinking that in fact the statement you wish to take down from me could lead to my being allowed to appear before Klamm. If that is the case, I'm prepared here and now to answer all questions. In fact, I'll do anything in that regard.' 'No,' said Momus, 'no such connections exist. For me, it is simply a matter of obtaining a precise account of this afternoon for Klamm's village records. The account is already complete, you are merely required to fill in a few gaps for form's sake, there's no other purpose, nor can any other purpose be achieved.' K. gave the landlady a silent look. 'Why are you looking at me,' she asked, 'did I say any different? He's like that all the time, Mr Secretary, all the time. Falsifies the information you give him, then says he's been given false information. I've always told him, today and every other day, that he hasn't the slightest chance of being seen by Klamm, so if no chance exists, he's not going to get one through this statement, either. What could be clearer? I say further that this statement is the one real official contact he can have with Klamm, that too is surely clear enough and beyond all doubt. But if he doesn't believe me, if he still – why and for what purpose I don't know – hopes to reach Klamm, then, to continue his train of thought, the only thing that can help him is the one real official contact he has with Klamm, namely this statement. That's all I have said, and anyone who claims otherwise is maliciously twisting words.' 'If that is so, ma'am,' said K., 'I beg your pardon, I misunderstood you, I thought, you see, mistakenly as it now turns out, that I detected from what you said earlier that there is some tiny hope for me after all.' 'Certainly,' said the landlady, 'I believe there is, too, you're twisting my words again, only this time in the opposite direction. I believe there is such a hope for you, and in fact this statement is the sole basis for it. But that doesn't mean you can simply spring the question on the secretary here: "Shall I be allowed to see Klamm if I answer the questions?" When a child asks that, people laugh, when a grown-up does so, it is an insult to the authorities, the secretary here simply had the grace to conceal it with the delicacy of his reply. However, the hope I'm talking about consists in the very fact that, through the statement, you have a kind of contact, possibly have a kind of contact with Klamm. Is that not hope enough? If you were asked about the merits that make you worthy of the gift of such a hope, would you have the slightest idea what to suggest? All right, nothing more precise can be said about this hope and particularly the secretary here will never, in his official capacity, be able to drop even the smallest hint about it. For him it is simply, as he said, a question of an account of this afternoon for form's sake, that's all he will say, even if you ask him about it right now in the light of what I've been saying.' 'Tell me, Mr Secretary,' said K., 'will Klamm be reading this statement?' 'No,' said Momus, 'why should he? Klamm can't read every statement, in fact he doesn't read any, "Stop plaguing me with your statements!" he always says.' 'Sir,' the landlady complained to K., 'you wear me out with such questions. Is it necessary or even desirable that Klamm should read this statement and learn about the trivia of your existence in so many words, wouldn't you rather submit a humble request that the statement be kept from Klamm – a request, by the way, that would be as stupid as the previous one, because who can keep anything from Klamm, though it would certainly reveal a more sympathetic character. And for what you call your hope, is that actually necessary? Didn't you state yourself that you'd be satisfied merely with the opportunity to speak to Klamm, even if he didn't look at you and didn't listen to what you said? And aren't you, with this statement, achieving at least that, possibly much more?' 'Much more?' asked K., 'in what way?' 'Merely by not,' the landlady burst out, 'forever wanting like a child to have things handed to you on a plate right away. Who can answer questions like that? The statement will go to Klamm's village record office, as you've heard, that's all that can be said about it for certain. But are you in fact aware of the whole significance of the statement, of the secretary here, of the village record office? Do you know what it means to have the secretary interrogate you? Possibly or probably he doesn't know himself. He sits here quietly and does his job – as he said, for the sake of form. Bear in mind, though, that Klamm appointed him, that he operates on Klamm's behalf, that what he does, even if it never gets as far as Klamm, nevertheless has Klamm's approval from the outset. And how can a thing have Klamm's approval that is not filled with his spirit? Far be it from me, in saying this, to seek in any crude way to flatter the secretary here, not that he'd have any truck with such an attempt, but I am talking not about his own person but about what he is when he has Klamm's backing, as now. He is then a tool on which the hand that rests is Klamm's, and woe betide anyone who does not do as he says.'

The landlady's threats did not alarm K., the hopes she was using to try to catch him out now wearied him. Klamm was remote, the landlady had once compared Klamm to an eagle and it had struck K. as absurd, but not any more, he thought of his remoteness, of his impregnable dwelling, of his silence broken only, perhaps, by such cries as K. had never heard before, of his piercing downward gaze that could never be proven, never refuted, of the indestructible circles that, viewed from down here where K. was, he traced in the air according to incomprehensible laws, visible only for moments – all this Klamm had in common with the eagle. But none of it, surely, had any relevance to this statement over which Momus was just then breaking a pretzel that he was enjoying with his beer, strewing salt and caraway seeds over all his papers.

'Good night,' said K., 'I dislike any kind of interrogation,' and this time he did actually walk to the door. 'He's really going,' Momus said almost anxiously to the landlady. 'He'll not dare,' she said, that is all K. heard, he was already out in the hallway. It was cold and a strong wind was blowing. From a door opposite the landlord emerged, he had apparently been keeping the hallway under observation through a peephole there. He had to flip his coat-tails around his body, so fiercely did the wind tug at them even here in the hallway. 'Off already, sir?' he said. 'Are you surprised?' asked K. 'Yes,' said the landlord, 'weren't you interrogated, then?' 'No,' said K., 'I wouldn't allow it.' 'Why not?' asked the landlord. 'I fail to see,' K. said, 'why I should allow myself to be interrogated, why I should play along with a joke or bow to an official whim. Another time I might have done so, likewise as a joke or in response to a whim, but not today.' 'Yes of course, I see,' said the landlord, but it was merely polite agreement, lacking any conviction. 'Now I must let the servants into the bar,' he said then, 'it's long past their time. I just didn't want to interrupt the interrogation.' 'You thought it was so important?' asked K. 'Oh yes,' said the landlord. 'Should I not have refused, then?' asked K. 'No,' said the landlord, 'you shouldn't have done that.' K. said nothing, so he added, either to make K. feel better or to get away sooner: 'Come now, it's not going to start raining fire and brimstone as a result.' 'No,' said K., 'the weather doesn't look like that.' And they parted laughing.

10

IN THE STREET

K. emerged on to the windswept steps and peered into the darkness. Awful, awful weather. Somehow associated with this, it occurred to him how the landlady had gone out of her way to bend his will in the matter of the statement, but he had stood firm. Her efforts had lacked frankness, of course, secretly she had at the same time been pulling him back from the statement, in the end there was no knowing whether one had stood firm or given in. A scheming sort of person, apparently operating blind like the wind, obeying distant, alien directives no one ever had sight of.

He had taken only a couple of steps up the road when he saw two swaying lights in the distance; well pleased with this sign of life, he hurried to meet them as they came floating towards him. He did not know why he was so disappointed when he recognized the assistants, but there they were, walking towards him, probably sent by Frieda, and the lanterns that released him from the darkness with its noisy assault from all sides were no doubt his property, still he was disappointed, he had expected strangers, not these old acquaintances who were a burden to him. The assistants were not alone, however, out of the darkness between them stepped Barnabas. 'Barnabas,' K. exclaimed, holding out a hand to him, 'are you looking for me?' Surprise at seeing him again temporarily obliterated the memory of all the trouble Barnabas had once caused K. 'I am,' said Barnabas, cordial as ever, 'with a letter from Klamm.' 'A letter from Klamm!' said K., throwing back his head, and eagerly he took it from Barnabas's hand. 'Light here!' he said to the assistants, who pressed close to right and left of him and lifted the lanterns. To read it, K. had to fold the large sheet of paper quite small, shielding it from the wind. Then he read: 'To the Land Surveyor at the Bridge Inn: Dear Sir, the land surveying operations that you have carried out so far meet with my approval.

The work of the assistants is also praiseworthy; you are good at keeping them at it. Do not let up in your zeal. Bring things to a successful conclusion. Any interruption would make me very angry. By the way, rest assured, the question of payment will be resolved shortly. I have you constantly in mind.' K. looked up from the letter only when the assistants, who read much more slowly than he did, celebrated the good news by shouting three cheers and waving the lanterns. 'Be quiet,' he said, and to Barnabas: 'There's been a misunderstanding.' Barnabas did not understand. 'There's been a misunderstanding,' K. repeated, and the afternoon's weariness returned, the schoolhouse still seemed so far off, and behind Barnabas his whole family now stood, and the assistants were still pressing against him so that he thrust them away with his elbows; how could Frieda have sent them to meet him when he had left orders that they should stay with her. He would have found his way home on his own, more easily on his own, in fact, than in this company. Also, one of them had now wound a scarf round his neck and the free ends of the scarf, flapping in the wind, had several times struck K. in the face, and though the other assistant had always promptly removed the scarf from K.'s face with his long, pointed, forever busy fingers he had not, in so doing, improved matters. They both even seemed to delight in the toing and froing, the wind and the wildness of the night generally exciting them. 'Let's go!' K. shouted, 'if you came out to meet me, why did you not bring my stick? How am I supposed to drive you home, eh?' They cowered behind Barnabas, yet they were not so fearful as not to have placed their lanterns to right and left on their protector's shoulders, he of course promptly shook them off. 'Barnabas,' said K., and it weighed on his mind that Barnabas clearly did not understand him, that when things were calm his coat was indeed a fine sight, but when they started to look bad there was no help to be found in him, only silent resistance, resistance it was impossible to combat since he himself was defenceless, only his smile shone brightly, but it was of no more use than the stars above against the whirlwind blowing down here. 'See what the man writes to me,' K. said, holding the letter up to his face. 'The gentleman is misinformed. I'm not doing any surveying work, and what the assistants are worth you can see for yourself. And, of course, work I am not doing I cannot interrupt, either, I can't even rouse the man's anger, how am I supposed to earn his approval! And I can never rest assured.' 'I'll give that message,' said Barnabas, who had spent the whole time looking past the letter, which he could not have read in any case since he had it right in front of his face. 'Ah,' said K., 'you promise me you'll give that message, but can I really believe you? I so badly need a trustworthy messenger, now more than ever!' K. bit his lips in his impatience. 'Sir,' said Barnabas with a gentle inclination of the neck – K. could almost have let it seduce him back into believing what Barnabas said – 'I certainly shall deliver that message, the instruction you gave me recently I shall also certainly be passing on.' 'What!' K. exclaimed, 'you haven't done that yet? You mean, you weren't in the castle next day?' 'No,' said Barnabas, 'my dear father is old, you saw him yourself, and there was a lot of work on, I had to help him, but I shall soon be going to the castle again.' 'But what do you think you're doing, you inscrutable fellow,' K. exclaimed, smacking himself on the forehead, 'don't Klamm's affairs take precedence over everything else? You hold the high office of messenger and execute it so shamefully? Who could care less about your father's work? Klamm is waiting for news, and you, instead of falling over yourself running, choose to muck out the stable.' 'My father is a shoemaker,' said Barnabas unperturbed, 'he had orders from Brunswick, and I am my father's journeyman.' 'Shoemaker–orders– Brunswick,' K. shouted grimly, as if rendering each word unusable for all time. 'And who here needs boots on these perpetually deserted streets. And what do I care about all this cobbling, I gave you a message, not for you to forget and fuddle on the workbench but for you to take straight to your master.' Here K. calmed down a little as it occurred to him that Klamm had probably not been in the castle the whole time but at the Count's Arms, but Barnabas irked him again when, as proof that he remembered it, he began to recite K.'s first message. 'That's enough, I don't want to know,' said K. 'Don't be cross with me, sir,' said Barnabas, and as if with the unconscious intention of punishing K. he took his eyes off him and looked down, though it was probably consternation caused by K.'s shouting. 'I'm not cross with you,' said K., and his agitation now turned against himself, 'not with you, but it's very bad for me, having only such a messenger as this for the things that matter.' 'Look,' said Barnabas, and it seemed that, to defend his honour as a messenger, he was saying more than he should, 'Klamm isn't waiting for the messages, in fact he's annoyed when I arrive, "yet more messages" he said once, and he usually gets up when he sees me coming in the distance, goes into the other room, and won't receive me. Nor is it laid down that I should come with every message immediately, if it were I should of course come immediately, but it is not so laid down and if I never came I'd not be admonished for it. When I bring a message, it is voluntarily.' 'Good,' said K., observing Barnabas and deliberately ignoring the assistants, who by turns would slowly rise up from behind Barnabas's shoulders, as if from nowhere, and then swiftly, with a little whistle in imitation of the wind, as if alarmed at seeing K., disappear again, this kept them amused for some time, 'how it is with Klamm, I don't know; I doubt whether you can know all about everything there, and even if you could, we could not improve these things. But you can deliver a message there, and that's what I'm asking. A very brief message. Can you deliver it tomorrow and also tomorrow tell me the answer or at least report on how you were received? Can you do that, and would you be prepared to? It would be of immense value to me. And I may yet get the opportunity to thank you properly, or perhaps you already have a wish I could fulfil.' 'Certainly I'll do the job,' said Barnabas. 'And are you prepared to make the effort to do it as well as possible, hand the message over to Klamm himself, receive the answer from Klamm himself, and do it all tomorrow, all of it, before noon, are you prepared to do that?' 'I shall do my best,' said Barnabas, 'but then I always do.' 'Let's not argue about that any more now,' said K., 'this is the message: Land Surveyor K. requests the Director's permission to call on him in person, he accepts in advance every condition that might be attached to such permission. He is forced to make his request because so far all intermediaries have failed completely, as evidence he cites the fact that he has not so far done any surveying work whatsoever and according to the mayor never will do, either; it was therefore with a desperate feeling of shame that he read the Director's last letter, only a personal visit to the Director can help here. The Land Surveyor is aware of what he is asking, but he will endeavour to render the disruption as nearly as possible imperceptible to the Director, he accepts any restriction in terms of time, he will even, should such be deemed necessary, comply with a limit on the number of words he may use during the interview, even ten words he believes will suffice for his purpose. In deep respect and the greatest impatience he awaits the outcome.' K. had spoken in a faraway manner, as if he had been standing at Klamm's door, addressing the doorman. 'It's come out much longer than I thought,' he said then, 'but you must pass it on verbally, I don't want to write a letter, it would only go through the endless official channels again.' So K. scribbled it just for Barnabas on a piece of paper on one assistant's back while the other shone a light, but K. was already able to take it down from Barnabas's dictation, Barnabas had remembered the whole thing and recited it with schoolboy correctness, ignoring the assistants' wrong prompts. 'You have an exceptional memory,' K. said, giving him the paper, 'please now prove yourself exceptional in the other matter too. What about wishes? Don't you have any? I'd find it, I'll be frank with you, somewhat reassuring as to the fate of my message if you did, you know?' At first Barnabas was silent, then he said: 'My sisters send you their regards.' 'Your sisters,' said K., 'ah yes, the big strong girls.' 'They both send their regards, but particularly Amalia,' said Barnabas, 'she also brought me this letter for you from the castle today.' Seizing on this information above all else, K. asked: 'Couldn't she take my message to the castle too? Or couldn't you both go and each try your luck?' 'Amalia's not allowed in the offices,' said Barnabas, 'otherwise she'd certainly be glad to.' 'I may come and see you tomorrow,' said K., 'but you come to me first with the answer. I'll be waiting for you at the school. Give your sisters my regards too.' K.'s promises seemed to make Barnabas very happy, after the farewell handshake he also touched K. briefly on the shoulder. As though everything was now back as it had been before, when Barnabas appeared in his splendour among the peasants in the bar, K. experienced this touch, if smilingly, as an accolade. His mood much improved, on the return journey he let the assistants do as they liked.

II

AT THE SCHOOL

He reached home frozen through, the whole place was in darkness, the candles in the lanterns had burned low, with the assistants guiding him, they already knew their way around here, he felt his way through to a classroom – 'Your first praiseworthy achievement,' he said, recalling Klamm's letter – half in her sleep, Frieda cried from one corner: 'Let K. sleep! Don't disturb him!' so much was K. in her thoughts, even though, overcome by drowsiness, she had not been able to wait up for him. The lamp was now lit, though it could not be turned up much because there was very little paraffin. The new household still had various shortcomings. The place was heated, but the big room, which was also used for PE – the pieces of apparatus stood around and hung from the ceiling – had already taken up all the available wood, it had also, K. was assured, been very pleasantly warm, but had unfortunately cooled right down again. There was in fact a large stock of wood in a shed, but the shed was locked and the key kept by the schoolmaster, who allowed wood to be taken only for heating during school hours. That would have been bearable if there had been beds in which to take refuge. In that respect, however, there was nothing but a single palliasse, covered nice and cleanly with one of Frieda's woollen shawls, but with no quilt and only two coarse stiff blankets, which gave little warmth. And even this poor palliasse received covetous looks from the assistants, though of course they had no hope of ever being allowed to lie on it. Frieda glanced anxiously at K.; she had shown back at the Bridge Inn that she could furnish even the most wretched room quite comfortably, but here there was nothing more she could have done, deprived as she had been of all resources. 'Our only decoration is the PE apparatus,' she said, making an effort to smile through her tears. But with regard to the greatest shortcomings, the inadequate sleeping arrangements and lack of heating, she confidently promised a remedy for the very next day and begged K. to be patient just till then. Not one word, not one hint, not one look on her face suggested that she bore even the least bitterness against K. in her heart, despite the fact that, as he had to admit to himself, he had torn her away both from the Count's Arms and now from the Bridge Inn too. However, because of this K. was at pains to find everything tolerable, which was not in fact too hard for him to do since in thought he was off with Barnabas, repeating his message word for word, though not as he had delivered it to Barnabas but as he believed it would sound in Klamm's presence. On the other hand, he did take a sincere delight in the coffee that Frieda made him on a tiny cooker, and leaning against the cooling stove he followed her deft experienced movements as she spread the inevitable white tablecloth on the schoolmaster's desk and set down a flowered coffee cup with, beside it, bread and ham and even a tin of sardines. Everything was now ready, Frieda herself had not eaten yet but had waited for K. There were two chairs, K. and Frieda sat on them at the desk, the assistants on the podium at their feet, they never remained still, though, even during the meal they were a nuisance; despite their having been given generous helpings of everything and being far from finished, they stood up from time to time to see if there was still plenty on the table and they might still expect something for themselves. K. took no notice of them, it was only Frieda's laughter that drew his attention to them. He covered her hand on the table caressingly with his own and asked gently why she forgave them so much, even cheerfully tolerating bad manners. That way they would never be rid of them, whereas by treating them in, so to speak, a forceful manner such as their behaviour did actually call for it might be possible either to restrain them or, as was more likely and even preferable, so to spoil the job for them that they would eventually run away. It didn't, K. went on, look like being a specially pleasant stay here in the schoolhouse, well, it wouldn't be a long one either, yet they would scarcely be aware of all the shortcomings if the assistants were not there and the two of them were alone in the silent building. Hadn't she noticed herself that the assistants were getting cheekier by the day, as if it was Frieda's presence that encouraged them, together with the hope that K. would not, with her there, act as firmly as he'd have done otherwise. There might, incidentally, be quite simple ways of getting rid of them immediately without further ado, maybe Frieda even knew of such, she was so familiar with the way things were hereabouts. Moreover, so far as the assistants themselves were concerned, they'd probably only be doing them a favour by somehow driving them away, because look, it was no great life of luxury they were living here and even the lazing around that they'd enjoyed up to now would at least to some extent come to an end in this place, surely, since they would have to work while Frieda, after the excitements of the last few days, must take it easy and he, K., would be busy finding a way out of their plight. However, he'd feel so relieved if the assistants left, he said, that he would easily manage all the caretaking work on top of everything else.

Frieda, who had been listening carefully, slowly stroked his arm and said she thought all that too but that possibly he was exaggerating the assistants' bad manners, they were young fellows, jolly and a bit simple, serving a foreigner for the first time, released from the strict discipline of the castle so slightly excited and surprised the whole time, and in this state they did occasionally do stupid things about which it was natural to get irritated, certainly, but more sensible to laugh. Sometimes she could not help laughing. Nevertheless, she agreed with K. entirely that the best course would be to send them away and just be the two of them. She moved closer to K. and buried her face in his shoulder. And there she said, so unintelligibly that K. had to bend down towards her, that no, she knew of no way of dealing with the assistants and was afraid that everything K. had suggested would fail. Anyway, so far as she knew K. had asked for them himself and now he had them and would be keeping them. The best thing was to accept them lightly as the lightweight folk they were, that was the best way of putting up with them.

K. was not happy with the answer, half jokingly, half seriously he said that she sounded as if she was in league with them or at least had a great fondness for them, well, they were handsome enough fellows but there was no one who could not be got rid of, given a modicum of good will, and he would prove it to her in the case of the assistants.

Frieda said she'd be most grateful to him if he succeeded. She wouldn't laugh at them any more in future, either, nor say an unnecessary word to them. In fact, she didn't find anything laughable about them any more, it really was no small matter to have two men watching you the whole time, she had learned to see the two of them through his eyes, she said. And she actually did flinch slightly as the assistants now stood up yet again, partly to check how much food was left, partly to discover the reason for the constant whispering.

K. used the occasion to put Frieda off the assistants, he drew Frieda to him and they finished their meal sitting close together. At this point they should have gone to bed, they were all very tired, one of the assistants had even fallen asleep over his food, this amused his colleague greatly and he tried to get the others to look at the sleeping man's stupid face, but in vain, K. and Frieda were sitting above him, their faces turned away. Also, with the cold becoming unbearable they were reluctant to go to bed, finally K. said the fire must be relit, otherwise it would be impossible to sleep. He looked around for some sort of axe, the assistants knew of one and brought it and off they all went to the woodshed. In a short while the flimsy door had been forced, delighted, as if they had never seen anything so lovely, chasing after and pushing each other, the assistants started carrying wood into the classroom, soon there was a big pile there, the fire was lit, they settled themselves down around the stove, the assistants were given a blanket to wrap themselves in, this was quite sufficient for them since it had been agreed that one should always be on watch and keep the fire going, soon it was so warm by the stove that the blankets were not even needed any more, the lamp was doused, and, pleased with the warmth and silence, K. and Frieda stretched themselves out to sleep.

When during the night K. woke up at some noise or other and in the first uncertain movement, still in sleep, felt for Frieda, he became aware that it was not Frieda but one of the assistants lying beside him. This gave him, probably as a result of the irritability that came from having been roused suddenly, the biggest fright he had experienced in the village so far. With a cry he half raised himself up and unthinkingly dealt the assistant such a blow with his fist that he began to cry. The whole episode was explained in an instant, in fact. Frieda had been wakened by – so at least it had seemed to her – some large animal, probably a cat, jumping on her chest and immediately running off. She had got up, lit a candle, and searched the whole room for the beast. One of the assistants had taken advantage of this to treat himself to the palliasse for a while, for which he was now paying dearly. Frieda found nothing, however, perhaps it had simply been an illusion, she returned to K., in passing she stooped, as if she had forgotten the evening's conversation, to give the hair of the crouching, whimpering assistant a consoling stroke. K. made no remark, merely telling the assistants to stop stoking the fire since through their having used nearly all the accumulated wood it was now too warm.

In the morning, they woke to find that the first schoolchildren had already arrived and were crowding curiously around the beds. This was awkward, because as a result of the great warmth, though in fact now, towards morning, this had given way to a noticeable chilliness, they had all stripped to their underwear and just as they were starting to get dressed Gisa, the schoolmistress, a tall fair-haired handsome if slightly stiff young lady, appeared in the doorway. She was clearly prepared for the new caretaker and had presumably also been given rules of behaviour by the schoolmaster, because before even crossing the threshold she said: 'I can't have this. This is a fine state of affairs. You merely have permission to sleep in the classroom, I on the other hand am under no obligation to teach in your bedroom. A caretaker's family lazing in their beds half the morning. Disgraceful!' Well, that was debatable, particularly as regarded the family and the beds, K. thought as together with Frieda – the assistants were no use here, they lay on the floor staring in amazement at the schoolmistress and the children – he hurriedly pushed the parallel bars and the horse across, covered both with the blankets, and thus constructed a little room in which they could be protected from the children's gaze while they at least got dressed. They were not left in peace for a moment, however, it started with the schoolmistress nagging because there was no clean water in the washbasin – K. had just had the idea of fetching the washbasin for himself and Frieda, he abandoned the idea for the moment in order not to irritate the schoolmistress too much, but this did him no good because shortly afterwards there was a tremendous crash, unfortunately they had neglected to clear the remains of their supper from the schoolmaster's desk, the schoolmistress removed it all using the ruler, everything went flying to the floor; the sardine oil and leftover coffee spilling out and the coffee pot smashing to pieces were no concern of the schoolmistress, the caretaker would soon tidy up.

Still not fully dressed, K. and Frieda leaned on the bars and watched the destruction of their few possessions, the assistants, who clearly had no thought of getting dressed, were to the children's huge delight peeking out from among the blankets down below. Frieda was of course most pained by the loss of the coffee pot, and it was not until K., to console her, promised to go straight to the mayor and request and obtain a replacement that she so far recovered herself as to leave the enclosure at a run, wearing only her vest and petticoat, to fetch the tablecloth at least and stop it getting any dirtier. She succeeded too, despite the fact that the schoolmistress, to deter her, kept hammering nerve-shatteringly on the desk with the ruler. When K. and Frieda had finished dressing they found that the assistants, who were as if bemused by events, not only needed to be urged to get dressed with orders and shoves but had to some extent even to be helped into their clothes. Once they were all ready, K. distributed the next jobs, the assistants were to fetch wood and relight the fire, but starting in the other classroom, from which much danger still threatened, because the schoolmaster was probably there already, Frieda was to wash the floor, and K. would fetch water and otherwise tidy up, breakfast was out of the question for the time being. However, to inform himself generally about the schoolmistress's mood K. wanted to go out first, the others were to follow only when he called them, he made this arrangement on the one hand because he did not wish to have the situation aggravated from the outset by stupidities on the part of the assistants and on the other hand because he was keen to protect Frieda as far as possible, for she had ambition, he had none, she was highly sensitive, he was not, she thought only about the current minor nastinesses, he was thinking about Barnabas and the future. Frieda obeyed all his orders precisely, hardly taking her eyes off him. Hardly had he emerged before the schoolmistress, amid the laughter of the children, which from this point on never stopped, called out: 'Had a good snooze, then?' and when K. took no notice, since it was not really a question, but made straight for the washbasin, the schoolmistress asked: 'What have you done to my pussycat, then?' A large, plump old cat lay stretched out inertly on the desk and the schoolmistress was examining its evidently slightly injured paw. So Frieda had been right after all, this cat had perhaps not leaped on her, it was no doubt past leaping, but had crawled over her, been frightened by the presence of people in the normally empty building, swiftly hid, and being unused to making swift movements injured itself. K. attempted to explain this calmly to the schoolmistress but she, seizing only on the outcome, said: 'There you are, you've injured her, that's a fine start, isn't it? Look here,' and she called K. up to the desk, showing him the paw, and before he realized what was happening she had made a mark across the back of his hand with the claws; the claws were blunt, in fact, but the schoolmistress, this time with no consideration for the cat, had pressed them in so hard that bloody weals did in fact result. 'And now get to work,' she said impatiently and bent over the cat once more. Frieda, who had been watching with the assistants from behind the bars, screamed at the sight of the blood. K. showed the hand to the children and said: 'Look what a wicked sly cat did to me.' He did not say it for the children's benefit, of course, their shrieking and laughing had already achieved such momentum that it needed no further cause or encouragement and not a word could be heard above or have any effect upon it. But since even the schoolmistress responded to the insult only with a swift sidelong glance and otherwise continued to busy herself with the cat, her initial anger seemingly appeased by the bloody punishment, K. summoned Frieda and the assistants and work began.

When K. had taken away the pail of dirty water, brought clean water, and was starting to sweep out the classroom, a boy of about twelve stepped from a desk, touched K.'s hand, and said something that was quite incomprehensible in the uproar. Suddenly, the whole uproar fell to nothing. K. turned. The thing he had been afraid of all morning had occurred. In the doorway stood the schoolmaster, each of the little man's hands holding one of the assistants by the collar. He had presumably caught them fetching wood, because in a powerful voice he shouted, leaving a pause after each word: 'Who dared to break into the woodshed? Where is he so I can pulverize the fellow?' Here Frieda got up from the floor, which she was struggling to wash clean at the schoolmistress's feet, looked across at K. as if seeking to draw strength, and said with something of the old superiority in her look and bearing: 'It was me, sir, I did it. I could see no alternative. If the classrooms were to be heated early the shed had to be opened, I didn't dare come and get the key from you during the night, my fiancé was at the Count's Arms, there was a chance he might be spending the night there, so I had to make a decision myself. If I did wrong, forgive my inexperience, I've already been well scolded by my fiancé when he saw what had happened. In fact he even forbade me to light the stoves in advance, believing that by locking the woodshed you had shown that you did not want any fires lit before you got here yourself. So it's his fault there's no heating but mine that the woodshed has been broken open.' 'Who broke the door open?' the schoolmaster asked the assistants, who were still trying in vain to shake off his grip. 'Him,' they both said, pointing at K. to remove any doubt. Frieda laughed, the laugh sounding even more conclusive than her words, then she took the cloth that she had been using to wash the floor and began to wring it out into the bucket, it was as if her explanation had ended the incident and the assistants' remark had been no more than a belated joke, not until she was down on her knees again, ready to resume work, did she say: 'Our assistants are children, for all their years they still belong in these school desks. No, I opened the door with the axe myself towards evening, it was very easy, I didn't need the assistants, they'd only have been in the way. But then during the night, when my fiancé arrived and went out to inspect the damage and if possible repair it, the assistants ran along too, probably because they were afraid to stay here on their own, saw my fiancé working on the forced door, and that's why they now say – well, they're children.' The assistants kept on shaking their heads throughout Frieda's explanation, again pointing at K. and trying by silently pulling faces to persuade Frieda to change her mind, but since they were unsuccessful in this they eventually accepted the situation, took Frieda's words as an order, and when the schoolmaster repeated his question no longer replied. 'So,' the schoolmaster said, 'you were lying, then? Or at least making a frivolous accusation against the caretaker?' Still they said nothing, but their trembling limbs and anxious glances appeared to suggest a guilty conscience. 'In that case I shall give you an immediate thrashing,' the schoolmaster said, and he dispatched a child into the next room for the cane. But then, as he raised the cane, Frieda cried out: 'The assistants were telling the truth,' threw the cloth into the bucket in despair, making the water splash up, and ran behind the parallel bars, where she hid. 'A bunch of liars,' said the schoolmistress, who had just finished

118

bandaging the paw and now took the creature on to her lap, for which it was almost too big.

'That leaves the caretaker,' said the schoolmaster, thrusting the assistants aside and turning to K., who had been listening the whole time, leaning on the broom: 'This caretaker who in his cowardliness has no qualms about allowing others to be falsely accused of his own dirty tricks.' 'Well,' said K., aware that Frieda's intervention had in fact tempered the schoolmaster's initial unbounded rage, 'if the assistants had had a bit of a thrashing I shouldn't have been sorry, if they've been spared on ten justified occasions they can pay for it on one unjustified one. But I'd have welcomed it anyway if an immediate clash between myself and yourself, sir, could have been avoided, it's even possible you'd have preferred it too. However, now that Frieda has sacrificed me to the assistants' – here K. paused, in the silence Frieda could be heard sobbing behind the blankets – 'the matter must of course be cleared up.' 'Incredible,' said the schoolmistress. 'I quite agree with you, Miss Gisa,' said the schoolmaster, 'you, caretaker, are of course fired immediately for this shameful breach of duty, I shall be deciding what punishment will follow, but now will you get out immediately and take all your stuff with you. It will be a real relief to us and lessons can at last begin. So be quick about it!' 'I'm not moving from this place,' said K., 'you may be my superior but you're not the one who gave me the job, that's the mayor, I shall accept my dismissal only from him. He, though, presumably didn't give me the job in order that I should freeze to death here with my people but – as you said yourself – to prevent any rash acts of desperation on my part. So firing me abruptly now would go clear against his intentions; until I hear to the contrary from his own lips, I shall not believe it. Besides, it will no doubt be greatly to your advantage, my not complying with your ill-considered dismissal.' 'So you won't do as I say?' asked the schoolmaster. K. shook his head. 'Think about it carefully,' said the schoolmaster, 'your decisions are not always for the best, remember yesterday afternoon, for instance, when you refused to be interrogated.' 'Why bring that up now?' asked K. 'Because I feel like it,' said the schoolmaster, 'and so I repeat for the last time: out!' When this too had no effect, the schoolmaster went over to the schoolmaster's desk and held a low-voiced discussion with the schoolmistress; she said something about the police, but the schoolmaster rejected it, eventually they agreed, the schoolmaster told the children to go across into his classroom, they would be having lessons there jointly with the other children, the change delighted them all, the room was vacated immediately amid laughter and shouting, the schoolmaster and schoolmistress bringing up the rear. The schoolmistress carried the register and on it what for all its bulk was the wholly apathetic cat. The schoolmaster would have liked to leave the cat behind, but a suggestion to this effect was firmly rebuffed by the schoolmistress with an allusion to K.'s cruelty, so that K. was also, to add to all the irritation, now lumbering the schoolmaster with the cat as well. No doubt this also influenced the final words that the schoolmaster directed at K. from the doorway: 'Miss Gisa is being forced to leave this room together with the children because you stubbornly refuse to comply with my dismissal and because no one can expect a young girl like her to give lessons surrounded by you and your filthy household. So you'll be on your own and can now, undisturbed by the revulsion of respectable onlookers, spread yourselves here as you wish. But it won't be for long, that I guarantee.' Whereupon he slammed the door.

12

THE ASSISTANTS

Scarcely had they all gone when K. told the assistants: 'Get out!' Startled by this unexpected command, they obeyed, but when K. locked the door behind them they tried to get back in, whimpering outside and knocking at the door. 'You're fired,' K. called out, 'I'll never take you into my service again.' They were not having that, of course, and they hammered on the door with hands and feet. 'Back to you, master!' they cried, as if K. were the dry land and they were sinking under the incoming tide. But K. was without pity, waiting impatiently for the intolerable din to force the schoolmaster to intervene. This soon occurred. 'Let your damned assistants in!' he shouted. 'I've dismissed them,' K. shouted back, which had the unlooked-for side effect of showing the schoolmaster what happened when someone was strong enough not simply to give notice of dismissal but actually to carry it out. The schoolmaster now tried in a friendly way to calm the assistants down, they should just wait there quietly, K. would eventually have to let them in again. Then he went away. And things might possibly now have stayed quiet had K. not started shouting at them again that they were now definitely dismissed and had no hope whatever of being taken on again. At this they again began to make as much noise as before. Back came the schoolmaster, but this time he no longer negotiated with them but, clearly using the dreaded cane, drove them from the building.

They soon appeared at the windows of the PE room, knocking on the panes and yelling, but the words could no longer be made out. However, they did not stay long there either, in the deep snow they were unable to leap about in the way their agitation demanded. So they hurried across to the fence around the school garden, jumped up on the low stone wall, where they also, though only from a distance, had a better view into the room, and ran to and fro along it, clinging to the railings, stopping now and then to stretch clasped hands pleadingly in K.'s direction. They went on like this for some time, heedless of the futility of their efforts; they were as if blind, they probably carried on even after K. had let down the curtains to rid himself of the sight of them.

In the now dimly lit room, K. went over to the parallel bars to find Frieda. Under his gaze she stood up, tidied her hair, dried her face, and wordlessly set about making coffee. Even though she knew about everything, K. formally advised her of the fact that he had dismissed the assistants. She merely nodded. K. sat in one of the desks and watched her weary movements. Always before it had been vigour and resolution that made her insignificant body beautiful, now that beauty was gone. A few days of living with K. had sufficed to achieve that. Working in the bar had not been easy, but it had probably suited her better. Or was being away from Klamm the real cause of her decline? It was Klamm's nearness that had made her so madly alluring, in that allurement she had snatched K. to her and now she was wilting in his arms.

'Frieda,' said K. She laid the coffee grinder aside immediately and came to K. in the desk. 'Are you cross with me?' she asked. 'No,' said K., 'I don't think you can help it. You were living happily at the Count's Arms. I should have left you there.' 'Yes,' Frieda said with a look of sadness, 'you should have left me there. I don't deserve to live with you. Free of me, you could achieve everything you want, possibly. Out of consideration for me, you place yourself under the tyrannical schoolmaster, accept this wretched job, strive to get an interview with Klamm. All for me, yet I repay you poorly.' 'No,' K. said, putting an arm round her consolingly, 'those are all minor matters, they don't hurt me, and it's not purely for your sake that I want to see Klamm. And look at all you've done for me! Before I met you I was completely adrift here. No one took me in and as soon as I imposed myself on someone they saw me off. And if there was someone I might have found a resting place with, it was people from whom I ran away myself, Barnabas's people, for instance –' 'You ran away from them? You did, didn't you? Darling!' Frieda threw in brightly before once again, after a hesitant 'Yes' from K., sinking into her weariness. But K. himself no longer had the resolution to explain how, as a result of his association with Frieda, everything had gone right for him. He slowly removed his arm from her and they sat in silence for a while, until Frieda, as if K.'s arm had been supplying a warmth she could no longer do without, said: 'I shan't be able to bear this life here. If you want to keep me, we have to emigrate, anywhere, to the South of France, to Spain.' 'I can't emigrate,' said K., 'I came here in order to stay here. I shall stay here.' And with an inconsistency he did not even attempt to explain he added, as if to himself: 'Because what could possibly have lured me into this desolate country but the desire to stay here.' Then he said: 'But you want to stay here too, after all it's your country. You just miss Klamm and that gives you despairing thoughts.' 'You think I miss Klamm?' said Frieda, 'there's a surfeit of Klamm here, too much Klamm; it's to escape him that I want to get away. I don't miss Klamm, I miss you. It's because of you I want to leave; because I can't get enough of you, with everyone tugging at me here. I'd rather the pretty mask were torn away, I'd rather my body were wretched, so I might live in peace with you.' K. heard only one thing in all this. 'Klamm's still in touch with you?' he asked promptly, 'he sends for you?' 'I don't know anything about Klamm,' said Frieda, 'I'm speaking of other people now, the assistants for example.' 'Aha, the assistants,' said K., surprised, 'they're pursuing you?' 'Hadn't you noticed?' asked Frieda. 'No,' K. said, trying vainly to recall details, 'they're randy, importunate young fellows, certainly, but I hadn't noticed them trying anything on with you.' 'No?' said Frieda, 'you didn't notice how there was no getting them out of our room at the Bridge Inn, how they kept a jealous eye on our relations, how one of them took my place on the palliasse this morning, how they gave evidence against you just now in order to drive you away, ruin you, and be alone with me. You didn't notice any of that?' K. looked at Frieda without replying. These charges against the assistants were real enough, no doubt, but at the same time they were all susceptible of a far more innocent interpretation in terms of the whole laughable, childish, fidgety, uncontrolled nature of the pair of them. And was the accusation not also belied by the fact that they had always sought to go everywhere with K. rather than stay behind with Frieda. K. mentioned something to this effect. 'Hypocrisy,' said Frieda. 'You didn't see through it? Why did you drive them away, then, if it wasn't for those reasons?' And she went to the window, moved the curtain aside a little, looked out, then called K. over. The assistants were still outside by the railings; tired though they clearly were by now, they still, from time to time, summoning all their strength, stretched their arms imploringly in the direction of the school. One of them, to avoid having to hold on all the time, had skewered the back of his coat on a spike.

'The poor things! The poor things!' said Frieda. 'Why did I drive them away?' echoed K. 'The immediate reason was you.' 'Me?' Frieda asked without averting her gaze from outside. 'Your over-familiar treatment of the assistants,' said K., 'excusing their bad manners, laughing about them, stroking their hair, constantly feeling sorry for them, "the poor things, the poor things," there you go again, and finally the most recent incident, when I was not too high a price for you to pay to ransom the assistants from a thrashing.' 'That's just it,' said Frieda, 'that's what I'm talking about, that's just what makes me so miserable, what's keeping me from you, when I know of no greater bliss for myself than to be with you, forever, without interruption, without end, when I dream, I really do, that there's no quiet place here on earth for our love, not in the village and not anywhere else, so I picture a grave, deep and narrow, in which we embrace as if clamped together, I bury my face against you, you yours against me, and no one will ever see us again. Here, though – look at the assistants! It's not for your benefit they clasp their hands together, it's for mine.' 'And it's not me,' said K., 'looking at them, it's you.' 'Of course it is,' Frieda said almost angrily, 'that's what I'm saying all the time; why otherwise would it matter, the assistants being after me, even if they are Klamm's envoys –' 'Klamm's envoys,' said K., to whom this description, natural though it immediately seemed to him, came as a great surprise. 'Yes, Klamm's envoys,' said Frieda, 'but even if they are, at the same time they're foolish youths who still need thrashings to train them. What nasty, dirty youths they are and what a revolting contrast between their faces, which suggest adults, even perhaps students, and their childishly silly behaviour. Do you think I don't see that? I'm ashamed of them. That's just it, though, they don't repel me, instead I'm ashamed of them. I always have to be looking at them. Where a person ought to find them irritating, I have to laugh. Where they should be beaten, I have to stroke their hair. And when I lie beside you at night, I can't sleep and have to look beyond you to where one of them is rolled tightly in the blanket, sleeping, and the other is kneeling at the open door of the stove, stoking it, and I have to lean forward so that I nearly wake you up. And it isn't the cat that scares me – I'm quite familiar with cats and I'm also familiar with the uneasy, constantly interrupted kind of dozing you get in the bar – it isn't the cat that scares me, I scare myself. And it doesn't even take that monster of a cat, the slightest sound makes me start. At one point I'm afraid you'll wake up and it will all be over, next minute I'm jumping up and lighting the candle to make sure you do wake up quickly and can protect me.' 'I knew nothing of all that,' said K., 'I had only an inkling of it when I drove them away, but now they've gone, now maybe everything will be all right.' 'Yes, at last they've gone,' said Frieda, but she looked tormented, not joyful, 'the trouble is, we don't know who they are. Klamm's envoys, that's what I call them in my thoughts, pretending, but maybe they really are. Their eyes, those artless yet twinkling eyes, somehow remind me of Klamm's eyes, yes, that's it, it's Klamm's look that sometimes goes right through me, coming from their eyes. So I was wrong when I said I'm ashamed of them. I only wish I were. All right, I know that anywhere else, in other people, the same behaviour would be stupid and offensive, in them it's not, I watch their stupidities with respect and admiration. Yet if they are Klamm's envoys, who will free us from them and would it even be a good thing if we were free of them? In which case, oughtn't you to fetch them in quickly and be glad if they still came?' 'You want me to let them in again?' asked K. 'No, no,' said Frieda, 'that's the last thing I want. The look on their faces as they came storming in, their delight at seeing me again, their hopping around like children and their stretching their arms out like men, all that might even be too much for me. But when I think that you may, if you go on being hard on them, be refusing Klamm himself access to you, I want to do my utmost to shield you from the consequences. Then I do want you to let them in. Then I can't wait for them to come in. Take no notice of me or what my interests are. I'll defend myself as long as I can, but if I lose, well, I'll lose, but in the knowledge that, again, I did it for you.' 'You simply confirm my opinion about the assistants,' said K., 'they'll never get back in if I have anything to do with it. Surely the fact that I got them out shows that they are sometimes controllable so can't have very much to do with Klamm. Only last night I received a letter from Klamm showing that he's quite wrongly informed about the assistants, which in turn must suggest he couldn't care less about them one way or the other, because if he did, surely he could have got hold of precise information about them. But your seeing Klamm in them proves nothing, because you're still, unfortunately, swayed by the landlady and see Klamm everywhere. You're still Klamm's mistress, still a long way from being my wife. Sometimes that makes me really depressed, I have the impression, then, that I've lost everything, I feel as if I'd only just arrived in the village, but not filled with hope as I was then in reality but knowing that only disappointments await me and that I'm going to have to taste them one after another to the last dregs.' But 'That's only sometimes, though,' K. added with a smile, seeing how Frieda was beginning to slump beneath his words, 'and basically it proves something good, namely how much you mean to me. And if you now ask me to choose between you and the assistants, that's because the assistants have already lost. What an idea, choosing between you and the assistants! What I want now is to be finally rid of them. By the way, who knows whether the feeling of weakness affecting us both doesn't come from our not having had breakfast yet?' 'Could be,' Frieda said with a weary smile, setting to work. K., too, reached for the broom again.

13

HANS

A short while later there was a quiet knock. 'Barnabas!' K. exclaimed, he tossed the broom aside and in a few steps was at the door. Alarmed by the name more than anything else, Frieda watched him. With his unsteady hands, K. could not immediately undo the old lock. 'I'm opening up,' he kept repeating, instead of asking who was actually there. And was then, having flung the door open, faced with the sight not of Barnabas coming in but the small boy who had tried to speak to K. earlier. K., however, had no wish to recall him. 'What are you doing here?' he said, 'the lesson's next door.' 'That's where I've come from,' said the boy, and his big brown eyes looked calmly up at K. as he stood there at attention, arms by his sides. 'So what do you want? Quick!' K. said, bending down slightly because the boy spoke in a quiet voice. 'Can I help you?' the boy asked. 'He wants to help us,' K. said to Frieda and then to the boy: 'What's your name?' 'Hans Brunswick,' said the boy, 'in the fourth class, son of Otto Brunswick, master shoemaker in Madeleine Street.' 'So, your name's Brunswick, is it?' said K., now more friendly towards him. It turned out that Hans had been so upset by the bloody weals the schoolmistress had scratched in K.'s hand that he had determined then and there to stand by K. He had now, on his own initiative, risked heavy punishment by slipping out of the adjacent classroom like a deserter. Possibly it was, in the main, such boyish ideas that governed all his actions. Similarly in keeping with them was the seriousness that came across in everything he did. Only initially had shyness held him back, he soon got used to K. and Frieda, and when he had been given some good hot coffee to drink he became lively and trustful and his questions keen and penetrating, as if he wanted to pick up the main points as quickly as possible in order to be able to make up his own mind on K. and Frieda's behalf. There was something of the commander about him too, but it was so blended with childish innocence that one found oneself, half sincerely, half as a joke, happy to do as he said. Certainly, he claimed their full attention, all work had ceased, breakfast became a very extended affair. Despite the fact that he was sitting in the school desk, K. up above on the schoolmaster's desk, and Frieda on a chair to one side, it looked as if Hans was the schoolmaster, as if he was checking and assessing the answers, a slight smile about his gentle mouth seemed to suggest that he was well aware this was only a game, but his concentration otherwise was all the more serious for that, maybe it was not a smile at all but the happiness of childhood that played around his lips. He was remarkably slow to admit that he knew K. already, had done since K. had called on Lasemann that time. K. was delighted at this. 'You were playing at the woman's feet, right?' K. asked. 'Yes,' said Hans, 'that was my mother.' And here he was obliged to talk about his mother, but he did so with reluctance and only when asked repeatedly, what now transpired was that he was indeed a small boy out of whom at times, it was true, particularly in his questions, possibly in anticipation of the future, though it may also have been simply a product of hallucination on the part of the uneasily tense listener, it almost seemed a vigorous intelligent far-sighted man spoke, but who then next minute, without transition, was a mere schoolboy who quite failed to understand a good many questions and got others wrong, who with a child's lack of consideration spoke too quietly, despite having had the mistake pointed out to him many times, and who finally, as if in defiance, said nothing at all in answer to several urgent questions, and did so without any embarrassment, as an adult could never have done. It was just as if, to his way of thinking, only he might ask questions; having the others ask questions breached some rule and was a waste of time. He was capable, then, of sitting still for a long time, body erect, head bowed, underlip pursed. Frieda liked this so much that she occasionally asked him questions that she hoped would make him fall silent in this way. She succeeded too, sometimes, but it annoyed K. Altogether, they did not learn much, the mother was poorly, but the nature of her illness remained vague, the child that Mrs Brunswick had had in her lap was little Hans's sister and was called Frieda (Hans's reaction to the identity of name with the woman quizzing him was hostile), they all lived in the village but not with Lasemann, they had simply been visiting him to be given a bath, because Lasemann had the big tub, bathing and larking around in which was a particular treat for the little children, of whom Hans, however, was not one; on the subject of his father, Hans spoke with either reverence or apprehension, but only when he was not at the same time talking about his mother, clearly, in comparison with the mother, the father did not count for much, though in fact all questions concerning family life, however slanted, went unanswered, with regard to the father's business they discovered that he was the biggest shoemaker in the locality, he had no equal, this was repeated several times, even in answer to quite different questions, in fact he supplied the other shoemakers, including for example Barnabas's father, with work, in the latter instance Brunswick presumably did it only as a special favour, at least that was what a proud toss of Hans's head suggested, prompting Frieda to jump down and give him a kiss. Asked whether he had ever been inside the castle, he replied only after many repetitions, his answer was 'no', the same question with regard to his mother he did not reply to at all. Eventually K. grew weary, he too began to see the questioning as futile, the boy was right there, and there was also something shameful about trying to uncover family secrets through the indirect medium of the innocent child, though what was doubly shameful was that even so one learned nothing. And when K. then, in conclusion, asked the boy what he was offering to help with, he was no longer surprised to learn that all Hans wanted was to help with the work here in order that the schoolmaster and the schoolmistress should not scold K. so much. K. explained to Hans that help of that kind was not required, scolding was no doubt in the schoolmaster's nature and there was little likelihood, even with the most meticulous work, of a person's being able to shield himself from it, the work itself wasn't difficult and it was only as a result of chance circumstances that he was behind with it today, besides, that kind of scolding didn't affect him as it did a pupil, he shook it off, it hardly mattered to him at all, also he hoped to be able, very soon, to escape from the schoolmaster altogether. So as it had simply been a question of help against the schoolmaster, Hans had his warmest thanks, he said, and might go back now, with any luck he would avoid punishment. K. certainly did not stress and only involuntarily suggested that it was merely help against the schoolmaster that he did not require, leaving the question of other kinds of help open, yet Hans sensed this clearly in K.'s words and asked whether K. needed any other kind of help, perhaps, he would be delighted to provide it and if not able to himself he would ask his mother, and then it would certainly be all right. Even his father, when he had problems, asked his mother for help. In fact, his mother had inquired after K. once, she hardly left the house herself, it had been an exception, her being at Lasemann's that time, though he, Hans, often went there to play with Lasemann's children and on one occasion his mother had asked him whether the land surveyor had perhaps been there again. His mother, he explained, being so frail and weary, must not be made to answer unnecessary questions, so he had simply said he hadn't seen the land surveyor there and there'd been no further mention of him; now, however, having found him at the school, he had had to speak to him in order to be able to report to his mother. Because that was what his mother liked best, having her wishes granted without an express command. K. thought for a moment, then replied that he did not require any help, he had everything he needed, but it was very kind of Hans to want to help him and he thanked him for his good intentions, it was always possible he might need something later, in which case he would turn to him, he had his address. On the other hand possibly he, K., could be of some help this time, he was sorry that Hans's mother was not well and clearly no one here knew what was wrong; often, when a case was neglected like that, a serious aggravation of what was in itself a mild complaint could set in. It so happened that he, K., had some medical knowledge and, even more valuably, experience in treating patients. Many times where doctors had failed, he had been successful. At home he had always, because of his healing powers, been dubbed the bitter herb. Anyway, he would be happy to look at Hans's mother and have a talk with her. He might be able to give some good advice, he would be glad to, simply for Hans's sake. At first, Hans's eyes lit up at this offer, encouraging K. to press it further, the outcome was unsatisfactory, though, because Hans said in answer to various questions, and was not even particularly sad as he did so, that his mother could have no visits from strangers, she needed very careful handling; K. had barely spoken to her that time, nevertheless she'd spent several days in bed afterwards, as happened now and again, Hans admitted.

His father, though, had been furious about K. on that occasion and would certainly never allow K. to visit his mother, in fact he had wanted to call on K. at the time to punish him for his behaviour, and only Hans's mother had prevented him from doing so. But above all his mother herself usually didn't want to speak to anyone, her asking about K. implied no exception to the rule, on the contrary she could, having mentioned him, have expressed a desire to see him, but hadn't done so, thus making her wish quite clear. She only wanted to hear about K., she didn't want to speak to him. It was not, by the way, an actual illness that she was suffering from at all, she was well aware of the cause of her condition and sometimes even alluded to it, it was no doubt the air here she couldn't tolerate, but neither did she wish to leave the place because of his father and the children, also it was better than it had been. That was about what K. learned; Hans's reasoning improved perceptibly as a result of his needing to protect his mother from K., from the man he had said he wanted to help; in fact, in the good cause of keeping K. away from his mother he even contradicted his own previous statements in many respects, for example regarding the illness. Nevertheless, K. was aware even now that Hans remained well-disposed towards him, it was just that his mother drove all other thoughts from his mind; anyone held up to his mother was instantly in the wrong, this time it had been K. but it might also be the father, for example. Wishing to test this latter possibility, K. said it was certainly very sensible of Hans's father to shield his mother from any disturbance and if he, K., had had the least inkling of any such thing at the time he would certainly not have made so bold as to address Hans's mother and would Hans please now convey his belated apologies to the family. However, he couldn't quite understand why Hans's father, if the cause of the complaint had been made as clear as Hans said, kept his mother from recovering in a different climate; it had to be said he was keeping her, because it was only for the children's and his own sakes that she did not leave, yet the children she could take with her, she needn't go away for long, nor need she go very far; just up on Castle Hill the air was already quite different. The father need not fear the cost of such an excursion, he was the biggest shoemaker in the locality and surely, too, either he or Hans's mother had relations or acquaintances in the castle who would be glad to have her. Why didn't he let her go? He ought not to underestimate such a complaint, K. had seen Hans's mother only briefly but her striking pallor and frailty had moved him to speak to her, he'd been surprised even at the time at Hans's father letting the sick woman stay in the stale air of the communal bathroom and washroom and not even curbing his own noisy speech. Presumably the father didn't realize what he was dealing with, the complaint may indeed have improved recently, a complaint like that has its ups and downs but will eventually, if not controlled, come back with full force and then nothing will help any more. If K. couldn't speak to the mother, it might be a good idea if he spoke to the father and drew his attention to all these things.

Hans had listened keenly, understood most of what he had heard, been powerfully aware of the threat of the incomprehensible remainder. Even so, he told K. that he could not talk to his father, his father had an aversion to him and would no doubt treat him as the schoolmaster had. He said this smilingly and shyly when speaking of K., grimly and sorrowfully when mentioning his father. He did add, though, that K. might be able to talk to his mother after all, but only without his father knowing. Then Hans thought for a moment, staring fixedly, very like a woman who has a wish to do something forbidden and is looking for a way of carrying it out unpunished, and said that it might be possible the day after tomorrow, his father went to the Count's Arms of an evening, he had to meet people there, in which case he, Hans, would come in the evening and take K. to his mother, provided, of course, that his mother agreed, which was still highly unlikely. Above all, she did nothing against his father's wishes, Hans said, she obeyed him in everything, including things that even he, Hans, clearly saw were unreasonable. Really, what Hans was after was K.'s help against his father, it was as if he had been deceiving himself in thinking that he wished to assist K., whereas in reality he had wanted to discover whether, since no one from his old surroundings had been able to help, this stranger who had appeared suddenly and had now even been mentioned by his mother might not be able to do so. He was as if unconsciously withdrawn, the lad, almost sly, this had scarcely been perceptible from his manner and his words up to now, it was only the almost resentful confessions extracted by chance and with intent that had brought it out. And now here he was, discussing at length with K.

what difficulties would need to be surmounted, with the best will in the world on Hans's part they were almost insurmountable difficulties, deep in thought but still seeking help, he kept his nervously blinking eyes trained on K. He could say nothing to his mother before his father had gone, otherwise his father would hear of it and the rest would become impossible, so he mustn't mention it till afterwards, but even then, out of consideration for his mother, not abruptly and quickly but gently, choosing the right moment, only then must he ask for his mother's consent, only then could he fetch K., but wouldn't that be too late already, wouldn't there already be a risk of his father returning? Oh, it was impossible. K., however, showed that it was not impossible. As to there not being enough time, they need have no fear, a brief chat, a brief instant together would do, nor need Hans come and get K. K. would be waiting in hiding somewhere near the house and at a sign from Hans would come immediately. No, said Hans, K. couldn't wait near the house – again it was over-sensitivity on his mother's account that influenced him – K. couldn't start out without his mother's knowledge, Hans couldn't make such a pact with K., keeping it a secret from his mother, he must fetch K. from the school and not earlier, before his mother knew of and agreed to it. Fine, said K., in that case it really was dangerous, there was a chance of Hans's father catching him in the house, and even if that didn't happen his mother, for fear of it, mightn't send for K. in the first place, so the whole thing would still fail because of the father. This time it was Hans who objected, and so the argument swung back and forth. K. had long since called Hans up to the schoolmaster's desk, drawn him between his knees, and been giving him the occasional soothing caress. This nearness was partly why, despite Hans's intermittent opposition, an agreement was reached. The two eventually agreed as follows: Hans would start by telling his mother the whole truth; however, to make it easier for her to agree he would add that K. also wanted to speak to Brunswick himself, not about the mother, though, about his own affairs. This was in fact correct, it had occurred to K. in the course of the discussion that Brunswick, who in other respects might well be a dangerous and evil person, could not actually be his enemy, because after all, according to the mayor at least, he had headed those who, even if it was for political reasons, had asked for a land surveyor to be appointed. K.'s arrival in the village must therefore be welcome so far as Brunswick was concerned; that did make the irritated greeting on the first day and the aversion Hans had spoken of almost incomprehensible, but perhaps Brunswick was offended precisely because K. had not turned to him first for help, perhaps there was another misunderstanding here that a couple of words might clear up. If that was what had happened, though, K. might very well receive Brunswick's backing against the schoolmaster, indeed even against the mayor, the whole official deception – because what else was it? – by means of which the mayor and the schoolmaster were keeping him from the castle authorities and had forced him into the job of school caretaker could be exposed, if it once again came to a fight over K. between Brunswick and the mayor, Brunswick would have to get K. on his side, K. would become a guest in Brunswick's house, Brunswick's instruments of power would be placed at his disposal, in defiance of the mayor, there was no knowing how far he might advance as a result, and in any case he would often be near where the woman was – thus he toyed with his dreams and they with him while Hans, thinking only of his mother, worriedly observed K.'s silence, the way one does with a doctor who is sunk in thought, trying to find a remedy for a serious case. This suggestion of K.'s that he wished to speak to Brunswick about the land surveyor job met with Hans's approval, though only because it protected his mother from his father and besides related only to an emergency, which he hoped would not arise. All he asked was how K. was going to explain to his father the lateness of his visit, and eventually he was satisfied, even if his face did darken slightly, by K.'s proposing to say that the intolerable position as school caretaker and the schoolmaster's humiliating treatment of him had made him suddenly desperate and driven all caution from his mind.

With everything, so far as one could see, now planned in advance and the possibility of success at least no longer out of the question, little Hans, the burden of thought removed, perked up and stayed chatting for a while, childishly, first with K. and then also with Frieda, who for a long time had been sitting there as if her thoughts were somewhere else entirely and only now started taking part in the conversation again. One of the things she asked him was what he wanted to be, he did not think for long before replying that he wanted to be a man like K. When then asked about his reasons he did not know how to answer, of course, and the question as to whether he wanted to be a school caretaker, say, met with a firm denial. Only after further questioning did it become clear by what route he had arrived at his wish. K.'s current situation was not the least bit enviable, it was wretched and contemptible, even Hans saw that clearly and had no need to look at other people in order to spot it, he himself would have preferred to shield his mother from every look and word of K.'s. Nevertheless, he came to K. and asked him for help and was glad when K. agreed, he believed he had spotted something similar in other people too, and above all his mother had mentioned K. herself. Out of this contradiction there arose in him the belief that, while K. at the moment was low and repulsive, in what was admittedly an almost inconceivably distant future he would outstrip everybody. And it was just this almost absurd remoteness and the proud development that should lead to it that Hans found attractive; for this price he was prepared to accept even the present K. The peculiarly precocious quality of this desire consisted in Hans's looking down on K. as if on someone younger, someone whose future stretched out farther than his own, the future of a small boy. And it was with an almost gloomy seriousness that, repeatedly prodded by questions from Frieda, he spoke of these things. K. was the one who cheered him up again, saying that he knew what Hans envied him for, it was his splendid gnarled stick, which lay on the table and with which Hans had been absent-mindedly playing as they talked. Well, said K., he could make such sticks, and once their plan had succeeded he'd produce an even finer one for Hans. It was now no longer entirely clear whether Hans had not really had only the stick in mind, so delighted was he by K.'s promise and gaily said goodbye, not without shaking K. firmly by the hand and telling him: 'Day after tomorrow, then.'

14

FRIEDA'S REPROACH

Hans had not gone a moment too soon, for shortly afterwards the schoolmaster tore open the door and, seeing K. and Frieda sitting quietly at table, shouted: 'Pardon the intrusion! But tell me, when is this room finally going to be tidied up. We're having to sit crammed together next door, lessons are suffering, meanwhile you stretch out at your leisure here in the big PE room and to give yourselves even more space have sent the assistants off too. Now will you both at least stand up and get moving!' And to K. alone: 'You'll fetch me my lunch from the Bridge Inn now.' All this was shouted angrily, yet the words were comparatively gentle, even in the somewhat coarse familiarity of the final command. K. was at once prepared to obey; however, to sound the schoolmaster out he said: 'But I've been fired.' 'Fired or not, fetch me my lunch,' said the schoolmaster. 'That's just what I want to know, am I fired or not?' said K. 'What are you talking about?' said the schoolmaster, 'you refused to accept dismissal.' 'That's enough to make it inoperative?' K. asked. 'Not in my eyes,' said the schoolmaster, 'take it from me, but it is in the mayor's, inexplicably. Now get a move on, or you'll really be out on your ear.' K. was satisfied, so the schoolmaster had had a word with the mayor in the meantime, or perhaps not even had a word but simply calculated the mayor's likely opinion and this was in K.'s favour. K. was keen to go running off for the lunch and was already out in the passage when the schoolmaster called him back, either because he was simply using this separate command to test K.'s willingness and whether he could continue to depend on it, or because he now felt a fresh desire to give orders and it pleased him to have K. go running off and then, at his command, have him, like a waiter, as quickly come running back. As for K., he realized that by giving in too readily he would make himself the schoolmaster's slave and whipping boy, yet he was now prepared to pander to the schoolmaster's whims up to a point because even if, as had transpired, the schoolmaster could not legally dismiss him he was certainly in a position to make the job agonizing beyond endurance. The fact was, the job now meant more to K. than it had done before. Talking to Hans had given him fresh, admittedly improbable, wholly groundless, yet henceforth indelible hopes, even eclipsing Barnabas, almost. If he pursued them, and he had to, he would need to gather all his strength for the purpose, not worry about anything else, not his meals, his accommodation, the village authorities, not even Frieda, and Frieda, basically, was what this was all about, all the other things concerned him only in relation to her. So this job, which gave Frieda a measure of security, was one he must try to keep, and he should have no regrets, with that end in view, about taking more from the schoolmaster than he would otherwise have been able to stomach. None of this was too painful, it was another of life's perpetual little torments, that was all, nothing when measured against what K. aspired to, he had not come to this place to lead a life of peace and honour.

As a result, where he had wanted to run to the inn immediately, at the amended command he was as immediately prepared to tidy the room first, in order that the schoolmistress might return with her class. However, the tidying-up had to be done very quickly because afterwards K. was still supposed to fetch the lunch and the schoolmaster was already very hungry and thirsty. K. promised that everything would be done as required; for a few minutes the schoolmaster watched as K. hurried about, clearing the beds away, pushing the PE apparatus back into place, sweeping as he went, while Frieda washed and scrubbed the rostrum. Apparently satisfied by this zeal, the schoolmaster pointed out that there was a stack of wood ready for the stove outside the door – he was unwilling to give K. access to the shed again, presumably – then, threatening that he would be back soon to check, went through to the children.

After working in silence for a while, Frieda asked why K. was now being so acquiescent towards the schoolmaster. The question was no doubt sympathetic and concerned but K., who was thinking how unsuccessful Frieda had been, after her original promise, at shielding him from the schoolmaster's orders and brutalities, merely said curtly that, having been made school caretaker, he must now do the job. Then all was quiet again, until K., reminded by the brief exchange that earlier Frieda had for so long been lost as if in anxious thought, particularly throughout most of the conversation with Hans, now asked her frankly, as he carried the wood in, what was on her mind. She replied, looking slowly up at him, that it was nothing specific, she was simply thinking about the landlady and about the truth of much of what she'd said. Not until K. pressed her, and then after several refusals, did she reply in more detail, but without pausing in her work, not through any diligence, it did not advance the job one bit, merely to avoid having to look at K. And she proceeded to tell K. how she had started listening to his conversation with Hans calmly, how she had then, startled by certain of K.'s words, begun registering the meaning of what he was saying more sharply, and how from then on she had been unable to stop herself hearing K.'s words as so many confirmations of a piece of advice she owed to the landlady but had never been willing to believe was justified. K., vexed by the generalities and even finding the tearfully plaintive voice more irritating than moving – mainly because the landlady was now meddling in his life again, at least through memories, having so far had little success in person – dropped his armful of wood on the floor, sat down on it, and in serious terms demanded total clarity. 'On several occasions,' began Frieda, 'right at the beginning, the landlady tried to make me doubt you, she didn't say you lie, on the contrary she said you're childishly frank, but you're so different from us by nature that even when you're speaking frankly we have trouble believing you, and if a kind woman friend doesn't come to our rescue first we must accustom ourselves to believing through bitter experience alone. Even she, with her keen eye for people, had fared little better, she said. However, after the last conversation with you at the Bridge Inn she had – I'm simply repeating her angry words – seen through your tricks, now you couldn't deceive her any more, even if you made an effort to conceal your intentions. "Yet he doesn't conceal anything," she kept saying, and then: "Make the effort, take any opportunity really to listen to him, not just superficially, I mean really listen to him." She'd done just that herself, she said, and so far as I was concerned this was what she'd heard, more or less: you made up to me – that was the humiliating expression she used – purely because I happened to cross your path, didn't exactly displease you, and because you see a barmaid, quite wrongly, as the preordained victim of any guest who holds his hand out. Also for whatever reason you were determined, as she learned from the landlord of the Count's Arms, to spend that night at the Count's Arms, and there was no other way of achieving that but through me. All this would have given you grounds for making yourself my lover for the night, but if something more was to come of it something more was needed, and that something was Klamm. The landlady doesn't claim to know what you want from Klamm, she merely claims that you were trying as hard to reach Klamm before you met me as after. The only difference was, previously you'd had no hope but now you thought you'd found, in me, a reliable way of actually getting through to Klamm soon, and even with a certain advantage. What a fright it gave me – only momentarily, though, not for any deeper reason – when you said today that before you met me you had lost your way here. They may be the very words the landlady used, she too said it was only since knowing me that you'd had any sense of purpose. It was the product, she said, of your thinking that in me you'd conquered a sweetheart of Klamm's and so held a pledge, redeemable only at the highest price. Negotiating that price with Klamm was your one aspiration. Since I was nothing to you, the price everything, over me you were prepared to make any concession, over the price you wouldn't budge. That's why you don't care about my losing the job at the Count's Arms, you don't care about my having to leave the Bridge Inn either, you don't care that I'm now going to have to do this heavy caretaking work at the school, you have no tenderness, no time for me any more, even, you abandon me to the assistants, you feel no jealousy, my one value in your eyes is that I used to be Klamm's mistress, in your ignorance you go out of your way not to let me forget Klamm, then at the end I shan't struggle too much when the crucial moment arrives, yet you also cross swords with the landlady, the only person you think capable of snatching me away from you, so you carry the quarrel with her to extremes in order to have to leave the Bridge Inn with me; that, so far as it's for me to say, I'm yours whatever happens, that you don't doubt. You picture the discussion with Klamm as a business deal, cash for cash. You're allowing for all possibilities; provided you get the price, you're prepared to do anything; if Klamm wants me, you'll give me to him, if he wants you to stay with me, you'll stay, if he wants you to throw me out, you'll throw me out, but you're also prepared to play-act, if there's any advantage in it, for example you'll pretend to love me, you'll seek to combat his indifference by stressing your own nothingness and shaming him with the fact of your having succeeded him or by telling him about my admissions of love regarding him, which I did in fact make, and asking him to take me back, on payment of the price, of course; and if all else fails, then on behalf of the K.s, husband and wife, you'll simply beg. But when afterwards, this was the landlady's conclusion, you realize that you've been wrong about everything, about your assumptions and your hopes, in your conception of Klamm and his relations with me, that's when my hell will begin, because that's when I really shall be the only possession left for you to depend on, but a possession that at the same time has proved worthless and that you'll treat accordingly, because you've no other feeling for me but that of an owner.'

K., tight-lipped, had been listening intently, the logs had begun to roll under him, he had almost slithered to the floor, he had taken no notice, only now did he get up, sit on the rostrum, take Frieda's hand, which she tried weakly to pull away from him, and say: 'I wasn't always able, in your account, to tell your opinion from the landlady's.' 'It was all the landlady's opinion,' said Frieda, 'I listened to everything because of my admiration for the landlady, but it was the first time in my life that I completely and utterly rejected her opinion. It seemed so pathetic, everything she said to me, so far removed from any understanding of how things were between the two of us. I was closer to seeing the exact opposite of what she said as correct. I thought of that bleak morning following our first night. The way you knelt beside me with a look as if all was now lost. And the way things did in fact turn out, how, try as I might, I was no help to you, more of a hindrance. Through me, the landlady became your enemy, a powerful enemy whom you still underestimate; because of me, being obliged to provide for me, you had to fight for your place, stood at a disadvantage with the mayor, had to submit to the schoolmaster, were put at the mercy of the assistants, but worst of all: on my account you had possibly offended Klamm. Your still wanting constantly to reach Klamm was simply an impotent striving somehow to placate him. And I told myself that the landlady, who surely knew all this far better than I did, was simply trying, with her insinuations, to save me from reproaching myself too terribly. Well-intentioned but superfluous concern. My love for you would have helped me over everything, in the end it would have carried you forward too, if not here in the village, then somewhere else, it had already proved its power once, rescuing you from Barnabas's family.' 'So that was your reaction at the time,' said K., 'and what has changed since?' 'I don't know,' Frieda said with a glance at K.'s hand, which held her own, 'maybe nothing's changed; when you're so close to me and ask so calmly, I think nothing's changed. In fact, though,' – she removed her hand from K., sat up straight facing him, and wept without covering her face; she openly presented this tear-drenched face to him as if she was not weeping for herself, she had nothing to hide, but as if she was weeping over K.'s betrayal, so it was fitting that he should also have this wretched sight of her – 'in fact, though, everything has changed since I heard you talking to the boy. You began so innocently, asking about things at home, about this and that, to me it was as if you'd just come into the bar, trusting, open-hearted, and were trying with childish eagerness to catch my eye. It was no different from then, and I just wished the landlady had been here, heard you talking, and then tried to hold to her opinion. But then suddenly, I don't know how it happened, I realized what you were after in speaking to the boy. With your sympathetic words you did what was not easy, you won his trust, you were then able to go straight for your goal, which was increasingly clear to me. That goal was the woman. Your ostensibly concerned remarks about her quite plainly expressed only regard for your affairs. You were betraying the woman even before you'd won her. Not only my past came back to me in your words, I also heard my future, to me it was as if the landlady was sitting beside me, explaining everything to me, and I was trying as hard as I could to push her away but was well aware of how hopeless my efforts were, and yet actually it wasn't me being betrayed any more, I wasn't even being betrayed, but the other woman. And when I then pulled myself together and asked Hans what he wanted to be when he grew up and he said he wanted to be like you, in other words already belonged to you so completely, where then was the big difference between him, the nice boy being taken advantage of here, and me back there in the bar?'

'Everything,' said K., his composure restored as he grew accustomed to the reproach, 'everything you're saying is correct in a sense, it's not untrue, simply hostile. These are the landlady's thoughts, my enemy's thoughts, even if you do think they're your own, I take consolation from that. But they are instructive, there's still much to be learned from the landlady. She has not said it to my face, though she's not spared me otherwise, clearly she entrusted this weapon to you hoping that you'd use it at a particularly awkward or critical time for me; if I'm taking advantage of you, so is she. But think, Frieda: even if everything were exactly as the landlady says it is, it would be truly awful only in one event, namely if you didn't love me. Then yes, it would be the case that I had won you with calculation and trickery in order to profit by such possession. Maybe it was even then part of my plan that, to excite your sympathy, I appeared before you arm-in-arm with Olga that time, and the landlady merely forgot to include this in my debit account. But if things were not in fact so bad and it was not a cunning predator seizing you that time but a question of you coming to me as I came to meet you and the two of us finding each other, both equally oblivious, then tell me, Frieda, how does that leave matters? It means I am pleading my cause as well as yours, there's no distinction here and only an enemy, the landlady, can draw one. That applies to everything, Hans included. By the way, your delicacy of feeling is such that you greatly exaggerate when judging the conversation with Hans, because if Hans's and my intentions aren't wholly identical, neither are they so far apart as to be actually opposed, also our own disagreement did not escape Hans's notice, if you thought it did you'd be badly underestimating the wary little fellow, and even if everything had escaped his notice, no one's going to suffer as a result, I hope.'

'It's so hard to tell what's what, K.', Frieda said with a sigh, 'I certainly didn't distrust you and if anything of the kind has transferred itself from the landlady to me I'll be only too happy to throw it off and beg your forgiveness on my knees, as in fact I do the whole time, whatever wicked things I may say. But it's true all the same: you do keep a lot of things secret from me; you come and you go, I don't know where from or where to. When Hans knocked that time you even called out the name Barnabas. If only you'd ever called me as lovingly as you did that hateful name, I can't understand why. If you don't trust me, how can I help but feel mistrust, it throws me back entirely on the landlady, whom your behaviour appears to bear out. Not in everything, I'm not saying you bear her out in everything, you did once chase off the assistants for my sake, didn't you? If you knew with what yearning I scrutinize everything you do and say, even if it's torture to me, for an inner core in my favour.' 'Frieda, above all,' said K., 'I don't conceal anything from you, not the least little thing. How the landlady hates me and does her best to tear you from me and what contemptible methods she uses and how you give in to her, Frieda, how you give in to her. Tell me, how do I conceal things from you? You know I want to reach Klamm, you also know you can't help me in this so I must manage it on my own, and you can see for yourself that I've not yet succeeded. Must I now, by recounting the futile attempts that already, in reality, amply humiliate me, humiliate myself twice over? Should I boast, for instance, of having spent a long afternoon waiting in vain, getting very cold, at the door of Klamm's sledge? Glad not to have to think about such things any more, I come hurrying to you and now have it all thrown back at me threateningly by yourself. And Barnabas? Certainly I'm expecting him. He's Klamm's messenger, I didn't make him that.' 'Barnabas again,' Frieda exclaimed, 'I can't believe he's a good messenger.' 'You could be right,' said K., 'but he's the only one I've been sent.' 'All the worse,' said Frieda, 'and all the more do you need to be on your guard against him.' 'Unfortunately, he's given me no opportunity for that up to now,' K. said with a smile, 'he doesn't come often and what he brings is of no consequence; only the fact of its stemming direct from Klamm gives it any value.' 'Yes, but look,' said Frieda, 'Klamm isn't even your goal any more, that's perhaps what bothers me most; it was bad enough, having you constantly pushing past me towards Klamm, seeing you now appear to give up on Klamm is much worse, it's something not even the landlady foresaw. According to the landlady my happiness, a dubious but very real happiness, would end the day you finally recognized that your hopes of Klamm were in vain. Now you're not even waiting for that day, along comes a small boy and you join battle with him over his mother as if you were fighting for your very life.' 'You've got it quite right, my conversation with Hans,' said K., 'that's really how it was. But is your whole life before so lost in oblivion (except for the landlady, of course, there's no shedding her along with it) that you've forgotten what a struggle it is to make any progress, especially for someone coming from a long way down? How everything must be exploited that gives any kind of hope? And this woman comes from the castle, she told me so herself when I blundered into Lasemann's house that first day. What more natural than to ask her for advice or even help; if the landlady has full knowledge only of all the obstacles keeping one from Klamm, this woman probably knows the way, I mean she herself came down by it.' 'The way to Klamm?' asked Frieda. 'To Klamm, yes of course, where else,' said K. He leapt to his feet: 'But now it's high time I fetched that lunch.' Urgently, far more so than the occasion demanded, Frieda begged him to stay, as if only his staying would confirm all the comforting things he had said to her. However, K. reminded her of the schoolmaster, indicated the door that might at any moment burst open with a noise like thunder, promised he would be right back, she needn't even light the stove, he would see to that himself. Eventually, Frieda accepted the situation, falling quiet. As K. trudged through the snow outside – the path should have been cleared long since, odd how slowly the work was progressing – he saw one of the assistants clinging to the railings, worn out. Only one, where was the other? Did this mean K. had at least broken the endurance of one of them? True, the one that was left still had his mind very much on the business in hand, this became clear when, stirred into life by the sight of K., he immediately recommenced the stretching out of arms and the wistful rolling of eyes. 'His stubbornness is exemplary,' K. told himself, though he could not help adding: 'such that he'll freeze to death at the railings.' Outwardly, however, all K. had for the assistant was a threatening wave of his fist, ruling out any approach, in fact the assistant timidly retreated some considerable way further. Frieda was just opening a window in order, as discussed with K., to air the room before lighting the stove. The assistant promptly left K. alone and, drawn irresistibly, stole towards the window. Her features contorted with kindliness towards the assistant and a plea of impotence for K.'s benefit, she gave a vague wave out of the upper part of the window, which might have been either rebuff or greeting, it was not even clear, nor did the assistant let this put him off approaching. Frieda then closed the outer window quickly but stayed where she was inside, hand on the catch, head at an angle, eyes wide, smiling fixedly. Was she aware that this attracted the assistant more than it scared him off? But K. did not look back again, he was more anxious to make as much haste as possible and be back soon.

15

AT AMALIA'S

At last – it was already dark, late afternoon – K. had cleared the garden path, piled the snow on both sides of the path and packed it solid, and had now finished the day's work. He stood at the garden gate, the only person anywhere in the vicinity. He had driven the assistant off hours ago, chasing him for some distance, the assistant had then hidden somewhere among the gardens and cottages, was no longer to be found, and had not emerged since. Frieda was at home, washing either the clothes already or still Gisa's cat; it had been a sign of great trust on Gisa's part, her giving Frieda this job, though it was unsavoury and unsuitable work that K. would certainly not have tolerated her taking on had it not been highly advisable, following various derelictions of duty, to exploit every opportunity of possibly putting Gisa in their debt. A satisfied Gisa had looked on as K. fetched the little baby bath from the attic, water was heated, and finally the cat was carefully lifted in. At that point, Gisa had even left the cat in Frieda's sole charge, because Schwarzer arrived, K.'s acquaintance from the first evening, he greeted K. with a mixture of timidity, for reasons dating from that evening, and the kind of boundless contempt that was a school caretaker's due, then accompanied Gisa into the other classroom. They were in there still. K. had learned at the Bridge Inn that Schwarzer, who was after all a governor's son, had for love of Gisa been living in the village for some time now, had contrived through his connections to have the municipality appoint him assistant schoolmaster, but performed that office chiefly by almost never missing a lesson of Gisa's, sitting either in a desk amongst the children or, for preference, on the rostrum at Gisa's feet. There was no awkwardness any more, the children had long since grown accustomed to it, perhaps all the more easily for the fact that Schwarzer neither liked nor understood children, hardly spoke to them, had taken over only the PE lessons from Gisa, and was otherwise content to live in Gisa's vicinity, Gisa's air, and Gisa's warmth. His greatest pleasure was to sit beside Gisa and mark exercise books with her. That was what they were doing today, Schwarzer had brought a huge pile of exercise books with him, the schoolmaster always gave them his too, and as long as it remained light K. had seen the two of them working at a table by the window, head to head, motionless, now all that could be seen there was two flickering candles. It was an earnest, taciturn love that bound them, the tone being set by Gisa, whose ponderous nature did occasionally, going wild, break all bounds, but who would not have tolerated anything of the sort in others, not ever, consequently even the lively Schwarzer had to submit, walk slowly, talk slowly, be silent a great deal, but he was richly rewarded for everything, that much was clear, simply by Gisa's quiet presence. Yet Gisa may not have loved him at all, certainly her round grey eyes, which quite literally never blinked, the pupils appearing to revolve instead, gave no reply to such questions, all one saw was that she put up with Schwarzer without protest, but the honour of being loved by a governor's son was something of which she certainly had no appreciation, and she carried her ample, opulent body about in the same steady fashion, whether Schwarzer's eyes were on her or not. Schwarzer, for his part, made her the permanent sacrifice of staying in the village; messengers from his father who arrived from time to time to fetch him back were dealt with as indignantly as if even the fleeting memory of the castle and of his filial duty that they aroused was a severe and irreparable disturbance of his happiness. Yet he had plenty of free time, in fact, because Gisa generally let him see her only during school time and at marking sessions, not of course in any calculated way but because she loved comfort and therefore solitude above all else and was probably happiest when she could stretch out on the couch at home in complete freedom with the cat beside her, the cat giving no trouble since it could hardly move any more. As a result, Schwarzer spent much of the day hanging around with nothing to do, but even this he enjoyed because it meant he always had the opportunity, of which he made very frequent use, to go round to Lion Street where Gisa lived, climb the stairs to her little attic room, listen at the invariably locked door, but then in fact go away again, having established that inside the room, every time, there was total, inexplicable silence. Even with him, however, the consequences of this way of life did occasionally manifest themselves, though never in Gisa's presence, taking the form of ludicrous outbursts at moments of reawakened official arrogance, which was quite out of place, of course, in the light of his present position; things usually turned out rather badly at such times, as K. had himself experienced.

The only surprising thing was that, at the Bridge Inn at least, Schwarzer was in fact spoken of with a certain respect, even when matters more ludicrous than estimable were involved, and Gisa was included in that respect. Even so, it was not right that as assistant schoolmaster Schwarzer should believe himself hugely superior to K., no such superiority existed, so far as the teaching staff is concerned, particularly a teacher like Schwarzer, a school caretaker is a very important person who cannot be shown disrespect with impunity and to whom such disrespect as is unavoidable for ranking purposes should at least be rendered tolerable with a suitable return. K. meant to bear this in mind, also Schwarzer was in his debt, had been since that first evening, nor was that debt any the less for the fact that the next few days had justified Schwarzer's reception. Because there was no forgetting that the reception may possibly have set the course for all that followed. Through Schwarzer, quite unreasonably, the full attention of the authorities had been turned on K. from the very beginning when, still a complete stranger to the village, knowing no one, having no refuge, tired out from the walk, utterly helpless as he lay there on the palliasse, he was at the mercy of any and every official action. Just one night later, everything might have passed off differently, smoothly, in semi-obscurity. At any rate, no one would have known anything about him, people would not have been suspicious, would at least not have hesitated to leave a journeyman alone for a day, they would have seen his usefulness and reliability, word would have gone round the neighbourhood, he would probably soon have found a position as hand somewhere. He would not have escaped officialdom, of course. But there was a big difference between central office or whoever had been on telephone duty being roused in the middle of the night on his account with a request for an on-the-spot decision, a request made with apparent humility but still with tiresome stubbornness, and by Schwarzer, too, a man who was no doubt unpopular up there, and the alternative, which was K. knocking on the mayor's door during office hours next day and registering in the proper way as an out-of-town journeyman who already had a bed with such-and-such a member of the community and would very likely be moving on again tomorrow, except in the highly unlikely event of his finding work here, only for a couple of days, of course, because under no circumstances did he wish to stay longer. That or something like it is how it would have been, but for Schwarzer. The authority would have continued to deal with the matter, but calmly, using official channels, untroubled by what it no doubt particularly disliked, namely impatience in the party. K. was of course innocent in all this, the guilt was Schwarzer's, but Schwarzer was a governor's son and on the face of it had acted quite correctly, so K. must be made to pay. And the ludicrous cause of it all? Possibly a bad mood on Gisa's part that day, as a result of which Schwarzer had been roaming around during the night, unable to sleep, and had proceeded to take his troubles out on K. On the other hand, of course, K. could also be said to owe much to Schwarzer's behaviour. It alone had made something possible that K. would never have achieved on his own, never have dared to achieve, and that the authority for its part was unlikely ever to have conceded, namely that he faced up to the authority from the outset without equivocation, openly, face to face, so far as the authority made such a stance possible. But this was a terrible gift, it did spare K. a lot of lying and secretiveness but it also made him virtually defenceless, at any rate put him at a disadvantage in the struggle and might on that account have caused him to despair had he not had to tell himself that the difference in power between the authority and him was so enormous that all the lying and trickery at his command could not have reduced that difference by much in his favour but must always have remained relatively imperceptible. However, this was just a thought with which K. consoled himself, Schwarzer was still in his debt; if he had harmed K. on that occasion, next time he might help him, K. was going to continue to need help at the most elementary level, with the most basic prerequisites, for example even Barnabas appeared to be failing again. Because of Frieda, K. had put off all day going to Barnabas's house to inquire; to avoid having to receive him in Frieda's presence, K. had been working outside here and had even stayed out here after work, waiting for Barnabas, but Barnabas had not come. Now he had no choice but to go and see the sisters, only for a moment, he only wanted to ask from the doorstep, he would be back before long. And he drove the shovel into the snow and ran. He reached Barnabas's house out of breath, knocked briefly, flung the door open, and without even taking in the scene in the room asked: 'Is Barnabas still not back?' Only then did he notice that Olga was not there, the two old people were once again sitting in a doze at the table set well back, had not yet worked out what had happened at the door, and were only now slowly turning to look, and finally that Amalia, lying under blankets on the bench by the stove, had started up in her initial alarm at K.'s appearance and was holding a hand to her forehead to give herself composure. If Olga had been there, she would have answered immediately and K. could have gone away again, as it was he had at least to take the few steps over to Amalia, give her his hand, which she pressed in silence, and ask her to prevent the startled parents from wandering off somewhere, which with a few words she then did. K. learned that Olga was outside chopping wood, an exhausted Amalia – she gave no reason – had had to lie down a moment before, and Barnabas was not in fact back yet but should be very soon, he never stayed in the castle overnight. K. thanked her for the information, he could now go, but Amalia asked whether he did not want to wait and see Olga, no, he hadn't time unfortunately, Amalia then asked whether in that case he had already spoken to Olga during the day, he said no in amazement and asked whether Olga had something special she wished to tell him, Amalia turned up her mouth as if mildly annoyed, gave K. a wordless nod, clearly in dismissal, and lay back down. From a reclining position, she surveyed him as if surprised that he was still there. It was a cold, clear gaze, inflexible as ever, not quite aimed at what she was looking at but passing – this bothered him – slightly, almost imperceptibly, but without any doubt to one side, it was apparently not weakness, not awkwardness, not dishonesty that caused this but a constant yearning, more powerful than any other emotion, to be alone, a yearning that perhaps she herself became aware of only in this way. K. thought he could remember the look preoccupying him that first evening, indeed the whole ugly impression that this family had instantly made on him probably stemmed from that look, which was not itself ugly but proud and sincere in its self-containment. 'You're always so sad, Amalia,' said K., 'is something tormenting you? Can you not say? I've never seen a country girl like you before. It's only today, only now that that's really struck me. Are you from this village? Were you born here?' Amalia said yes as if replying to K.'s last question only, then she said: 'So you will wait for Olga?' 'I don't know why you keep on asking the same thing,' said K., 'I can't stay any longer because my fiancée's waiting at home.' Amalia propped herself up on her elbows, she was not aware of a fiancée. K. mentioned the name, Amalia had never heard of her. She asked whether Olga knew of the engagement, K. thought she did, yes, in fact Olga had seen him with Frieda, anyway news like that spread rapidly in the village. However, Amalia assured him that Olga didn't know and that it would make her extremely unhappy since she appeared to be in love with K. She hadn't spoken about it openly because she was very reserved, but love gave itself away spontaneously, did it not. K. was sure Amalia was mistaken. Amalia smiled, and that smile, although sad, lit up the darkly furrowed face, made the silence voluble, made the remoteness familiar, was the divulgence of a secret, the surrender of a hitherto protected possession, which though it might be taken back could never be so entirely. Amalia said she was certainly not mistaken, in fact she knew something else, she knew that K. was himself fond of Olga and that his visits, made on the pretext of messages of some kind from Barnabas, were actually only for Olga's benefit. However, now that she knew everything, Amalia said, he need no longer be so strict about it and could come more often. That was all she'd wanted to say to him. K. shook his head and mentioned his engagement again. Amalia appeared not to waste much thought on this engagement, the immediate impression of K., who was the only person standing before her, was what mattered so far as she was concerned, she merely asked when K. had met the girl, he had only been in the village a few days. K. told her about the evening at the Count's Arms, to which Amalia simply said briefly that she had been very much against his being taken to the Count's Arms. She appealed to Olga to corroborate this, Olga who had just come in with an armful of wood, fresh, her face stung by the cold wind, lively and vigorous, as if transformed by physical labour in comparison with her previously leaden stance there in the room. She threw the wood down, gave K. an unembarrassed greeting, and promptly asked after Frieda. K. glanced at Amalia, but she did not seem to think she had been proved wrong. Slightly irritated by this, K. spoke of Frieda in greater detail than he would otherwise have done, described the difficult circumstances under which she was nevertheless keeping house after a fashion at the school, and so far forgot himself in his haste to tell his story – he was anxious to leave for home immediately – that by way of saying goodbye he invited the sisters to visit him some time. Here he did become alarmed and falter for a moment, while Amalia, leaving him no time to say another word, at once announced her acceptance of the invitation, then Olga had to chime in too and did so. K., however, still plagued by the thought of needing to make a swift getaway and feeling uncomfortable under Amalia's gaze, had no hesitation in admitting baldly that the invitation had been issued quite without thinking, prompted purely by his personal feelings, but that unfortunately he could not stand by it since there was great and, so far as he was concerned, wholly incomprehensible enmity between Frieda and the Barnabas household. 'It's not enmity,' Amalia said, getting up from the bench and flinging the blanket behind her, 'it's not that big a thing, it's an unthinking reflection of the general view, that's all. Off you go, then, go to your fiancée, I can see what a hurry you're in. And don't worry about us coming, I only meant it as a joke from the start, I only said it out of spite. You can visit us often, though, there's nothing to stop you doing that, you can always make Barnabas's messages your excuse. I'll make it even easier for you by saying that Barnabas, even if he does bring a message for you from the castle, can't go on to the school to report it to you. He can't do so much running about, poor lad, the job's eating him up, you'll have to come and fetch the news yourself.' K. had not heard Amalia say so much all of a piece before, also it sounded different from her usual speech, there was a kind of majesty in it that not only K. felt but obviously Olga too, her sister who was quite used to her, she was standing a little to one side, hands clasped before her, having resumed her usual spread-legged, slightly stooping posture, her eyes were fixed on Amalia, who was looking only at K. 'It's a mistake,' said K., 'a big mistake, your thinking that I'm not serious about waiting for Barnabas, sorting out my affairs with the authorities is my highest, in fact my only wish. And Barnabas is to help me do it, much of my hope is in him. He's already disappointed me badly once, I know, but that was more my fault than his, it happened in the confusion of the first few hours, I thought at the time that I could accomplish everything with a quick evening stroll, and when the impossible turned out to be just that, I blamed him. It even influenced me in judging your family, in judging you. That's behind me, I believe I understand you better now, in fact you're' – K. searched for the right word, did not find it immediately, and settled for an approximation – 'you're possibly better-natured than any of the other villagers, those I've met up to now. But look, Amalia, you're confusing me again by the way you make light, if not of your brother's work, certainly of its significance so far as I am concerned. Maybe you're not in on Barnabas's affairs, in that case, fine, I'll let the matter rest, but maybe you are – which is rather the impression I have – and that's bad, because it would mean your brother is deceiving me.' 'Don't worry,' said Amalia, 'I've not been initiated, nothing could persuade me to have myself initiated, nothing, not even regard for you, for whom there's a great deal I would do, because as you were saying we're good-natured folk. But my brother's affairs are his business, I know nothing about them except what I happen, willy-nilly, to hear now and then. Olga, on the other hand, can give you all the details, she's his confidante.' And Amalia walked away, going first to her parents, with whom she exchanged whispers, then into the kitchen; she had left K. without saying goodbye, as if she knew he would be staying a lot longer and no goodbye was necessary.

16

K. was left standing there, looking surprised, Olga laughed at him, pulled him over to the bench by the stove, she seemed really happy to be able to sit with him there alone now, but it was a peaceable happiness, quite unclouded by jealousy. And this very absence of jealousy and hence of any kind of intensity did K. good, he enjoyed looking into those blue, unseductive, unimperious, shyly reposeful, shyly steadfast eyes. It was as if the warnings of Frieda and the landlady had made him not more susceptible to everything here but more alert, more resourceful. And he laughed with Olga when she wondered why he had called Amalia of all people good-natured, Amalia was many things, she said, but good-natured was not actually one of them. At this, K. explained that the compliment had of course been intended for her, Olga, but that Amalia was so imperious, not only did she usurp for herself everything that was said in her presence but one also, spontaneously, assigned it to her. 'True,' said Olga, becoming more serious, 'in fact, truer than you think. Amalia is younger than me, younger than Barnabas too, but she's the one who makes the decisions in the family, in good times and in bad, she also carries more of it than the rest of us, of course, the good as well as the bad.' K. thought this exaggerated, hadn't Amalia just been saying that she didn't concern herself with their brother's affairs, for instance, whereas Olga knew all about them. 'How can I explain it?' Olga said, 'Amalia bothers neither about Barnabas nor about me, in fact she doesn't bother about anyone except our parents, she looks after them day and night, she was asking what they wanted just now and has gone into the kitchen to cook them something, it was for their sake she forced herself to get up, because she's been feeling unwell since noon and has been lying down on the bench here. Even so, despite her not bothering about us, we're governed by her as if she were the eldest, and if she were to give us advice regarding our affairs we'd certainly follow it, but she doesn't, we're strangers to her. Look, you have a lot of experience of people, you're from foreign parts, doesn't she also strike you as particularly shrewd?' 'She strikes me as particularly miserable,' said K., 'but how does it fit in with your awe of her that for example Barnabas does this messenger job that Amalia disapproves of, maybe even despises.' 'If he could think of something else to do, he'd quit the messenger job immediately, he gets no satisfaction out of it.' 'Isn't he a qualified shoemaker?' asked K. 'He is,' said Olga, 'in fact he even works for Brunswick on the side and would have work day and night if he wanted it and earn plenty.' 'Well, then,' said K., 'in that case he'd have an alternative to the messenger job.' 'To the messenger job?' asked Olga in amazement, 'you think he took that on for money?' 'Maybe,' said K., 'but surely you said something about it not satisfying him.' 'It doesn't satisfy him, and for a variety of reasons,' said Olga, 'but it is a castle job, a kind of castle job, anyway, so at least one's led to believe.' 'What do you mean?' said K., 'you even doubt that?' 'Well, no,' said Olga, 'not really, Barnabas goes to the offices, mixes with the servants on an equal footing, sees individual officials too, from a distance, has relatively important letters, indeed even messages for oral transmission entrusted to him, that's certainly a great deal and we could take pride in the way he's achieved so much at such an early age.' K. nodded, he had forgotten all about going home. 'Does he have his own livery as well?' he asked. 'You mean the jacket?' said Olga, 'no, Amalia made that for him before he became a messenger. But there you touch on the sore point. He should long since have been issued not with a livery, they don't have a livery in the castle, but with an official suit, he's been promised one, but they're very slow in the castle in that respect, and the trouble is, you never know what that slowness means; it may mean the matter's receiving official attention, but it may also mean the procedure has not even begun, in other words that, say, they still want to try Barnabas out first, but it may also, finally, mean the official procedure is already finished with, the promise has for some reason been withdrawn, and Barnabas will never get the suit. You can discover nothing more precise than that, or only after a long time. There's a saying here, perhaps you know it: "official decisions have the shyness of young girls".' 'That's a good observation,' K. said, taking it even more seriously than Olga, 'a good observation, the decisions may also have other properties in common with girls.' 'Possibly,' said Olga, 'though I don't know what you mean by that. You may even mean it as praise. But as regards the uniform, that's one of Barnabas's worries and, since we share our worries, also mine. Why does he not get a uniform, we ask ourselves in vain. But you see, this whole question is far from simple. Officials, for example, appear not to have a uniform at all; so far as we're aware here and from what Barnabas tells us, the officials go around in ordinary if rather splendid clothes. Well, you've seen Klamm. Now Barnabas, of course, is no official, not even of the lowest category, nor does he presume to aspire to be one. But even high-ranking servants, whom of course we never get to see here in the village, do not have official suits, according to Barnabas; that is some comfort, you might think at first, but it's deceptive, because is Barnabas a high-ranking servant? No, never mind how fond you are of him, you can't say that, he's not a high-ranking servant, the mere fact that he comes to the village, even lives here, is proof to the contrary, high-ranking servants are even more reserved than officials, perhaps rightly so, they may even outrank many officials, there's some evidence for that, they do less work, and according to Barnabas it's a marvellous sight to see these exceptionally tall, powerfully-built gentlemen slowly pacing the corridors, Barnabas always sneaks round them. In a word, there can be no question of Barnabas being a high-ranking servant. So maybe he's one of the lowlier servants, but they do have official suits, at least when they come down to the village they do, it's not a proper livery, also there are many variations, nevertheless the castle servant is instantly recognizable by his clothes, you've seen such people at the Count's Arms. The most striking thing about the clothes is that they're usually tight-fitting, a farmer or manual worker would have no use for such a garment. Well, Barnabas does not have one, which is worse than simply embarrassing or degrading, that one could stand, it makes you – particularly when times are bad, as they sometimes are, quite often in fact, for Barnabas and me – it makes you doubt everything. Is it even castle work that Barnabas does, we wonder then; all right, he goes to the offices, but are the offices the castle proper? And even if offices do belong to the castle, is it those offices Barnabas is allowed into? He's admitted to offices, but that's only part of it, then come barriers and beyond them there are other offices. He's not actually forbidden to proceed farther but he can't proceed any farther, can he, once he's found his superiors and they have dealt with him and dismiss him. Besides, you're under constant observation there, at least you have that impression. And even if he did proceed farther, what would be the use when he has no official business there and would be an intruder. And you mustn't think of the barriers as a definite dividing-line, that's something Barnabas is always drawing my attention to. There are barriers in the offices he enters too, so some barriers he passes and they look no different from the ones he's yet to surmount, which is another reason for not assuming from the outset that beyond those latter barriers lie fundamentally different offices from the ones Barnabas has already been in. Except that, when times are bad, that's just what you do think. And then the doubts go further, you can't help yourself. Barnabas talks to officials, Barnabas receives messages. But what sorts of official, what sorts of message are they. Now he's assigned to Klamm, he says, and is personally instructed by him. Well, that would certainly mean a lot, even high-ranking servants don't get that far, it would almost mean too much, that's the worrying thing. Think of it, being assigned directly to Klamm, speaking with him person to person. But is that really how it is? Well, yes it is, but why in that case does Barnabas doubt that the official referred to there as Klamm really is Klamm?' 'Olga,' said K., 'you're joking, surely; how can there be any doubt about Klamm's appearance, everyone knows what he looks like, I've seen him myself.' 'Not at all, K.,' said Olga, 'I'm not joking here, these are my deepest, deepest fears. But neither am I telling you this to lighten my heart and possibly burden yours but because you were asking after Barnabas, Amalia told me to tell you, and because I believe it's also useful for you to have more details. I'm doing it for Barnabas as well, to prevent you from placing too many hopes in him and him disappointing you and then suffering himself as a result of your disappointment. He's highly sensitive; for instance, he didn't sleep last night because you were unhappy with him yesterday evening, you apparently said it was very bad for you, "having only such a messenger as this", meaning Barnabas. Those words kept him awake, you hardly noticed how upset he was yourself, I expect, castle messengers have to keep themselves under tight control. But he doesn't have an easy time of it, even with you. I'm sure that, as you see it, you don't ask too much of him, you brought specific ideas about messenger work with you, and you gauge your requirements accordingly. But in the castle they have different ideas about messenger work, incompatible with yours, even if Barnabas were to sacrifice himself to the job utterly, as he seems prepared to do sometimes, more's the pity. We'd have to go along with that, couldn't raise any objection, were it not for the one question: is it really messenger work that he does? He can't voice doubts on the matter to you, of course, he'd be undermining his whole existence if he did that, grossly violating laws he believes still apply to him, and even with me he won't speak freely, I have to fondle and kiss his doubts out of him, and even then he'll not admit the doubts are doubts. There's a bit of Amalia in him. And he certainly doesn't tell me everything, despite my being the only one who's close to him. But we do occasionally talk about Klamm, I've not seen Klamm yet, Frieda doesn't much like me, as you know, and would never have given me that pleasure, but of course it's well-known in the village what he looks like, some people have seen him, everyone's heard of him, and from eye-witness accounts, rumours, and also a good many distorting ulterior motives a picture of Klamm has emerged that is probably correct in its essentials. Only in its essentials, though. Otherwise it varies, maybe not even as much as Klamm's actual appearance. Apparently, he looks quite different when he arrives in the village and different when he leaves it, different before he's been drinking beer, different afterwards, different awake, different asleep, different alone, different in conversation, and, understandably after all this, almost totally different up in the castle. And even within the village itself, fairly major differences are reported, differences of height, posture, girth, differences in his beard, only as regards clothing do the reports agree, fortunately, he's always wearing the same suit, a black two-piece with long tails. Well, all these differences are not of course due to magic, they're very understandable, arising out of the mood, degree of excitement, countless gradations of hope or despair in which the spectator, who in any case is usually permitted only a glimpse of Klamm, finds himself at the time, I'm telling you all this the way Barnabas has often explained it to me, and generally, if you're not directly involved in the case at a personal level, there's comfort to be had from it. Not for us, it's vitally important to Barnabas whether he's really talking to Klamm or not.' 'As it is to me,' said K., and they moved even closer together on the bench. While not unaffected by all Olga's bad news, K. saw some recompense largely in the fact that he found here people who, at least superficially, were in much the same situation as himself, with whom he could therefore ally himself, to whom he could talk about many matters, not just some, as with Frieda. True, he was gradually losing hope as regarded Barnabas's message succeeding, but the worse things went for Barnabas up there, the closer he came to him down here, K. would never have thought that even so sorry an endeavour as that of Barnabas and his sister could spring from the village. Of course, it was by no means fully explained as yet and might eventually turn into its converse, it was important not to let Olga's undoubtedly innocent nature promptly tempt one into believing that Barnabas was sincere, too. 'The reports about Klamm's appearance,' Olga went on, 'are very familiar to Barnabas, he's collected and compared a great many of them, possibly too many, he saw Klamm himself once in the village, through a carriage window, or thought he did, so he'd had adequate preparation for recognizing him, and yet – how do you explain this? – when he entered an office in the castle and they pointed out to him one official among a number, saying that was Klamm, he failed to recognize him and for a long time afterwards just could not accept that it really had been Klamm. But if you ask Barnabas how that man differs from the usual idea people have of Klamm, he can't answer, or rather he does answer and describes the official in the castle, but the description exactly matches the description of Klamm as we know him. "Come on, Barnabas," I say, "why these doubts, why do you torment yourself." At which he then, clearly distressed, starts to list peculiarities of the official in the castle, but giving the impression that he's inventing them more than reporting them, and anyway they're so minor – concerning a particular sort of nod, say, or simply the jacket being undone – that it's impossible to take them seriously. Even more significant, it seems to me, is the way Klamm is with Barnabas. Barnabas has often described this to me, even drawn it. Usually, Barnabas is shown into a large office, but it's not Klamm's office, it's not anyone's office in particular. The room is divided in two across its width by a single high desk running from wall to wall, there's a narrow part where two people can only just get past each other, that's the officials' space, and a wide part, which is for the parties, the spectators, the servants, the messengers. Lying open on the desk are great big books, one next to the other and with officials standing by most of them, reading. They don't stay with the same book all the time, though, but they change not books but places, the thing Barnabas finds most extraordinary is the way, when they're doing this, because of the narrowness of the space they have to squeeze past one another. Right in front of the desk are low tables where clerks sit who, when the officials require, write to their dictation. Barnabas is always amazed at how this happens. There's no explicit command from the official, nor is the dictating done aloud, you're scarcely aware that dictation is being given, the official appears to be reading as before, only he also whispers as he does so and the clerk picks it up. Often the official dictates so quietly that the writer can't hear at all sitting down, he has to keep jumping up to catch the words, sitting down again quickly to write, then jumping up, and so on. The whole thing is so peculiar! It's almost incomprehensible. Barnabas has plenty of time to take it all in, of course, because he stands there in the spectators' part of the room for hours and sometimes days on end before Klamm's eye falls on him. And even if Klamm has already spotted him and Barnabas is standing at attention, nothing is decided yet because Klamm may turn away from him, back to the book, and forget him, that often happens. But what kind of messenger service is it that matters so little? It saddens me to hear Barnabas say in the morning that he's off to the castle. The probably pointless journey, probably wasted day, probably empty hope. What's it all for! And here there's a pile of shoemaking work with no one to see to it and Brunswick insisting that it's done.' 'All right,' said K., 'Barnabas has to wait a long time before he's given a task. That's understandable, there seem to be too many people employed here, not all of them can be given a task every day, you needn't complain about that, presumably it applies to everyone. In the end, though, even Barnabas gets tasks, he's brought me two letters already.' 'Quite poss-ibly,' Olga said, 'we're wrong to complain, especially me, knowing everything as I do only from hearsay and also, as a girl, not being able to understand it as well as Barnabas, who also keeps quite a lot back, in fact. But now listen to what happens with the letters, with letters to you for instance. He receives those letters not from Klamm direct but from the clerk. On a certain day, any day, at a certain time, it can be any time – that's why, easy though the job appears, it's very tiring, because Barnabas has to be constantly on the alert – the clerk will think of him and beckon him. Klamm doesn't appear to be behind this at all, he's calmly reading his book, although sometimes, but this he does anyway from time to time, he's just polishing his pince-nez when Barnabas arrives and may glance at him as he does so, that's assuming he can see at all without his pince-nez, which Barnabas doubts, Klamm has his eyes nearly shut at such times, he looks as if he's asleep and polishing the pince-nez in a dream. Meanwhile the clerk searches among the many files and papers he has beneath the table for a letter for you, so it's not a letter he's just written, in fact from the look of the envelope it's a very old letter that has been lying there for ages. If it is an old letter, though, why has Barnabas been kept waiting for so long? And you too, presumably? And finally the letter as well, because presumably it's already obsolete. And the upshot is, Barnabas gets the reputation of being a poor messenger because a slow one. The clerk, incidentally, makes it easy for himself, hands Barnabas the letter, says: "Klamm to K." and with that Barnabas is dismissed. Well, Barnabas comes home, then, out of breath, the letter he has at last got hold of tucked inside his shirt against the bare skin, and we sit down on the bench here, as we are now, and he tells his story and we then study every detail and try to work out what he has achieved and in the end find it's very little and even that much is dubious, and Barnabas puts the letter on one side, he doesn't feel like delivering it, but neither does he feel like going to bed, he gets out the shoemaking work and spends the night there on the stool. That's how it is, K., and those are my secrets, and now I suppose you're no longer surprised at Amalia forgoing them.' 'And the letter?' asked K. 'The letter?' said Olga, 'well, after a while, when I've urged Barnabas enough, days and weeks may have passed in the meantime, he does pick up the letter and goes off to deliver it. In externals like that he's very dependent on me. You see I, once I've got over the initial impression of his story, can pull myself together again, which he, probably because he knows more, isn't able to do. That means I can always say to him something like: "What do you really want, then, Barnabas? What sort of career, what sort of goal do you dream of? Do you perhaps want to get so far that you have to abandon us, abandon me, altogether? Is that your aim? Isn't that what I'm forced to believe, because otherwise it would make no sense that you're so appallingly dissatisfied with what you've already achieved? Look around you, has any of our neighbours got so far? All right, they're in a different situation from us and have no call to aspire beyond it, but even without comparing, no one can deny that in your case everything is going superbly. There are obstacles, there are doubtful aspects, there are disappointments, but all that means is what we've known from the outset, that you'll get nothing handed to you on a plate but must fight for every iota yourself, yet another reason to be proud, not defeated. And then you're also fighting for us, right? Does that mean nothing to you? Doesn't it give you fresh strength? And the fact that I'm glad to have, am almost arrogant about having such a brother, doesn't that give you confidence? I tell you, it's not in what you've achieved in the castle but in what I've achieved with you that you disappoint me. You're admitted to the castle, you're a regular visitor to the offices, you spend whole days in the same room as Klamm, you're a publicly accepted messenger, you're entitled to a uniform, you're given important letters to deliver, you're all of that, you're allowed to do all those things, and you come back down and, instead of us lying in each other's arms, weeping with happiness, all your courage seems to desert you the minute you see me, you have doubts about everything, the only thing that tempts you is the shoemaker's last, and the letter, the guarantee of our future, you leave lying around." That's how I talk to him, and when I've repeated that for days on end, at some point he'll sigh, pick up the letter, and go. Only it's probably nothing to do with my words, he just gets the urge to return to the castle and without having performed the task he wouldn't dare to.' 'But surely you're also right in everything you tell him,' said K., 'it's marvellous, how accurately you've summed it all up. How amazingly clearly you think!' 'No,' said Olga, 'you're deceived, and maybe I deceive him in the same way. Because what has he achieved? He's allowed into an office, but apparently it's not even that, more an outer office for the offices proper, maybe not even that, maybe a room where all the people are to be detained who are not allowed in the actual offices. He talks to Klamm, but is it Klamm? Isn't it rather someone who simply looks like Klamm? A secretary, perhaps, if that, who looks a bit like Klamm and in his efforts to look even more like him pretends to be important in the dozy, daydreamy way Klamm does. That part of his character is the easiest to imitate, lots of people attempt it, the rest of his character they wisely keep away from. And a man so often aspired to and so seldom attained as Klamm easily takes on different forms in people's imaginations. For instance, Klamm has a village secretary here by the name of Momus. Really? You've met him? He's another very reserved person, though I have seen him a few times. A young man, powerfully built, right? In other words, he probably looks nothing like Klamm. Yet you can find people in the village who would swear on oath that Momus is Klamm and none other. That way, people contribute to their own confusion. And is it any different in the castle, necessarily? Someone told Barnabas that that official is Klamm, and there is indeed a resemblance between them, though it is a resemblance Barnabas always questions. And there's every reason for him to question it. Is Klamm supposed to have to squeeze into this public room amongst other officials, a pencil behind his ear? Surely that's most unlikely. Barnabas has the rather childish habit – he's got to be in a confident mood, though – of sometimes saying: "The official does look very like Klamm, if he had his own office, with a desk of his own and his name on the door – I'd no longer have any doubts." It is childish, but you can understand it. However, it would be a great deal easier to understand if, when up there, Barnabas asked a number of people straight out what was really going on, there are enough people standing about in the room, from what he says. And even if their statements were not much more reliable than that of the person who pointed Klamm out to him unasked, at least the diversity of them would inevitably throw up certain clues, certain points of comparison. The idea is not mine, it's Barnabas's, but he daren't carry it out; he's so afraid he might lose his job by unintentionally violating some obscure code, he doesn't dare speak to anyone; that's how unsure of himself he feels; it's that unsureness, which is pathetic, actually, that for me sheds more light on his position than any amount of description. How dubious and threatening everything must look to him there if he daren't even open his mouth to ask an innocent question. Thinking about it, I blame myself for leaving him on his own in those unfamiliar rooms, where things are such that even he, who's more daredevil than coward, probably quakes with fear.'

'There I think you hit on the crucial point,' said K. 'This is it. From all you've told me, I believe I see clearly now. Barnabas is too young for this job. Nothing of what he says can be taken seriously as it stands. He's scared to death up there, he can't take things in, and if he's forced even so to give an account down here, the result is a tangle of made-up stories. It doesn't surprise me. A deep respect for the authority is something you're all born with here, more of it gets instilled into you in all sorts of ways and from every direction throughout your lives, you also do your best to help the process along yourselves. Not that I'm saying anything against that, basically; if an authority is good, why shouldn't people respect it? Only you can't then take an uneducated youth like Barnabas, who has never set foot outside the village, suddenly dispatch him to the castle, and expect to get truthful reports out of him and analyse his every word as if it were a revelation and make your own future happiness hang on the interpretation. Nothing could be more wrong. I admit, I let him mislead me too, just as you did, I both placed hopes in him and suffered disappointments at his hands, neither on the basis of anything more than his words, which is to say virtually without foundation.' Olga said nothing. 'It's not going to be easy for me,' K. said, 'to shake your confidence in your brother, I can see how you love him and how much you expect of him. But it has to be done, not least because of your love and because of your expectations. Look, there's always something – I don't know what it is – that prevents you from acknowledging what Barnabas has not achieved, I don't say achieved, but been accorded. He's allowed in the offices or, if you like, in an outer office, all right, so there's an outer office, but it has doors that lead farther, barriers a person can pass through, given the skill. To me, for instance, that outer office is totally inaccessible, at least for the moment. Whom Barnabas talks to there I don't know, he may be the lowest of the servants, that clerk, but even if he is the lowest he may lead to the next one up, and if he can't lead to him he can at least give his name, and if he can't give his name he'll be able to point to someone who can give his name. The man alleged to be Klamm may not have the least thing in common with the real Klamm, the resemblance may exist only in Barnabas's eyes, blinded as they are by excitement, he may be the lowest of the officials, he may not even be an official, but he does have some kind of job at the desk there, he is reading something in his big book, he does whisper something to the clerk, something occurs to him when once in a long while his gaze falls on Barnabas, and even if none of this is true and he and his actions mean nothing at all, somebody put him there and did so with something in mind. What I'm trying to say in all this is that there's something there, something is being offered to Barnabas, something at least, and that only Barnabas is to blame if he can make nothing of it but doubt, dread, and despair. And I'm still assuming the least favourable case here, which seems highly unlikely. Because we do after all have the letters in our possession, not that I place much faith in them, but a lot more than I do in Barnabas's words. Even if they're old, worthless letters, pulled at random from a pile of equally worthless letters, at random and as mindlessly as fairground canaries peck a person's – any person's – fortune out of a heap, even if that is the case, at least these letters have something to do with my work, are clearly meant for me, if perhaps not for my benefit, were in fact, as the mayor and his wife have testified, personally written by Klamm, and possess, again according to the mayor, a significance that may be purely private and not particularly obvious but is nevertheless great.' 'The mayor said that?' Olga asked. 'He did,' replied K. 'I'll tell Barnabas,' Olga said quickly, 'that'll encourage him no end.' 'But he doesn't need encouraging,' said K., 'encouraging him is like telling him he's right, he has only to go on as before, but the fact is, he'll never achieve anything that way, if a person is blindfolded, no matter how much you encourage him to stare through the blindfold he'll never see a thing; only when the blindfold is removed will he be able to see. Barnabas needs help, not encouragement. Just think for a minute, up there is the authority in its inextricably complex magnitude – I thought I had some idea of it before I came here, how childish I was – there's the authority, then, and up to it comes Barnabas, no one else, only him, pitifully alone, he's already over-rewarded, not spending his whole life pushed into a dark corner of the offices, forgotten.' 'Rest assured, K.,' said Olga, 'we appreciate the difficulty of the job Barnabas has taken on. We're not lacking in respect for the authority, you said as much yourself.' 'But it's a misguided respect,' said K., 'respect in the wrong place, that kind of respect debases its object. Can you still call it respect when Barnabas abuses the gift of entry into that room to spend his days there doing nothing, or when he comes down and proceeds to suspect and disparage the very people in whose presence he has just been trembling, or when from despair or fatigue he doesn't deliver letters immediately and immediately pass on messages that have been entrusted to him? That's surely no longer respect. But the reproach goes beyond that, it touches you too, Olga, I can't pretend it doesn't, it was you, despite your belief that you respect the authority, who for all Barnabas's youth and frailty and friendlessness sent him off to the castle or at least didn't hold him back.'

'The reproach you level at me,' Olga said, 'is one I also level at myself, always have done. Though not that I sent Barnabas off to the castle, that's not what I'm to be reproached with, I didn't send him, he went himself, but you're right: I ought to have used every means, persuasion, guile, force, to hold him back. I ought to have held him back, but if today were that day, that crucial day, and I felt Barnabas's poverty, our family's poverty, as I did then and do now, and Barnabas once again, clearly aware of all the responsibility and danger, smiled and gently took leave of me to go, I shouldn't hold him back today either, despite everything I've experienced in the meantime, and I don't think you could have done any differently in my place. You don't know how poor we are, that's why you do us all, but mainly Barnabas, such injustice. We had more hope then than we do today, but even then we didn't have a lot of hope, the only thing we had a lot of was poverty, still is. Didn't Frieda tell you anything about us?' 'Only hints,' said K., 'nothing specific, but just your name upsets her.' 'And the landlady said nothing, either?' 'No, nothing.' 'Nor anyone else?' 'No one.' 'Of course not, how could anyone have said anything? They all know something about us, either the truth, so far as people have access to it, or at least some rumour that they've adopted or usually invented themselves, and they all think about us more than they need, but no one will actually say anything, they shrink from mentioning such things. And they're right. It's difficult to come out with it, even to you, K., and isn't there then a chance, too, that when you've heard it you'll go away and not want to hear of us again, however little it seems to concern you. Then we'll have lost you, you who, I'll be honest with you, mean almost more to me than Barnabas's castle work did before. And yet – the contradiction has haunted me all evening – it's something you must learn, because otherwise you'll have no overall view of our situation, you'll continue, this would particularly hurt me, to be unfair to Barnabas, we'd lack the total unity we need, and you could neither help us nor accept our help, unofficially speaking. But there's still one question: do you in fact want to know?' 'Why do you ask?' said K., 'if it's necessary, I want to know, but why do you ask like that?' 'Superstition,' said Olga, 'you'll be drawn into our affairs, innocently so, not much more to blame than Barnabas.' 'Hurry up and tell me,' said K., 'I'm not afraid. Anyway, with your womanish timidity you're making it worse than it is.'

17

AMALIA'S SECRET

'Judge for yourself,' said Olga, 'actually, it sounds very simple, it's not immediately obvious how it can be of any great importance. There's an official in the castle called Sortini.' 'I've heard of him,' said K., 'he was involved in my appointment.' 'I doubt it,' said Olga, 'Sortini hardly ever appears in public. Aren't you getting confused with Sordini, with a "d"?' 'You're right,' said K., 'it was Sordini.' 'Yes,' Olga said, 'Sordini is very well-known, one of the hardest-working officials, he's much talked about, Sortini is different, extremely retiring and a stranger to most people. I saw him for the first and last time more than three years ago. It was the third of July, at a fire-brigade gala, the castle had also got involved, donating a new fire-engine. Sortini, who apparently has something to do with fire-brigade matters, though he may just have been there as a stand-in – the officials usually stand in for one another, which makes it difficult to know what a particular official's responsibility is – took part in the handing-over of the fire-engine, other people from the castle were there too, of course, officials and servants, and Sortini, true to his nature, was very much in the background. He's a short, frail-looking, pensive gentleman, one thing that struck everyone who noticed him at all was the way his forehead wrinkled, all the wrinkles – and he had lots, although he's certainly not above forty – ran in straight lines across his forehead towards the bridge of his nose, forming a fan, I've never seen anything like it. Well, that was the fire-brigade gala. Amalia and I had been looking forward to it for weeks, some of our Sunday clothes had been spruced up, Amalia's outfit in particular was very beautiful, the white blouse billowing out in front with layers and layers of lace, mother had lent all her lace for the purpose, I was jealous at the time and cried half the night before the gala. It was only when the landlady from the Bridge Inn came to inspect us next morning –' 'The landlady from the Bridge Inn?' asked K. 'Yes,' said

Olga, 'she was a great friend of ours, she arrived, then, had to admit that Amalia had the edge, and so, to pacify me, lent me her own necklace of Bohemian garnets. As we stood ready to go out, however, Amalia in front of me, all of us admiring her and father saying: "Today, mark my words, Amalia will find a husband", I suddenly, I don't know why, took off the necklace, my pride and joy, and put it on Amalia, not a bit jealous any more. I was bowing to her victory, do you see, and I was sure everyone would bow before her; we were surprised, perhaps, that she looked different from usual, because she wasn't actually beautiful, not really, but her sombre look, which she's kept the same ever since, passed high above our heads and we almost literally and from instinct bowed down before her. Everyone noticed it, even Lasemann and his wife, who came to fetch us.' 'Lasemann?' asked K. 'Yes, Lasemann,' said Olga, 'we were much respected, you see, the gala could scarcely have started without us, for instance, because father was number-three instructor in the fire-brigade.' 'Your father was still so sprightly?' asked K. 'Father?' asked Olga as if not quite understanding, 'three years ago he was still almost a young man, when there was a fire at the Count's Arms, for example, he carried an official, a heavy man, Galater, out on his back at the double. I was there myself, there was no danger of the building going up, it was just the dry wood beside a stove that started smoking, but Galater became anxious, called from the window for help, the fire-brigade arrived, and my father had to carry him from the building, even though the fire was already out. Galater isn't an agile man, you see, and needs to be careful in such cases. The only reason I'm telling you this is because of my father, not much more than three years have passed since then and now see how he sits there.' Only at this point did K. notice that Amalia was back in the room, but she was a long way off, by the parents' table, she was feeding her mother, who had no movement in her rheumatic arms, and talking to her father as she did so, asking him to be patient for his food a little longer, she would be with him in a moment and feed him too. Her urging was unsuccessful, however, for her father, now very keen to get at his soup, conquered his weakness in an attempt first to slurp the soup from his spoon, then to drink it straight from the bowl, and muttered angrily when he could manage neither the one thing nor the other, the spoon was empty long before reaching his mouth and it was never his lips, always only his drooping moustache that dipped in the soup and dripped and sprayed it everywhere except into his mouth. 'Three years have done that to him?' K. asked, but still he felt no compassion for the old people and for that whole corner of the family table, only revulsion. 'Three years,' Olga said slowly, 'or more precisely, a couple of hours at one gala. The festivities were held in a field beyond the village, down by the stream, there was already a huge crowd when we arrived, lots of people had come from neighbouring villages as well, the noise was overwhelming. First, of course, father took us to see the fire-engine, he laughed with delight when he saw it, a new fire-engine made him happy, he began touching it and telling us about it, he'd not be contradicted and tolerated no lack of enthusiasm from others, if there was something to be inspected beneath the fire-engine we all had to bend down and virtually crawl under it, Barnabas, who refused, got a thrashing. Only Amalia showed no interest in the fire-engine, she just stood there in her beautiful outfit and no one dared say anything to her, I ran to her occasionally and took her arm, but she said nothing. To this day I can't explain how it happened that we were standing by the fire-engine for so long and it was only when father detached himself from it that we became aware of Sortini, who had clearly been leaning on a pump-handle behind the fire-engine all the time. The noise was dreadful, admittedly, worse than at most galas; you see, the castle had also presented the fire-brigade with a number of trumpets, special instruments on which with a minimum of effort, a child could do it, the most savage sounds could be produced; listening, you thought the Turks were invading, and there was no getting used to the din, each fresh blast made you jump like the first time. And because the trumpets were new, everyone wanted to try them out, and it being a gala they were able to. Just where we were, maybe Amalia had attracted them, there were several folk blowing away, it was a job to keep your wits together, and if you were also, father insisted on it, meant to be paying attention to the fire-engine, that was as much as you could manage, which is why we'd not noticed Sortini, whom in any case we'd never met previously, for such an unusually long time. "There's Sortini," I eventually heard Lasemann, I was standing with them, whisper to father. Father bowed low, making frantic signals to us to bow too.

Without having met him before, father had always had a great deal of respect for Sortini as an expert in fire-brigade matters and had often mentioned him at home, so it was a big surprise and an important moment for us, seeing Sortini in the flesh like this. But Sortini took no notice of us, not that this was anything peculiar to Sortini, most officials appear apathetic in public, also he was tired, only his official duty was keeping him down here, nor are they the worst officials who find just such public duties particularly irksome, other officials and servants, now that they were there, circulated among the villagers, but he stayed by the fire-engine, and anyone who tried to approach him with a request of some kind or a flattering remark he repulsed by his silence. As a result, he took even longer to became aware of us than we had of him. It was only when we bowed respectfully and father attempted to apologize on our behalf that he looked at us, looked us over one after another, wearily, as if sighing that, after each one, there invariably came another, until his gaze reached Amalia, at whom he had to look up, she was much taller than he was. He gave a sudden start, leapt over the shafts to get closer to Amalia, we misunderstood at first and all tried to approach him, led by father, but he held us at a distance with an upraised hand and then waved us away. That was it. Afterwards, we teased Amalia a lot, saying now she really had found a husband, we were foolish enough to be very happy all afternoon, though Amalia was quieter than ever, "oh, she's fallen well and truly in love with Sortini," said Brunswick, who's always a bit coarse and has no feeling for people like Amalia, but this time his remark struck us as just about right, we were rather silly that day altogether and except for Amalia all in a bit of a daze from the sweet castle wine when we got home after midnight.' 'And Sortini?' asked K. 'Right, Sortini,' said Olga, 'I saw Sortini in passing several more times during the gala, he was sitting on the shafts with his arms folded across his chest, and that was how he stayed until the castle carriage arrived to fetch him. He didn't even attend the fire-brigade drills, in which father, hoping that Sortini was watching, did strikingly better than all the men of his age.' 'And have you not heard from him since?' asked K. 'You seem to have a great admiration for Sortini.' 'Admiration, yes,' said Olga, 'I do, and we did hear from him again. Next morning we were roused from a heavy sleep by a cry from Amalia, the others slumped back under the covers immediately but I was wide awake and ran to Amalia, she was standing by the window holding a letter that a man had just handed her through the window, the man was still there, waiting for a reply. Amalia had read the letter – it wasn't a long one – already and was holding it in a hand that dangled loosely; how I loved her whenever she was weary like that. I knelt beside her and read the letter. I'd just finished when Amalia, after a quick glance at me, raised it to her eyes again but could no longer bring herself to read it, tore it up, threw the pieces at the man outside, hitting him in the face, and closed the window. That was the crucial morning. I call it crucial, but that instant the previous afternoon had been equally crucial.' 'And what did the letter say?' K. asked. 'Right, I haven't told you that yet,' said Olga, 'the letter was from Sortini, addressed to the girl with the garnet necklace. I can't give you the exact wording. It was a request that Amalia come to him at the Count's Arms, immediately, because in half an hour Sortini had to leave. The letter was written in the most vulgar language, using expressions I'd never come across before and only half guessed at from the context. A person who, not knowing Amalia, had read only that letter would feel inevitably that the girl whom someone dared address in such terms was dishonoured, even if she'd apparently not been touched. And it was not a love letter, there were no compliments in it, in fact Sortini was clearly angry that the sight of Amalia had so stirred him, keeping him from his business. We worked out later that Sortini had probably intended to drive to the castle that evening, had only stayed in the village because of Amalia, and in the morning, furious that even during the night he'd not been able to forget Amalia, had written the letter. Faced with that letter, even the most cool-headed person's first reaction had to be indignation, but subsequently, in anyone else but Amalia, no doubt fear would have gained the upper hand, fear at the angry, threatening tone, Amalia was simply indignant, she knows no fear, not for herself, not for others. And as I then crept back into bed, saying the incomplete final sentence over to myself: "So be sure to come immediately, otherwise –!" Amalia remained on the window seat, looking out, as if she expected further messengers and was prepared to treat them all exactly as she had the first.' 'That's what the officials are like, then,' K. said hesitantly, 'they include specimens like that. What did your father do? I hope he lodged a vigorous complaint about

Sortini in the right quarter, if he didn't prefer the shorter, more certain course of a visit to the Count's Arms. The ugliest thing of all about the episode isn't the insult to Amalia, is it, that would be easy to put right, I don't see why you stress that particular aspect so inordinately; why should Sortini have permanently compromised Amalia with a letter like that, from your account one might think he had, but it's simply not possible, making amends to Amalia would have been easy and in a few days the incident would have been forgotten, Sortini didn't compromise Amalia, he compromised himself. So it's Sortini that scares me, the way such an abuse of power is possible. What failed in this case because it was put in plain terms and was totally transparent and because it found, in Amalia, a superior opponent, may in a thousand other cases, given only slightly less favourable circumstances, be totally successful and escape everyone's notice, even that of the person being abused.' 'Quiet,' said Olga, 'Amalia's looking this way.' Amalia had finished feeding the parents and was now busy undressing her mother, she had just loosened her skirt and proceeded to hang her mother's arms around her neck, lift her a little way in that position, pull the skirt off, and lower her gently back down. Her father, still unhappy about mother being attended to first, though clearly the only reason why this happened was that she was the more helpless of the two, now tried, perhaps partly to punish his daughter for what he felt was her slowness, to undress himself, but in spite of his beginning with the easiest, least necessary items, the enormous slippers in which his feet were only loosely encased, he simply could not get them off, he was soon wheezing hoarsely, had to give up, and leaned back stiffly in his chair. 'You're missing the crux of the matter,' Olga said, 'you may be right in everything you say, but the crux of the matter was that Amalia did not go to the Count's Arms; the way she'd treated the messenger, that she might have got away with, it could have been hushed up; but the fact that she didn't go laid a curse on our family, and because of that the treatment of the messenger also became something unpardonable, in fact for the public it was even thrust into the foreground.' 'What!' K. exclaimed, promptly lowering his voice when Olga gestured imploringly, 'surely you, as her sister, aren't saying Amalia should have done what Sortini said and gone running to the Count's Arms?' 'No,' said Olga, 'may it never be suspected of me, how could you think such a thing. I know no one so firmly in the right as Amalia in everything she does. If she had gone to the Count's Arms, I'd have thought her right too, of course; however, her not going was heroic. Personally, I'll be honest with you, if I had received such a letter I'd have gone. I couldn't have borne the fear of the future, only Amalia could do that. There were plenty of alternatives, after all, someone else might have got herself up really beautifully, say, and it would have taken some time, and she would have arrived at the Count's Arms to learn that Sortini had already left, possibly that he'd driven off immediately after dispatching the messenger, in fact that's highly likely, the gentlemen's whims are short-lived. But Amalia didn't do that or anything like it, she was too deeply insulted and answered without reserve. If she'd just made some pretence of obeying, just crossed the threshold of the Count's Arms at the right moment, the disaster might have been averted, we have very clever lawyers here, capable of taking nothing and turning it into whatever you like, but in this case there wasn't even a nothing in our favour, quite the opposite, we were left with the dishonouring of Sortini's letter and the insulting of the messenger.' 'But what do you mean, a disaster,' said K., 'what lawyers; surely Amalia couldn't be charged, much less punished, because of Sortini's criminal behaviour?' 'She could,' said Olga, 'and was, not in the context of a proper trial, of course, nor was she punished directly, but she was punished in another way, she and our whole family, and how hard that punishment is you're no doubt now beginning to see. To you it seems unjust and monstrous, in the village that's a quite isolated opinion, it's greatly in our favour and ought to be a comfort to us, and so it would if it didn't clearly spring from errors. I can prove that to you easily, forgive me mentioning Frieda in this context but, apart from the way things turned out eventually, something very similar occurred between Frieda and Klamm as occurred between Amalia and Sortini, and yet you find, even though you may have been alarmed to begin with, that's now quite all right. And it's not habit does that, a person won't become so inured through habit in a matter of simple judgement; it's just shedding errors.' 'No, Olga,' said K., 'I don't know why you bring Frieda into this, hers was another case entirely, don't confuse such utterly different things, just go on with your story.' 'I'm sorry,' said Olga, 'don't be cross with me if I insist on the comparison, it's a residue of errors in this case regarding Frieda that makes you think you have to defend her against a comparison. She doesn't need defending, she deserves nothing but praise. When I compare the two cases, I'm not saying they're the same, they relate to each other like white and black, white being Frieda. At worst a person can laugh at Frieda the way I was rude enough – I deeply regretted it later – to do in the bar, but even someone laughing here is either spiteful or envious, still, a person can laugh, but Amalia, if you're not tied to her by blood, can only be despised. That's why, although the cases are utterly different, as you say, in fact they're also similar.' 'They're not even similar,' said K., shaking his head indignantly, 'leave Frieda out of this. Frieda received no pretty letter like Amalia had from Sortini, and Frieda really loved Klamm, anyone in doubt can ask her, she loves him to this day.' 'Are those major differences, though?' asked Olga. 'Don't you think Klamm might have written to Frieda in the same way? When the gentlemen get up from their desks, that's the way they are; they don't know how to cope with the world; in their absent-mindedness, they then say the coarsest things, not all, but many of them. Look, the letter to Amalia may have been dashed down on paper in thought form, quite without regard to what was actually written. What do we know of the gentlemen's thoughts! Haven't you heard yourself or heard tell of the tone Klamm used with Frieda? Klamm's known to be extremely coarse, he can be silent for hours, apparently, then all of a sudden come out with something so coarse it makes you shudder. Sortini's not known for that, in fact very little is known about him altogether. Actually, the only thing we do know is that his name resembles Sordini's; but for that similarity of name, he'd probably never have been heard of. Even as a fire-brigade expert, people probably confuse him with Sordini, the actual expert, who exploits the similarity of name to unload particularly his public-appearance duties on Sortini, enabling him to get on with his work undisturbed. Well, when a man as unversed in the ways of the world as Sortini is suddenly seized with love for a village girl, naturally it takes different forms from when the joiner's mate next door falls in love. Another thing you need to bear in mind is that between an official and a shoemaker's daughter there's a big gap that must somehow be bridged, Sortini tried to do it this way, another man might go about it differently. I know they say we all belong to the castle and there is no gap and nothing to be bridged, and it may well be true in the normal course of events but we, unfortunately, have had occasion to see that, just when it matters, it's not true at all. Anyway, after all that, Sortini's conduct will be easier for you to understand, less monstrous, and indeed it is, compared with Klamm's, much more understandable and even for those intimately involved much easier to bear. When Klamm writes a tender letter, it's more embarrassing than the coarsest letter of Sortini's. Don't get me wrong, I'm not passing judgement on Klamm, I wouldn't dare do that, I'm simply comparing, because you won't have any comparison. Klamm is like a commanding officer with women, ordering this one or that one to come to him, not tolerating any of them for long, and as he orders their coming, also ordering them to go. Oh no, Klamm wouldn't even bother to write a letter first. Now then, compared to that, is it still so monstrous if Sortini, who lives in complete seclusion, whose feelings for women are at best unknown, sits down one day and in his fine official hand writes what I admit was a shocking letter? And if no difference emerges here in Klamm's favour, quite the reverse, how is Frieda's love going to make it do so? Women's relations with the officials are, believe me, very hard or rather always very easy to judge. There's no shortage of love here, not ever. There is no such thing, for officials, as unrequited love. In this respect it's no compliment when they say of a girl – I'm not just talking about Frieda here, far from it – that she gave herself to the official only because she loved him. She loved him and she gave herself to him, that's how it was, there's no place for praise. Ah, you'll object, but Amalia didn't love Sortini. All right, she didn't love him, but maybe she did love him in fact, who can tell? Not even she can. How could she think she loved him when she rejected him so firmly, probably more firmly than any official was ever rejected before. Barnabas says she still trembles sometimes, even now, from the movement with which she slammed that window three years ago. It's true too, and it's why we can't ask her; she's finished with Sortini, that's all she knows; whether she loves him or not, that she doesn't know. We know, though, that women can't help loving officials, once the officials turn their attention to them, in fact even before, try as they may to deny it, and Sortini didn't just turn his attention to Amalia, did he, he leapt over the shafts when he saw Amalia, with his legs all stiff from desk work he leapt over the shafts. But Amalia's an exception, you'll say. She is, yes, she showed that when she refused to go to Sortini, that's exceptional enough; but the suggestion that she didn't even love Sortini, well, that would be almost too exceptional, that would defy belief. We were struck blind that afternoon, I know, but the fact that we did at the time, through all the mist, believe we sensed something of Amalia's being in love, surely that shows we had some of our wits about us. But when you look at all that together, what difference is left between Frieda and Amalia? Only that Frieda did what Amalia refused to do.' 'Possibly,' said K., 'for me, though, the main difference is that Frieda's my fiancée, while Amalia, when all's said and done, concerns me only in so far as she is Barnabas's sister, Barnabas is a castle messenger, and her fate may be intertwined with Barnabas's job. If an official had done her so glaring an injustice as I initially, from your account, believed to be the case, that would have weighed on my mind, but even then far more as a public issue than as a personal misfortune of Amalia's. Now, though, from your account, the picture's changing in a way I'll admit I don't entirely understand but, since it's you doing the telling, I find sufficiently credible, so I'll be delighted to overlook the matter completely, I'm not a fireman, what do I care about Sortini. I care about Frieda, though, which is why I find it strange that you, whom I trusted completely and shall be happy to go on trusting, should keep trying, through Amalia, to mount indirect attacks on Frieda and make me suspicious about her. I don't suppose you do it on purpose, or even with malice aforethought, otherwise I'd have had to leave long since, you're not doing it on purpose, circumstances encourage you to do it, your love of Amalia makes you want to elevate her to a position high above all women, and not finding enough praiseworthy features in Amalia herself, you resort to belittling other women. What Amalia did is remarkable, but the more you talk about it the less one's able to decide whether it was a lot or a little, clever or stupid, heroic or cowardly, Amalia keeps her motives locked in her heart, no one's going to get them out of her. Frieda, on the other hand, did nothing remarkable at all but simply obeyed her feelings, that much is clear to anyone taking a well-meaning interest, anyone can verify it, there's no room for gossip. I'm not trying either to disparage Amalia or to defend Frieda but simply to explain to you how I stand towards Frieda and how any attack on Frieda is an attack on my own existence. I came here of my own volition, and it's of my own volition that I've got caught up here, but all that's happened since and above all my future prospects – gloomy they may be but they still exist – I owe it all to Frieda, no amount of talking will alter that. All right, I was taken on here as a land surveyor, but that was mere pretence, I was a plaything, I was driven from every house, I'm still a plaything now, but how much more elaborate it is, I've gained in substance, as it were, and that certainly means something; after all, insignificant though it may all be, I've got a home, a job with real work to do, I have a fiancée who, when I'm on other business, relieves me of my professional obligations, I shall marry her and become a member of the community, I have not only my official relationship to Klamm but also a personal relationship, though it's one I've not been able to exploit as yet. That's quite something, is it not? And when I come to you people, who is it you welcome? Olga, who is it you're confiding the history of your family to? Who is it you're looking to for the possibility, however minute, however unlikely, of some kind of help? Surely not to me, the land surveyor, whom only a week ago, for example, Lasemann and Brunswick threw out of their house, you're looking to the man who already has some sort of power, but you see, I owe that power to Frieda, Frieda who's so modest that, if you were to quiz her on the subject, would certainly not claim to know anything about it. And yet it would appear from all this that Frieda has done more in her innocence than Amalia in all her arrogance, because do you know, it's my impression you're looking for help for Amalia. And from whom? None other, as it happens, than Frieda.' 'Was I really being so horrible about Frieda?' Olga asked, 'I certainly didn't mean to be, nor did I think I was, but I may have been, it's in the nature of our situation that we've fallen out with everyone, and if we start complaining, we get carried away, we don't know where we'll end up. And you're right, there is a big difference now between us and Frieda, and it's good that that should be highlighted for once. Three years ago, we were nice middle-class girls and Frieda, the orphan, was a maid at the Bridge Inn, we'd pass her in the street without a glance, we were too proud, undoubtedly, but it was the way we'd been brought up. That evening at the Count's Arms, though, you may have seen how things stand currently: Frieda wielding a whip and me amid the crowd of hands. But in fact they're even worse. Frieda may despise us, that tallies with her position, present circumstances compel her to. But then who doesn't despise us! Anyone who decides to despise us immediately has company, plenty of it. Do you know the girl who's taken Frieda's place? She's called Pepi. I met her two evenings ago for the first time, she used to be a chambermaid. She outdoes Frieda, I'm sure of it, in despising me. She saw me from the window as I arrived to buy beer, she ran to the door and bolted it, I had to beg for ages and promise her the ribbon I was wearing in my hair before she let me in. But then when I gave it to her, she tossed it in the corner. Well, me she may despise, to some extent I'm dependent on her goodwill and she is the barmaid at the Count's Arms, only temporarily, of course, she surely lacks the necessary qualities to be employed there on a permanent basis. You only have to listen to the way the landlord talks to Pepi and compare it with the way he used to talk to Frieda. But that doesn't stop Pepi despising Amalia too, when a mere glance from Amalia would make little Pepi, with all her bows and pigtails, quit the room faster than she'd ever have managed just on her short chubby legs. What a scandalous load of gossip I had to hear from her again yesterday on the subject of Amalia before eventually the customers took care of me, even if it was in the way you've already seen on one occasion.' 'You're so afraid,' said K., 'all I was doing was giving Frieda the place she deserves, I wasn't trying to talk down your family the way you're taking it now. There's something special about your family for me too, I've made no secret of that; but how that something special could ever give rise to contempt, that I don't under-stand.' 'Oh K.,' said Olga, 'you will, I'm afraid, even you will come to understand it; can you just not see that it was Amalia's behaviour towards Sortini that first occasioned that contempt?' 'But that would be too peculiar,' said K., 'Amalia might be admired for that reason or condemned, but despised? And if as a result of some feeling I don't understand people do despise Amalia, why extend that contempt to the rest of you, the innocent family? For instance, Pepi despising you, Olga, is really a bit strong, and I intend to have it out with her on my next visit to the Count's Arms.' 'Look, K.,' said Olga, 'if you wanted to dissuade all the people who despise us, you'd have a difficult job, because it all stems from the castle. I still remember exactly what happened later that morning. Brunswick, who was our assistant at the time, had arrived as he did every day, father had given him some work and sent him home, we then sat down to breakfast, everyone except Amalia and myself was very animated, father went on and on about the gala, he had various plans regarding the fire-brigade, the castle has its own fire-brigade, you know, which had also sent a delegation to the gala, there had been a lot of discussion with them, the gentlemen who were there from the castle had seen what our fire-brigade could do, spoken of it very favourably, looked at the performance of the castle fire-brigade in comparison, the outcome was in our favour, there'd been talk of the need to reorganize the castle fire-brigade, which would require instructors from the village, various people were considered for this but father had hopes of the choice falling on him. That's what he was talking about, then, and in that lovely way he had of really spreading himself at table, he sat there with his arms taking up half the tabletop, and as he gazed through the open window up at the sky his face was so young and hopeful, I was never to see him like that again. Suddenly, with a haughtiness we didn't recognize in her, Amalia said no one should place much faith in such talk on the gentlemen's part, they liked to come out with something pleasant on occasions like that, but it meant little or nothing at all, it was forgotten for ever as soon as spoken, though people were taken in by them again, of course, on the next occasion. Mother scolded her for such talk, father simply laughed at her precociousness and air of worldly wisdom, but then he hesitated, seemed to be looking for something he'd only just noticed was missing, only there was nothing missing, and said Brunswick had mentioned something about a messenger and a letter being torn up, and he asked whether we knew anything about it, who had been involved, and how things stood now. We said nothing, Barnabas, who was then a young lambkin, made some particularly silly or cheeky remark, the talk turned to other things, and the matter was forgotten.'

18

AMALIA'S PUNISHMENT

'But before long we were being bombarded with questions about the letter business from all sides, friends and enemies came, acquaintances and strangers, they didn't stay long, though, the best friends leaving in the biggest hurry, Lasemann, normally always slow and dignified, came in as if he simply wished to check the dimensions of the room, one look around and he'd finished, it was like some awful children's game when Lasemann took to his heels and father, disengaging himself from some other people, went hurrying after him as far as the threshold of the house and there gave up, Brunswick came and gave father notice, he wanted to set up on his own, he said quite sincerely, smart fellow, he knew when to seize the moment, customers came and started searching father's storeroom for boots that they'd left to be mended, at first father tried to change the customers' minds – and we all backed him up as best we could – later he gave up trying and in silence helped the customers look, line after line was crossed out in the order book, the stocks of leather that people had with us were handed over, debts settled, it all passed off without the least argument, people were happy if they could sever the connection with us swiftly and completely, even if they made a loss doing it, that didn't matter. And finally, as might have been predicted, Seemann appeared, the chief of the fire-brigade, I can picture the scene even now, Seemann tall and powerfully-built but with a slight stoop and tubercular, invariably serious, he's incapable of laughter, standing in front of my father, whom he admired, to whom in a moment of familiarity he had held out the prospect of becoming deputy fire chief, and having now to tell him that the association is discharging him and wants its diploma back. The folk who were in the house at the time left off what they were doing and pressed in a circle around the two men. Seemann is speechless, just keeps tapping father on the shoulder as if trying to tap out of father the words he should be saying himself and cannot find. And all the time he's laughing, presumably in an attempt to calm himself and everyone else down a bit, but since he's incapable of laughing and no one has ever heard him laugh before, no one thinks for a moment that it is laughter. But father's already too tired and desperate from the day to be able to help Seemann out, in fact he seems too tired even to wonder what's going on. We were all of us similarly desperate, I know, but being young we simply couldn't believe in so complete a collapse, we kept thinking that in the stream of visitors eventually someone would come who would call a halt and make everything go into reverse. In our ignorance, Seemann seemed to us just the man for this. We waited eagerly for that constant laughter to give way at last to a clear command. Because what was there to laugh about at that moment, surely only the stupid injustice being done to us. Mr Fire Chief, Mr Fire Chief, get on and tell the people, we thought as we pressed around him, but this only made him launch into curious twisting motions. In the end, though, not so much to satisfy our secret wishes as in response to people's encouraging or irritating yells, he did begin to speak. We were still hopeful. He started by heaping praise on father. Called him a credit to the association, a matchless exemplar for the younger generation, an irreplaceable member whose retirement would inevitably almost bring the association down. That was all very fine, if he'd ended there. But he went on. The fact that the association had nevertheless decided to ask father, if only provisionally, to seek a discharge indicated the gravity of the reasons compelling the association to take this step. It was possible that, without father's dazzling achievements at the previous day's gala, things would not have had to come to this, but it was those very achievements that had particularly attracted official attention, the association was now very much in the spotlight and must be even more mindful of its purity than before. And now there'd been the insult to the messenger, the association had been left with no alternative, and he, Seemann, had taken upon himself the difficult task of announcing that fact. He hoped father was not going to make it even more difficult for him. How glad Seemann was to have got this out, in his satisfaction at having done so he was not even overly considerate any more, he pointed to the diploma hanging on the wall and beckoned with a finger. Father nodded and went to fetch it, but with his trembling hands couldn't get it off the hook, I climbed on a chair and helped him. And from that moment, it was all over, he didn't even remove the diploma from the frame but gave the whole thing to Seemann as it was. Then he sat down in a corner, did not stir and spoke to no one any more, we had to negotiate with people on our own as best we could.' 'And where do you see the influence of the castle in this?' asked K. 'There's no sign of it having intervened as yet. What you've talked about so far was simply people's mindless apprehension, delight at a neighbour's downfall, unreliable friendship, things that are found everywhere, and also, incidentally, on your father's part – so it seems to me, at least – a certain pettiness, because what was it, that diploma? Confirmation of his abilities and they were surely still his, if they rendered him indispensable so much the better, and the only way he'd have made things really difficult for the fire chief is if he'd tossed the diploma at his feet as soon as he started speaking. But what seems to me particularly significant is the fact that you don't even mention Amalia; Amalia, who was to blame for the whole thing, probably stood quietly in the background, watching the devastation.' 'No, no,' said Olga, 'no one should be criticized, no one could have acted any differently, it was castle influence, the whole thing.' 'Castle influence,' repeated Amalia, who had come in from the yard unnoticed, the parents were long since in bed, 'is someone telling castle stories? You two still sitting together? And you meant to leave immediately, K., and now it's almost ten. Can you even be bothered with such stories? There are people here who feed off stories like that, they sit down together the way you two are sitting here and regale each other with them. You don't strike me as one of those people, though.' 'Oh I am,' said K., 'that's just what I am, one of them, whereas people who can't be bothered with such stories and leave it to others, they don't impress me very much.' 'I see,' said Amalia, 'but people's interests vary enormously, don't they, I once heard of a young man who was preoccupied with thoughts about the castle day and night, he neglected everything else, people feared for his sanity because his whole mind was up there in the castle, but in the end it turned out he'd not actually meant the castle at all, merely the daughter of a woman who does washing-up in the offices, he got her, by the way, and everything was all right again.' 'I think I'd like the fellow,' said K.

'I doubt whether you would,' said Amalia, 'you might like his wife, though. Well, don't let me disturb you but I'm going to bed, and I'll need to turn out the light because of the parents, I know they fall fast asleep immediately, but after an hour their proper sleep is over and the least glimmer disturbs them. Good night.' And indeed, there was darkness immediately, Amalia presumably lying down to sleep on the floor somewhere, near the parents' bed. 'So who is this young man she was talking about?' K. asked. 'I don't know,' said Olga, 'Brunswick, possibly, though it doesn't fit him entirely, but maybe someone else. It's not easy to understand exactly what she means, because often you don't know whether she's speaking ironically or in earnest, it's usually in earnest, but it sounds ironic.' 'Never mind the interpretations,' said K. 'How did you personally come to be so dependent on her? Was it like that before the disaster? Or only afterwards? And do you never wish you could become independent of her? And does that dependence have any rational basis? She's the youngest, and as such should be submissive. Guilty or not, it was she brought disaster on the family. Instead of, with each new day, begging forgiveness from each of you afresh, she holds her head up higher than anyone, bothers about nothing except at a pinch, out of pity, your parents, refuses to be initiated into anything, as she puts it, and if she does eventually address you for once, it's "usually in earnest, but it sounds ironic". Or does she dominate because of her beauty, say, which you mention from time to time? Look, you're very alike, all three of you, but the thing that distinguishes her from both of you is very much to her disadvantage, the first time I saw her I was put off by the dull, unloving look in her eye. And then, she may be the youngest, but nothing of that shows in her appearance, she has that ageless look of women who scarcely age at all, but who were also never really young. You see her every day, you don't even notice the hardness in her face. That's why, come to think of it, I can't take Sortini's sudden liking very seriously either, maybe he only meant to punish her with the letter, not summon her.' 'I don't want to talk about Sortini,' said Olga, 'with the castle gentlemen anything's possible, whether it's the most beautiful or the ugliest girl involved. But otherwise you're completely wrong about Amalia. Look, I have no reason for winning you over to Amalia particularly, and if I try all the same, I'm only doing it for you. In one way or another, certainly, Amalia caused our misfortune, yet not even father, who was after all hardest hit by the disaster and has never had much control over his language, particularly not at home, not even father had one word of reproach for Amalia, even when things were at their worst. And it wasn't that he approved of Amalia's action, either; how could an admirer of Sortini possibly have approved of it, he couldn't begin to understand it, he'd probably have been glad to sacrifice himself and everything he possessed to Sortini, though not the way it was happening now, with Sortini very likely furious. I say very likely furious because that was the last we heard of Sortini; if he'd been withdrawn before, from now on it was as if he no longer existed. And you really should have seen Amalia during that time. We all knew no specific punishment would ensue. Everybody simply withdrew from us. The people here, and also the castle. But whereas we noticed the withdrawal of people here, of course, from the castle there was no sign. We'd not, you see, been aware of any solicitude on the castle's part before, so how should we have noticed any drastic change now. That silence was the worst thing. It wasn't people withdrawing from us, not at all, we knew they hadn't done so out of any kind of conviction, they may not even have had anything against us to speak of, there was nothing like today's contempt then, they'd only done it through fear and were now waiting to see how things turned out. Nor was poverty a threat at this stage, our debtors had all paid up, the settling of accounts had been to our advantage, whatever food we lacked relatives helped us with in secret, it was simple, this was harvest-time after all, not that we had any fields, nor would anyone give us employment, for the first time in our lives we were condemned to idleness, almost. So there we all sat, behind closed windows, in the heat of July and August. Nothing happened. No summons, no news, no visit, nothing.' 'Well,' said K., 'if nothing happened and no specific punishment was to be expected either, what were you all afraid of? I mean, what kind of people are you!' 'How can I explain it to you?' Olga said. 'We weren't afraid of something in the future, we were suffering purely from the present, our punishment was all around us. You see, the village people were simply waiting for us to come to them, for father to reopen his workshop, for Amalia, who could sew very beautiful clothes, only for the poshest people, mind you, to start coming round for orders again, they were all sorry for what they'd done, you see; when a respected family in the village is all of a sudden totally excluded, everyone is disadvantaged in some way; in repudiating us, they'd simply done what they saw as their duty, we should have done the same in their place. They hadn't even known in any detail what it had been about, the messenger had simply arrived back at the Count's Arms with a handful of scraps of paper, Frieda had seen him go out and then return, exchanged a few words with him, and immediately put about what she'd learned, but again, not out of any hostility towards us, not at all, simply out of duty, as it would have been anyone's duty in the same case. And, do you see, what people would have most welcomed, as I said, would have been a happy resolution of the whole thing. If we'd suddenly turned up with the news that everything was now all right, that it had simply been a misunderstanding, say, which had since been completely cleared up, or that there had been an offence, yes, but action had already been taken to put it right, or – even this would have been enough for people – that we'd managed through our contacts in the castle to quash the matter – we should quite certainly have been taken back with open arms, kisses, hugs, there'd have been parties, I've seen such things more than once with other folk. But not even that kind of announcement would have been needed; if we'd just come along freely and offered ourselves, resumed the old contacts without wasting so much as a word over the letter business, that would have been enough, they'd all have been delighted to refrain from discussing the affair, as well as the fear, do you see, it had mainly been the awkwardness of the affair that had caused people to cut themselves off from us, simply in order not to have to hear anything about it, nor have to talk about it, nor think about it, nor be affected by it in any way. If Frieda had given the affair away, she'd not done so in order to take any delight in it but to protect herself and everyone else against it, to draw the council's attention to the fact that something had happened here from which people should be very careful to keep their distance. It wasn't we as a family who were considered here, it was the affair only, and we only because of the affair in which we'd become entangled. So if we had simply re-emerged, allowed the past to rest, shown by our behaviour that we'd got over the affair, never mind how, and people had in this way become convinced that, whatever form the affair may have taken, never again would it come up for discussion, again everything would have been all right, we'd have experienced the old helpfulness everywhere, and even if we'd only partially forgotten the affair, people would have forgotten it and would have helped us to forget it completely. But instead of that, we sat at home. I don't know what we were waiting for, Amalia's decision, I suppose, she'd taken command of the family that morning and kept a firm grip on it. Without any special arrangements, without orders, without requests, almost entirely through silence. The rest of us had plenty to discuss, of course, there was continuous whispering from morning till evening, and occasionally father called me to him in a sudden state of alarm and I spent half the night by the bedside. Or sometimes we would sit together, Barnabas and I, he understood very little of the whole thing, of course, and kept clamouring for explanations, always the same ones, well aware that the carefree years that others of his age could look forward to no longer existed for him, there we would sit, very much as we're sitting here now, K., and forget all about night falling and then morning coming. Mother was the weakest of us all, no doubt because she felt not only our joint plight but also the plight of each one of us, so that to our dismay we saw changes occurring in her that were presumably in store for the whole family. Her favourite place was the corner of a couch, we haven't had it for ages now, it stands in Brunswick's big parlour, there she sat and – you couldn't tell which, exactly – dozed or, as her restless lips seemed to suggest, held long conversations with herself. It was so natural, do you see, that we should have talked constantly of the letter business, going back and forth over all its definite details and indefinite possibilities, and that we should constantly have outdone one another in devising means to a good solution, it was natural and inevitable, but no good, it just got us deeper and deeper into the thing we were trying to escape. And what was the use of such ideas, however excellent, none of them was feasible without Amalia, they were no more than preliminary discussions, meaningless in that their conclusions never even reached Amalia, and if they had got that far they'd have met with nothing but silence. Well, fortunately I understand Amalia better now than I did then. She bore more than any of us, it's incomprehensible the way she put up with it and is still living with us today. Mother may have borne our common plight, she bore it because it overtook her, and she didn't bear it for long; she can't be said to be in any way bearing it still, and even at the time her wits were blurred. But Amalia not only bore our plight, she also had the intelligence to see through it, we saw only the consequences, she saw the reason, we hoped for some small contrivance, she knew that everything had been decided, we had to whisper, she needed only to stay silent, she stood face to face with the truth and lived and endured this life then as she does today. How much better off we were, for all our misery, than her. Granted, we had to leave our house, Brunswick moved in, we were given this cottage, we brought our belongings round here in a handcart, taking several journeys, Barnabas and I pulled, father and Amalia helped behind, mother, whom we'd brought right at the start, met us sitting on a chest, yammering quietly the whole time. Yet I remember that, even during those laborious journeys – which were also very humiliating, because we kept meeting harvest carts whose crews fell silent at the sight of us and looked away – even during those journeys we couldn't stop talking, Barnabas and I, about our troubles and sometimes, deep in conversation, we came to a complete standstill and only father's "hey you" reminded us of our duty. But the endless deliberating did nothing to change our lives after the move, either; all that happened was, we now became gradually acquainted with poverty too. The contributions from relatives stopped coming, our resources had almost run out, and that was precisely when the kind of contempt for us that you've witnessed began to develop. People became aware that we lacked the strength to work our way back from the business of the letter, and they took that very much amiss, they didn't under-estimate the hardness of our lot, even without knowing the details, had we got over it they'd have held us in correspondingly high regard, but since we hadn't managed to, what people had done only on a provisional basis before, they now made final, they excluded us from every circle, they knew they would probably have stood the test no better than we had, but that made it all the more necessary for them to sever relations with us completely. From then on, we were no longer spoken of as individuals, people stopped using our surname; when they had to speak of us, they called us after Barnabas, the most innocent member of the family; even our cottage got a bad name, and if you think about it you'll admit that you too, when you first came in, felt such contempt justified; later, when people began visiting us again, they would turn up their noses over quite trivial things, for instance the fact that the little oil lamp hung above the table there. I mean, where else should it hang but above the table; to them, though, it seemed insufferable. However, if we hung the lamp in a different place, their distaste didn't alter. Everything we were and had, met with the same contempt.'

19

APPROACHES

'And what did we do meanwhile? The worst thing we could have done, a thing we'd have deserved to be despised for more than the one we were actually despised for – we betrayed Amalia, we broke free from her silent command, we couldn't go on living like that, with no hope whatever we couldn't go on living, and we began, each in his own way, to beg or besiege the castle, asking for pardon. Oh, we knew we were in no position to put anything right, we also knew that the one promising contact we had with the castle, namely through Sortini, the official who was well-disposed towards father, events had now pushed beyond our reach, but we set to work none the less. Father began, that was the beginning of the futile petitions to the mayor, the secretaries, the lawyers, the clerks, usually no one would see him, and when by some ruse or accident he was received – how we cheered at such news and rubbed our hands together – he was turned down very swiftly indeed and never received again. In any case, it was all too easy to answer him, the castle always finds it so easy. What did he want, then? What had happened to him? What did he want to be pardoned for? When and through whom had the castle so much as lifted a finger against him? All right, he was impoverished, he'd lost his customers, etc., but these were manifestations of everyday life, trade and market matters, was the castle supposed to attend to everything? In fact it did attend to everything, but it couldn't just barge in and take a hand in developments, purely and for no other purpose than to serve the interests of a particular individual. Was it supposed to dispatch its officials, say, and were these then to chase up father's customers and bring them back to him by force? But, father then objected – we all discussed these things in detail at home, before and after, squeezed in a corner as if hiding from Amalia, who although she noticed everything did nothing to stop it – but, father then objected, he wasn't complaining about the impoverishment, was he, everything he'd lost here he meant to make up quite easily, none of that would matter if he was simply pardoned. But what was he supposed to be pardoned for? came the reply, no report had been filed as yet, at least there was no mention of it yet in the records, not, at any rate, in the records publicly available to the legal profession, consequently no action, so far as could be ascertained, had been taken against him, nor was any in train. Could he perhaps name an official order that had been passed against him? Father could not. Or had there been any intervention on the part of an official agency? Father knew of none. Well then, if he knew nothing and if nothing had occurred, what did he want? What could he be pardoned for? At most, for the fact that he was now pestering the authorities to no purpose, but precisely that was unpardonable. Father didn't let up, he was still very vigorous then and the enforced idleness gave him plenty of time. "I shall retrieve Amalia's honour for her, it won't take much longer," he told Barnabas and me several times a day, but only very quietly, Amalia must not hear; even so, it was said solely for Amalia's benefit, because in reality he was not thinking at all about retrieving honour, only about being pardoned. But to obtain a pardon he first had to establish guilt, and up in the offices that was being denied him. He conceived the idea – and this showed he was already not all there, mentally – that the guilt was being kept secret from him because he was not paying enough; up until then, you see, he'd always paid only the fixed charges, which were steep enough, at least for our circumstances. Now he felt he must pay more, which was surely wrong, because with our authorities, although they do, for simplicity's sake, to avoid pointless discussion, take bribes, nothing can be achieved that way. But if that was what father hoped, we didn't want to spoil it for him. We sold what we still had – virtually only essentials were left – to fund father's inquiries, and for a long time we had the daily satisfaction of knowing that, when father set out each morning, he always at least had a few coins in his pocket to jingle. We starved all day, of course, while the only additional thing we achieved by raising the money was that father was sustained in a state of some optimism. This was scarcely an advantage, though. They were hard work, his visits, and what without the money would very soon have come to a well-deserved end now dragged on and on. Since there was actually nothing out of the ordinary that people could do in return for the extra payments, the odd clerk would at least try to look as if he was doing something, he'd promise inquiries, hint that certain leads had in fact been traced that they would follow up not because they were obliged to but purely for father's sake – and he, instead of growing more sceptical, became increasingly credulous. He'd come back with this kind of patently empty promise as if he were in fact bringing full blessing into the house again, and it was harrowing to watch as, from behind Amalia's back, pointing at Amalia with a contorted grin and big round eyes, he tried repeatedly to make us see that Amalia's deliverance, which would surprise no one more than herself, was now, through his efforts, actually imminent, but it was all still a secret and we should guard it strictly. Things would surely have gone on like that for a very long time had we not, in the end, been totally incapable of finding father the cash. True, in the meantime Barnabas had after much pleading been taken on by Brunswick as an assistant, though only for the purpose of collecting the orders in the evenings, after dark, and delivering the finished work, also after dark – all right, so far as his business was concerned Brunswick was taking a certain risk here for our sakes, but in return he paid Barnabas very little, didn't he, and Barnabas's work is faultless – however, the wages were only just enough to keep us from complete starvation. Very gently and after many preliminaries, we told father we were discontinuing our financial support, but he took it very calmly. In his mind, he was no longer capable of seeing the futility of his interventions, but certainly the constant disappointments had wearied him. He did in fact tell us – he no longer spoke as distinctly as before, he used to speak almost too distinctly – that he'd spent very little money so far, tomorrow or even that day he'd have found out everything, and now it had all been in vain, purely because of the money, etc., but his tone of voice suggested that he didn't believe any of it. Also he immediately, that instant, had other plans. Since he'd failed to prove guilt so could achieve nothing further through official channels, he must fall back on pleading alone and approach the officials personally. There were surely some among them with kindly, sympathetic hearts that they were of course not allowed to listen to while performing their official duties, but no doubt could outside that context, if you caught them at the right moment.'

At this point K., who had been listening to Olga in total absorption, interrupted her account with the question: 'And you don't think that's right?' The way the account went on would inevitably have given him the answer, of course, but he wanted to know right away.

'No,' Olga said, 'there can be no question whatever of sympathy or anything of that sort. Young and inexperienced we may have been, but we knew that, and of course father knew it too, but he'd forgotten, as he had most things. What he planned to do was stand by the road near the castle, where the officials' carriages passed, and at every opportunity make his request for pardon. Quite honestly, the plan made no sense at all, even if the impossible were to occur and the request actually reach the ears of an official. I mean, can an individual official grant a pardon? At best, that might be a matter for the authority as a whole, though even it can probably not grant a pardon, only issue a directive. But how can an official, even if he is prepared to climb out and deal with the matter, going only on what father, a poor, tired, elderly man, comes up to him and mumbles, possibly form a picture of the case? The officials are highly educated men, but it's only one-sided, their education, in his field an official will instantly, from a single word, grasp whole trains of thought, but things from another department may be explained to him for hours, he'll perhaps nod politely but he won't understand a word. All this is obvious, of course, a person need only look at the minor official matters that concern himself, trivial stuff that an official will dispatch with a shrug, a person need only try to reach a thorough understanding of that and he'll have a job for life and still not be done. But if father had found a competent official, without preliminary papers the official can do nothing, particularly not at the roadside, he can't grant a pardon, you see, he can only deal with a thing officially, and to do that he can only refer to official channels, but down that route father had already failed to achieve anything at all. How far things must have gone with father already, that he meant somehow to get through with this new plan. If there were even the remotest possibility of any such thing, that bit of road would be teeming with supplicants, but since we're dealing here with an impossibility that even the most elementary schooling will impress upon a person, it's quite empty. Maybe that was another thing that confirmed father in his hope, he fed it from every source. So he needed to, very much, a sound mind would surely never have got involved in such major considerations, the impossibility would have been clear to it at the most superficial level. When officials drive to the village or back to the castle, those aren't pleasure trips, there's work waiting for them in the village and the castle, so they travel at top speed. Nor does it occur to them to glance out of the window, looking for petitioners outside; the fact is, the carriages are stuffed with files that the officials study.'

'Ah,' said K., ' but I've seen inside an official's sledge, there were no files there.' In Olga's account, there opened up before him a world so vast and scarcely plausible that he could not resist reaching out and touching it with his little experience, in order to convince himself more clearly not only of its existence but also of his own.

'That may be,' said Olga, 'but if so, it's even worse, it means the official is about such important business that the files are too valuable or too fat to be taken along, officials like that arrange to be driven at a gallop. Certainly, none would have any time to spare for father. And another thing: there are several roads leading to the castle. Now one will be in vogue, so most people use it, now another, and they'll all throng that way. What rules govern the change have yet to be discovered. One morning at eight o'clock, everyone will be using one street, half an hour later they're all using another, ten minutes later a third, then half an hour later they're perhaps back on the first one, and that's how it will stay for the rest of the day, except that each moment there's a chance it will change. All the access roads do join up near the village, but at that point the carriages are all racing along, whereas nearer the castle their speed's a bit more moderate. But just as the leaving arrangements with regard to the roads are irregular and totally obscure, it's the same with the number of carriages. Many days there's not a carriage to be seen, then there'll be crowds of them again. Now, given all this, just imagine our father. Wearing his best suit, soon to be his only one, he leaves the house every morning with our blessings accompanying him. He takes a small fire-brigade badge with him, which he really had no right to keep, and pins it on outside the village, in the village itself he's afraid to show it, despite its being so small that from two paces you can hardly see it, but father reckons it will be just the thing to draw the officials' attention to him as they drive by. Not far from the castle entrance there's a market garden, it belongs to a man called Bertuch, he supplies vegetables to the castle, it was there, on the narrow stone pedestal of the garden fence, that father chose to sit. Bertuch let him because he'd once been friends with father as well as being one of his most loyal customers; he has a slightly deformed foot, you see, and believed only father was capable of making him a boot that would fit. So there father sat, day after day, it was a dismal, rainy autumn, but he took absolutely no notice of the weather, at a set time each morning he had his hand on the latch and was waving us goodbye, in the evening he returned, his stoop seeming worse every day, soaked to the skin and collapsed in a corner. At first he used to tell us his little adventures, perhaps that out of sympathy and former friendship Bertuch had tossed him a blanket over the railings, or that he thought he'd recognized this or that official in the carriage driving past, or that the occasional coachman had recognized him and as a joke touched him lightly with the thong of his whip. Later he stopped telling these stories, clearly he no longer expected to achieve anything at all there, he simply saw it as his duty, now, his dreary calling, to go and spend the day there. That was when his rheumatic pains began, winter was approaching, snow fell early, winter does begin very early here, so there he sat, one day on the wet stones in the rain, next day in the snow. During the night he'd groan with pain, some mornings he was unsure whether to go, but then managed to pull himself together and did. Mother clung to him, refusing to let go, he'd probably lost his nerve because of his limbs no longer obeying him so he allowed her to come along, the result was that the pains gripped mother too. We often went to see them, taking something to eat or simply visiting or trying to persuade them to come home, how often we'd find them there, slumped together, supporting each other on their narrow seat, huddled in a thin blanket hardly big enough for them both, all around them nothing but the grey of snow and fog, and far and wide and for days on end not a single person or carriage, what a sight, K., what a sight! Till one morning father just couldn't get his stiff legs out of bed any more; he was inconsolable, with his mind wandering in a mild fever he imagined he saw a carriage drawing to a halt up by Bertuch's that very moment, an official getting out, looking up and down the railings for father, shaking his head, and climbing crossly back into the carriage. As he did so, father uttered such shrieks that it seemed he was trying to attract the official's attention from here and explain how blameless his absence was. It turned into a lengthy absence, too, he never went back there, he had to keep to his bed for weeks. Amalia took over waiting on him, looking after him, giving him his treatment, everything, in fact with interruptions she's done it to this day. She knows herbs that soothe pain, she needs almost no sleep, never panics, is scared of nothing, won't ever lose patience, she used to do all the work for our parents; and while we, without managing to help at all, would flap around nervously, she stayed cool and calm throughout. Once the worst was over, though, and father was able carefully, with someone supporting him on either side, to wrestle his way out of bed again, Amalia promptly withdrew and left him to us.'

20

OLGA'S PLANS

'Once again it was a question of finding something for father to do that was still within his powers, something that at least sustained him in the belief that it was helping to shift the blame off the family. It wasn't difficult, finding something like that, basically anything was as much use as sitting outside Bertuch's garden, but I found something that gave even me some hope. Whenever there'd been talk of our guilt among officials or clerks or elsewhere, the only thing ever mentioned was the insulting of Sortini's messenger, no one ventured any further. Well, I thought to myself, if public opinion, even if only seemingly, is aware only of the insult to the messenger, everything might be put right – again, even if only seemingly – if the messenger could be placated. After all, no report has been filed, so we're told, so no department has the matter in hand as yet, it's therefore still open to the messenger, so far as he personally is concerned, and that's all we're talking about here, to forgive and forget. None of this could have any decisive importance, of course, it was mere appearance and again couldn't lead anywhere, but it would please father, and the many purveyors of information who'd been such a torment to him might possibly, and for him satisfyingly, be driven into something of a corner by it. First, of course, the messenger had to be found. When I told father about my plan he was very angry at first, he'd turned very obstinate, you see, partly he believed, this had developed during his illness, that we'd always prevented him from ultimately succeeding, first by discontinuing our financial support, now by keeping him in bed, partly he'd become quite incapable of fully taking in other people's ideas. I hadn't even finished explaining before my plan was rejected, his view was that he must go on waiting outside Bertuch's garden, and since he'd certainly not be able to walk up there every day any more, we'd have to take him in the handcart. I didn't give up, though, and gradually he came round to the idea, the one thing that upset him about it was that in this matter he was wholly dependent on me, because I was the only one who'd seen the messenger that time, he didn't know him. Of course, one servant looks much like another, and even I wasn't certain I'd know that one again. So we started going to the Count's Arms and looking among the servants there. It had been one of Sortini's servants, of course, and Sortini no longer came to the village, but the gentlemen often change their servants, we might very well find him in another gentleman's group, and if he wasn't to be found in person it might be possible to gather news of him from the other servants. To do that, though, we had to be at the Count's Arms every night, and we weren't welcome anywhere, let alone in a place like that; nor could we pose as paying guests. But it turned out they did have a use for us after all; you know youself what a trial the servants were to Frieda, they're basically quiet folk for the most part, spoiled and also dulled by undemanding work, "may you lead a servant's life" is a form of blessing among officials and in fact, as regards good living, the servants are reckoned to be the real kings of the castle; they appreciate it too, and in the castle, where their behaviour is governed by its laws, they are silent and dignified, that's been confirmed to me many times, and even here you still find traces of it among the servants, only traces, though, otherwise the fact that the castle laws no longer fully apply to them in the village almost transforms them; they're a wild, unruly lot here, governed not by the laws but by their own insatiable desires. Their shamelessness knows no bounds, luckily for the village they're only allowed to leave the Count's Arms under orders, but inside the Count's Arms you have to try to get along with them; well, Frieda used to find that very hard, so she was very glad to be able to use me to calm the servants down, for more than two years I've spent at least a couple of nights a week with the servants in the stable. Before, when father was still able to accompany me to the Count's Arms, he'd sleep in the bar somewhere and wait there for the news I'd bring in the morning. It wasn't much. We haven't found the messenger we're looking for yet, he's still in Sortini's service, apparently, Sortini thinks very highly of him, and he went with Sortini when he withdrew to more remote offices. Most of the servants haven't seen him any more recently that we did, and when one of them does claim to have seen him in the meantime, it's probably an error. So my plan would seem to have been a failure and yet wasn't entirely, it's true we didn't find the messenger, and all the walking to the Count's Arms and spending the night there, maybe even feeling for me in so far as he was still capable of it, unfortunately finished father off and he's been in the state you saw him in for almost two years now, but he may be in better shape than mother, whose end we expect daily, only Amalia's superhuman efforts are delaying it. But what I did achieve at the Count's Arms was a certain connection with the castle; you mustn't despise me for saying I don't regret what I did. What great connection with the castle might that be, you'll perhaps wonder. And you're right, it isn't a great connection. I do know lots of servants now, the servants of virtually all the gentlemen who've visited the village in recent years, and if I do ever get into the castle I'll not be a stranger there. That's only servants in the village, of course, in the castle they're quite different and probably no longer recognize anyone there, particularly not someone they used to associate with in the village, even if they've sworn a hundred times in the stable that they look forward very much to meeting again in the castle. Anyway, I've already learned how little such promises mean. But that's not the most important thing. It's not just through the servants themselves that I have a connection with the castle but also possibly, I hope this is true, in that someone who is observing me and what I do from up there – and of course administering the vast body of servants is an extremely important and worrying aspect of the authority's work – in that the person who's observing me in this way will perhaps reach a more lenient judgement about me than others have, that he'll perhaps recognize that I am, pathetically I admit, also fighting for our family and continuing father's efforts. If it's looked at in that light, perhaps I'll also be forgiven for accepting money from the servants and spending it on the family. And there's another thing I've achieved, though it's something even you hold against me. I've learned a lot from the hands about indirect ways of getting on to the castle payroll, avoiding the laborious public admittance procedure, which takes years, I know a person's not a public employee in that case, you're only secretly and partly authorized, you have neither rights nor duties, having no duties is the worst, but you do have one thing, being always around, whatever's going on, means you can spot and make use of favourable opportunities, you're not an employee, but some job or other may crop up, no employee is available just then, there's a call, you come running, and what you weren't a moment ago, now you are, you're on the payroll. When does such an opportunity arise, though? Sometimes straightaway, you've scarcely arrived, scarcely looked around you, the opportunity's there already, in fact not everyone has the presence of mind, as a novice, to seize it immediately, but another time it will take more years than the public admittance procedure, and a person who's been semi-authorized like that cannot then be publicly admitted any more, not properly. So there's plenty to think about here; but it's nothing compared to the fact that public admittance involves a meticulous choice, and a member of a family that's in any way notorious is rejected from the start, say such a person subjects himself to the procedure, he spends years in terror of the outcome, everyone asks him in astonishment from day one how he dared embark on so hopeless an undertaking, he has his hopes, though, how could he live otherwise, but many years later, maybe as an old man, he hears he's been rejected, hears that all is lost and his life has been in vain. Again, there are of course exceptions, which is why one's so easily tempted. It can happen that people who are in fact notorious are eventually admitted, there are officials who literally against their will adore the smell of such game, during examinations they'll sniff the air, curl their lips, roll their eyes, such a man will seem as it were hugely appetizing to them, and they must stick very closely to the codes if they're to resist him. Sometimes, though, this helps the man to gain not admittance but only an endless prolongation of the admittance procedure, which is then never completed but only broken off following the man's demise. In other words, both regular admittance and the other sort are full of obvious and concealed difficulties, and before a person gets involved in something like that it is most advisable to weigh everything up very carefully. Well, we spared no pains there, Barnabas and I. Every time I came back from the Count's Arms we sat down together, I told him what news I'd heard, we spent days discussing it, and the work Barnabas had in hand was often left for longer than it should have been. And here I may bear some blame in your sense. I realized that the hands' stories weren't very reliable. I knew they never really wanted to talk to me about the castle, they were always changing the subject, making me coax every word out of them, but then, of course, once they got going they let rip, talked a lot of nonsense, boasted, vied with one another in exaggerations and inventions, with the obvious result that, in the constant uproar in which one took over from another in that dark stable, there'd at most be the odd meagre hint at the truth. Yet I passed everything on to Barnabas as I remembered it, and he, who was quite incapable of telling truth from lies as yet and with the family in its present situation was all but parched with longing for such things, he lapped it all up and was avid for more. As a matter of fact, it was on Barnabas that my new plan was based. There was nothing more to be achieved with the hands. Sortini's messenger was not to be found, nor would he ever be, Sortini and consequently the messenger too seemed to withdraw further and further, often people forgot what they looked like and what they were called and I often had to describe them at length, only to achieve nothing in the process except that people did laboriously recall them but beyond that could say nothing about them. And as to my life among the hands, naturally I had no influence over how it was judged, I could only hope it would be taken in the way I'd lived it and that a tiny bit of the blame would be lifted from our family in return, yet I received no outward sign of this. Still, I kept at it because I saw no other chance of my achieving anything for us in the castle. For Barnabas, though, I did see such a chance. I was able if I felt like it, and I felt very much like it, to work out from what the hands said that a person who is taken on to the castle payroll can do a great deal for his family. All right, how much of what they said was worth believing? Impossible to tell, except that it was clearly very little. Because if, say, a hand whom I would never see again, or even if I did would scarcely recognize, solemnly assured me that he'd help my brother find a position in the castle or at least, if Barnabas got into the castle some other way, give him support, for example by reviving him, because according to the hands it sometimes happens that job applicants are kept waiting so long they faint or become confused and are then done for unless friends look after them – if such things and much more were told me, they were no doubt legitimate warnings but the promises that went with them were totally empty. Not for Barnabas, I did warn him against believing them, but the mere fact of my telling them to him was enough to win him over for my plans. What I said myself for that purpose influenced him less, mainly he was influenced by the stories the hands told. Really, then, I had to fend entirely for myself, no one was capable of communicating with our parents apart from Amalia, the more I pursued father's old plans after my fashion, the more Amalia cut herself off from me, in front of you or other people she'll talk to me, never alone any more, the hands at the Count's Arms saw me as a toy and tried furiously to smash me, not one friendly word did I exchange with any of them over the two years, only sneaky or false or crazy talk, that left me with Barnabas, and Barnabas was still very young. When I was reporting to him and saw the gleam in his eye, which he's kept ever since, I was scared and yet didn't leave off, too big a thing seemed to me to be at stake. Of course, I didn't have my father's grand if also empty plans, I didn't have that determination men have, I stuck to making amends for the insult to the messenger and even expected credit for such modesty. But what I had failed in alone, I now wanted to achieve differently and for sure through Barnabas. We'd insulted one messenger and driven him from the front offices, what better idea than to offer a fresh messenger in the person of Barnabas, have Barnabas do the work of the insulted messenger, and so make it possible for the insulted one to stay away for as long as he wanted, for as long as he needed to get over the insult. I quite realized that there was presumption in the very modesty of this plan, that it might give the impression that we were trying to dictate to the authority how it should organize staff matters or doubted that the authority was capable of making the best arrangement on its own and would in fact have made such an arrangement already, long before it had even occurred to us that something might be done in this area. But then I went back to thinking that it was impossible the authority should misunderstand me so badly or, if it did, should be doing so deliberately, i.e. that everything I did was dismissed from the outset without closer examination. So I kept at it, and Barnabas's ambition helped. In that period of preparations, Barnabas became so arrogant that he found shoemaking work too dirty for someone who was about to become a castle-office employee, in fact he even, when Amalia said something to him, which was pretty rarely, dared to contradict her, and roundly too. I didn't begrudge him that moment of joy, because from the first day he entered the castle, enjoyment and arrogance, as anyone could have foreseen, were things of the past. That was the beginning of the pretend work I was telling you about. What was amazing was how Barnabas had no trouble entering the castle for the first time or rather the particular office that has become his, so to speak. This success made me almost crazy at the time, I went running, when Barnabas whispered it to me on arriving home that evening, to Amalia, grabbed her, pushed her into a corner, and kissed her with lips and teeth till she wept with pain and fright. I was speechless with excitement, in any case we'd not been speaking for so long that I put it off for a few days. But of course, over the next few days there was no more to say. That success, so swiftly achieved, was it. For two years Barnabas led this monotonous, oppressive existence. The hands were quite useless, I gave Barnabas a short letter in which I commended him to the hands' attention, at the same time reminding them of their promises, and whenever Barnabas saw one of them he took the letter out and held it up to him, and if he did presumably sometimes come across hands who didn't know me and if even to those that did his way of presenting the letter in silence, because he doesn't dare speak up there, was annoying, even so it was disgraceful that no one helped him, and it was a great relief, which of course we could have brought about ourselves long since, when one of the hands, who may already have had the letter thrust at him on a number of occasions, screwed it up and threw it in a wastepaper basket. He might almost, I thought, have said as he did so: "That's what you do with letters yourselves, right?" But however fruitless that whole period was in other respects, the effect on Barnabas was good, if you can call it a good thing that he aged prematurely, became a man before his time, in fact in many ways acquired a gravity and understanding beyond manhood. It often makes me very sad to look at him and compare him with the youth he was two years ago. And yet I have none of the comfort and support that as a man he might have given me. Without me, he'd scarcely have got into the castle, but since he did he's been independent of me. I'm his only close friend, but I'm sure he doesn't tell me more than a fraction of what's on his mind. He tells me a lot about the castle, but his accounts, the bits and pieces he shares with me, come nowhere near explaining how it could have changed him so much. It's particularly unclear why the pluck he had as a youngster, to the despair of us all, has now so completely deserted him up there as a man. All right, the futile standing around and waiting day after day, always starting again from scratch with no prospect of change, that wears a man down and makes him unsure of himself and eventually incapable of anything but that hopeless standing around. But why did he put up no resistance, even before? Particularly as he soon saw I'd been right and there was nothing there for ambition, whereas there might be something as regarded improving our family's situation. Because there, apart from the servants' moods, everything is modest and unassuming, ambition seeks fulfilment in work and since the job itself receives priority it is absorbed completely, no room there for childish desires. But Barnabas, as he told me, thought he saw clearly how great was the power and knowledge even of the very dubious officials whose rooms he was permitted to enter. The way they dictated, at speed, with half-closed eyes, curt gestures, the way they used no more than an index finger, not saying a word, to deal with the grumpy servants who at such moments, breathing hard, smiled contentedly, or the way, finding an important passage in their books, they pounced on it, and so far as possible in the restricted space the others came hurrying over and craned their necks to see. These and other similar things gave Barnabas big ideas about these men, and he had the impression that, if he could get to the point of being noticed by them and being allowed to have a few words with them, not as a stranger but as an office colleague, of the most subordinate kind, of course, then incalculable advantages might be obtained for our family. However, things have yet to reach that point, and Barnabas doesn't dare do anything that might bring him closer to it, even though he's well aware that, despite his youth, as a result of our unfortunate circumstances he's risen within the family to the very responsible position of paterfamilias, no less. And now for my last confession. A week ago, you arrived. I heard someone mention it at the Count's Arms but took no notice; a land surveyor had arrived, I didn't even know what that was. But the next evening Barnabas – I usually went part of the way to meet him at a prearranged time – got home earlier than usual, saw Amalia in the living-room so dragged me out into the street, and there pressed his face against my shoulder and wept for minutes on end. He was the little boy from the old days once again. Something had happened to him that he wasn't equal to. It was as if a whole new world had suddenly opened up before him and he couldn't stand the happiness and cares of so much novelty. Yet all that had happened to him was that he'd been given a letter to deliver to you. But of course it was the first letter, the first job, he'd ever been given.'

Olga broke off. There was silence except for the heavy, occasionally wheezy breathing of the parents. K. merely slipped in, as if to amplify Olga's account: 'You all hid your true feelings from me. Barnabas handed me the letter like a senior, extremely busy messenger and you and Amalia, who in other words was in agreement with you both on this occasion, behaved as if the messenger work and the letters were something purely incidental.' 'You have to distinguish between us,' said Olga, 'Barnabas has become a happy child again as a result of the two letters, despite all his doubts about what he's doing. He has those doubts only for himself and me, but with you he makes it a point of honour to appear as a real messenger, the way he imagines real messengers appear. For example, even though his hopes of a uniform are now rising, I was given two hours to alter his trousers in such a way that they at least resembled the tight-fitting trousers of the official suit and he could get away with them in your presence, you of course being still easily deceived in this respect. That's Barnabas. Amalia is different, she really does despise messenger work, and now that he seems to be having some success, as she can easily tell from Barnabas and me and the way we sit together whispering, now she despises it more than ever. So she's telling the truth, don't ever let yourself be deceived into doubting that. But K., if I've at times disparaged messenger work, it was not with the intention of deceiving you but from fear. Those two letters that have so far passed through Barnabas's hands are the first sign of forgiveness, dubious though it is, that our family has received for three years. This change, if it is a change and not an illusion – illusions are more common than changes – is connected with your arrival here, our fate has to some extent become dependent on you, possibly these two letters are just the start and Barnabas's activities will expand beyond the messenger work concerning you – let's hope so, as long as we're allowed to – but for the time being everything is directed at you. Up there we have to be content with what we're given, but down here it may be that we can also do something ourselves, namely secure your goodwill or at least guard against your aversion or, most importantly, protect you to the best of our ability and experience in order to keep your contact with the castle – which might mean our livelihood – from being lost. So, what was the best way of setting about all that? To avoid making you suspicious of us when we approach you, because you're a stranger here so bound to be full of suspicion in all directions, quite legitimate suspicion. What is more, we're despised and you're influenced by public opinion, particularly through your fiancée, how are we to reach you without, for instance, even quite unintentionally, opposing your fiancée and thus offending you? And the messages, which I carefully read before you received them – Barnabas didn't read them, as messenger he wouldn't allow himself to – seemed at first glance to be not very important, outdated, even undermining their own importance by referring you to the mayor. So, how ought we to behave towards you in this regard? If we stressed their importance, we rendered ourselves suspect by overrating something so obviously unimportant, talking ourselves up in your eyes as the bearers of such news, pursuing our aims rather than yours, it was even possible that in so doing we'd be belittling the news itself in your estimation and thus very much against our will deceiving you. But if we declined to attach much value to the letters, we rendered ourselves equally suspect because why in that case did we bother to deliver these unimportant letters, why did our actions and our words contradict each other, why were we deceiving not only you, the addressee, but also our principal, who had certainly not given us the letters for us to devalue them in the addressee's eyes by what we said. And steering a middle course between the two exaggerations, in other words assessing the letters correctly, is impossible, they're constantly changing in value themselves, the considerations they prompt are endless and where one draws the line only chance decides, in other words one's opinion is itself a matter of chance. And when in addition worrying about you gets in the way, everything becomes blurred, you mustn't judge my words too harshly. When, for example, as happened once, Barnabas arrives with the news that you're unhappy with his messenger work and he, in his initial alarm and also, unfortunately, not without a messenger's touchiness, has offered to resign from your service, then, mind you, I'm capable, in order to rectify the mistake, of cheating, lying, deceiving, committing any wickedness if it'll only help. But then I'll be doing it, at least this is what I believe, as much for your sake as for ours.'

Someone knocked. Olga ran to the door and flung it wide. Out of the night, a ray of light fell from a signalling lantern. The late visitor asked whispered questions and was answered in a whisper, but not content with this he attempted to push his way into the room. Presumably Olga felt unable to restrain him any longer so called Amalia, clearly hoping that she, to protect their parents' sleep, would make every effort to oust the visitor. She did indeed come hurrying across, pushed Olga aside, stepped out into the street, and shut the door behind her. A moment passed, and already she was back inside, so swiftly had she achieved what Olga had found impossible.

K. then learned from Olga that the visit had concerned him, it had been one of the assistants, looking for him on Frieda's orders. Olga had wanted to protect K. from the assistant; if K. meant to own up to Frieda subsequently about his visit there, let him do so, but it shouldn't be discovered by the assistants; K. agreed. But Olga's offer that he should spend the night there and wait for Barnabas, that he refused; other things being equal, he might have accepted, it was already late at night and it seemed to him he was now, willy-nilly, so involved with this family that spending the night here, though perhaps awkward for other reasons, was in fact, considering that involvement, the most natural place for him in the entire village, all the same he refused, the assistant's visit had alarmed him, he failed to understand how Frieda, who surely knew what he wanted, and the assistants, who had learned to fear him, had grown so close again that Frieda did not shrink from sending one of the assistants after him, only one though, while the other had presumably stayed with her. He asked Olga if she had a whip, she did not, but she did have a stout willow rod, he took that; then he asked if there was another way out of the house, there was such a way out through the yard, except that you then had to climb over the fence of the next-door garden and walk through that garden before you came to the street. K. decided to do that. As Olga led him across the yard to the fence, K. tried quickly to reassure her regarding her worries, told her he was not a bit cross with her over her little tricks in the account she had given but quite understood her, thanked her for the confidence she had in him and had demonstrated with her account, and asked her to send Barnabas round to the school as soon as he returned, even if it was still night. Barnabas's messages were not his only hope, things would look bad for him if they were, but he was reluctant to dispense with them, very reluctant, he wanted to hold on to them and at the same time not forget Olga, because what mattered to him almost more than the messages was Olga herself, her courage, her prudence, her shrewdness, the way she sacrificed herself for the family. If he had to choose between Olga and Amalia it wouldn't, he told her, cost him much thought. And he pressed her hand warmly while already swinging himself up on the fence of the next-door garden.

Out on the street he looked up and, so far as the murky night allowed, saw the assistant still pacing to and fro outside Barnabas's house, from time to time the man would stop and try to shine his light through the curtained window into the living-room. K. called to him; showing no sign of alarm, he left off spying on the house and approached K. 'Who are you looking for?' K. asked as he tested the suppleness of the willow rod against his thigh. 'You,' said the assistant, coming closer. 'Who are you, then?' said K. suddenly, because it did not appear to be the assistant. He looked older, wearier, more wrinkled and yet fatter in the face, also his walk was quite different from the nimble, almost electric-jointed walk of the assistants, it was slow, with a slight limp, genteelly infirm. 'You don't recognize me?' the man asked, 'Jeremiah, your old assistant.' 'Really?' K. said and pulled the willow rod out again a little, having put it out of sight behind his back. 'But you look quite different.' 'It's because I'm alone,' said Jeremiah, 'If I'm alone, my merry youth has left me too.' 'So where's Arthur?' K. asked. 'Arthur?' asked Jeremiah, 'the little dear? He's quit. Well, you were a bit hard on us, you know. He couldn't take it, the delicate soul. He's gone back to the castle and is making a complaint about you.' 'And you?' asked K. 'I was able to stay,' said Jeremiah, 'Arthur's making the complaint for me too.' 'What is it you're complaining about?' asked K. 'About the fact,' said Jeremiah, 'that you've no sense of humour. I mean, what did we do? Joked a bit, laughed a bit, teased your fiancée a bit. All according to orders, by the way. When Galater sent us to you –' 'Galater?' asked K. 'Yes, Galater,' said Jeremiah, 'he was standing in for Klamm at the time. When he sent us to you, he said – I made a careful note of this, because it's what we're basing our complaint on – he said: You're going as the land surveyor's assistants. We said: But we don't know anything about that kind of work. He came back with: That's not the most important thing; if it becomes necessary, he'll teach you. The most important thing is that you cheer him up a bit. I'm told he takes everything very seriously. He's now arrived in the village, and immediately this is a big event for him, whereas in reality of course it's nothing at all. That's what you're to teach him.' 'Well,' said K., 'was Galater right and have you carried out your orders?' 'I don't know,' said Jeremiah. 'I doubt it was even possible in that short time. All I know is that you were extremely rude, and that's what we're complaining about. I don't understand how you, who are only an employee yourself and not even a castle employee, can fail to see that such a job is hard work and that it's most unfair to start mischievously, almost childishly hampering the worker in his work as you did. Your ruthlessness in letting us get so cold out by the railings or the way you treated Arthur, who's someone an angry word will pain for days, almost striking him dead on that mattress with your fist, or the way you chased me up and down through the snow this afternoon so that it took me an hour to recover from all the running. I'm not a youngster any more!' 'My dear Jeremiah,' said K., 'you're right about everything, only it's Galater you should be taking it up with. It was his idea, sending you, I didn't ask him for you. And not having requested you, I was also able to send you back and should have preferred to do so in peace rather than by force, but that was clearly the way you both wanted it. Incidentally, why didn't you speak as frankly as this as soon as you came to me?' 'Because I was in service,' said Jeremiah, 'surely that's obvious.' 'And now you're no longer in service?' asked K. 'Not any more,' said Jeremiah, 'Arthur's given notice at the castle or at least proceedings are in hand that will finally release us.' 'But surely you're still looking for me now as if you were in service?' said K. 'No,' said Jeremiah, 'I'm looking for you simply to pacify Frieda. You see, when you left her for the Barnabas girls she was very unhappy, not so much because of the loss as because of your betrayal, although she'd seen it coming for a long time and had already suffered badly as a result. I went back to the classroom window at one point to see whether you had perhaps come to your senses. But you weren't there, only Frieda, sitting at a desk and weeping. So I went to her and we reached an agreement. It's all been implemented already, too. I'm a room-waiter at the Count's Arms, at least until my case has been dealt with at the castle, and Frieda's back behind the bar. It's better for Frieda. There was no sense in her becoming your wife. And you were incapable of appreciating the sacrifice she was prepared to make for you. But the poor thing still has occasional misgivings as to whether you've not been done an injustice, whether perhaps you really weren't with the Barnabas girls. There couldn't of course be any doubt where you were, but I still went round there to establish the fact once and for all; because after all the upheavals, Frieda deserves a quiet night's sleep for once, as do I. So along I went and not only found you but at the same time discovered that the girls automatically do what you tell them. Particularly the dark-haired one, a real wildcat, has taken your side. Well, each to his taste. Anyway, there was no need for you to go round via the next-door garden, I know the way.'

21

So now it had happened, predictably but unavoidably. Frieda had left him. It need not be final, it was not that bad, Frieda could be won back, she was easily influenced by others, even by these assistants, who saw Frieda's situation as similar to their own and now that they had given notice had induced Frieda to break it off too, but K. had only to confront her, remind her of all the things in his favour, and she would contritely be his once more, especially if, say, he could have justified the visit to the girls by some success he owed to them. Yet despite these thoughts, with which he sought to reassure himself about Frieda, he was not reassured. A moment ago he had been singing Frieda's praises to Olga, calling her his sole support, well, it was not the firmest of supports, it had not taken the intervention of anyone powerful to rob him of Frieda, this not particularly savoury assistant had been enough, this lump of flesh that at times gave the impression it was not properly alive.

Jeremiah had already started walking off, K. called him back. 'Jeremiah,' he said, 'I want to be quite frank with you, give me a straight answer, will you, to one question. We're not in a master–servant relationship any more now, you're not the only one who's glad about that, I am too, so there's no reason why we should deceive each other. Here in your sight I break the rod that was meant for you, because it wasn't for fear of you I chose the way through the garden, it was to catch you by surprise and use the rod on you a few times. Well, don't hold it against me now, that's all over; if you hadn't been a servant forced on me officially but just an acquaintance, even if I do find your appearance disconcerting at times I've no doubt we'd have got on famously. In fact, we could make up now for what we've missed in this regard.' 'You think so?' said the assistant, yawning and rubbing tired eyes, 'I could lay it out for you in more detail but I haven't time, I must go to Frieda, the dear child's waiting for me, she hasn't started work yet, she was all for throwing herself into the job immediately, probably to forget, but the landlord let me persuade him to give her a bit of convalescence, we want to spend that at least together. As to your proposal, I certainly have no reason to lie to you, but equally I've no reason to confide in you at all. It's different for me, you see. As long as I was in service to you, you were a very important person for me, naturally, not because of any qualities of yours but because of the job, and I'd have done anything for you that you wanted, but now I don't care about you. Even the breaking of the rod leaves me unaffected, it simply reminds me of what a rough master I had; it isn't the sort of thing that is going to win me over to you.' 'You talk,' said K., 'as if it was quite settled that you'll never have anything to fear from me again. But that's not actually how it is. You probably aren't free of me yet, in fact, things aren't dealt with that fast here –' 'Even faster, sometimes,' Jeremiah objected. 'Sometimes,' said K., 'but there's nothing to suggest that has happened this time, at least neither you nor I have our hands on a written settlement. So proceedings have only just begun, and I haven't even used my contacts to intervene yet, though I will. If the decision goes against you, you won't have done much in advance to get your master on your side, and it may even have been uncalled-for, breaking the willow rod. All right, you've taken Frieda away, which makes you particularly cocky, but for all the respect I have for you personally, even if you've ceased to have any for me, a couple of words of mine in Frieda's ear will be enough, I know they will, to tear the lies you've ensnared her with to shreds. And only lies could have alienated Frieda from me.' 'These threats don't scare me,' said Jeremiah, 'you don't even want me as an assistant, you're afraid to have me as an assistant, you're afraid of assistants altogether, it was fear made you hit poor Arthur, that's all.' 'Possibly,' said K., 'did it hurt any the less for that? Perhaps I'll have many more opportunities of showing my fear of you in this way. If I see that being an assistant gives you little pleasure, it'll give me, over and above any fear, the most tremendous fun to force you into it. In fact, this time I'll make it my business to get you on your own, without Arthur, then I'll be able to devote more attention to you.' 'Do you suppose,' said Jeremiah, 'that I'm the least bit scared of any of that?' 'Oh, I think so,' said K., 'you're certainly a little scared, and if you're smart, a lot. Why otherwise would you not have gone straight to Frieda? Tell me, are you in love with her?' 'Love?' said Jeremiah, 'she's kind and intelligent, an ex-mistress of Klamm's so a respectable girl in any event. And if she constantly pleads with me to free her from you, why should I not do her that favour, particularly since I'm doing you no harm in the process, now that you've consoled yourself with the Barnabas girls, curse them.' 'Now I can see you're afraid,' said K., 'really pitifully afraid, you're trying to catch me out with lies. Frieda asked for one thing only, to be delivered from those by now maddened, lascivious dogs of assistants, unfortunately I didn't have time to carry out her request in full and am faced with the consequences of my failure.'

'Sir! Mr Land Surveyor!' someone called up the street. It was Barnabas. He arrived, out of breath but not forgetting to bow to K. 'I managed it,' he said. 'What have you managed?' asked K. 'You mean, you put my request to Klamm?' 'That didn't work,' said Barnabas, 'I tried hard, but it was impossible, I pushed through to the front, spent all day, uninvited, standing so close to the desk that at one point a clerk whose light I was in even shoved me aside, announced my presence, which is forbidden, by raising my hand whenever Klamm looked up, stayed on longest in the office, was even there with the servants and no one else, had the further pleasure of seeing Klamm come back, but it wasn't because of me, he just wanted to look something up in a book quickly and left again immediately, in the end, when I still didn't move, the servant virtually swept me out of the door with the broom. I'm owning up to all this because I don't want you being unhappy with my performance again.' 'What good is it to me how hard you work, Barnabas,' said K., 'if it brings no results.' 'But I did get a result,' said Barnabas. 'As I was leaving my office – I call it my office – I saw a man slowly approaching out of the depths of the corridors, except for him everything was already empty, it was very late by now, I decided to wait for him, it was a good excuse to stay there a bit longer, I'd rather have stayed there for ever than have to bring you the bad news. But it was worth waiting for the gentleman in any case, it was Erlanger. You don't know him? He's one of Klamm's first secretaries. A frail little man, has a slight limp. He recognized me instantly, he's famous for his memory and his knowledge of human nature, he just knits his brows, that's all he has to do to recognize anyone, often including people he's never seen, people he's only heard of or read about, he can hardly have seen me before, for instance. But even though he recognizes everyone immediately, at first he asks as if unsure. "Aren't you Barnabas?" he said to me. And then he asked: "You know the land surveyor, right?" And then he said: "That's very convenient. I'm just off to the Count's Arms. The land surveyor is to come and see me there. I'll be in room 15. But he should come right away. I've only a few appointments there, and I'll be driving back at five in the morning. Tell him I'm very keen to have a word with him." '

Suddenly, Jeremiah set off. Barnabas, who in his excitement had taken very little notice of him before, asked: 'What's Jeremiah up to?' 'Trying to beat me to Erlanger,' said K. as he ran after Jeremiah, caught him up, took his arm, and said: 'Is it missing Frieda that's come over you all of a sudden? I feel it too, so we'll be in step.'

Outside the dark Count's Arms stood a small group of men, two or three carried hand lanterns, as a result several faces could be distinguished. K. saw only one person he knew, Gerstäcker, the coachman. Gerstäcker greeted him with the question: 'You're still in the village, then?' 'Yes,' said K., 'I'm here for the duration.' 'None of my business, of course,' said Gerstäcker, clearing his throat vigorously and turning to some of the others.

It emerged that they were all waiting for Erlanger. Erlanger had already arrived but was still in discussion with Momus, prior to receiving the parties. The general conversation revolved round the fact that they were not allowed to wait inside but had to stand out there in the snow. It was not particularly cold, but even so it was inconsiderate to make the parties stand outside at night, possibly for hours on end. This was not Erlanger's fault, of course, he was extremely obliging, probably knew nothing about it, and would certainly have been furious had it been reported to him. It was the fault of the landlady of the Count's Arms, who in her pathological striving for refinement was not prepared to have a lot of parties entering the Count's Arms at one time. 'If it has to be and they have to come,' she would say, 'then for heaven's sake let it be just one by one.' And she had managed to get the parties, who at first had simply waited in a corridor, later on the stairs, then in the hallway, and finally in the bar, ultimately pushed out into the street. And even that did not satisfy her. She found it intolerable to be forever 'under siege', as she put it, in her own house. She could not understand why there was this coming and going of parties at all. 'To dirty the front steps,' an official had once answered her, probably in irritation, but to her that had been most enlightening and she was fond of quoting the remark. Her ambition, which of course ran counter to the wishes of the parties, was to have a building erected opposite the Count's Arms where the parties might wait. She would have been happiest if the discussions and interviews with the parties could also have taken place somewhere other than at the Count's Arms, but that was opposed by the officials, and when the officials put up serious opposition, the landlady did not of course get her way, even though in side issues, thanks to her tireless yet, since she was a woman, tender zeal, she exerted a kind of minor tyranny. However, it looked as if the landlady would have to continue to tolerate discussions and interviews at the Count's Arms because the gentlemen from the castle refused, so far as official affairs in the village were concerned, to quit the Count's Arms. They were always in a hurry, it was very much against their will that they were in the village, they had not the slightest desire to prolong their stay there beyond what was absolutely necessary, consequently they could not be required, purely out of consideration for the domestic peace of the Count's Arms, to make a temporary move, together with all their documents, across the street into some other building, thus wasting time. The officials were actually happiest dealing with official matters in the bar or in their rooms, if possible during mealtimes or from their beds before they went to sleep or in the morning when they were too tired to get up and felt like lying in bed a bit longer. On the other hand, the question of the construction of a waiting-hall appeared to be nearing a favourable conclusion, though of course it was a harsh punishment for the landlady – there was some laughter over it – that the matter of the waiting-hall itself necessitated many discussions and the passages of the house were rarely empty.

All these things were being talked about in low voices among the people waiting. K. was struck by the fact that, although there was discontent in plenty, no one had any objection to Erlanger's summoning the parties in the middle of the night. He asked why and was told they should even be extremely grateful to Erlanger for this. It was purely his good will and the exalted view he took of his office that prompted him to come to the village at all, had he wished he could instead – in fact, this might have been more in keeping with the regulations – have sent some junior secretary and had him take the statements. But no, for the most part he refused to do that, wanting to see and hear everything for himself, but that meant he had to give up his nights for the purpose, his official schedule allowed no time for village trips. K. objected that surely Klamm himself came to the village during the day and even stayed for several days; was Erlanger, a mere secretary, more indispensable up there? One or two laughed good-humouredly, others, embarrassed, said nothing, the latter eventually prevailed and K. got little answer. Only one man said hesitantly that of course Klamm was indispensable, in the castle as much as in the village.

At this point the front door opened and Momus appeared, flanked by two servants carrying lamps. 'The first ones admitted to see Secretary Erlanger,' he said, 'are: Gerstäcker and K. Are they both here?' They said they were, but then Jeremiah, with an: 'I'm a room-waiter here,' and receiving a welcoming pat on the shoulder from a smiling Momus, slipped into the house ahead of them. 'I must keep more of an eye on Jeremiah,' K. said to himself, though he remained aware that Jeremiah was probably far less dangerous than Arthur, who was in the castle, working against him. It might even be better to let oneself be plagued by them as assistants than have them wandering about in this uncontrolled fashion, free to conduct their intrigues, for which they seemed to have a particular talent.

As K. passed, Momus pretended that only now did he recognize him as the land surveyor. 'Ah, the land surveyor!' he said, 'the man who's so averse to examinations is now eager to be examined. It would have been simpler with me that time. Of course, it's difficult, choosing the right examinations.' When K., thus addressed, looked like stopping, Momus said: 'Move along, move along. I could have used your answers then, I can't now.' Nevertheless, provoked by Momus's behaviour, K. said: 'All you think about is yourselves. If it's purely for official purposes, I'll not answer, not then, not now.' Momus said: 'Who are we supposed to think about? Who else is there in this place? Move along, now.'

A servant met them in the hallway and led them along the route K. already knew across the courtyard, then through the door and into the low, slightly downhill passage. Clearly, only the higher officials stayed on the upper floors, while the secretaries stayed on this passage, Erlanger too, even though he was one of the highest of them. The servant doused his lantern because here there was bright electric light. Everything here was small but daintily constructed. The best possible use was made of space. The passage was just high enough for a person to walk upright. Down the sides, the doors almost touched. The walls on either side stopped short of the ceiling; this was no doubt for ventilation purposes, because in this deep, cellar-like passage the tiny rooms presumably had no windows. The disadvantage of these not quite complete walls was the noise in the passage and inevitably also in the rooms. Many rooms seemed to be occupied, in most the people were still awake, you heard voices, hammering, the clink of glasses. Yet there was no impression of any special merriment. The voices were muffled, no more than the odd word could be made out, nor did there seem to be conversations going on, probably somebody was just dictating something or reading something out, particularly from the rooms giving out the sound of glasses and dishes not a word could be heard and the hammering reminded K. of something that he had been told somewhere, namely that many officials, to relax from the constant mental exertion, from time to time did a little carpentry, light engineering, that sort of thing. The passage itself was empty except for a tall pale thin man sitting outside one of the doors in a fur, under which his nightclothes showed, probably it had got too stuffy for him in the room so he had come to sit outside and was reading a newspaper, albeit inattentively, from time to time he would stop reading with a yawn, bend forward, and look along the passage, possibly he was expecting a particular party whom he had summoned and who was late arriving. Once they were past him the servant, referring to the man, said to Gerstäcker: 'Pinzgauer!' Gerstäcker nodded; 'he's not been down here for a long time,' he said. 'Not for ages,' the servant confirmed.

Eventually, they came to a door that was no different from the rest but behind which, the servant informed them, Erlanger stayed. The servant had K. lift him on to his shoulders and looked through the open gap into the room. 'He's lying,' the servant said, climbing down, 'on the bed, he's dressed but I rather think he's asleep. Sometimes tiredness overtakes him like that here in the village, with its different way of life. We shall have to wait. He'll ring when he wakes up. It has happened that he's spent his whole time in the village sleeping and had to drive back to the castle as soon as he woke up. It is voluntary work he does here, after all.' 'Let's hope this time he sleeps right through,' said Gerstäcker, 'because when he does have a little time for work after waking, he's very indignant about having slept, tries to deal with everything in a rush, and a person scarcely has time to speak out.' 'You've come about the award of the cartage contracts for the building?' the servant asked. Gerstäcker nodded, drew the servant aside, and spoke quietly to him, but the servant, barely listening, gazed beyond Gerstäcker, he was more than a head taller than him, and gravely and slowly passed a hand through his hair.

22

At this point K., looking aimlessly around him, saw Frieda, off in the distance at a bend in the passage; she acted as if she did not recognize him, simply staring at him, holding a tray of empty dishes. He told the servant, who took absolutely no notice – the more the servant was spoken to, the more absent-minded he seemed to become – that he would be back in a moment, then ran to Frieda. Reaching her, he seized her by the shoulders as if retaking possession of her, asked a number of inconsequential questions, and as he did so gazed intently into her eyes. But her rigid bearing relaxed hardly at all, after a few distracted attempts to rearrange the crockery on the tray, she said: 'What do you want from me, then? Go on, go to those – well, you know what they're called, you've just come from them, I can tell from looking at you.' K. swiftly changed the subject, not wanting their talk to start so abruptly and with the very worst things of all, those least in his favour. 'I thought you were in the bar,' he said. Frieda looked at him in surprise and gently ran her free hand over his brow and cheek. It was as if she had forgotten what he looked like and this was her way of reminding herself, her eyes even had that clouded expression of an effort of memory. 'I have been taken on again for the bar,' she said then, slowly, as if it did not matter what she said, beneath the words she was conversing with K. again, and that mattered more, 'this job doesn't suit me, besides anyone can do it; anyone who can make beds and put on a friendly face and who doesn't mind being pestered by the guests but even encourages it, anyone like that can be a chambermaid. In the bar, things are rather different. Also, I was taken on again for the bar immediately, even though I'd left it not too honourably before, this time I had backing, of course. But the landlord was delighted that I had backing and it was therefore easy for him take me on again. In fact, I even needed urging to accept the job; if you consider what the bar reminds me of, you'll understand. In the end I did accept the job. I'm here only temporarily. Pepi asked to be spared the disgrace of having to leave the bar at once, so we decided, because she has worked hard and looked after everything to the very best of her ability, to give her twenty-four hours' notice.' 'Everything's been arranged admirably,' said K., 'except that first you quit the bar because of me, and now, with our wedding imminent, you're going back there, is that it?' 'There'll be no wedding,' said Frieda. 'Because I've been unfaithful?' K. asked. Frieda nodded. 'Look here, Frieda,' said K., 'we've discussed this alleged infidelity several times now and you've always, in the end, had to admit the suspicion was unfounded. Well, nothing's changed on my side since then, everything is still as innocent as it always was and can never be otherwise. So something must have changed on your side, as a result of people's insinuations or for some other reason. In any case, you're not being fair to me, because look, how are things really with those two girls? One of them, the dark-haired one – I'm almost ashamed to have to make this detailed defence, but you've asked for it – the dark-haired one, then, is probably no less of an embarrassment to me than to you; if there's any way I can keep my distance from her, I do, and she actually makes it easier, there couldn't be a shyer person.' 'Yes,' Frieda exclaimed, the words bursting from her as if against her will; K. was pleased to see her so distracted; she was different from the way she wished to be, 'you may see her as shy, the world's most brazen creature you call shy, and you honestly mean it, incredible though it is, I know you're not pretending. The Bridge Inn landlady says about you: I can't abide him, but I can't abandon him either, it's like when you see a little child who can't walk properly yet and ventures a long way ahead, you can't control yourself, you have to do something.' 'Take her advice this time,' said K. with a smile, 'but that girl, whether she's shy or shameless we can leave aside here, I don't wish to know about her.' 'But why do you call her shy?' Frieda asked adamantly, K. took this interest as a sign in his favour, 'have you put it to the test, or is this your way of disparaging others?' 'Neither,' said K., 'I call her that out of gratitude because she makes it easy for me to take no notice of her and because, even if she asked me repeatedly, I couldn't bring myself to go back there, which would definitely be a major loss so far as I'm concerned since I need to go there because of our joint future, as you know. And that's why I also need to talk to the other girl, of whom I admit I think highly for her competence, prudence, and selflessness, but who could never be depicted as a temptress.' 'The hands think differently,' said Frieda. 'In this and I dare say in many other respects too,' said K. 'You'd infer I'd been unfaithful from the cravings of the hands?' Frieda said nothing but allowed K. to take the tray from her, place it on the ground, slip his arm beneath hers, and begin slowly pacing up and down with her, keeping to a small area. 'You don't know what being faithful is,' she said, resisting his closeness slightly, 'however you choose to behave towards the girls, that's not what really matters; the mere fact of your visiting that family at all and coming back with the smell of their parlour in your clothes is for me an intolerable disgrace. And you go running from the school without a word. And even stay with them half the night. And then, when someone asks after you, have the girls disown you, passionately disown you, particularly the one who's so shy. Sneak secretly out of the house, possibly even to protect the girls' reputations, the girls' reputations! No, let's not talk about it any more!' 'Not about that,' said K., 'but about something else, Frieda. Anyway, there's no more to be said about that. You know why I have to go there. It isn't easy for me, but I force myself. You shouldn't make it harder for me than it is. Today I thought I'd go there just for a moment and ask whether Barnabas, who should have brought an important message long ago, had finally come. He hadn't, but soon would, I was credibly assured, very soon. I was reluctant to have him come on to me at the school, wanting to avoid bothering you with his presence. Hours went by, and unfortunately he didn't come. Someone else did, though, someone I detest. I didn't feel like having him spy on me so I went through the next-door garden, but nor did I wish to hide from him, instead I went straight up to him on the street, though with, I admit, a nice bendy willow rod. That's all, so there's nothing further to be said about it, but about something else there is. What's the situation with the assistants, mentioning whom I find almost as repellent as you find any mention of that family? Compare your relationship with them to the way I behave towards the family. I understand your dislike of the family and can share it. It's only because of this business that I go to them, sometimes it almost seems to me I'm doing them an injustice, exploiting them. But take you and the assistants. You've never denied they persecute you and have admitted that it attracts you to them. I wasn't cross with you for that, I could see forces were at work here that you were no match for, I was glad you at least put up a fight, even helped you defend yourself, and just because I relaxed my attention for a couple of hours, confident of your loyalty but also hoping that the building really was locked and that the assistants had been driven off for good – I'm afraid I still underestimate them – just because I relaxed my attention for a couple of hours and that Jeremiah, who on closer inspection is a none-too-healthy, quite elderly fellow, had the cheek to come to the window, just because of that I'm to lose you, Frieda, and find myself greeted with the words: "There'll be no wedding." Surely I'm the one who could make accusations and yet doesn't, still doesn't.' And again K. thought it was time to take Frieda's mind off things a bit, so he asked her to bring him something to eat, he hadn't eaten since lunchtime. Clearly relieved by the request herself, Frieda nodded and ran off to fetch something, not farther down the passage, where K. had assumed the kitchen to be, but down some steps to one side. She was soon back with a plate of cold meat and a bottle of wine, but it was only the remains of a meal, presumably, the individual slices had been hastily rearranged to conceal the fact, there were even discarded sausage skins, and the bottle was three-quarters empty. However, K. said nothing about this and fell to with a hearty appetite. 'You went to the kitchen?' he asked. 'No, to my room,' she said, 'I have a room down here.' 'I wish you'd taken me with you,' said K., 'I'll go down there and sit a bit while I eat.' 'I'll bring you a chair,' said Frieda and turned to go. 'No, thanks,' K. said, holding her back, 'I'll not be going down there, nor do I need a chair.' Sulkily, Frieda endured his grip, bowing her head low and biting her lips. 'All right, he's down there,' she said, 'what did you expect? He's lying in my bed, he caught a chill outside, he's shivering, he's hardly eaten. It's all your fault, basically, if you hadn't chased the assistants away and gone running after those people, we could now be sitting peacefully in the school. You're the one who's destroyed our happiness. Do you suppose Jeremiah would have dared seduce me as long as he was in service? If you do, you've got the system here completely wrong. He wanted to come to me, he was in agony, he'd lie in wait for me, but it was just a game, the way a hungry dog will fool around but not actually go so far as to jump on the table. And I was the same. I was drawn to him, he's my playmate from childhood – we used to play together on the slopes of Castle Hill, marvellous times, you've never asked me about my past – but none of that mattered so long as Jeremiah was restrained by his position, I knew my duty as your wife-to-be. But then you drove the assistants off and even boasted about it as if you'd done something for me, well, in a sense you had. In Arthur's case, you got what you wanted, if only temporarily, he's delicate, he lacks Jeremiah's passion, which defies every difficulty, also when you punched him during the night – that blow was also levelled at our happiness – you almost destroyed him, he fled to the castle to complain, and although he'll soon be back he's away for now. But Jeremiah stayed. On duty he's afraid if his master twitches an eyebrow, off duty he's afraid of nothing. He came and took me; abandoned by you, dominated by him, my old friend, I couldn't help myself. I didn't unlock the school door, he smashed the window and pulled me out. We fled here, the landlord thinks highly of him, and what better for the guests than to have such a room-waiter, so we were taken on, he's not living with me but we share a room.' 'In spite of everything,' said K., 'I don't regret having driven the assistants from our service. If the relationship was as you describe it, in other words your fidelity due only to the assistants' obligation to us as our servants, then it was good that everything came to an end. It would hardly have been a happy marriage, between two beasts of prey only whipping could tame. In which case, I'm also grateful to the family that unintentionally contributed towards splitting us up.' They fell silent and began pacing up and down again, and this time there was no telling who had started it. Frieda, close beside K., appeared irked that he did not take her arm again. 'That way everything would be all right,' K. went on, 'and we could say goodbye, you to go to your lord and master Jeremiah, who probably still has a chill from the school garden and whom in that respect you've left alone far too long, and I on my own to the school, or else, since without you I've no business there, to some other place where they'll have me. If I hesitate, it's because I still, with good reason, have my doubts about what you've told me. I have the opposite impression of Jeremiah. As long as he was in service he was after you, and I don't think in the long run the job would have kept him from making a serious assault on you at some time. Now, though, since he's regarded the job as over, it's different. Forgive me, but this is how I see it: now that you're no longer his master's fiancée, you've ceased to be such a temptation to him. You may be his girlfriend from childhood but in my view – I know him only from a brief conversation this evening, really – he sets no great store by such emotional factors. I can't think why you see him as a passionate person. The way his mind works strikes me as unusually calculating. Regarding myself, he's been given some commission by Galater, possibly none too favourable to me, which he's trying hard to perform with what I'll admit is a certain passion for the job – it's not all that rare here – part of it being to wreck our relationship; he may have tried it in various ways, one was that he attempted to entice you with his leching, another, in which he had the landlady's backing, that he told stories about my infidelity, his attack succeeded, some memory of Klamm surrounding him may have helped, true, he lost his job, but possibly just when he no longer needed it, now he reaps the fruits of his labours and pulls you out of the schoolroom window, but with that his work is done and, his passion for the job deserting him, he feels weary, would rather be in Arthur's place, Arthur who is not lodging a complaint at all but collecting praise and fresh commissions, someone has to stay behind, though, and see how things develop. It's a rather tiresome duty for him, looking after you. There's no trace of love for you, he's openly admitted as much to me, as Klamm's mistress you're of course a respectable figure in his eyes, and installing himself in your room and feeling like a lesser Klamm for once no doubt does him a lot of good, but that's as far as it goes, you yourself mean nothing to him now, it's only on top of his main job that he's found accommodation for you here; to avoid unsettling you, he stayed on himself, but only temporarily, just till he receives fresh news from the castle and you've made his cold better.' 'How you slander him!' Frieda said, striking her little fists together. 'Slander him?' said K., 'no, I'm not trying to slander him. I may be doing him an injustice, of course, that's possible. You see, it's not all obvious on the surface, what I've been saying about him, it's open to another interpretation. But slander him? Surely, the only point of that would be to combat your love for him. Were it necessary and were slander a suitable means, I shouldn't hesitate to slander him. No one could condemn me for that, given the person he takes his orders from he has such an advantage over me that I might well, having no other resource, be allowed a bit of slandering. It would be a relatively innocent and, when all's said and done, also impotent means of defence. So you can put your fists down.' And K. took Frieda's hand in his; Frieda tried to pull it away, but smilingly and not making any great effort. 'But I don't need slander,' said K., 'because you don't in fact love him, you only think you do, and you'll thank me for freeing you from the illusion. Look, if someone wanted to get you away from me not by force but with the most careful calculation possible, he'd have to do it using both assistants. Ostensibly kind-hearted, childlike, cheerful, feckless young men who've blown in from above, from the castle, with a dash of childhood memory added, it's all very endearing, of course it is, particularly when I'm the opposite of all that, constantly preoccupied with matters you don't fully understand, that irritate you, that bring me into contact with people you find hateful and who, for all my innocence, pass on something of that to me too. The whole thing is simply a malicious though most ingenious exploitation of the flaws in our relationship. Every relationship has its flaws, even ours; we came together from quite different worlds, after all, and since we've known each other, our lives have each taken an entirely fresh turn, we're still unsure of ourselves, everything's too new. I'm not talking about myself, that's not so important, as a matter of fact I've been receiving gifts ever since you first turned to look at me, and that's not a hard thing to get used to, receiving gifts. But you, apart from anything else, were torn away from Klamm, I can't gauge what that means, but I have gradually acquired some sense of it, the upheaval, the feeling of being unable to cope, and although I was prepared always to take you in, I wasn't always there, and if I was you were sometimes in the grip of your dreams or something more substantial, the landlady, say – in short, there were times when you looked away from me, longing to penetrate some half-indeterminate sphere, poor child, and during such interludes it only needed suitable people to be lined up in the direction of your gaze for you to be lost to them, falling for the illusion that what were only moments, ghosts, old memories, basically past, indeed increasingly passing former existence, that this was still your real life now. An error, Frieda, merely the last and, looked at properly, contemptible problem facing our eventual union. Wake up, pull yourself together; you may have thought the assistants had been sent by Klamm – it's not true, they came from Galater – and they may, aided by that illusion, have managed to bewitch you in such a way that even in their smut and obscenity you felt you found traces of Klamm, the way a person thinks he sees a once mislaid gemstone in a dungheap, whereas in reality he could never find it there, even if that was where it really was – the fact remains, they're only lads, much like the hands in the stable, except they lack their health, a bit of fresh air makes them ill and puts them in bed, a place their servile cunning is adept at seeking out anyway.' Frieda had laid her head on K.'s shoulder, they were walking up and down in silence, arms round each other. 'If only,' Frieda said slowly, quietly, almost contentedly, as if aware that she had been granted only the briefest period of peace on K.'s shoulder but wishing to savour it utterly, 'if only we'd left here immediately, that night, we might be somewhere in safety, together the whole time, your hand always near enough to grasp; how I need your nearness, how much, since I met you, I've felt abandoned without your nearness; believe me, your nearness is all I ever dream of, the only thing.'

There was a shout in the side passage, it was Jeremiah, he was standing on the bottom step, wearing only a shirt but with one of Frieda's shawls around him. The way he was standing there, hair dishevelled, skimpy beard as if rain-soaked, eyes painfully wide, pleading and reproachful, dark cheeks flushed but as if the flesh hung too loosely, bare legs shivering from the cold so that the long fringes of the shawl shivered with them, he was like a patient escaped from hospital, for whom one's only thought, probably, would be getting him back into bed. Which was just how Frieda assessed the situation, she slipped away from K. and was down there with him immediately. Her nearness, the care with which she pulled the shawl more tightly round him, the urgency with which she tried to push him straight back into the room, seemed in themselves to make him a little stronger, it was as if he recognized K. only at this point, 'Ah, the land surveyor,' he said, with Frieda, loath to allow any more talk, stroking his cheek to soothe him, 'sir, forgive the interruption. I'm not at all well, though, that's my excuse. I think I'm running a temperature, I must take an infusion and sweat it out. Those wretched railings in the school garden,

I'll have cause to remember them, and now, with a chill already, I've been running around at night. We all, without noticing what we're doing, sacrifice our health for things that are truly not worth it. But, sir, you mustn't let me interrupt you, come into our room with us, visit a sick man, and while you're at it tell Frieda what remains to be said. When two people who are used to each other come to part, then of course, in the final moments, they have so much to say to each other that a third person, particularly one who's lying in bed, waiting for the infusion he's been promised, cannot possibly know what it's like. Do come in, though, I'll be quite quiet.' 'All right, that's enough,' said Frieda, tugging at his arm, 'he's feverish and doesn't realize what he's saying. But don't come in, K., please. This is my and Jeremiah's room or rather my room alone, I forbid you to come in with us. You're persecuting me, K., why are you persecuting me. I'll never come back to you, not ever, just thinking of the possibility makes me shudder. Go to your girls, why don't you; dressed only in their chemises, so I'm told, they sit with you on the bench by the stove, and when someone comes to fetch you they spit in his face. That's clearly where you belong if you're drawn there so much. I always kept you away from there, not very successfully, still, I kept you away, now that's over, you're free. You've a fine life ahead of you, you may have a bit of a tussle with the hands for one of them, but as far as the other's concerned, no one in heaven or on earth will begrudge you her. The alliance is blessed from the outset. Don't say a word to the contrary, oh I know, you can deny everything, but in the end nothing is denied. Imagine, Jeremiah, he's denied everything!' They exchanged nods and smiles. 'However,' Frieda went on, 'supposing he had denied everything, what would that achieve, what do I care? How things go with them in that place is entirely their and his affair, not mine. Mine is to look after you until you're well again, the way you were once, before K. started tormenting you on my account.' 'Are you really not coming then, sir?' Jeremiah asked, but here Frieda, who did not even turn to face K. again, finally pulled him away. A small door could be seen down below, even lower than the doors in the passage, not just Jeremiah, even Frieda had to stoop to enter, inside it looked bright and warm, whispering was heard for a while, no doubt tender persuasions to get Jeremiah into bed, then the door was shut.

23

Only now did K. notice how quiet it had become in the passage, not just in this part of the passage where he had been with Frieda and that seemed to belong to the utility rooms but also in the long passage with the rooms that had previously been so busy. So the gentlemen had gone to bed at last. K. was very tired himself, possibly it was through tiredness that he had failed to stand up to Jeremiah as he should have done. It might have been wiser to copy Jeremiah, who was obviously exaggerating his chill – his wretchedness did not come from a chill, it was innate and not to be cured by herb tea – to copy Jeremiah exactly, make a similar show of his really extreme tiredness, sink to the floor here in the passage, which would surely have done a lot of good on its own, doze for a bit and then perhaps also get a bit of attention. The trouble was, it would not have turned out as well as it had for Jeremiah, who would surely and no doubt rightly have won this competition for sympathy in addition, clearly, to winning the other contest. K. was so tired, he wondered whether he might not try to enter one of these rooms, many of which he was sure were vacant, and have a good sleep in a nice bed. That might have made up for a lot, he thought. He even had a nightcap ready. The tray Frieda had left lying on the floor had had a small decanter of rum on it. Not worrying about the effort of getting back, K. drained the little bottle.

Now he at least felt strong enough to face Erlanger. He looked for the door to Erlanger's room, but since the servant and Gerstäcker were no longer to be seen and all the doors were identical, he could not find it. However, believing he remembered more or less where in the passage the door had been, he decided to open a door that was probably, he thought, the one he was looking for. There was no harm in trying; if it was Erlanger's room, Erlanger would no doubt receive him, if it was someone else's room, he could always apologize and leave again, and if the guest was asleep, as was most likely, K.'s visit would pass quite unnoticed, the only potential problem was if the room was vacant, because then K. would scarcely be able to resist the temptation to lie down on the bed and sleep for hours. He gave one more look to right and left along the passage, someone might be coming who could tell him what he needed to know and remove the need for any risk, but the long passage was silent and empty. Next, K. listened at the door, not a sound there either. He knocked softly enough not to wake anyone who might have been asleep, and when even then nothing happened he very carefully opened the door. Here, though, a shriek greeted him. It was a small room, more than half occupied by a wide bed, the lamp on the bedside table was switched on, beside it stood a small travelling bag. In the bed, but completely hidden under the quilt, someone shifted uneasily and whispered through a gap between quilt and sheet: 'Who is it?' Now K. could no longer simply leave, he contemplated the ample but unfortunately not empty bed with displeasure, then remembered the question and gave his name. This seemed to have a positive effect, the man in the bed pulled the quilt away from his face a little, but timidly, all ready to cover himself up again immediately if there was something not right outside. Then, however, he threw the quilt back without further thought and sat up. It was certainly not Erlanger. This was a small, fit-looking man whose face presented a certain inherent contradiction in that the cheeks were round like a child's, the eyes merry like a child's, but the high forehead, pointed nose, narrow mouth with lips that barely met, and almost non-existent chin were not childish at all but suggested a superior intelligence. It was no doubt contentment on that score, contentment with himself, that had preserved in him a large measure of healthy childishness. 'Know Friedrich?' he asked. K. said he did not. 'He knows you, though,' the man said with a smile. K. nodded, there was no shortage of people who knew him, in fact that was one of the greatest obstacles in his path. 'I'm his secretary,' the man said, 'name's Bürgel.' 'Forgive me,' said K., reaching for the doorhandle, 'I'm afraid I mistook your door for another. I've been summoned to Secretary Erlanger, in fact.' 'What a shame!' said Bürgel. 'Not your being summoned elsewhere, your mistaking the doors. You see, once I'm awake, there's no chance I'll get back to sleep. Well, you mustn't let that distress you, that's my bad luck. Anyway, why can't the doors here be lockable? you're wondering. There's a reason, of course. Because, according to an old saying, the secretaries' doors should always be open. Still, there was no need to take it so literally.' Bürgel gave K. an inquiring and quite happy look, in contrast to his complaint he seemed perfectly rested, probably Bürgel had never in his life been as tired as K. was now. 'Right, where do you want to go?' Bürgel asked. 'It's four o'clock. Anyone you wanted to go to now you'd have to wake up, they aren't all as used to being disturbed as I am, they won't all take it as patiently, they're a highly-strung lot, the secretaries. So stay awhile. People here start getting up around five, that'll be the best time for you to answer your summons. So please, let go of that doorhandle and sit down somewhere, there's not much room here, I grant you, the best thing will be if you sit on the edge of the bed here. You're surprised I have no table and chair in here? Well, I was given the choice of having either a fully furnished room with a narrow hotel bed or this big bed and nothing else but the washstand. I chose the big bed; in a bedroom, surely the main thing is the bed. Ah, if a person could stretch out and sleep well, for a good sleeper this bed would have to be truly exquisite. But even I, who am tired all the time without being able to sleep, find it does me good, I spend much of the day in it, do all my letters here, take people's statements. It works very well. There's nowhere for the parties to sit, of course, but they get over that, in fact it's more agreeable for them too if they're standing and the person taking the statement is at his ease, instead of them sitting comfortably but being yelled at. Then I just have this space on the edge of the bed available, but that's not an official place, it's only for talks at night. But you're so quiet, Mr Land Surveyor.' 'I'm extremely tired,' said K., who as soon as invited had rudely, disrespectfully sat down on the bed and leaned back against the post. 'Of course you are,' said Bürgel with a smile, 'everyone's tired here. For example, it was no mean job I did yesterday and that I've already done today. As I said, there's no question of my falling asleep now, but in the utterly unlikely event that I should fall asleep while you're here, please just keep quiet and don't open the door either. However, worry not, I certainly shan't fall asleep, at best it'll only be for a few minutes. That's the way it is with me, you see, probably because I'm so used to parties coming and going, I fall asleep most easily when I have company.'

'Please, just go ahead and sleep, sir,' said K., delighted by this announcement, 'in which case, if it's all right with you, I'll sleep a little myself.'
'No, no,' Bürgel said, laughing again, 'I'm afraid it takes more than an invitation to make me fall asleep, it's only in the course of an interview that the opportunity may arise; an interview is the thing most likely to put me to sleep. I'm telling you, the nerves suffer in our business. Take me, I'm a link secretary. You don't know what that is? Well, I'm the strongest link' – here he swiftly rubbed his hands together in involuntary merriment – 'between Friedrich and the village, I'm the link between his castle and village secretaries, I'm mostly in the village though not permanently, I have to be ready to return to the castle at any time, you see the travelling bag, a restless life, doesn't suit everyone. On the other hand, the fact is I couldn't be without this kind of work now, any other kind would seem stale to me. What's land surveying like?' 'I don't do that job, I'm not working as a land surveyor,' said K., scarcely thinking about what he was saying, actually he was longing for Bürgel to fall asleep, but even that was only out of a certain sense of duty towards himself, deep down he felt he knew that the moment of Bürgel's falling asleep was still immeasurably distant. 'That's amazing,' Bürgel said with much tossing of his head as he pulled a notepad from under the quilt to jot something down, 'you're a land surveyor and have no land surveying work?' K. nodded mechanically, he had stretched his left arm out on top of the bedpost and laid his head on it; he had tried various ways of getting comfortable, but this position was the most comfortable of all, also he could now pay slightly more attention to what Bürgel was saying. 'I'm prepared,' Bürgel went on, 'to take this matter further. It's most certainly not our way here to let a skilled man go unused. And you must find it hurtful yourself, do you not suffer as a result?' 'Oh, I suffer,' K. said slowly, smiling to himself because at the moment he was not suffering at all. Also, Bürgel's offer made little impression on him. It was so amateurish. Knowing nothing of the circumstances in which K.'s appointment had occurred, of the problems it had met with in the municipality and in the castle, of the complications that in the time K. had been here had already arisen or had announced themselves – knowing nothing of all this, in fact giving no indication that, as might well have been assumed of a secretary, he had at least an inkling of it, here he was, offering off the cuff, with the aid of his

notepad, to sort matters out. 'You seem to have had a number of disappointments already,' Bürgel said at this point, proving that he did after all have some understanding of human nature, and indeed K. had been telling himself on and off since entering the room not to underestimate Bürgel, though in his condition it was hard to form a just view of anything beyond his own weariness. 'No,' said Bürgel, as if replying to a thought of K.'s and considerately wishing to spare him the effort of voicing it, 'you mustn't let disappointments put you off. A lot of things here seem designed to put one off, and when a person first arrives the obstacles look insuperable. I don't want to go into how things actually stand in this regard, it may be that the appearance does in fact match the reality, in my position I lack the proper distance to judge, but note this, other opportunities arise from time to time that almost don't accord with the overall situation, opportunities whereby a word, a glance, a sign of trust may achieve more than a lifetime of exhausting endeavour. I assure you, that's how it is. Then again, of course, such opportunities do in fact accord with the overall situation in that they're never made use of. But why aren't they made use of, I keep wondering.' K. did not know, he was aware, of course, that what Bürgel was talking about probably concerned him closely, but at the moment he had a great aversion to all things concerning himself, he jerked his head slightly to one side as if in so doing he was leaving the way clear for Bürgel's questions and could no longer be affected by them. 'It is,' Bürgel continued, stretching his arms and yawning, which conflicted bewilderingly with the gravity of his words, 'it is a constant complaint of the secretaries that they're obliged to conduct most village examinations at night. But why do they complain about it? Because it's a strain for them? Because they'd rather use the night for sleeping? No, that's certainly not what they're complaining about. Of course, some of the secretaries are diligent, others less so, it's the same every-where, but none of them is going to complain of too much strain, particularly not in public. It's just not our way. In this respect, we see no difference between ordinary time and working time. Such distinctions are alien to us. So what is it the secretaries have against night-time examinations? Consideration for the parties, say? No, no, that's not it, either. With regard to the parties, secretaries are ruthless, though no more ruthless than with regard to themselves, not a bit of it, precisely as ruthless. Actually, that very ruthlessness, which is in fact strict compliance with and execution of a secretary's duties, is the highest consideration the parties could ever wish for. Basically, too – a superficial observer will not notice this, of course – the fact is fully recognized; for instance, in this case it's the night-time examinations in particular that the parties like, no complaints of principle against night-time examinations are received. So why the secretaries' aversion?' K. did not know this either, he knew so little, he could not even tell whether Bürgel was seriously demanding an answer or only appearing to, 'If you let me lie in your bed,' he was thinking, 'tomorrow noon or better still in the evening I'll answer all your questions.' But Bürgel seemed to be paying no attention to him, he was altogether too taken up with the question he had put to himself: 'So far as I can see and so far as my own experience goes, the secretaries have more or less the following reservation about night-time examinations. The reason why night-time is less suitable for hearing parties is because at night it's difficult if not impossible fully to preserve the official character of such hearings. This has nothing to do with externals, the formalities can of course, if we wish, be observed quite as strictly at night as during the day. So it's not that; on the other hand, official judgement suffers at night. There's an instinctive tendency to judge things from a more individual standpoint at night, the parties' submissions carry greater weight than is appropriate, totally irrelevant considerations to do with the parties' wider situations, their cares and concerns, interfere in the judgement, the requisite barrier between parties and officials, even if outwardly present and correct, is more relaxed and where normally, as should be the case, only questions and answers pass back and forth, sometimes a curious, quite unsuitable exchange of identities seems to occur. So, at least, the secretaries say, i.e. people professionally endowed with a quite exceptional sensitivity regarding such things. But even they – this is something we've often talked about amongst ourselves – remain largely unaware of these unfavourable influences during night-time examinations, on the contrary, they strive from the outset to counteract them and feel in the end that they've turned in particularly good performances. However, reading through the statements later, one's frequently amazed at their patent shortcomings. And these are errors, often in fact semi-unjustified gains by the parties, that under our rules at least can no longer be rectified by the usual short cut. They're sure to be corrected by a control bureau at some stage, but that will only benefit the law, it can't harm the party any more. Under the circumstances, aren't the secretaries' complaints highly justified?' K. had already been half-dozing for a while, now he was disturbed again. 'What's this all about? What's this all about?' he wondered and from beneath lowered eyelids considered Bürgel not as an official who was discussing difficult questions with him but simply as something that was keeping him from sleeping, the further significance of which escaped him. Bürgel, on the other hand, absorbed in his train of thought, was smiling as if he had just succeeded in misleading K. slightly. However, he was ready to guide him back on to the right path again immediately. 'Still,' he said, 'neither can we call these complaints entirely justified and leave it at that. All right, nowhere are night-time examinations actually prescribed, so a person is not violating any rule in seeking to avoid them, but circumstances, the vast amount of work, the way officials are employed in the castle, the difficulty of getting hold of them, the rule that examination of parties is to take place only after the rest of the investigation has been completed in full, but must then be conducted immediately, all these things and others too have made night-time examinations an unavoidable necessity. However, if they have become a necessity – this is what I say – it's partly, at least indirectly, a consequence of the rules, and carping at the fact of night-time examinations would be almost tantamount – I exaggerate slightly, of course, the reason being that as an exaggeration I'm permitted to voice it – would be tantamount to carping at the rules themselves. On the other hand, let it be said that the secretaries do, within the rules, seek to protect themselves against night-time examinations and the perhaps only apparent disadvantages of them so far as they can. Indeed they do and to a quite enormous extent, they admit only matters at issue from which there's a minimum to fear in that regard, check themselves carefully before hearings and then, if the result of the check requires it, order even last-minute postponements of all examinations, fortify themselves by summoning a party often as many as ten times before actually conducting the examination, happily have colleagues represent them who are not responsible for the case in question and can therefore deal with it more easily, fix hearings at least for the early or latter part of the night, avoiding the hours in between – there are many more such measures; they're not easy to get the better of, the secretaries, they're almost as robust as they are vulnerable.' K. was asleep, not properly, of course, he could hear Bürgel's words if anything better than before, when he had been awake but dead-tired, word upon word struck his ear, but the burden of consciousness had disappeared, he felt free, it was not Bürgel holding him now, it was himself still occasionally reaching out for Bürgel, he was not yet in the depths of sleep but he was immersed in it, no one was going to take that away from him now. And he felt as if he had carried off a great victory here, and people had already gathered to celebrate it and he or possibly someone else was raising a champagne glass to toast the victory. And in order that everyone should know what was going on, the battle and the victory were being re-enacted once again or possibly not re-enacted at all, they were happening for the first time and had already been celebrated before and it was not being taken as a reason for not celebrating them that the outcome was fortunately beyond doubt. A secretary, naked and looking very like a statue of a Greek god, was being pressed by K. in combat. It was very comical, and K. smiled gently in his sleep at the way the secretary was constantly being startled out of his proud bearing by K.'s thrusts and had to make swift use of, say, his upstretched arm and clenched fist to cover his nakedness, yet every time was too slow in doing so. The fight did not last long; step by step, and they were huge steps, K. advanced. Was it a fight at all, in fact? There was no serious obstacle, just the odd squeal from the secretary. He squealed, this Greek god, like a young girl being tickled. And in the end he was gone; K. was alone in a large room, in fighting stance he turned around, looking for his opponent, but there was no one there any more, even the people had dispersed, only the champagne glass lay on the ground, broken, K. crushed it underfoot. But the pieces stabbed him, with a start he did now wake up, he felt sick, the way a child does when woken, yet even so the sight of Bürgel's bare chest prompted the thought, coming from the dream: 'Here is your Greek god! Come on, haul him out of bed!' 'However,' said Bürgel, his face raised thoughtfully towards the ceiling as if he was searching his memory for examples but could find none, 'there is nevertheless, despite all precautionary measures, a chance of the parties turning this nocturnal weakness on the part of the secretaries, always supposing it is a weakness, to their advantage. A very slim chance, admittedly, or rather, one that almost never occurs. It consists in the parties arriving unannounced in the middle of the night. Perhaps you're surprised that what seems so obvious should happen so rarely. Yes, well, you're not familiar with our circumstances here. Still, even you must have been struck by the completeness of the official organization. One result of that completeness, though, is that everyone who has any kind of request or who for other reasons needs to be examined about something will instantly, without hesitation, usually even before he has himself prepared his case, indeed before he is aware of it himself, receive a summons. He won't be examined this time, not as a rule, the business has usually not got as far as that yet, but he's received his summons, so arriving unannounced, i.e. entirely unexpected, is no longer an option, the most he can do is arrive at the wrong time, in which case, well, he'll simply have his attention drawn to the date and hour of the summons, and if he then comes back at the right time he's generally sent away, that's no longer a problem, the summons in the party's hand and the entry in the records are, for the secretaries, perhaps not always adequate but certainly powerful weapons of defence. That applies only to the particular secretary with competence for the case, though, it would still be open to anyone to approach the others unexpectedly at night. But very few do that, it makes almost no sense. For one thing, the effect would be to infuriate the competent secretary, not of course that we secretaries are jealous of one another so far as work is concerned, we all carry far too big a workload for that, heaped on us really quite unstintingly, but with regard to parties we're simply not allowed to countenance any irregularities over competence. Many a party has lost his chance because, feeling he was getting nowhere with the competent agency, he tried to slip past one that was not. Anyway, such attempts are bound to fail since a non-competent secretary, even if he's caught unawares at night and really wants to help, can scarcely, for the very reason that it is not his responsibility, take any further action than your average lawyer could, or rather, when all's said and done, a great deal less because, even if he might otherwise do something, knowing the secret avenues of the law as he does better than any of the legal crowd – he simply, regarding things outside his competence, has no time, not so much as a moment can he spend on them. So who, given such prospects, would utilize his nights going around non-competent secretaries, and anyway the parties are fully employed if, in addition to their usual occupations, they want to comply with the summonses and suggestions of the competent agencies, "fully employed" in the parties' sense, that is, which is of course nothing like the same as "fully employed" in the secretaries' sense.' K. nodded, smiling, now he thoroughly understood everything, he thought, not that it bothered him but because he was now convinced that in the next few moments he would fall asleep completely, this time with no dreaming and interruption; between the competent secretaries on the one hand and the non-competent on the other, and faced with the throng of fully-employed parties, he would sink into a deep sleep and in that way elude them all. He was so used to Bürgel's voice by now, soft, self-satisfied, and evidently labouring in vain as regarded putting its owner to sleep, that it would induce sleep for him more than disturb it. 'Clack away, little mill, clack away,' he thought, 'clacking just for me.' 'So where,' said Bürgel, playing on his underlip with two fingers, eyes wide, neck outstretched, almost as if after an arduous journey he was approaching some delightful vantage point, 'where, then, is that chance I mentioned, so rare it almost never happens? The secret lies in the rules governing competence. You see, it is not and in a large, living organization cannot be the rule that only one particular secretary is competent in each case. It's just that one has the main competence but many others have competence too, in certain aspects, if to a lesser degree. Who, on his own, however great a worker, could gather all the strands of even the most minor incident together on his desk at one time? Even what I said about the main competence itself goes too far. Doesn't even the smallest competence already encompass the whole? Isn't the crucial thing here the fervour with which the matter is addressed? And isn't that always the same, always present with full intensity? There may be all sorts of differences among the secretaries, there are indeed such differences, masses of them, but not in terms of fervour, there's not one of the secretaries will be able to hold back when faced with a request that he deal with a case for which he possesses the slightest competence. For external purposes, of course, there needs to be a tidy procedural option;

consequently, for the parties it is always one particular secretary who comes to the fore, to whom they're officially meant to turn. However, this needn't even be the one with the greatest competence in respect of the case, that will be decided by the organization and its specific immediate requirements. That's the position. And now, sir, consider the possibility of a party, as a result of certain circumstances, any circumstances, and despite the obstacles that have been described to you and that usually prove quite adequate, nevertheless, in the middle of the night, surprising a secretary who possesses a certain competence regarding the case concerned. Presumably such a possibility never occurred to you before, am I right? I quite believe it. Nor need it have done, since it almost never ever happens. What an oddly and very specifically shaped, agile little granule such a party would need to be to pass through the supreme sieve. You think it can't happen at all? You're right, it can't. But one night – who can vouch for everything? – it does happen. Though I know of no one, among my acquaintance, to whom it's ever occurred; all right, that proves very little, my circle of acquaintance is limited, measured against the numbers involved here, and anyway it's by no means certain that a secretary to whom something of the sort has occurred will want to admit as much, it's a very personal matter, after all, and one that touches closely on official nakedness, if you like. Still, what my experience does perhaps show is that we're talking about something so rare, which is actually only rumoured to exist and is not corroborated by anything else, that it's a great exaggeration to be afraid of it. Even if this thing really did occur, it's possible – so we're told – literally to render it harmless by showing it, which is very easy to do, that there's no room for it in this world. At any rate, it's morbid to be so scared of it that one hides under the quilt, say, and daren't look out. And even if total improbability had suddenly materialized, does that mean all is lost? On the contrary. Everything being lost is even less likely than the least likely thing of all. Of course, if the party is in the room, things are bad, very bad. One's chest tightens. "How long will your resistance last?" one asks oneself. But it won't be resistance, one's aware of that. Look, just picture the situation as it really is. There he sits, the party, never seen before but always expected, I mean really thirsted after, and always sensibly regarded as out of reach. The man's silent presence is itself an invitation to penetrate his wretched life, to look around in it as if one were the owner, and to suffer with him from his futile demands. That invitation, in the silence of night, is an enchantment. One accepts it and has actually ceased, then, to be an official. It's a situation in which it quickly becomes impossible to turn down a request. To be precise, one is in despair, to be even more precise, one's extremely happy. In despair, because the defenceless way one sits there, waiting for the party's request and knowing that, once voiced, it must be granted, even if, so far as one's own vision goes, at least, it literally rips the official organization apart – that is probably the worst thing one comes up against, doing this job. Above all – apart from anything else – because it's also an incredible jump in rank that one's here, for a moment, forcibly laying claim to. Our position simply doesn't give us the authority to grant requests such as we're talking about here, but through the proximity of this party at night it's as if our official powers grow too, we commit ourselves to things that lie outside our province, indeed we'll even implement them, the party extorts sacrifices from us in the night like the robber in the forest, sacrifices we'd never be capable of normally – all right, that's how it is then, when the party's still there, still giving us strength and coercing us and egging us on, and everything is still progressing half unconsciously, but how will it be afterwards, when it's over, the satisfied, carefree party has left us, and there we stand, alone, defenceless in the face of our misuse of office – that doesn't bear thinking about. And yet we're happy. How suicidal happiness can be! I mean, we could make an effort to conceal the true situation from the party. He is hardly going to notice anything on his own. He probably thinks he's just somehow, never mind how, found his way, exhausted, disappointed, reckless and apathetic from exhaustion and disappointment, into a different room from the one he wanted, he's sitting there unsuspecting, busy thinking, if he's busy at all, about his mistake or about how tired he is. Couldn't one just leave him to it? No, it's impossible. With the garrulousness of the happy man, one must explain everything to him. One must show him, in detail, with no chance of sparing oneself, what has happened and the reasons why it has happened, what an exceptionally unusual and uniquely great opportunity this is, one must show how, having stumbled upon this opportunity with all the helplessness of which no other creature, only a party, is capable, he can now, if he wishes, Mr Land Surveyor, sir, control everything, all he need do is somehow make his request, the granting of which is already prepared, is in fact reaching out towards him – all those things must be shown, it's the official's hour of trial. But when one's managed that too, sir, then the essential has been done, one must be content to wait.'

That was all K. heard, he was asleep, cut off from everything that was happening. His head, which had initially been resting on his left arm on top of the bedpost, had slid off in his sleep and now hung free, slowly sinking lower, the support of the arm up above was no longer adequate, instinctively K. gave himself a fresh one by bracing his right arm against the quilt, but he happened, in the process, to grasp hold of Bürgel's foot, which stuck up under the cover at just that point. Bürgel looked across and let him have the foot, irksome though this was.

There was a knocking then, several heavy blows on the side wall, K. started up and looked at the wall. 'Isn't that the land surveyor in there?' a voice asked. 'Yes,' said Bürgel, freeing his foot from K. and stretching, suddenly unruly and mischievous, like a small boy. 'Right, let's have him,' the voice came again; no consideration was shown to Bürgel or to the possibility that he might still need K. 'It's Erlanger,' Bürgel said in a whisper; the fact that Erlanger was in the next room seemed not to surprise him, 'go straight round there, he's already upset, try and calm him down. He sleeps soundly, but we've been talking too loud, it's impossible to keep oneself and one's voice under control on certain subjects. Well, go on then, you look as if you're having trouble waking up. Go on, what are you waiting for? No, you needn't apologize for being sleepy, why should you? The body will only keep going for so long, no one can help it if that particular frontier is significant for other reasons as well. No, that can't be helped. It's the way the world adjusts its course and keeps its balance. It's an excellent, always unimaginably excellent arrangement, is it not, albeit bleak in other respects. Off you go, now, I don't know why you're looking at me like that. If you leave it any longer, Erlanger will be after me, that's something I'd much rather avoid. Go on, who knows what awaits you there, it's all opportunities in this place. Only of course some opportunities are too big to be taken advantage of, as it were; there are things that fail for no reason other than themselves. Oh yes, it's amazing. Also, I'm hoping I may get a little sleep now. It's already five o'clock, of course, and the noise will start soon. Just go, will you!'

Dazed through being roused abruptly from deep sleep, still vastly in need of sleep, his body hurting all over as a result of his awkward posture, for some time K. could not make himself get up, he held his forehead and looked down into his lap. Not even Bürgel's incessant dismissals could have persuaded him to leave, only a sense of the utter futility of remaining in the room any longer slowly brought him round to it. The room seemed indescribably desolate to him. Whether it had become so or had always been so, he did not know. He would not even be able to fall asleep again here. In fact, it was this conviction that clinched matters, with a little smile at the fact he stood up, supported himself wherever he could, on the bed, on the wall, on the door, and not saying a word, as if he had long since taken his leave of Bürgel, went out.

24

Probably he would as apathetically have walked straight past Erlanger's room had not Erlanger, standing in the doorway, signalled to him. A curt signal given with a forefinger, once only. Erlanger was all ready to leave, he wore a black fur coat with a tight collar buttoned right up. A servant was just handing him his gloves and still held a fur hat. 'You should have been here long ago,' said Erlanger. K. tried to apologize, Erlanger indicated by wearily closing his eyes that he would rather he did not. 'The issue is as follows,' he said, 'someone called Frieda used to serve in the bar, I only know the name, the person is unknown to me, she is no concern of mine. This Frieda sometimes served Klamm's beer. Now there appears to be another girl there. The change is trivial, of course, probably in everyone's eyes and most certainly in Klamm's. However, the bigger a job, and don't forget that Klamm's job is the biggest, the less strength it leaves for defending oneself against the outside world; as a result, any trivial change in the most trivial matters can cause a serious upset. The slightest change on the desk, the removal of a stain that had always been there, anything like that can cause an upset, and so can a new serving-girl. Now, of course, none of that, even if it would upset anyone else, doing any old job, upsets Klamm, there can be no question of that. Nevertheless, it is our duty to keep so close an eye on Klamm's well-being that even upsets that do not affect him as such – and there are probably none that do – we remove if they strike us as potential upsets. It's not for his sake or for the sake of his job that we remove them but for our own sake, for the sake of our conscience and our peace of mind. For that reason, the girl Frieda must return to the bar immediately, it may be that her return will in itself cause an upset, in which case we shall send her away again, but for the time being she must return. You live with her, I'm told, so see to it that she returns immediately. Personal feelings cannot be considered here, that goes without saying, so I'll not get involved in any further discussion of the matter. I'm already doing far more than I need by pointing out that, if you prove yourself in this small thing, it may be useful to you some time as regards your making progress. That's all I have to say to you.' He dismissed K. with a nod, donned the fur hat the servant now handed him, and with the servant following him walked quickly, if with a slight limp, off down the passage.

Sometimes, orders were issued here that were very easy to comply with, yet such ease gave K. no joy. Not only because the order concerned Frieda, and though meant as an order sounded to K. like a jibe, but above all because it offered K. a glimpse of the futility of all his endeavours. The orders were issued over his head, the unfavourable ones as well as the favourable, and even the favourable ones no doubt had an ultimately unfavourable core; at any rate, they were all issued over his head, and he was far too lowly to be able to intervene in them, let alone silence them and make his own voice heard. If Erlanger waves you aside, what are you going to do, and if he didn't wave you aside, what could you tell him? K. was still aware that his weariness had done him more harm today than any unfavourable circumstances, but why was he incapable, having believed he could rely on his body, indeed without that conviction he would never have set out in the first place, why could he not tolerate a couple of poor nights and one sleepless one, why did he become so uncontrollably weary here of all places, where no one was weary or rather where everyone was weary the whole time without it harming their work in the least, in fact it seemed to help it. The inference was that theirs was a quite different kind of weariness from K.'s. Here it was presumably weariness in the context of happy work, something that looked like weariness from outside and was really indestructible calm, indestructible peace. Feeling a bit weary at midday is part of the happy, natural course of the day. For the gentlemen here, it's midday all the time, K. told himself.

And it was very much in line with this that things began at this point, around five o'clock, to become lively everywhere off the passage. There was something thoroughly cheerful about this babble of voices in the rooms. At one point it sounded like the merriment of children getting ready for an outing, at another like dawn in the hen-house, like the joy of being in total harmony with the breaking day, somewhere a man even imitated the call of a cockerel. The passage itself was empty as yet, but the doors were already in motion, every now and again one would be opened a little way and swiftly shut again, there was a whirring in the passage from doors being opened and closed like this, here and there K. also saw, in the gaps at the tops of the walls where they stopped short of the ceilings, dishevelled early-morning heads appearing and immediately vanishing. Slowly advancing out of the distance, steered by a servant, came a little trolley loaded with files. Another servant walked alongside, he had a list in his hand and was clearly using it to compare the numbers on the doors with those on the files. The trolley stopped outside most of the doors, usually the door then opened and the appropriate files, though sometimes it was only a single sheet – in such cases a brief conversation developed between room and passage, probably the servant being told off – were handed into the room. Where the door remained closed, the files were carefully stacked on the sill. In such cases, K. had the impression that the motion of the doors in the vicinity did not diminish, despite the fact that the files had already been distributed there too, rather it increased. It could be that the others were peering covetously at files that still, inexplicably, lay unclaimed on the sill, they failed to understand someone needing only to open the door to get hold of his files and not doing so; it could even be that files never claimed were later distributed among the other gentlemen, who were keen to satisfy themselves now, by making frequent checks, as to whether the files still lay on the sill and there was thus still hope for them. Actually, the files that remained on the sills were in most cases particularly large bundles, and K. assumed that there was an element of boasting or malice or even of justified pride, serving as a spur to colleagues, in their having been left lying there temporarily. He was supported in this assumption by the fact that occasionally, always when he was not looking in that direction, the pile, having been left on show for long enough, was suddenly and very swiftly pulled into the room and the door again became as motionless as before; the doors in the vicinity then calmed down too, disappointed or indeed pleased that an object of constant provocation had at last been removed, but then they gradually resumed their motion.

K. considered all this not merely with curiosity but with active interest. He felt almost at ease amid the bustle, looking this way and that and following – at an appropriate distance, of course – behind the servants, who of course had several times already turned to face him with harsh looks, lowered heads, and pursed lips, watching their work of distribution. This went less and less smoothly, the further it proceeded, either there was something not quite right about the list or the files were not always easy for the servants to distinguish or the gentlemen raised objections on other grounds, at any rate certain allocations had to be withdrawn, in which case the trolley reversed and negotiations through the gap above the door were held regarding the return of files. These negotiations caused difficulties enough in their own right, but it frequently happened that, when it came to returning files, the very doors that had previously been in the liveliest motion now remained stubbornly closed as if they wished to hear no more of the matter. It was only then that the real difficulties began. The person who thought he was entitled to the files showed extreme impatience, made a great deal of noise in his room, clapped his hands together, stamped his feet, and kept shouting through the gap above the door out into the passage, reiterating a particular file number. The trolley was then often left entirely abandoned. One servant was busy pacifying the impatient gentleman, the other fighting outside the closed door for the return of the files. Both had problems. The impatient gentleman often became even more impatient as a result of the pacification attempts, incapable of listening to the servant's empty words any more, he did not want consolation, he wanted files, one such gentleman, using the gap above the door, emptied a whole washbasin over the servant. But the other servant, clearly the higher-ranking one, had a far bigger problem. Where the gentleman concerned was prepared to negotiate, business-like discussions ensued in which the servant referred to his list and the gentleman to his notes as well as to the very files he was required to return but for the time being clung to so firmly that very little of them was visible to the servant's covetous eyes. The servant was also, in such a case, obliged to run back and fetch fresh evidence from the trolley, which on the slightly descending floor of the passage had invariably rolled on a little way on its own, or he had to go to the gentleman who was claiming the files and there swap the current owner's objections for fresh counter-objections. Such negotiations took a very long time, occasionally agreement was reached, with the gentle-man perhaps surrendering some of the files or receiving another file in compensation, there having simply been a mistake, but it also happened that a person had to relinquish all the files demanded without further ado, either because he was driven into a corner by the servant's evidence or because he grew tired of the endless haggling, but in that case he did not hand the files to the servant but with sudden determination hurled them a long way out into the passage so that the strings came undone and papers flew about and the servants had a great deal of trouble tidying everything up again. Still, it was all relatively simpler than if the servant's request for return received no answer at all, then he stood outside the closed door, pleading, imploring, citing his list, appealing to regulations, all in vain, not a sound came from the room and without permission to enter the servant clearly had no rights. Then even this model servant occasionally lost his self-control, he went over to his trolley, sat down on the files, mopped the sweat from his brow, and for a while did absolutely nothing except swing his feet helplessly. There was great interest in the matter all around, whispering could be heard everywhere, hardly a door was still, and from up above, where the walls ended, faces that, oddly, were almost completely swathed in scarves and never kept still for an instant followed everything that went on. Amid all this bustle, it struck K. that Bürgel's door remained closed the whole time and that the servants had already done that part of the passage; Bürgel, however, had not been allocated any files. Possibly he was still asleep, though in this din that would have indicated a very sound sleep, but why had he received no files? Only very few rooms, probably unoccupied ones at that, had been passed over in this way. On the other hand, in Erlanger's room there was already a new and particularly restless guest, Erlanger must literally have been driven out by him during the night; this scarcely accorded with Erlanger's chilly, urbane manner, but his having had to wait for K. on the threshold did point in that direction.

From all abstract observations, K. always came back before long to the servant; indeed, so far as this servant was concerned none of the things applied that K. had otherwise been told about servants in general, about their idleness, their comfortable existence, their arrogance, no doubt there were also exceptions among the servants or, as was more

246

likely, different groups among them, because here, K. noticed, many distinctions existed of which he had received little indication before. Particularly the intransigence of this servant pleased him enormously. Struggling with those stubborn little rooms – it often seemed to K. like a struggle with the rooms, since he saw hardly anything of the occupants – the servant did not give up. He weakened occasionally – who would not have done? – but he quickly recovered, slid down from the trolley, and strode erect, teeth clenched, back towards the door to be conquered. It happened, in fact, that he was repulsed two or three times, and in a very simple manner, merely by that awkward silence, yet he was not beaten, not a bit of it. Seeing that he could achieve nothing by open assault, he went about it another way, using cunning, for example, if K. understood correctly. He then appeared to give that door up, letting it exhaust its power of silence, as it were, and turned his attention to other doors, but after a while he came back, called to the other servant, all of this very obviously and out loud, and began piling files on the sill of the closed door, as if he had changed his mind and the gentleman ought by rights not to have something withdrawn but instead have something issued. Then he moved on, still keeping an eye on the door, however, and if then, as usually happened, the gentleman soon cautiously opened the door to pull the files inside, in two bounds the servant was there, shoved a foot between door and jamb, and thus forced the gentleman at least to negotiate with him face to face, which then generally led to a reasonably satisfactory outcome. And if this failed or if at a particular door he felt it was the wrong approach, he tried something different. He switched to the gentlemen who were claiming the files, for instance. In which case he gave the other servant, who was still working in a purely mechanical fashion, an utterly worthless helper, a push to one side and started in on the gentleman himself, speaking in whispers, furtively, sticking his head well into the room, probably making the man promises as well as assuring him that at the next distribution the other gentleman would be penalized accordingly; at least, he pointed towards the adversary's door now and again and laughed, so far as his fatigue allowed. But then there were instances, once or twice, where admittedly he abandoned every attempt, though here again K. thought it was only an apparent abandonment or at least an abandonment for good reason, because he went calmly on, tolerating the din from the disadvantaged gentleman without looking round, only an occasionally more prolonged lowering of the eyelids indicating that the din caused him hurt. However, the gentleman did then gradually calm down; just as the uninterrupted crying of a child gradually turns into increasingly isolated sobs, so it was with his yelling, except that even after he had fallen quite silent there was still the occasional isolated yell or swift opening and slamming of that door. Anyway, it transpired that here too the servant had probably acted quite correctly. In the end, only one gentleman refused to calm down, for a long time he was silent, but only in order to recover himself, then off he went again, no less vigorously than before. It was not entirely clear why he was yelling and protesting in this way, it may have had nothing to do with the distribution of files. Meanwhile, the servant had completed his work, only one file, actually only a scrap of paper, a page torn from a notebook, was left in the trolley through the fault of the helper, and now they did not know whom to give it to. The thought occurred to K.: 'That could well be my file.' The mayor had spoken repeatedly, had he not, of this smallest of small cases. And K., arbitrary and ridiculous though he himself felt his assumption to be, deep down, tried to approach the servant as he perused the note; this was none too easy, K.'s interest in him was poorly repaid; even in the middle of the hardest work, the servant had still found time to cast angry or impatient glances at K., twitching his head nervously. Only now that the distribution was complete did he appear to have forgotten K. to some extent, as indeed he had become more apathetic in other ways as well, his great exhaustion making this understandable, even with the note he hardly put himself out, he may not even have read it right through, merely pretending to, and despite the fact that he could probably, by distributing the note, have pleased any of the occupants of the rooms off the passage, he decided otherwise, he had had enough of distributing, putting a forefinger to his lips he signalled to his companion to say nothing, ripped – K. was nowhere near him yet – the note into little pieces, and stuffed them in his pocket. It was probably the first irregularity that K. had witnessed here in terms of office procedure, though it could be that he got this wrong too. And even if it was an irregularity, it was excusable, in the conditions that prevailed here the servant could not operate impeccably, at some point the accumulated anger, the accumulated agitation had to break out, and if it found expression merely in a little note being ripped up, that was harmless enough. The voice of the gentleman whom nothing would soothe still rang through the passage, and his colleagues, who in other respects behaved with no particular friendliness towards one another, seemed in regard to the din to be entirely of one mind, gradually it was as if this gentleman had taken on the task of making a din for them all, and they were simply encouraging him with cheers and nods to keep it up. Now, however, the servant no longer minded about him, he had done his job, he pointed to the handle of the trolley, indicating that the other servant should take hold of it, and away they went, as they had come, only looking happier and moving so fast that the trolley bounced in front of them. Only once did they flinch and glance back, when the still yelling gentleman, outside whose door K. had lingered because he would have liked to understand what the man wanted, clearly ceased to find satisfaction in yelling, no doubt discovered the button of an electric bell, and in his delight, presumably, at this relief now stopped yelling and launched into a continuous ringing. At this, a great murmur arose in the other rooms, apparently signifying approval, the gentleman seemed to be doing something they had all wanted to do for a long time and had only had to forbear from doing for reasons unknown. Was it perhaps room service, perhaps Frieda, that the gentleman was ringing for? In which case he could be ringing for some time. Frieda was busy wrapping Jeremiah in wet towels, and even if he was already better she had no time, for then she'd be lying in his arms. However, the ringing did have an immediate effect. The landlord of the Count's Arms was himself already visible in the distance, hurrying on to the scene, dressed in black and buttoned up as usual; but it was as if he had forgotten his dignity, the way he was running; his arms were half outflung as if he had been summoned because of a major misfortune and was arriving to seize it and immediately stifle it against his chest; and at every little irregularity in the ringing he appeared to make a little hop in the air and hurry even more. A good way behind him, his wife now also came into view, she too was running with arms outflung but her steps were short and dainty and K. felt she would arrive too late, the landlord would already have done everything necessary. And to leave the landlord room to run past, K. stood close to the wall. However, the landlord stopped right beside K. as if here was his objective, and next moment the landlady was there too and they were both heaping reproaches on him, which in the rush and surprise he failed to grasp, particularly since the gentleman's bell intervened as well and other bells began to ring too, no longer from necessity but for fun and in an outburst of joy. K., who set great store by achieving a thorough understanding of his guilt, was strongly in agreement with the landlord's taking his arm and going off with him, away from that din, which went on getting louder since behind them – K. never turned round because the landlord and even more the landlady on his other side kept going on at him – the doors now opened wide, the passage came alive, a coming and going appeared to develop there as in a busy little alley, the doors ahead of them were clearly waiting impatiently for K. to pass at last in order that they might release the gentlemen, and into all this fell the ringing, repeatedly recommenced, of the bells as if in celebration of some victory. Now at last – they were back in the silent white courtyard, where several sledges waited – K. gradually learned what was going on. Neither the landlord nor the landlady could understand how K. had dared do such a thing. But what was it he had done? K. asked over and over again but was for a long time unable to discover because, his guilt being all too obvious to them both, they did not remotely think that his conscience might be clear. Only very slowly did K. come to see the whole thing. He'd had no right to be in the passage, in general terms he was allowed no farther than the bar, and that was only as a favour, subject to revocation. If he was summoned by one of the gentlemen, he must of course appear at the place of summons, but he should remain aware – presumably he possessed at least the usual amount of common sense? – that he was in a place where he did not really belong, to which he had merely been invited, with much reluctance, simply because an official matter required and excused the fact, by one of the gentlemen. Consequently, it was for him to appear swiftly, submit to examination, but then vanish again even more swiftly if possible. So had he not, there in the passage, had a feeling of severe impropriety? And if he had, how could he have hung around there like an animal put out to grass? Had he not been summoned to a night-time examination, he was asked, and was he unaware why night-time examinations had been introduced? Night-time examinations – and here K. was given a fresh explanation of their purpose – had the sole object of allowing parties, the sight of whom the gentlemen would have found quite intolerable by day, to be heard swiftly at night, under artificial light, with the chance, as soon as the examination was over, of forgetting all nastiness in sleep. But K.'s behaviour, he was told, had made a mockery of all precautions. Even ghosts disappear towards morning, but K. had remained there, hands in pockets, as if expecting that, since he did not go away, the whole passage with all the rooms and gentlemen would go away. And this would indeed – let him not doubt it – quite certainly have occurred if at all possible, because the gentlemen's sensitivity was limitless. None of them, for instance, would drive K. away or even say what really went without saying, namely that he should finally go, none of them would do that, despite the fact that for as long as K. remained they were probably in a quiver of excitement and the morning, their favourite time, was ruined for them. Rather than take action against K., they chose to suffer instead, though no doubt a factor in this was the hope that in the end surely even K. must gradually accept the glaringly obvious and, as the gentlemen suffered, inevitably suffer himself, to the point where it became unbearable, from standing there with such hideous inappropriateness, visible to all, in the passage in the morning. Vain hope. They did not or in their kindliness and condescension had no wish to know that there are also insensitive, hard hearts whom awe will never soften. Did not even the moth, poor creature, seek out a quiet corner when day came, flatten itself, ask for nothing more than to disappear, and experience sadness that it could not? K., by contrast, stuck himself where he was most visible, and had he been able to stop the dawn coming up by doing so, they added, he'd have done so. Stopping it was beyond him, but unfortunately he had been able to delay it, make it more difficult. Had he not witnessed the distribution of the files? Something that no one was allowed to witness, except those immediately involved. Something not even the landlord and the landlady had been allowed to see in their own home. Of which they had only heard tell obliquely, as for example this morning from the servant. Surely he'd noticed the difficulties that had accompanied the distribution of files, something incomprehensible in itself because every one of the gentlemen was devoted to the cause, never considered his private advantage, and therefore inevitably worked with all his might towards ensuring that the distribution of files, that vital, fundamental task, went swiftly and easily and without snags? Had it really not remotely occurred to K. that the chief cause of all the difficulties was the fact that distribution had to be effected with the doors as good as closed and no possibility of direct communication among the gentlemen, who would of course have been able to reach agreement in no time, whereas distribution by the servants inevitably took hours, almost, could never be completed without some complaining, was a perpetual torment to gentlemen and servants, and would probably have harmful consequences as regarded subsequent work. And why were the gentlemen not able to communicate with one another? What, K. still didn't get it? The landlady had never, she said – and the landlord corroborated this for his own part – come across anything like it, and they'd had dealings with a variety of intractable folk. Things one normally dared not utter had to be said to K. openly, otherwise he did not understand the absolute essentials. All right, since it had to be said: it was because of him, simply and solely because of him, that the gentlemen had been unable to emerge from their rooms, because in the morning, having just woken up, they were too ashamed, too vulnerable to be able to expose themselves to strange eyes, they literally, no matter that they were fully dressed, felt too naked to show themselves. It was difficult to say why they were ashamed, it could be that they were ashamed, those perpetual workers, merely of having slept. But perhaps even more than of showing themselves they were shy of seeing other people; the thing they had happily avoided with the aid of night-time examinations, namely the sight of parties whom they found so hard to bear, they were reluctant to have now, in the morning, suddenly, unexpectedly, and large as life, intrude on them anew. They were simply not up to it. What sort of person would fail to respect that? Well, it had to be someone like K. Someone who disregarded everything, the law as much as the most ordinary human consideration, with this dull indifference and sleepiness, someone who did not care that he was making the distribution of files almost impossible as well as damaging the reputation of the establishment and who caused the unprecedented to happen in that the gentlemen, now made desperate, began to defend themselves, and following what for ordinary people would have been an inconceivable act of willpower reached for the bell and rang for help in order to drive K., whom nothing else would unsettle, right away. They, the gentlemen, rang for help! Truly, the landlord and landlady and their entire staff would have come running long since, had they only dared to appear before the gentlemen in the morning unsummoned, even if only to bring help and then vanish again immediately. Quivering with indignation over K., inconsolable on account of their impotence, they had waited here at the end of the passage, they said, and the ringing, which they had never in fact expected, had been a release for them. It meant the worst was over! If they might have just a glimpse of the merry bustle among the gentlemen, now free of K. at last! For K., of course, it was not over, he would certainly have to answer for what he had done here.

They had now reached the bar; why the landlord, for all his anger, had nevertheless brought K. here was not entirely clear, he may have realized that for the moment K.'s weariness made it impossible for him to leave the building. Immediately, without waiting for an invitation to sit down, K. literally collapsed on one of the barrels. There in the half-dark, he felt contented. The only light still burning in the large room was a feeble electric bulb above the beer taps. Outside too it was still pitch-dark, it looked like driving snow. Being here in the warm was cause for gratitude, he must be careful not to get himself thrown out. The landlord and landlady continued to stand in front of him as if he still represented a certain threat, as if, given his utter unreliability, it was entirely possible he might suddenly take off and attempt to force his way back into the passage. Also, they were themselves weary from the night's alarm and from getting up so early, especially the landlady, who wore a rustling, silk-type dress, full-skirted, brown in colour, rather untidily buttoned and fastened – where had she found it in the rush? – leaned her head as if dejectedly on her husband's shoulder, and was dabbing at her eyes with a dainty pocket handkerchief between darting childishly malevolent glances at K. To calm the couple down, K. said that everything they had just told him was quite new to him, but that despite his ignorance of it he had not in fact spent all that much time in the passage, where he really had no business and had certainly not wished to torment anyone, but that it had all happened purely as a result of overtiredness. He thanked them for having brought the embarrassing scene to an end. Were he to be called to account, he would be very glad, since that was the only way he could avoid universal misinterpretation of his behaviour. Only weariness and nothing else had been to blame, he assured them. That weariness, however, stemmed from his not yet being used to the strain of examinations. He'd not been here long, after all. Once he had a certain amount of experience, nothing of the kind could ever reoccur. He might be taking the examinations too seriously, but presumably that was no bad thing in itself. He'd had to undergo two examinations in quick succession, he said, one with Bürgel and the second with Erlanger, particularly the first he had found very tiring, the second had not lasted very long, in fact, Erlanger had simply asked him a favour, but both together had been more than he could stand at one time, something like it might even have been too much for someone else – you, sir, for example, K. suggested to the landlord. He had actually left the second examination staggering. It had been almost a kind of intoxication – he'd been seeing and hearing the two gentlemen for the first time and had nevertheless had to give them answers. It had all turned out very well, so far as he knew, except that then the accident happened; surely, though, given what had preceded it, that could hardly be blamed on him. Unfortunately, only Erlanger and Bürgel had seen the state he was in, they would undoubtedly have looked after him and prevented all the rest but Erlanger had had to leave immediately after the examination, clearly in order to drive to the castle, and Bürgel, probably tired from the examination itself – so how should K. have survived it unscathed? – had fallen asleep and had even slept through the entire distribution of files. If K. had had a similar opportunity he would have been delighted to take advantage of it and gladly have forgone any forbidden glimpses, all the more easily, indeed, for the fact that in reality he had been quite incapable of seeing anything at all, so that even the most sensitive of the gentlemen might have shown themselves in his presence without fear.

The mention of the two examinations, particularly the one by Erlanger, and the respect with which K. spoke of the gentlemen disposed the landlord in his favour. In fact, he seemed to be on the point of complying with K.'s request for permission to lay a board on the barrels and sleep there at least until dawn, but the landlady was firmly against it; only now becoming aware of the disorder of her dress, she plucked at it uselessly here and there, shaking her head repeatedly, what was evidently an old dispute concerning the tidiness of the establishment was about to break out once again. For K., in his weariness, the couple's conversation assumed excessive importance. Being driven away again from this place struck him as a disaster transcending everything he had experienced up to now. It must not happen, even if the landlord and landlady united against him. Slumped there on the barrel, he eyed them both furtively. Until with her unusual touchiness, which K. had long been aware of, the landlady suddenly stepped to one side and – she had no doubt been talking to the landlord about other matters – cried out: 'Look how he's eyeing me! Send him packing, why don't you!' But K., seizing the opportunity and now wholly convinced, almost to the point of indifference, that he would be staying, said: 'I'm not eyeing you, only your dress.' 'Why my dress?' the landlady asked in fury. K. shrugged. 'Come away,' the landlady said to the landlord, 'the lout's drunk. Let him sleep it off here,' and she ordered Pepi, who at her summons appeared out of the darkness, dishevelled, weary, trailing a broom, to throw K. a cushion.

25

When K. woke up, his first thought was that he had hardly slept at all, the room was unchanged, empty and warm, all the walls in darkness, a single light bulb above the beer taps, dark outside the windows as well. But when he stretched, and the cushion fell to the floor, and the board and the barrels creaked, Pepi came to him immediately and he learned that it was already evening and he had slept for well over twelve hours. The landlady had asked after him a number of times during the day; Gerstäcker, too, who had been waiting here in the dark over a beer that morning when K. had spoken to the landlady but had then not dared bother K. further, had looked in once in the meantime to see K., and finally Frieda had also been, apparently, and had stood beside K. for a moment, though she had not exactly come on K.'s account but because she needed to get various things ready, she was due to resume her old job that evening. 'She doesn't care for you any more, presumably?' Pepi asked as she brought coffee and cakes. However, she no longer asked maliciously, as before, but sadly, as if in the meantime she had come to know the malice of the world, beside which all personal malice collapses and becomes futile; she spoke to K. as if to a fellow sufferer, and when he tasted the coffee and she thought she saw it was not sweet enough for him she ran and fetched him the full sugar bowl. Her sadness had not prevented her from adorning herself possibly even more today than the last time; she had a mass of bows and ribbons woven in her hair, the hair itself had been carefully curled over her forehead and at her temples, and round her neck she wore a little chain that dangled down to meet the low neckline of her blouse. When K., in his contentment at having had a decent sleep at last and being able to drink a nice cup of coffee, surreptitiously reached for one of the bows and tried to undo it, Pepi said wearily: 'Oh, don't,' and sat down on a barrel beside him. And K. did not even have to ask her what was wrong, she promptly began telling him herself, staring fixedly at K.'s coffee pot as if, even while telling her story, she needed a diversion, as if, even preoccupied as she was with her suffering, she was unable to abandon herself to it completely, that would be beyond her strength. The first thing K. learned was that really he was the one to blame for Pepi's misfortune, but that she did not hold it against him. And she nodded eagerly as she spoke to forestall any protest on K.'s part. To start with, he'd taken Frieda away from the bar, making Pepi's promotion possible. There was otherwise no conceiving what might have persuaded Frieda to give up her position, she sat there in the bar like a spider in her web, she had threads all over the place, only she knew where; removing her against her will would have been quite out of the question, it had taken love for an inferior, in other words something incompatible with her situation, to push her out. And Pepi? Had it ever occurred to her to go for the job herself? She was a chambermaid, had an unimportant job with few prospects, she dreamed of a great future like every other girl, no one can help dreaming, but she had no serious plans to get on, she'd come to terms with what she had achieved. And then suddenly Frieda had disappeared from the bar, so suddenly that the landlord had not had a suitable substitute available right away, he'd looked around and his eye had fallen on Pepi, who had of course pushed herself forward accordingly. At the time, she loved K. as she had never loved anyone before, for months on end she'd been sitting in her gloomy little room downstairs, prepared to spend years and at worst her entire life there, quite unheeded, and then, all of a sudden, along had come K., a hero, a rescuer of maidens, and had cleared the way for her to rise in the world. He knew nothing about her, of course, he'd not done it for her sake, but that took away none of her gratitude, the night before her appointment – the appointment was uncertain as yet but already looked very likely – she had spent hours talking to him, whispering her thanks in his ear. And it further enhanced what he'd done in her eyes that it was Frieda he had burdened himself with, there was something incredibly selfless about the fact that, to bring Pepi out, he had taken Frieda as his lover, Frieda, an unlovely, no longer young, rather thin girl with short wispy hair, a sneaky sort of girl, too, who always had some secret or other, it seemed to go with her looks; face and body might be pitiful beyond question, but she must at least have other secrets that no one could check, her alleged relationship with Klamm, for instance. And even thoughts like these had occurred to Pepi at the time: was it possible that K. really loved Frieda, was he not deceiving himself, or possibly deceiving only Frieda, and would perhaps the sole result of all this be in fact Pepi's promotion, and would K. then notice his mistake or no longer wish to conceal it and not see Frieda any more but only Pepi, which was not necessarily a mad fancy on Pepi's part, not at all, for on a girl v. girl basis she was more than a match for Frieda, as no one would deny, and it had mainly been Frieda's situation, had it not, and the brilliance Frieda had contrived to bring to it that had dazzled K. at the time. Pepi's dream then had been that, once she had the situation, K. would come pleading to her and she would have the choice of either yielding to K. and losing the job or rejecting him and climbing further. And she'd decided to renounce everything and turn back down to him and teach him true love, which he had never been able to experience with Frieda and which was independent of all the prestigious offices in the world. However, things had worked out differently. And where did the blame for that lie? With K. mainly, and of course also with Frieda's cunning. With K. mainly, because what did he want, what sort of strange fellow was he? What was he striving for, what were these weighty matters that preoccupied him and made him forget his nearest, finest, and loveliest of all? Pepi was the one who suffered and it was all stupid and hopeless and anyone who had the strength to set fire to the whole Count's Arms and burn it to the ground, leaving no trace, burn it like a scrap of paper in the stove, would today be Pepi's darling. So then, Pepi had arrived in the bar four days ago, shortly before lunch. It wasn't easy, the work here, you might say it was almost killing, but what could be achieved was no small thing either. Even before, Pepi had not lived for the moment, and if she would also never in her wildest dreams have claimed this job for herself she had made plenty of observations, she knew what the job entailed, she'd not have taken it on unprepared. Not that it was a job you could take on unprepared, if you did you'd lose it in the first couple of hours. Particularly if you tried to behave like a chambermaid, doing it. As a chambermaid, you began to feel quite forlorn and forgotten as time went on, it was like working down a mine, at least that was how it was on the secretaries' corridor, all day long there, apart from the few daytime parties scurrying back and forth, not daring to look up, you saw no one but the two or three other chambermaids, and they were equally bitter. Mornings you were not even allowed out of your room, the secretaries wished to be alone then, the hands fetched them their food from the kitchen, that meant the chambermaids usually had nothing to do, even during mealtimes they weren't allowed to show themselves on the corridor. Only while the gentlemen were working were the chambermaids allowed to tidy up, but of course not in the occupied rooms, only in those that happened to be empty, and the work must be done very quietly in order that the gentlemen's work shouldn't be disturbed. But how could they tidy up quietly when the gentlemen spent days on end in the rooms, also the hands, that filthy bunch, hung around in them, and when the chambermaid was finally admitted, the room was in such a state that not even the Deluge could have washed it clean. Honestly, these were important gentlemen, but you had to force down your disgust before you could tidy up after them. Chambermaids did not have too much work to do, but what they had was tough. And never a kind word, nothing but complaints, notably that most hurtful and frequent complaint of all: that during cleaning files had gone missing. In reality, nothing went missing, every scrap of paper was handed in to the landlord, files did go missing, of course they did, but not through the maids' doing. Then committees arrived and the maids had to vacate their room while the committee rummaged in the beds; the maids had nothing of their own, their few things fitted into one back pannier, but the committee still spent hours searching. They found nothing, of course; how were files going to find their way in there? What would the maids want with files? Even so, the invariable result was simply insults and threats on the part of the disappointed committee, passed on by the landlord. And never quiet – not in the daytime, not at night. Noise half the night and noise from first thing in the morning. If at least you hadn't needed to live there, but you did, because in between times, depending on orders, it was the chambermaids' job to fetch bits and pieces from the kitchen, especially at night. Always the sudden hammering on the chamber-maids' door, the dictating of the order, the running down to the kitchen, the shaking the sleeping kitchen boys awake, the laying of the tray with the things ordered outside the chambermaids' door, where the hands came to fetch it – what a misery it all was. But that wasn't the worst of it, oh no, the worst was when no order came, when what happened was that at dead of night, when everyone should have been asleep and most people had in fact gone to sleep at last, sometimes there'd be this creeping around outside the chambermaids' door. Then the maids climbed out of bed – the beds were one above the other, there was very little space anywhere, the whole maids' room was actually nothing but a big closet with three shelves – listened at the door, knelt down, clung together in fear. And all the time they could hear the creeping around outside the door. They'd all have been glad if whoever it was creeping around had finally come in, but nothing happened, no one came in. And you had to admit, there wasn't necessarily any threat involved here, it might just be someone pacing to and fro outside the door, wondering whether to place an order and then not being able to make up his mind after all. Perhaps that was all it was, but it might be something quite different. You didn't really know the gentlemen at all, you'd hardly seen them. At any rate, the maids inside were scared to death, and when at length it was quiet outside they leaned against the wall, not having the strength to climb back into bed. That was the kind of life that awaited Pepi once more, she was to move back into the chambermaids' room that very evening. And why? Because of K. and Frieda. Back to the life from which she'd only just escaped, she'd had K.'s help to escape, admittedly, but she'd also made an enormous effort herself. The fact was, in that job girls neglected themselves, even those who were normally the most careful. For whose benefit should they adorn themselves? No one saw them, or at best the kitchen staff; if that was all a girl wanted, let her adorn herself. The rest of the time, though, forever in their little room or in the gentlemen's rooms, which it would have been a foolish extravagance to enter even simply in clean clothes. And constantly in artificial light and breathing that stuffy air – the stove was alight the whole time – and, to tell the truth, constantly tired. Your one afternoon off a week you spent at best sleeping, calm and free from worry, in a quiet corner of the kitchen. So what was the point of adorning yourself? You scarcely even got dressed. And then, all of a sudden, Pepi had been transferred to the bar where, assuming you wanted to make your mark there, the exact opposite was required, where you were constantly in people's sight, some of them very fastidious and sharp-eyed gentlemen, and where you must therefore always look as neat and attractive as possible. Well, that had been a big change. And Pepi felt able to say that she hadn't wasted the opportunity. How things might turn out subsequently had not concerned her. She had known she had the skills the position called for, she'd been quite sure of that, she was still convinced of it even now and no one could take that away from her, not even today, the day of her downfall. The only problem had been how she was going to prove herself initially, that had been difficult, because after all she was only a poor chambermaid with no clothes and no jewellery and because the gentlemen didn't have the patience to wait and see how you developed but wanted immediately, without transition, to have a proper barmaid, otherwise they'd go elsewhere. You might have supposed their demands were not exactly high, since Frieda had managed to satisfy them. That was not true, though. Pepi had often thought about it; after all, she'd met Frieda on occasion and for a while had even slept with her. Frieda was not an easy person to fathom and anyone who was not very careful – and how many of the gentleman were very careful? – she promptly misled. No one was more aware than Frieda herself of how wretched she looked; for instance, the first time you saw her let down her hair you clapped your hands together in sympathy, by rights such a girl shouldn't even get to be a chambermaid; she knew it too, and many a night she had cried over it, clinging to Pepi and draping Pepi's hair round her own head. But when she was at work all doubts disappeared, she thought of herself as the loveliest girl in the world and knew just how to plant the idea in every head. She understood people, that was her real skill. And lied promptly and practised deceit in order that people shouldn't have the time to examine her closely. That wouldn't do in the long run, of course, people had eyes and these would eventually prevail. But as soon as she spotted such a danger she had another weapon ready – recently, for example, her relationship with Klamm. Her affair with Klamm! Oh yes, if K. didn't believe it, he could check for himself by going and asking Klamm! Very clever, very clever. And if perhaps K. didn't dare go to Klamm with such a question and was possibly not admitted with vastly more important questions and Klamm was even entirely inaccessible to him – only to him and his kind, since Frieda, for example, popped in to see him whenever she liked – if that was the case, he could still check the matter, he only needed to wait. Klamm wouldn't be able to tolerate that sort of false rumour for long, he undoubtedly took a keen interest in what was being said about him in the bar and in the guest rooms, it was all of the greatest importance to him, and if it was wrong, he'd promptly correct it. This he didn't correct, though, which meant there was nothing *to* correct and it was the honest truth. All you saw, admittedly, was Frieda carrying beer into Klamm's room and coming out again with the money, but what you didn't see, Frieda told you and you had to believe it. Not that she told you herself, no, she would never let such secrets out, the secrets let themselves out around her and once they were out, all right, she was no longer afraid to talk about them herself, but modestly, without making any kind of claim, citing only what was in any case common knowledge. Not citing everything, for instance she didn't mention the fact that, since she had been in the bar, Klamm had been drinking less beer than before, not a lot less but still significantly less, she didn't mention that, there might in fact have been various reasons for it, a time had simply come when Klamm liked beer less or even, because of Frieda, forgot all about beer-drinking. So Frieda, amazing though it might be, really was Klamm's mistress. But what was good enough for Klamm was bound, surely, to be admired by everyone else, so that in no time at all Frieda had become a great beauty, just the kind of girl the bar needed, almost too beautiful, actually, too powerful, the bar was now scarcely enough for her. Indeed, it struck people as remarkable that she was still in the bar; being a barmaid was a big thing; it made the connection with Klamm seem very plausible; but once the barmaid was Klamm's mistress, why did he leave her – and for so long, too – in the bar? Why didn't he raise her higher? You could tell people a thousand times that there was no contradiction in this, that Klamm had specific reasons for acting in this way or that some time, maybe in the immediate future, Frieda's elevation would suddenly come about, but none of it had much effect, people had set ideas and refused in the long run to be diverted from them, however skilfully this was tried. The fact was, no one doubted any longer that Frieda was Klamm's mistress, even those who clearly knew better were by now too weary to doubt it. 'Damn it, be Klamm's mistress,' they'd thought, 'but if you are, we want to see it in your promotion too.' They had seen nothing, however, and Frieda had remained in the bar as before, secretly delighted to do so. But she'd begun to lose people's respect, as of course she couldn't help noticing, usually she noticed things before they happened. A truly beautiful, truly charming girl would not, once she'd settled down in the bar, need to use any tricks; so long as she remained beautiful, unless a particular unhappy accident occurred, she would be barmaid. A girl like Frieda, though, had to be constantly worried about her job, she didn't show it, of course, that was understandable, instead she tended to complain and curse the job. But in secret she'd been monitoring the atmosphere the whole time. And what she'd seen was how people grew indifferent, her appearance was no longer worth even glancing up for, not even the hands bothered about her any more, understandably sticking to Olga and girls like her, she'd noticed from the landlord's behaviour too that she was less and less indispensable, nor could she go on inventing fresh stories about Klamm, there were limits to everything – and so dear Frieda had decided on something new. Which of them could possibly have seen through it from the beginning! Pepi had had her suspicions, but sadly she'd not seen through it. Frieda had decided to create a scandal, she, Klamm's mistress, would throw herself at just anyone, if possible the lowest of the low. That would cause a stir, that would be something people talked about for a long time and eventually, eventually they would remember what it meant to be Klamm's mistress and what it meant to discard that honour in the ecstasy of a fresh love. The only problem had been finding the right man to play this clever game with. It couldn't be anyone Frieda knew, not even one of the hands, he would probably have stared at her wide-eyed and passed on, above all he'd not have taken the matter seriously enough and it would have been impossible for even the glibbest of tongues to put it about that Frieda had been pounced on by him, been unable to fend him off, and in a moment of madness succumbed to him. And even if the person had to be one of the lowest of the low, he must still be somebody of whom it could plausibly be said that, for all his stolid, unrefined ways, he did in fact yearn for Frieda and Frieda alone and had no greater desire than – God in heaven! – to wed her. But even so, even if he was a common fellow, even lower than a hand if possible, far lower than a hand, he must still be somebody on whose account she'd not have all the girls laughing at her, somebody in whom another girl, one with judgement, might also find something attractive. But where was such a man to be found? A different girl would probably have spent her whole life looking for him without success, Frieda's luck had brought the land surveyor into her bar on the very evening, possibly, when the plan first occurred to her. The land surveyor! Really, what had K. been thinking of? What had he had in mind, particularly? Had he been out to achieve something specific? A good position, a distinction of some kind? Had he been after something like that? If so, he should have gone about it differently right from the start. He was nothing, nothing at all, his situation brought tears to the eyes. He was a land surveyor, all right, that was something, perhaps, so he had studied something, but if a person didn't know what to do with it, even that counted for nothing. And yet there he was, making demands; without anything at all behind him he'd been making demands, not outright, but he had clearly been advancing claims of some kind, and that had been a provocative thing to do. Didn't he realize that even a chambermaid lost face if she spoke to him for any length of time? And with all those special demands, the very first evening he had fallen straight into the biggest trap of all. Wasn't he ashamed of himself? What was it about Frieda that had so ensnared him? He could confess now. Had she really contrived to please him, the skinny sallow creature? Surely not, he'd not even looked at her, she had merely told him she was Klamm's mistress, he'd been impressed by what was for him still news and that had been it, he was lost. But she'd then had to move out, there was no room for her now at the Count's Arms, of course. Pepi had seen her the morning before the move, the staff had all assembled, everyone was curious to watch. And such had been her power, still, that people felt sorry for her, they all, even her enemies, felt sorry for her; that was how right their assessment had proved from the outset; throwing oneself away on a man like that had seemed incomprehensible to them all, a real blow of fate, the little kitchen maids, who of course looked up to any girl who worked in the bar, had been inconsolable. Pepi herself had been affected, not even she was completely impervious, even if her attention had actually been drawn to something else. She'd noticed how far from sad Frieda actually was. Basically, an appalling disaster had befallen her, and she had indeed acted as if she was very unhappy, but it hadn't been enough, the act hadn't fooled Pepi. So what had been keeping her going? The happiness of her new love, perhaps? As it happened, that idea was out of the question. But what else had it been? What had given her the strength even to treat Pepi, already seen as her successor, with the same cool friendliness as before? Pepi had not had time to think about it just then, she'd been too busy making preparations for the new job. She was probably going to have to start in a couple of hours, and she still had no pretty hair-do, nothing smart to wear, no delicate underthings, no decent shoes. All these items she would need to get hold of in a couple of hours, if you couldn't kit yourself out properly it was better not to take the job at all, you were bound to lose it in the first half hour. Well, she'd not been unsuccessful. When it came to doing hair, she had a special aptitude, the landlady had even sent for her to do her hair once, she was blessed with a unique lightness of touch; of course, with her luxuriant hair you could do anything. For the dress, too, help had been at hand. Her two colleagues had stood by her, it was an honour for them too, in a way, when a girl from their particular group became a barmaid, also Pepi would be able, later on, once she was in a position of power, to secure a good many advantages for them. One of the girls had had some expensive material tucked away for a long time, it was her treasure, she'd had the others admire it occasionally, no doubt she dreamed of making splendid use of it herself some time, and – this had been really nice of her – now that Pepi needed it, she'd given it up. And they'd both helped willingly with the sewing, they couldn't have been keener if they had been sewing for themselves. It had been very happy, satisfying work, in fact. There they had sat, each on her own bed, one above the other, sewing and singing, and they'd handed the finished sections and the bits and pieces up and down to one another. Thinking back, Pepi felt even more dejected that it had all been for nothing and she was returning to her friends empty-handed. What a disaster it had been and how thoughtlessly occasioned, mainly through K.'s fault. How pleased they'd all been with the dress then. It seemed to guarantee success, and when they'd subsequently found room for yet another ribbon, the last doubt disappeared. And was it not truly beautiful, the dress? It was creased now and a bit stained; the fact was, Pepi had no spare dress, she'd to wear that one day and night, but you could still see how beautiful it was, not even those damned Barnabas girls would have made a better one. And the way it could be gathered and let out again as required, above and below, in other words that, though just a dress, it was so versatile, that was a particular advantage and had actually been her idea. And of course it hadn't been difficult to sew, Pepi wasn't boasting about that, everything fitted healthy young girls. What had been much more difficult was getting hold of underwear and boots, in fact this was where things had begun to go wrong. Again, her friends had helped out as best they could, but they'd not been able to do much. It had only been coarse linen that they had collected together and mended, and instead of high-heeled bootees she'd had to make do with slippers of the kind a girl would rather hide than show off. To console Pepi, people had told her that Frieda was not particularly well dressed either and sometimes went about in so slovenly a state that the guests preferred to have the cellarmen serve them instead. It was quite true, but Frieda had been able to do that, she was already in favour and an object of respect; if a lady appeared in public dirty and sloppily dressed, it only made her more alluring, but with a novice like Pepi? Anyway, Frieda had been quite incapable of dressing well, she had no taste at all; of course, if a girl had sallow skin she was stuck with it, but she didn't have to do as Frieda had done and wear a low-cut cream-coloured blouse as well, making your eyes water with all that yellow. And even apart from that, she'd been too mean to dress well, everything she earned she'd hung on to, no one knew what for. She hadn't needed any money at work, she'd got by with lies and ruses, it was an example Pepi would not and could not follow, so she'd been right to adorn herself as she did in order to make the most of herself, especially at the start. If she'd only had more resources to do it with she would still, for all Frieda's shrewdness, all K.'s stupidity, have come out on top. Things had begun well enough. The few skills and scraps of knowledge needed she'd learned in advance. She'd felt like a fixture from the moment she arrived in the bar. No one had missed Frieda working there. Not until the second day had some of the guests inquired after Frieda's whereabouts. No mistakes had been made, the landlord had been happy, in his anxiety he'd been in the bar constantly that first day, afterwards he had come only occasionally, and in the end, seeing that the till added up – average takings had even shown a slight improvement on Frieda's time – he was leaving everything to Pepi. She'd made some changes. Frieda, not because she was industrious but because she was mean, domineering, and anxious not to cede any of her rights to anyone, had even, at least to some extent, particularly when she was being watched, looked after the hands; Pepi had given that whole job to the cellarmen, who were much better at it. That way she'd left more time free for the gentlemen's rooms, guests had been served quickly but still with her managing to exchange a few words with each one, not like Frieda, who had apparently saved herself entirely for Klamm and seen every word, every overture by anyone else as an insult to Klamm. That had been shrewd too, of course, because if she did ever allow someone to approach her it was an enormous favour. But Pepi hated such tricks, anyway there'd been no place for them at the beginning. Pepi had been friendly to everyone and everyone had repaid her with friendliness. They had all been visibly delighted with the change; when the work-weary gentlemen were finally able to sit down for a moment over a beer she'd been able, with a word, a glance, a shrug of the shoulders, positively to transform them. So eagerly had everyone's hands run through Pepi's curls that she'd had to redo her hair probably ten times a day, they'd none of them been able to resist the temptation of those curls and bows, not even the usually so absent-minded K. In this way, several exciting, strenuous, but successful days had flown by. If only they'd not flown by so fast, if only there'd been a few more of them. Four days had been too few, even working yourself to a standstill, maybe just the fifth day would have been enough, but four days had been too few. Granted, Pepi had won patrons and friends in those four days, if every glance was to be believed, had even floated, as she arrived with the mugs of beer, on a sea of friendship, a clerk by the name of Bratmeier had been crazy about her, he'd given her this necklace and pendant and put a picture of himself in the pendant, though that had been cheeky – those and other things had occurred, but there'd been only the four days, in four days Frieda might, had Pepi applied herself, have been almost, perhaps, but not quite forgotten, and so she would have been, possibly even sooner, had she not taken care, by causing such a scandal, to keep her name on people's lips, it had made her a novelty, simple curiosity had made people keen to see her again; what had become tedious to them to the point of nausea had now, thanks to the otherwise quite indifferent K., acquired fresh appeal in their eyes, not of course that they'd have given Pepi up on that account, so long as she stood there and made her presence felt, but they were mostly elderly gentlemen, set in their ways, and for them to get used to a new barmaid, no matter how positive the change, took a few days, against the gentlemen's own will it took a few days, maybe only five, but four were not enough, Pepi was still, despite everything, seen as the stand-in. And then what had perhaps been the greatest misfortune of all, over those four days Klamm, even though he spent the first two in the village, had not come down to the lounge. Had he done so, that would have been Pepi's crucial test, and it was one she did not fear in the least, in fact she'd been looking forward to it. She would – these were of course things that it was best never to touch on in words – not have become Klamm's mistress, nor would she have lied her way into such a position, but she'd have known how to set the beer glass down on the table at least as nicely as Frieda, without Frieda's pushy ways she'd have said a pretty greeting and a pretty farewell, and had Klamm been on the lookout for anything in a girl's eyes, then he'd have found it in Pepi's eyes, as much as he wanted. But why had he not come? By chance? That was what Pepi had thought herself at the time. For those two days she had expected him at every moment, even waiting at night. 'Now Klamm will come,' she had thought constantly, and she'd run to and fro for no other reason than the restlessness of anticipation and the desire to be the first to see him as soon as he entered the room. This continuous disappointment had made her extremely tired, perhaps that had been why she'd not performed as well as she might. She'd sneaked, whenever she had a moment, up to the corridor, where staff were strictly forbidden to go, and there squeezed into a corner and waited. 'If Klamm would only come,' she'd thought, 'if I could just take the gentleman from his room and carry him down to the lounge in my arms. That's one burden I would not collapse under, no matter how great it was.' But he hadn't come. It was so quiet up in those corridors, it was impossible, if you'd never been there, to imagine how quiet. It was so quiet you couldn't bear it there for long, the silence drove you away. But again and again, driven away a dozen times, a dozen times Pepi had climbed back up there. And there'd been no point. If Klamm had wanted to come, he'd have come; but if he didn't want to come, Pepi was never going to tempt him out, even if she did half suffocate in the corner with palpitations. It was pointless, but if he didn't come, surely almost everything was pointless. And he did not come. Had not come. Now Pepi knew why. How Frieda would have laughed if she'd been able to see Pepi up in the corridor, squeezed into a corner with both hands over her heart. Klamm had not come down because Frieda hadn't let him. It had not been her pleas that achieved that result, her pleas had not got through to Klamm. But she'd had contacts, the little spider, contacts no one knew about. When Pepi had said something to a guest, she'd said it openly, the next table had been able to hear it too; Frieda had had nothing to say, she'd set the beer down on the table and gone; only her silk petticoat, the one thing she did spend money on, had rustled slightly. But when she had occasionally said something it had not been openly, she'd whispered it to the guest, bending down, making the people at the neighbouring table prick up their ears. What she'd said was probably immaterial, not always, though, she'd had connections, had backed one up with another, and if most of them had failed – who was going to worry about Frieda the whole time? – now and again one had worked. She'd started to make the most of those connections, K. had given her the opportunity, instead of staying with her and making sure she was all right he'd spent hardly any time at home, gone roaming about, had meetings here and there, attended to everything except Frieda, and eventually, to give her even more freedom, moved out of the Bridge Inn into the empty school. A fine start to the honeymoon that had been. Well, Pepi would certainly be the last to criticize K. for being unable to stand it with Frieda; no one could have stood it with Frieda. But why in that case had he not left her completely, why had he kept coming back to her, why had he given the impression, with his roamings, that he was fighting for her. It had looked, in fact, as if he had only discovered his true nothingness through contact with Frieda, wanted to make himself worthy of Frieda, wanted somehow to hoist himself up, had for that reason deprived himself of her company for the time being in order to be able to reward himself for such sacrifices later, at his leisure. Meanwhile, Frieda had wasted no time, she'd sat in the school, to which she had probably steered K. deliberately, and kept one eye on the Count's Arms and the other on K. She'd had excellent messengers available, K.'s assistants, whom he – this defied belief, even if you knew K. it defied belief – left entirely to her. She had dispatched them to her old friends, reminded them of her existence, complained of being held prisoner by such a man as K., stirred up feeling against Pepi, announced her imminent arrival, asked for help, implored them to give nothing away to Klamm, acted as if Klamm needed to be protected and must therefore on no account be allowed down to the bar. What to some she'd passed off as protecting Klamm, she'd persuaded the landlord to see as her success, drawing attention to the fact that Klamm no longer came; how could he come, when a mere Pepi was serving downstairs; oh, it wasn't the landlord's fault, Pepi had still been the best substitute to be found, she was just not good enough, not even for a few days. K. had been unaware of all this activity on Frieda's part; when not roaming around, he'd lain unsuspecting at her feet as she counted the hours that still separated her from the bar. But the assistants had provided more than just this messenger service, they had also served to make K. jealous, keep him interested. Frieda had known the assistants since childhood, they certainly had no more secrets from one another, but for K.'s sake they had begun to pine for one another and there'd been the risk, so far as K. was concerned, of this becoming a great love. And K. had done everything to please Frieda, even the most contradictory things, he'd allowed the assistants to make him jealous but at the same time tolerated the three of them remaining together while he went off roaming by himself. It was almost as if he'd been Frieda's third assistant. At this point Frieda had finally, on the basis of her observations, decided on her big move, she would make a comeback. And it really was high time, it was marvellous how Frieda, in her cunning, had seen that and exploited it, this power of watching and coming to a decision was Frieda's inimitable skill; had Pepi possessed it, how differently her life would have turned out. If Frieda had remained in the school for another day or two, there'd have been no driving Pepi out, she'd have been barmaid for good, universally loved and in demand, she'd have earned enough money to make dazzling additions to her meagre get-up, another day or two and no amount of intrigue would have kept Klamm away from the lounge any longer, he'd have come down, had a drink, felt at ease, and, if he noticed Frieda's absence at all, been highly satisfied with the change, another day or two and Frieda and her scandal, her connections, the assistants, the whole lot, would have been utterly and completely forgotten, never to re-emerge. She might then have held to K. that much more firmly, perhaps even, assuming she had it in her, really learnt to love him? No, not that either. Because a day had been as long as even K. needed to grow tired of her, to realize how shamefully she'd deceived him in every way, in her supposed beauty, her supposed loyalty, and above all her supposedly having the love of Klamm, and one more day, that had been all he needed to chase her out of the house with the whole filthy crew of assistants, just imagine, not even K. had needed longer. And because, between those two perils, with the grave virtually closing over her already, K. had been naïve enough to hold the last narrow passage open, Frieda had absconded. Suddenly – something hardly anyone had expected any more, it went against the grain – suddenly it had been she who'd thrown K. out, K. who still loved her and was still pursuing her, and with the backing of friends and assistants she'd appeared to the landlord as his salvation, much more alluring than before as a result of her scandal, a proven object of desire among the humblest and highest-ranking alike, yet submitting to the humblest only for a moment, soon quite properly thrusting him aside, becoming for him and all the rest as unattainable as before, the only difference being that, before, people had rightly doubted all of this, whereas now they were sure of it again. So back she'd come, the landlord had hesitated, glancing at Pepi – should he sacrifice her, now that she'd proved her worth? – but had soon been persuaded, there was too much in Frieda's favour, particularly the fact that she'd win Klamm back for the lounge. They'd just been having supper. Pepi was not going to wait until Frieda arrived and made a triumph of the takeover. She'd already handed the landlady the till receipts, she was free to go. The sleeping compartment in the maids' room downstairs was ready for her, she would go down there, be greeted by her weeping friends, and pull the dress off and the ribbons from her hair and stuff everything in a corner where it would be well hidden and not needlessly remind her of times best forgotten. Then she'd take the big bucket and the broom, grit her teeth, and get down to work. But first she must tell K. everything in order that he, who without help would not have grasped this even now, should see clearly for once how badly he had behaved towards Pepi and how miserable he'd made her. Admittedly, he too had simply been abused in the process.

Pepi had finished. Heaving a sigh, she wiped tears from her eyes and cheeks and then looked at K., nodding her head as if to say that, deep down, this was not about her misfortune at all, that she would bear without needing anyone's help or comfort to do so, least of all K.'s, she knew about life, despite her youth, and her misfortune merely confirmed what she knew, no, this was about K., it was him she had wanted to confront with himself, even after the collapse of all her hopes she'd felt she had to do that.

'What a crazy imagination you have, Pepi,' said K. 'It's quite untrue that you've only just discovered all these things, they're simply dreams from your dark little maids' room downstairs, they're in the right place there but they look odd here in the empty bar. You'd never have survived here with such thoughts, that goes without saying. Even the dress and the hair-do you so pride yourself on are simply monstrous products of that darkness and those beds in your room; there I've no doubt they're very fine, but here everybody secretly or openly laughs at them. And what else was it you were saying? That I'd been abused and betrayed? No, Pepi dear, I've no more been abused and betrayed than you. You're right that Frieda has left me for the moment or, as you put it, absconded with one of the assistants, an inkling of the truth you do have, and also, yes, it's most unlikely she'll ever become my wife, but it is utterly and completely untrue that I'd got tired of her, let alone that I drove her out next day or that she betrayed me as a wife might ordinarily betray a husband. You chambermaids are always spying through keyholes, and it's put you in the habit of taking a tiny detail that you actually see and from it grandly but quite wrongly deducing the whole picture. The upshot is that in this case, for instance, I know very much less than you. I can't explain anywhere near as precisely as you can why Frieda left me. The most likely explanation seems to me the one you touched on yourself but did not use, namely that I neglected her. It's true, unfortunately, I did neglect her, but there were particular reasons for that, reasons that have no place here, I'd be happy if she came back to me, but I should immediately begin neglecting her again. That's the way it is. When she was with me, I was always roaming about in the way you ridiculed; now that she's gone, I have virtually nothing to do, I feel tired, I long for an ever more complete idleness. Have you no advice for me, Pepi?' 'Yes, I do,' said Pepi, suddenly becoming animated and seizing K. by the shoulders, 'we've both been betrayed, let's stick together, come down with me to the girls.' 'Until you stop moaning about being betrayed,' said K., 'I can't communicate with you. You always want to have been betrayed because it flatters you and you find it moving. The fact of the matter is, you're wrong for the job. And how obvious that wrongness must be if even I, in your view the most ignorant of men, am aware of it. You're a good girl, Pepi, but it's not entirely easy to see that, I for example found you cruel and arrogant at first, you're not, though, it's just that this job confuses you because you're the wrong person for it. I'm not saying the job's too good for you, it isn't so exceptional a job after all, it may, looked at closely, carry slightly more honour than your previous job but on the whole there's not much difference, the two are almost indistinguishable, in fact the chambermaid's existence might almost be said to be preferable to the bar, because there you're always among secretaries whereas here, even if in the lounges you get to serve the secretaries' superiors, you also have to bother with really humble folk, me for instance; legally, I'm not allowed anywhere else but in the bar here, and is the opportunity of associating with me supposed to be such an incredible honour? You only think it is, and you may have your reasons. But that's precisely what makes you unsuitable. It's a job like any other, but for you it's like being in heaven, consequently you set about everything far too eagerly, decking yourself out the way you think angels are adorned – in reality, they're different – you tremble for your job, feel persecuted the whole time, try by being tremendously friendly to win over everyone you think might support you but in fact irritate them and put them off because they've come to the pub for some peace, they don't want the barmaid's worries on top of their own. It's possible that, following Frieda's departure, none of the important guests actually noticed anything had happened, they know about it now, though, and really do miss Frieda, because no doubt Frieda did operate quite differently. However she may have been in other respects and however much she valued her job, in her work she was experienced, cool, and in control, you stress that yourself, though without turning the lesson to advantage. Did you ever notice the look in her eye? That wasn't the look of a barmaid, that was the look of a landlady, almost. She saw everybody, and in so doing she also saw each individual, and the look she had left for the individual still had the power to bring him into submission. What did it matter that she was perhaps a bit thin, a bit on the old side, that her hair might conceivably have been more luxuriant, these were details compared to what she did actually possess, and anyone worried about such shortcomings would simply have been displaying his want of feeling for higher things. Klamm certainly cannot be accused of that, and it's only the mistaken viewpoint of a young, inexperienced girl that prevents you from believing in Klamm's love for Frieda. Klamm, to you – and rightly so – seems unattainable, so you think Frieda could never have approached Klamm either. You're wrong. I'd simply take Frieda's word for it, even if I did not have irrefutable proof. Incredible though it may seem to you, and however difficult to reconcile with your ideas of the world and officialdom and rank and the power of female beauty, the fact is that, as we two are sitting side by side today, with me taking your hand between mine, so too, as if it had been the most natural thing in the world, did Klamm and Frieda sit together, and he came down of his own accord, indeed hurried down, no one was lying in wait for him in the corridor, neglecting other work, Klamm had to make the effort to come down himself, and the defects in Frieda's dress that so upset you didn't bother him in the least. You're determined not to believe her! And you don't realize how that gives you away, how that's precisely what reveals your inexperience. Even someone who knew nothing of the relationship with Klamm would inevitably see by its nature that it had moulded someone who was more than you and me and anyone else in the village, and that their exchanges went beyond the banter that usually passes between guests and waitresses and appears to constitute your goal in life. But I'm being unfair to you. You're well aware of Frieda's advantages yourself, you've noticed her gift of observation, her decisiveness, her influence over people, only of course you misinterpret it all, you think she's selfishly using everything purely for her own advantage, to evil ends, or even as a weapon against you. No,

Pepi, even if she had such arrows, she'd not be able to shoot them from such close range. And jealous? On the contrary, it could be said that, in sacrificing what she had and what she might look forward to, she gave us two the opportunity to prove ourselves in higher positions, but that we've let her down and are almost forcing her to return here. I don't know if that is so, nor is my guilt at all clear to me, it's only when I compare myself with you that anything of the sort occurs to me; as if we'd both tried too hard, too noisily, too childishly, and with insufficient experience, by weeping, scratching, tugging, to obtain something that with Frieda's calm, say, and Frieda's straightforwardness would have been achieved easily and imperceptibly, the way a child tugs at the tablecloth but achieves nothing except simply to hurl the whole splendid display to the floor and put it beyond reach for ever – I don't know whether that's how it is, but I'm sure it's more like that than the way you tell it.' 'All right,' said Pepi, 'you're in love with Frieda because she ran away from you, it's not hard to be in love with her when she's not there. But however it is, and even if you're right about everything, including your making a fool of me – what do you intend to do now? Frieda's left you, neither my account nor your own offers you any hope of her coming back, and even if she does, you must spend the intervening period somewhere, it's cold and you have neither a job nor a bed, move in with us, you'll like my friends, we'll make it comfortable for you, you can help us with our work, which is really too strenuous for girls on their own, and we shan't have to fend for ourselves and be frightened at night any more. Move in with us. My friends know Frieda too, we'll tell you stories about her till you can't listen to any more. Oh, do! We've even got pictures of Frieda, we'll show you them. Frieda used to be even plainer than she is today, you'll scarcely recognize her, by her eyes you might, they've always had a furtive look. Will you come, then?' 'You mean, I'm allowed to? Yesterday there was a terrible fuss, remember, because I got caught on your corridor.' 'Because you got caught; if you're with us, you won't get caught. No one will know about you, only we three. Oh, it'll be fun! Already, living there seems much more tolerable to me than a moment ago. Maybe I'm not losing so much after all, having to leave this place. Hey, we didn't have a bad time even with the three of us, you need to sweeten life's bitterness for yourself, life's made bitter for us in our youth to stop our tongues getting spoiled, so we stick together, the three of us, we live as well as it's possible to live there, you'll like Henrietta particularly, but so you will Emily, I've already told them about you, stories like that sound unbelievable there, as if nothing real could happen outside the room, it's warm and snug there, and we also press together closely, no, even though we're so dependent on one another we haven't grown tired of one another, quite the opposite, when I think about my friends I almost don't mind going back; why should I be promoted above them; that was the very thing that kept us together, the fact that the future was barred to all three of us identically, and then I did in fact break through and was separated from them; I didn't forget them, of course, my first thought was how I might do something for them; my own position was still uncertain – just how uncertain I had no idea – when I first talked to the landlord about Henrietta and Emily. Regarding Henrietta, the landlord wasn't entirely inflexible, but for Emily, who is much older than us, she's around Frieda's age, he held out no hope. But listen, they don't actually want to leave, they realize it's a wretched life they lead there but they've accepted it, the loves, I believe their tears when we said goodbye were mostly due to sadness that I must leave the room we shared, go out into the cold – to us, there, everything outside our room seems cold – and in those great big unfamiliar spaces contend with important, unfamiliar people for no other purpose than to eke out my life, as I'd been managing to do quite well before, with the three of us living together. They probably won't even be surprised if I come back now, and it'll only be to humour me that they'll cry a bit and bemoan my bad luck. But then they'll see you and realize it's been a good thing I went away after all. The fact that we now have a man to help and protect us will please them no end, and they'll be absolutely delighted that it must all remain a secret and that as a result of that secret we'll be bound together even more tightly than before. Do come, please; move in with us. There'll be no commitment so far as you're concerned, you won't be tied to our room for ever, as we are. When spring comes, if you find accommodation elsewhere and you're no longer happy living with us, you'll be free to go, the only thing is, you must keep the secret even then and not give us away, because that would be our last hour at the Count's Arms; in other ways too, of course, you must be careful when you're with us, never show yourself anywhere we don't consider harmless, and generally follow our advice; that's the only tie you'll have, anyway you'll surely be as keen on that as we are, otherwise you're completely free, the work we'll give you won't be too hard, you needn't be afraid of that. So will you come?' 'How long is it till spring?' K. asked. 'Till spring?' echoed Pepi, 'our winters are long here, very long and very monotonous. But we don't complain about it downstairs, we're shielded against the winter. Oh, spring does come eventually, and summer, and they last for a while, but now, looking back, spring and summer seem so short, as if they were not much more than a couple of days, and even on those days, no matter how lovely the day, it still snows occasionally.'

Just then the door opened, making Pepi jump, mentally she'd moved too far away from the bar, but it was not Frieda, it was the landlady. She pretended to be astonished to find K. still there, K. excused himself on the grounds that he had been waiting for the landlady, at the same time he thanked her for letting him spend the night there. The landlady failed to understand why K. had been waiting for her. K. said he had been under the impression that the landlady wished to speak to him again, he apologized if this had been an error, in fact he must go now, he'd left the school where he was caretaker unattended for too long, it was all the fault of the previous day's summons, he still had insufficient experience in these matters, it would certainly not happen again that he caused the landlady so much unpleasantness as yesterday. And he bowed, preparatory to leaving. The landlady was gazing at him as if in a dream. One result of this gaze was that K. was detained longer than he had intended. She then added a quiet smile, and it was only K.'s look of astonishment that roused her, so to speak, she might almost have been expecting a response to her smile and it was only when none came that she woke up. 'I believe yesterday you had the impertinence to say something about my dress.' K. did not remember. 'You don't remember? So, first impertinence, then cowardice.' K. said he was sorry, he'd been tired the day before and it was quite possible he'd gone on a bit, he couldn't remember. Anyway, what could he have said about ma'am's clothes? That they were finer than any he'd ever seen? He'd certainly never seen a landlady working in such attire before. 'That's enough,' the landlady said quickly, 'I don't want to hear another word

277

from you on the subject of clothes. It's not for you to concern yourself about my clothes. I forbid you to, once and for all.' K. bowed again and walked to the door. 'And what's that supposed to mean,' the landlady called after him, 'you've never seen a landlady working in such attire before? Why do you make such pointless remarks? That really is utterly pointless. What are you trying to say?' K. turned and begged the landlady not to upset herself. Of course the remark had been pointless. In any case, he didn't know the first thing about clothes. In his situation, any garment that was clean and hadn't been mended looked sumptuous. He'd simply been astonished to see the landlady appear there in the passage, at night, among all those scantily dressed men, in such a beautiful gown, that was all. 'I see,' said the landlady, 'it appears you do remember your remark of yesterday at last. And you top it off with yet more nonsense. It's true, you don't know a thing about clothes. But in that case, will you also – I ask this seriously of you – stop passing judgement on what constitutes sumptuous dresses, unsuitable gowns, etc. In fact' – here it was as if a cold shudder ran through her – 'you're to leave my dresses alone altogether, do you hear?' And as K., saying nothing, was on the point of turning away again, she asked: 'Where do you get your knowledge of clothes from, anyway?' K. shrugged, he had no knowledge. 'No, you don't,' said the landlady, 'and nor should you pretend to. Come into the office, I've something to show you, then I hope you'll stop your impertinence for good and all.' She went out through the door first; Pepi sprang to K.'s side; using the pretext that K. was paying his bill, they quickly made an arrangement; it was very simple, K. knew the courtyard where the gate led into the side street, beside the gate there was a little door, Pepi would be behind the door in, say, an hour and open it to three knocks.

The private office was opposite the bar, there was only the hallway to be crossed, the landlady was already standing in the office with the light on, looking impatiently in K.'s direction. However, there was a further hold-up. Gerstäcker had been waiting in the hallway to speak to K. It was not easy, shaking him off, the landlady helped too and admonished Gerstäcker for his pushiness. 'Where to, then? Where to?' Gerstäcker could be heard calling even after the door had closed, and the words formed an ugly confusion with sighing and coughing.

It was a small, overheated room. Against the end walls stood a high desk and an iron safe, against the side walls a closet and a couch. The closet took up most space, it not only filled the entire side wall but was also so deep that it made the room very narrow, three sliding doors were needed to open it completely. The landlady pointed to the couch, indicating that K. should sit down, she herself sat in the swivel chair by the desk. 'Didn't you learn dressmaking once?' asked the landlady. 'No, never,' said K. 'So what are you, actually?' 'A land surveyor.' 'What's that, then?' K. explained, the explanation made her yawn. 'You're not telling the truth. Why are you not telling the truth?' 'You're not telling it, either.' 'Me? More of your impertinence, I take it. Even if I haven't been telling the truth – must I answer to you? In what way am I not telling the truth, then?' 'You're not just a landlady, as you pretend.' 'Well, you're full of discoveries, you are. What else am I, then? Your impertinence really is getting out of hand.' 'I don't know what else you are. All I can see is that you're a landlady and also that you wear dresses that don't suit a landlady and are like no one else in this village wears, so far as I know.' 'Ah, now we're coming to the point, you can't keep quiet about it, can you, maybe you're not impertinent at all, you're just like a child that knows some piece of nonsense and can't anyhow be persuaded to keep quiet about it. Go on, then. What's so special about these dresses?' 'You'll be cross if I tell you.' 'No I won't, I'll laugh, it'll only be childish prattle. What are they like then, my dresses?' 'You really want to know. Well, they're made of fine material, very sumptuous, but they're outmoded, ornate, often over-elaborate, shabby, and they suit neither your age, nor your figure, nor your position. They struck me immediately, the first time I saw you, a week or so ago, here in the hallway.' 'So there we have it. They're outmoded, ornate, and what else was it? And how do you come by all this knowledge?' 'I can see it. One doesn't need to be taught these things.' 'You just see it. You don't need to ask, you know immediately what fashion demands. In that case you'll be indispensable to me, I happen to have a weakness for fine dresses. And what have you got to say about this closet being full of dresses?' She pushed the sliding doors aside to reveal dresses, crammed tightly together, filling the whole breadth and depth of the closet, most of them were dark-coloured, grey, brown, and black, all of them were carefully hung up and spread flat. 'My dresses, which you say are all outmoded and ornate. But these are only the dresses I don't have space for in my room upstairs, there I have another two closets full, two closets, each nearly as big as this one. Surprised?' 'No, I expected something of the kind, I told you, you're not just a landlady, you have some other aim in mind.' 'My only aim is to dress well, and you're either a fool or a child or an extremely wicked, dangerous person. Go on, get out!' K. was already out in the hallway and Gerstäcker had him by the sleeve again when the landlady called after him: 'I'm getting a new dress tomorrow, I may send for you.'

Gerstäcker, gesticulating angrily as if in an attempt to silence the landlady from out here and stop her being a nuisance, asked K. to come with him. He refused to be more specific for the moment. K.'s objection that he should be off to the school now was virtually ignored. It was only when K. put up some resistance to being dragged away that Gerstäcker told him he mustn't worry, he'd have everything he needed at his place, he could give up the caretaking job, would K. please just come, finally, he'd spent the whole day waiting for him, his mother had no idea where he was. K., slowly giving in to him, asked why he should want to give him board and lodging. Gerstäcker made only the briefest of replies, he needed K.'s help with the horses, he himself had other things to do now, but would K. please stop making him drag him along like this and not cause him needless difficulties. If he wanted payment, then he'd pay him. But at this point K. halted, despite all the tugging. He knew nothing whatever about horses, he said. Nor did he need to, Gerstäcker said impatiently, wringing his hands in irritation to persuade K. to go with him. 'I know why you want to take me with you,' K. said finally. Gerstäcker did not care what K. knew. 'Because you think I can get somewhere with Erlanger for you.' 'Of course,' said Gerstäcker, 'why else would you matter to me.' K. chuckled, took Gerstäcker's arm, and let the man lead him through the dark.

The living-room of Gerstäcker's cottage was lit only dimly by the fire in the stove and a stump of candle, by the light of which someone sat hunched in a corner under the crooked rafters that protruded there, reading a book. It was Gerstäcker's mother. She held a trembling hand out to K. and made him sit down beside her, she spoke with an effort, it was an effort to understand her, but what she said

READ MORE IN PENGUIN

In every corner of the world, on every subject under the sun, Penguin represents quality and variety – the very best in publishing today.

For complete information about books available from Penguin – including Puffins, Penguin Classics and Arkana – and how to order them, write to us at the appropriate address below. Please note that for copyright reasons the selection of books varies from country to country.

In the United Kingdom: Please write to *Dept. EP, Penguin Books Ltd, Bath Road, Harmondsworth, West Drayton, Middlesex UB7 0DA*

In the United States: Please write to *Consumer Sales, Penguin Putnam Inc., P.O. Box 12289 Dept. B, Newark, New Jersey 07101-5289*. VISA and MasterCard holders call 1-800-788-6262 to order Penguin titles

In Canada: Please write to *Penguin Books Canada Ltd, 10 Alcorn Avenue, Suite 300, Toronto, Ontario M4V 3B2*

In Australia: Please write to *Penguin Books Australia Ltd, P.O. Box 257, Ringwood, Victoria 3134*

In New Zealand: Please write to *Penguin Books (NZ) Ltd, Private Bag 102902, North Shore Mail Centre, Auckland 10*

In India: Please write to *Penguin Books India Pvt Ltd, 11 Community Centre, Panchsheel Park, New Delhi 110017*

In the Netherlands: Please write to *Penguin Books Netherlands bv, Postbus 3507, NL-1001 AH Amsterdam*

In Germany: Please write to *Penguin Books Deutschland GmbH, Metzlerstrasse 26, 60594 Frankfurt am Main*

In Spain: Please write to *Penguin Books S. A., Bravo Murillo 19, 1° B, 28015 Madrid*

In Italy: Please write to *Penguin Italia s.r.l., Via Benedetto Croce 2, 20094 Corsico, Milano*

In France: Please write to *Penguin France, Le Carré Wilson, 62 rue Benjamin Baillaud, 31500 Toulouse*

In Japan: Please write to *Penguin Books Japan Ltd, Kaneko Building, 2-3-25 Koraku, Bunkyo-Ku, Tokyo 112*

In South Africa: Please write to *Penguin Books South Africa (Pty) Ltd, Private Bag X14, Parkview, 2122 Johannesburg*

READ MORE IN PENGUIN

Published or forthcoming:

Swann's Way Marcel Proust

This first book of Proust's supreme masterpiece, *A la recherche du temps perdu*, recalls the early youth of Charles Swann in the small, provincial backwater of Combray through the eyes of the adult narrator. The story then moves forward to Swann's life as a man of fashion in the glittering world of *belle-époque* Paris. A scathing, often comic dissection of French society, *Swann's Way* is also a story of past moments tantalizingly lost and, finally, triumphantly rediscovered.

Metamorphosis and Other Stories Franz Kafka

A companion volume to *The Great Wall of China and Other Short Works*, these translations bring together the small proportion of Kafka's works that he thought worthy of publication. This volume contains his most famous story, 'Metamorphosis'. All the stories reveal the breadth of Kafka's literary vision and the extraordinary imaginative depth of his thought.

Cancer Ward Aleksandr Solzhenitsyn

One of the great allegorical masterpieces of world literature, *Cancer Ward* is both a deeply compassionate study of people facing terminal illness and a brilliant dissection of the 'cancerous' Soviet police state. Withdrawn from publication in Russia in 1964, it became a work that awoke the conscience of the world. 'Without doubt the greatest Russian novelist of this century' *Sunday Times*

Peter Camenzind Hermann Hesse

In a moment of 'emotion recollected in tranquility' Peter Camenzind recounts the days of his youth: his childhood in a remote mountain village, his abiding love of nature, and the discovery of literature which inspires him to leave the village and become a writer. 'One of the most penetrating accounts of a young man trying to discover the nature of his creative talent' *The Times Literary Supplement*